The Mad Trinkets

The Mad Trinkets

Cameron Scott Kirk

THE MAGE'S
LANTERN
LOS ANGELES

Copyright © 2021 by The Mage's Lantern, LLC

The Mage's Lantern, LLC
P.O. Box 361012
Los Angeles, CA 90036
www.themageslantern.com

Edited by M.L. Anderson
Cover Illustration © Jodie Muir

The Library of Congress Cataloging-in-Publication Data is available upon request.

ISBN 978-0-9992809-7-3 (Hardcover)
ISBN 978-0-9992809-6-6 (Paperback)
ISBN 978-0-9992809-5-9 (eBook)
ISBN 978-0-9992809-9-7 (Audiobook)

First Edition: September 2021

0 9 8 7 6 5 4 3 2 1

For Cody

ACKNOWLEDGMENTS

A special thank you to my wife Penny for pushing me to be better.

Huge appreciation to Ronnie Smart for his support in the early stages of my writing career and for his time spent reading the novel from start to finish and offering crucial feedback.

I would like to extend my sincere gratitude to Matthew Anderson, my editor and publisher, for his leap of faith in choosing my manuscript among many others and making it a better novel than I alone was capable of producing. I can honestly say that his input has changed the course of my life.

Thanks to Kaelyn and everyone on the team at The Mage's Lantern.

A shoutout to Mark Lanegan, whose music provided the backdrop for much of this novel and inspired scene, character, and dialogue.

1

Broadford the Key

The gibbet creaked in the wind, its rusty iron squeak unhurried—for the dead are always unhurried. Creak, squeak. The metal cage and its corpse slowly rotated one way, then another, in the sharp breeze coming from the Western Sea.

Broadford Higgins steadied his horse, turned to face the wind, and adjusted his gentleman's top hat against the breeze. He could sense the coast just beyond his vision, just beyond the old road winding its way down and then upwards over the distant horizon. The sporadic trees along the path were bent backward by the sea wind, and no other soul walked the dirt road, no other soul to see him sitting there on his black mount, only two crows balancing atop the metal cage, watching him with malevolent eyes, jealously guarding their perch and its contents.

Patches of sodden ground marked the place where the local townsfolk had stomped, churned the grass to mud, assassinated it carelessly. A crowd had gathered here a few days ago to witness judicial retribution at the very spot where the innocent young child was murdered. They had screamed for blood, shook their fists, laughed as the prisoner hanged in the air—jerking, choking, dying.

Broadford watched as they stuffed the still-warm corpse into its cold iron cage. The body twitched within and opened its eyes. "He's here," it said and pointed a malignant finger. "There! behind you, I see him. The Hungry King comes! He comes for you!"

Laughter turned to screams, and women and children tripped over themselves to get away from the living corpse, from his threats, from death itself. Men stood slack jawed.

The flustered hangman strung the man up a second time to finish the job, and hardened veterans of the Great War went pale and puked as they held onto the criminal by his ankles, pulling him down, again and again, against the rough hemp rope until his neck cracked and splintered, until it was finally over.

Broadford nodded. That was Malcolm, stubborn till the last breath.

Malcolm Dewar had maintained his innocence right to the end, but the evidence was overwhelming, including a reliable and trustworthy eyewitness who had testified to seeing the horrific murder of the girl.

That eyewitness, none other than the esteemed Broadford Higgins himself, walked his horse under the scaffold. The crows hopped from foot to foot, ready to defend their treasure trove, but he waved his arms and shouted, and the birds took flight, shrieking their displeasure, promising to pick at his corpse one day if he weren't more respectful.

Watch your back, dandy, they cawed.

The dead man's bare feet poked limply through the gibbet.

"Poor Malcolm," Broadford said with an exaggerated plum in his mouth. "Someone has purloined your favorite boots." He clucked his tongue in mock disapproval. "Really, is there no respect for the dead?"

Smiling and standing in his stirrups, he grabbed the iron cage to steady himself. His horse whinnied and stomped, causing the gibbet to judder and shake, the putrefying corpse within jiggling.

"Easy," he said. "Easy."

He removed a knife from his black leather overcoat. Even without his top hat, Broadford was tall, his head now level with that of the slumped corpse. The dead man's eye sockets were bloody black holes—eyes now food for the disgruntled crows—yet somehow managed an accusing gaze.

Broadford took a breath, reached within the iron framework, and stabbed the dead man in the stomach. He twisted the knife, cutting, sawing, carving. Cold blood and bile streamed over his hand and under his sleeve as foul gas issued into the air, and the corpse seemed to shrink, to decompress.

"Why are you doing this?"

Broadford whirled, spraying droplets of near-frozen blood from his knife. His horse, startled by the sudden movement, kicked and shied, causing him to lose his grip on the gibbet.

Swing, creak, squeak.

The girl was there, looking up at him, then glancing at his bloodied hands. She was small, fragile, pale faced in her nightdress, the clothes she'd been wearing when she was murdered on this exact spot, merely seven years of age at the time of her death.

Broadford closed his dark brown eyes and breathed. He clenched his jaws, ground his teeth, heartbeat slowing to something akin to normal. He concentrated on the air washing across his face and then opened his eyes.

She was gone, as he knew she would be.

He eased his unsettled horse back under the gibbet, the mare snorting and whinnying. "Steady, steady. It's nothing. There's nothing there, all in your head." The horse settled, and with a last glance around at the empty, wind-blown country road, he delved back into the guts of Malcolm Dewar. "Come on, you bastard. I know it's in here somewhere."

The smell was vile, but Broadford was used to the stink of guts and shit, the Great War having given him a sturdy insight into the workings of the human body. This wasn't the first time he'd been elbow deep in a man. He put the knife in his left hand and massaged the intestines with his right, squeezing them like a sausage maker. And then he felt it, the hard thing inside.

He sliced once, twice, and removed a section of intestine or bowel, he couldn't be sure; he was, after all, an ex-soldier, a killer, not an anatomist. He kneaded the object out of its organic casing along with molding human muck.

"Thanks for looking after this, my friend," he said, casting aside the dead man's innards. The guts landed on the dirt road with a pathetic slap.

With a rag, he cleaned shit and blood from the small metal object.

He held the key up to the wind and smiled. The trinket was luminous, a dim light radiating from the oddly textured metal, which pulsed first blue, then purple, then a lustrous brown. A myriad of colors came and went. The longer the key remained in his fingers, the more vibrant each hue.

"All right, Malcolm. Let's see what this is all about."

He gripped the trinket, and a warm calmness bubbled up, turning to heat within him. His lungs expanded and kept expanding; he tasted the air in a way that was unfamiliar, fresher, sharper. The scent of sea salt, mud, and patchy grass filled his nostrils. A hare scampered somewhere in the distance. He could hear it, smell it! Stars appeared where a moment before there had been nothing but blue skies and scudding clouds.

The stars, in a blue sky?

He felt giddy, as if the universe were closing in on him or he were expanding outwards to fill it. Then came a surge of health and power, an erection out of nowhere. Suddenly, he felt invincible.

Broadford grinned, enjoying this new state of being. He looked one last time at the gutted corpse swinging slowly in its rusty, airy sepulcher, its mass of sandy hair subjected to the whims of the wind.

"You should have shared this, Malcolm." He urged his horse around. "But I can see why you didn't."

He put the key in his pocket, wiped his hands on the rag, and threw it into the air. He settled his top hat firmly on his head and rode away, toward the horizon, toward fortune and glory.

He gave Malcolm Dewar no more thought.

And the girl Broadford Higgins had murdered, the one the innocent man had swung for? He gave her the same consideration.

2

Warrior Scholar

From the height of a sandy clifftop, two figures sat upon two very different horses and watched the girl running for her life along the beach below. She sprinted into the strong wind, her light brown hair streaming behind her, her white tunic flapping like a feverish beating heart. She looked back desperately at the men pursuing her. She had a twelve horse-length lead and was not letting it lapse.

The tall woman astride the white horse, hands on pommel, turned to her male companion on his smaller brown mare. He was clothed like a monk, his habiliments those of the Order of the Yellow Scholars, butter-colored robes that hung loosely on his thin frame.

"She wants to live," the woman said. She wore her long blonde hair in the Norse style, a tightly wound and braided ponytail, shaved head above the ears.

"As do I," the thin man said. "Those are King Bruwaert's men, highly trained. This isn't our affair."

"There are four of them, and she but a girl." She nodded toward the pursuit. "What would your conscience tell you to do, William?"

The tall woman now looked to the gray clouds scurrying through the chill blue sky. Despite using his name, William Barding knew she was not talking to him; rather, she was consulting her ancestors, asking their advice, the only advice that mattered to the Norse. In his experience, such advice usually ended in bloodshed.

William pointed eastwards to the far end of the beach where it curved out of sight. "Six," he said. Two riders on horseback had appeared in the salty beach haze, kicking at their horses, making frantic speed. They were King Bruwaert's Personal Guard, lethal experts in any kind of named warfare and a few more besides.

The girl now had no chance.

"Brynhild, we're outnumbered."

"So is she." Her tone was flat, brooking no protestation, but William offered one last objection before his companion launched them both into a situation with unfavorable odds.

"This isn't our fight. You're going to get yourself killed."

Brynhild Grimsdotter smiled at the lean monk in the butter-colored robes. "Then, as my personal poet and historian, you will record and sing of my deeds, and I shall be immortal. Make this a grand tale, won't you?" Still smiling, she kicked at her horse and disappeared over the lip of the sandy cliff.

The monk spit wind-blown sand from his mouth and muttered, "Provided I don't get killed along with you."

After a final, surprisingly secular curse, he urged his horse downwards after the tall Norsewoman and caught up to her.

She rocked back and forth in the saddle, her long braided ponytail lazily slapping her wide back, left, right, left again, a back as muscular as William had ever seen on a man, not unattractive on a woman by any means. Her brown leather jerkin was sleeveless, exposing the backs of her arms and muscles that he had yet to read about in any anatomist's tome. And he had read many, even written one. Her waist was narrow, her legs long, lithe, and supple, her buttocks—

The thin monk nearly fell from the saddle as his horse stumbled on the narrow, crumbling path.

Steady, William. Concentrate. He was a scholar, for God's sake.

His attention finally came to rest on the sword at her powerful hip, a sword born in the Far East. In that place, it was known as a *katana*. It was the finest weapon William had ever known, in the hands of the finest warrior he had ever known.

The Easterners called her *Kita No Ki*, the Northern Tree. That would be the title of William's book. Rather clever, not even the abbot could fail to approve. Could he, the fat bastard?

The tall warrior and the willowy monk made for the beach, and their horses broke into a gallop, her white courser accelerating away from his smaller brown mount.

The soldiers on foot had discarded their armor and weapons to lighten their load and catch the girl, but she was strong, and they made no ground. The leather-armored knights on horseback raced up the beach, and the desperate girl increased her speed, but the effort was futile, as they'd be upon her in mere moments.

Brynhild and William were close enough now to make out King Bruwaert's insignia on the body armor of the pursuing horses: two keys crossed. The men on foot cheered as the King's Personal Guard thundered past them. It wouldn't be long before they harried their prey to ground and took what they wanted, each in turn.

The girl changed direction, heading toward the sea, perhaps to drown herself before she could be run down, tortured, raped, but Brynhild headed her off. The girl stopped, breathless, but her courage did not wilt; she withdrew a knife from somewhere and put it to her own throat.

Brynhild reined in her horse and reached her palm outwards. "Stay the knife, girl, I mean you no harm!"

The girl, no more than fifteen years old, scowled at the Norsewoman, clearly mistrusting and yet hope glimmering in her youthful aspect.

William rode up behind Brynhild. "We're not with them," he said. "We wish to help."

The girl cast a look with brilliant amber eyes from the Norsewoman to the scholastic monk and back again; perhaps it was William's gentle tone of voice or his monastic robes, but she took the knife from her neck.

William smiled, reassuringly he hoped.

"Give me the knife," Brynhild said.

The young woman seemed to snap out of a dream and pressed the blade to her pulsing throat, her breath rasping like a shingle slide upon a steep hill.

The two knights on horseback were approaching.

"We must act before the foot soldiers gather upon us," the monk said. "Even you cannot defeat six men. We must even the odds, and quickly."

The Norsewoman nodded sharply. "I understand."

The two men on horseback arrived, pulling up heavily, sending sand-spray into the cool mid-morning wind. Neither wore helmets. The lead rider was a huge man with a patchy red beard. "Stand back! This is king's business!" he shouted.

Brynhild saluted the lead rider, fist on chest. "My liege, I have her. She is yours."

The young girl shot a venomous glance at the Norsewoman and turned in circles, the knife beginning to draw blood from her neck.

Red Beard narrowed his eyes in an ugly display of confusion and contempt. His horse was snorting, its breath curling into the frigid coastal air. "Who are you?" the man barked.

"A landowner in these parts, most devoted to King Bruwaert," Brynhild said.

"And you?" said the other rider, a young man with close-cropped black hair, cold blue eyes, and a cruel mouth, looking at William. "Who are you? Her bodyguard?"

The monk nearly laughed out loud. The man couldn't be serious. William simply smiled and bowed his head. Raising it again, he said, "Her biographer."

The man twisted his harsh face in puzzlement.

William didn't believe in physiognomy, but if he did, the features of the rider betrayed him as a right prick, callous beyond measure.

Brynhild got down from her horse. "Remember what I said," she whispered to the frightened girl and held out her hand.

Reaching for the sword at his waist, Red Beard moved his horse forward. "Stand back, this is not your affair!"

"Certainly, sire." Brynhild bowed, pulled the katana from its scabbard, and sliced the foreleg clean off the man's horse, just below the animal's body armor. The mare screamed and dropped with its rider to the wind-blown sands, trapping him beneath its floundering bulk, Red Beard's scream joining that of his horse, his left leg and arm broken.

William threw a dagger at the second man and hit him in the shoulder, piercing his boiled leather armor. He didn't drop but turned his horse to flee.

With the bloody blade in her hands, the Norsewoman moved toward the second horse, preparing to chop it down.

"Please don't hurt the horse!" the girl shouted, the breath back in her lungs.

Brynhild hesitated, and the rider moved away, out of reach.

The monk grabbed for another dagger, but before he could free it, the callous-faced young soldier had fallen backward off his horse, a knife jutting from the back of his neck, dead before he hit the sand. William looked at Brynhild, but her attention was on the girl moving like a cat, leaping forward to retrieve the blade she'd thrown.

The girl pulled the knife out of the body and moved to Red Beard, who was still trapped beneath the wildly flailing horse, the mare's blood spraying like a fountain. She grabbed the man's hair and tried to pull his head backward, but Red Beard had his right arm free and pushed the girl away.

The four men on foot were now nearly upon them and screaming, "King's Guard, leave that man alone!"

The girl looked up at the tall woman. "Hold his arm."

Brynhild nodded, knelt on Red Beard, braced herself, and heaved the big man's arm behind his back. The girl swiftly sliced the man's throat from ear to ear. He screamed, gurgled, and just before he passed, the girl stabbed him in both eyes, blood spraying on her, on the Norsewoman, on the monk several yards away.

William's skin went cold and prickled. What kind of child could dispatch a man so viciously?

Brynhild merely chuckled quietly.

The four soldiers on foot made their belated arrival and stopped, horrified expressions on their faces, only yards away as Brynhild got back on her horse.

"You're outnumbered!" one of the soldiers screamed. "Give your-selves up!"

Brynhild laughed. "Outnumbered? I believe the odds are now in our favor. Two on horseback against four on foot."

"And one murderous child with a kitchen knife," William said.

The king's soldiers all stared at the girl, their fear showing. Suddenly, she was no longer a fragile child. Now, Death sat on her blood-spattered shoulder, sharpening his teeth.

"And I believe," Brynhild said, easing her horse forwards, "you've discarded your weapons in pursuit of the girl. That was very foolish, and the gods of war are unforgiving."

For a moment there was a pause in aggression, the men seeming to weigh up their fate, waiting for someone to act, whether on their side or the other. Then one of them broke and ran, the other three losing their nerve and having no choice but to join him.

Brynhild reached down and pulled the young woman onto the back of her horse, and the monk spurred his mount to run down one of the soldiers.

William didn't like killing. He liked poetry and prose. He enjoyed having his fellow scholars copy out his words and send his books abroad. That filled him with pride, to know that somebody some-where was reading his work. Killing was distasteful, often necessary, but distasteful. On this occasion, however, he suffered very little compunction.

He took out another dagger from his sleeve and embedded it in the back of one of the fleeing soldiers, dropping him instantly.

Brynhild had thrown the child from her horse, or the child had jumped, William couldn't be sure, onto another of King Bruwaert's men, knife in her hand, falling upon the man's back, slashing and hacking. The soldier dropped, trying to fend off the wild creature, but she seemed to know where his arteries lay hidden beneath his skin. She nearly beheaded the man.

Another soldier was running toward the ocean. Fleeing was a wise move, the only thing to do under the circumstances, but Brynhild cut him down before he reached the salty waters—one horizontal strike from the katana, almost gently delivered. The man probably didn't feel a thing, a blade that sharp would have disconnected body from brain with almost humane speed.

The final soldier stopped, dropped to his knees, and begged for his life. "I have a wife and child," he blubbered.

Brynhild approached slowly on her white courser, and the girl moved swiftly on foot, closing in on the man.

"Please keep her off me," he said.

"Wait," Brynhild held out her hand.

The girl stopped and gestured with her bloody knife at the dead soldiers. "They killed my father, they . . . they killed my father." The girl looked eastwards. "There," she said, indicating a point where smoke rose from somewhere along the coast.

"Let me question him first."

The girl screwed her face, anger slowly blossoming through.

Brynhild pierced the terrified soldier with her stare. "Why do you pursue this girl?"

The man had his hands out, knees sinking into the sand, as if attempting to dig himself to safety. "For the m-metal."

"What metal?"

"The trinket her father . . ." He looked at the girl and gulped. "Her father possesses something that belongs to King Bruwaert. Please, Sarah waits for me, and little—"

"Stop!" Brynhild commanded. "I do not wish to know their names. Hold out one arm."

"What?"

"Hold out one arm."

"Why?"

"Hold it out and close your eyes. You shall die now if you refuse."

"Oh God." He did as he was asked, and Brynhild sliced the man's hand off at the wrist. He screamed.

She nodded to the girl, and the girl closed in on the now defenseless man and stabbed the soldier in places that wouldn't kill him quickly.

Eventually, the man bled out.

The girl was covered in blood; her eyes shining through crimson gave her a devilish appearance. "Why did you kill the horse?" she asked, turning on Brynhild, her teeth bared.

"He was a big man. I needed to bring him down quickly."

"That was very cruel."

Brynhild raised an eyebrow and looked at William. "Well, here I am having to explain myself to a child." She turned back to the girl. "You do realize that William and I have just saved your life?"

The girl seemed to collapse in on herself, deflating. She sank to the sand and bowed her head. "I am grateful." She began to cry, gently at first and then in great heaving sobs.

The tall Norsewoman eased her horse away, toward the waves rolling in, giving the girl privacy within which to grieve.

William got off his horse and wrapped his arms around the crying child. His was not the way of the staunch Norse. The girl clasped him, though a stranger, as if he were her dead father returned. The waves crashed in.

Brynhild was gazing far away on the sea horizon, and the thought crossed William's mind that she might be thinking of her own father. William knew he had died long ago, when she was but a girl. He would include him in the book. Sagran Grimsdotter had been a hero of note, and William sometimes wondered if Brynhild had grown to be a fierce warrior in his image simply to live up to the reputation of her famous father. The monk wasn't trained in the confessional, but he thought the father-daughter angle might provide an interesting emotional element to his book.

The girl's tears were wetting William's robes, and for a moment, the monk felt guilty that his thoughts were floating away to his work, that he was not mentally present for the weeping child. Still, he hoped he was of some comfort.

Brynhild came out of her own reverie and approached the scholar-monk and girl. She spoke to William. "What is the metal the soldier spoke of? I wish I'd had more time with the man, but the girl needed vengeance."

Before the monk could answer, the sniffling girl got to her feet and removed a necklace. "This," she said, holding up a small trinket carved from some kind of eerily glowing metal. It was designed in the shape of a book, its pages caught mid-turn in exquisite detail. Unless William was mistaken, the object appeared to be changing color from dark red to sunset orange.

"What is your name, child?" he asked.

"I am Rebecca Occitane. My father was Robert Occitane."

"Why would King Bruwaert send men to kill for this trinket?" Brynhild said.

"I don't know. I don't understand anything." The girl sounded drowsy, shock setting in.

William pulled his robes over his head, arranged it upon her. She collapsed and William caught her. He looked up at Brynhild. "She needs to rest."

"Rest? Why?"

The monk was slightly startled that he had to justify his statement. "She needs time to accept what's happened." He felt the cold morning air begin to envelop him, his white undershirt flapping in the wind.

"She'll never accept what's happened, nor should she."

William sighed, becoming irritated. "I may not be a fearsome warrior, but I know the girl needs rest, quiet, and food."

Brynhild nodded eastwards, and William followed her gaze to the smoke.

"You can't seriously want to take her back there?" he said.

"She has to bury her father. Wouldn't you agree?"

William sighed again. He couldn't disagree. "Perhaps if you showed a little mercy, it might..."

"Might what?"

"Make things more..." The thin monk shook his head. He wasn't sure what mercy could deliver right now.

"We take her back. She buries her father. Then she can grieve in her own time and fashion."

"At least help me get her up on my horse," William muttered in exasperation.

"That I can do."

Together they lifted a trembling Rebecca Occitane onto William's brown mare, the monk sitting behind and supporting her. The trinket at her chest was now a strange color between silver and white.

As they rode toward the smoke spiraling into the bitter coastal air, Brynhild said to William, "I don't think I've ever seen such clean undergarments in all my years." She looked him up and down.

He found the comment strange. Was she attempting to make a joke, to provide a moment of levity? It was badly timed, if that were the case. He felt oddly uncomfortable, as if he were being measured, in what capacity he wasn't sure, and found wanting.

"You need to eat more, priest, if you ever want a woman to lie with you," she said.

So, the look was a sexual appraisal. Fascinating. "I'm a monk, not a priest, but mostly a scholar, and we don't particularly make a habit of lying with women."

Brynhild smiled from one side of her mouth. "Who doesn't? Monks or scholars?"

"Both. Neither."

She shrugged, as if to suggest a lack of sexual intimacy was William's loss, and dug her boots into her horse's flanks. She pulled away, and William had to make haste to stay with her, his own horse now burdened with two bodies.

The monk thought he heard Brynhild Grimsdotter's laughter on the cooling beach breeze, but it might have been the call of the gulls. He had to admit that he was finding her behavior inappropriate, strangely unattuned to the present circumstances, as if she occupied a different plane and remained emotionally unaffected by the events unfolding around her.

Yes, indeed, she would provide excellent source material for his new book.

3

Tristan the Crown

In darkness, an hour before dawn's first rays, the fishmonger walked his usual circuitous route to the fish market with his knife set strapped to the prosperous girth of his waist. He was following the well-trodden sailors' path from pub to port when he came upon the slumped silhouette of a man against a stone wall. The fishmonger scratched his muttonchops, looked around, then knelt and rifled through the man's pockets.

The collapsed drunk was a sailor by scent, all brine and rum, and cold to the touch. Whether dead or deeply in slumber, the fishmonger didn't know or care. If the sailor woke, he fully intended on cutting his throat—a man had to make a living. His targets were never local or likely to be missed, and the blood of his victims covering his apron was indistinguishable from that of the fish he worked with every day.

But the drunk seaman carried nothing of value, no coin, no trinkets, and the fishmonger contemplated stabbing him out of frustration. He stood up, relinquishing the search, then jumped back in fright despite himself.

A tall figure draped in a heavy traveling cloak seemed to float above the ground in the half light, wordless, just watching, its face buried in hood-shaped blackness.

The fishmonger raised his knife. "He was already like this when I f-found him. I didn't do nothing." His heart was hammering within his chest. Something under the darkness of the hood terrified him, a glint of something menacing. His stomach, his strength, dissolved within him, his knees buckling.

Then the thing spoke in a dark, mellifluous voice. "The Gorgon?"

The fishmonger wanted to run, but his body wouldn't respond. It took him a few moments to realize that the creature was referring to the slumped sailor. He puzzled hard. The Gorgon? The ship recently docked? "Aye, he could be one of the crew. I don't know."

The hood nodded, and the fishmonger watched the thing glide across the street as if on air, making no sound, and then it was gone. The fat peddler of fish glanced around and ran as fast as his heavy jelly-like legs would carry him—the other way.

The shadow that had so frightened the fishmonger had a name: Tristan Drogos de Merlon. He stood now in the early morning sun, watching the Gorgon slowly rolling in her berth.

The ungainly ship was large, flaking, and gloom surrounded the aging vessel as shadows enveloped de Merlon. The ship was a converted trader, now a prison hulk carrying a cargo of one. Tristan knew that most of her crew were ashore, still drinking themselves senseless, trying to forget the floating hell their lives had become. He understood that not all the crew would return; sailors half-mad with fear would abandon ship, only to be replaced by an ignorant local or two blinded by the coin, until they too would flee the forsaken ship at the next port of call.

Tristan walked along the jetty toward the prison hulk, his long black cloak floating behind him in the salty sea breeze. The air was chilly despite the sunshine, but he felt nothing.

He withdrew a piece of paper from within his cloak and waved it at the nervous sailor watching him from the deck of the Gorgon. The wind tore at the paper, but the hand holding it did not relent.

"Piss off," the sailor said, glancing about.

"I am on the king's business," Tristan shouted across the gap from pier to vessel, waving the flapping paper above his head.

The young sailor scoffed. "What king? I have no idea where in White Cloud we anchor, nor do I care. King's business or no, you don't want aboard this ship, mate. Trust me." The sailor peered intently at the hand holding the paper, the hand which resembled a claw, and shivered.

Tristan looked back down the pier. The other ships in the dock rested apart from the Gorgon, seemingly unwilling to share the same water the prison vessel floated in. Still, there were too many eyes.

"You're in Stollot, King Tremain's territory. Your head, friend, if I don't get on board in the next five minutes, it'll be on a pike in the king's shithouse."

"I have orders not to let anyone on."

"This order abrogates yours, friend."

The young fellow gave a puzzled scowl. "Abrogates?"

"Dissolves. Overturns. Trumps."

A minute passed in which the man on the Gorgon seemed to weigh up his options. Finally, he took a deep breath. "All right." The fidgeting sailor let down the gangplank with a rotting thud.

Tristan made the crossing, and a sword greeted him as he stepped onto the deck, the tip pointing at his chest.

"The order, show it to me."

"Certainly, now where did I put it?" Tristan pulled back his hood, revealing a gray, pock-marked face, sunken cheeks, hairless skull.

The young sailor backed away. "Oh shit, have you got the plague?"

"Plague, leprosy, take your pick, but I am fully recovered on both counts, thank the Savior." He looked skyward.

The young sailor's unblemished face turned white. "People don't just recover from leprosy or the Black Death."

"Well, young fellow, I did. Truly blessed . . . Ah, here it is," Tristan said, producing the king's order from thin air and handing it over.

The sailor shook his head and took another step back, keeping his sword aimed at Tristan's chest. "I don't want to touch nothing of yours, no offense."

"None taken." Tristan smiled, showing his sharp jagged teeth.

"Oh, Lord Almighty!" The sailor looked as if he'd just shat his britches. "You look like him down below. I suppose that's why you're here?"

"Indeed."

"I'm having second thoughts about all this. This doesn't seem right."

Tristan once again offered the king's order, and once again the sailor shook his head. "Listen, friend, I simply want to talk to the prisoner." He spoke in a placating tone, hands upturned. "Five minutes, and I'll be gone."

The young man kept the sword tip level with Tristan's heart, the sharpened steel of the blade wavering. A moment later, he let the sword fall to his side. "All right, all right. Five minutes. Follow me, but not too close. For your benefit. And mine."

"Of course." He gestured for the sailor to lead the way.

Down they went, down creaking steps twisting back on themselves, down into the musty darkness of the hold, and then deeper. Finally, they came to a long passageway. The bright morning sun was now an eternity away. Tristan let the king's order fall onto the molding floorboards, into the shadows, unnoticed by the nervous young sailor a few paces in front of him.

"Watch the inmate, now," the sailor said. "He can speak in your head, get in there, twist your thoughts and your guts."

Tristan nodded.

"They've left me here alone. Supposed to be three of us at all times to guard the prisoner. Them's the rules. The bastards are out whoring and drinking. So I'm glad for the company, if I were honest. Even if you are a . . ."

"A leper?"

"Uh, no offense."

Tristan sharpened a smile. It had been a long time since anyone was glad for his company.

They came to a solid oak door with scratch marks in the wood and a sliding panel at about head height of the young man. The sailor moved the panel while keeping his face well back, revealing a slit through which one could view the interior were it not so dark. But dark it was.

"Don't get too close," the sailor said, moving back down the passageway. "I'll be up top when you've finished."

Tristan waited until the young sailor disappeared.

"Good morning," he said, leaning down to look within at the small shadowed figure.

"Is it?" said a dry croaking voice, long unused to the civilities of social chit-chat. "It's always night in this place."

"It's a fine morning, you can take my word for it."

The voice merely grunted.

The shape within the cell entered a patch of lighter gloom closer to the door. The figure wore the garb of the eremite, or possibly that of the monastic order. It was hard to tell which from simple observation, but Tristan knew what the robes represented. He knew.

He peered inside the cell but couldn't make out the eyes of the bent and twisted figure.

The wizened creature inside whispered, "Come closer to the door."

"I wouldn't do that if I were you."

Tristan turned to see the young sailor approaching with the discarded king's order in his hand. He was holding it up for him to see.

"Hey, this paper, there's nothing on it. It's blank. Who are you?"

When the young man was close enough, Tristan lunged and casually slashed the sailor's throat with a hidden knife. The boy sank to his knees and tried to stem the blood spurting from his neck, over Tristan's boots, and into the cracks of the molding floor. His face displayed confusion and irritation. He tried to speak, a wet gurgle, unintelligible to any normal pair of ears. But Tristan Drogos de Merlon possessed unusual senses and was well-versed in hearing a dying man's last words.

"S'posed to be three of us."

The man fell forward and died, the knife that had taken his life cleaned and concealed before the body hit the floorboards.

Tristan searched the fresh corpse.

"There is no key to this door," said the shadowed figure within. "If there was, that idiot wouldn't be entrusted with it. And I echo his question and add one of my own. Who are you, and what do you want?"

"Do not fear me," Tristan said, moving close to the door.

Cackling laughter. "You misunderstand. I do not fear you."

"Good. I'm about to open this door."

Silence. Then, "Why?"

"To free you."

The creature asked the same question. "Why?"

"You have something I want."

"What is that precisely?"

Tristan reached within his cloak at the neck, pulled out a chain with a small pendant at the end, and held it up to the slit in the door. The pendant was fashioned from a strange glowing metal, shaped like a king's crown.

A soft moan escaped the monk's thin lips. He said, "If you open this door, what makes you think I won't kill you?"

"Who says you can? Besides, I have something you want."

"You have nothing I want."

"I beg to differ. I have your freedom."

A snort. "Worth nothing to me after all this time."

"You must desire something."

"What I desire you cannot provide."

Tristan pressed a palm against the door. "I can help you. You merely have to tell me."

The monk-thing came closer still to the aperture, stood on tip-toes, and looked down at the cherub-faced dead sailor. The creature's eyes at the slit were yellow, bloodshot. "Innocence," it said. "We long always for innocence. But I warn you, fairly, if you open this door, I'll be inclined to suckle on the innocence within your breast. I can't help myself."

A parchment-dry grin stretched across Tristan's wrecked face, over pointed cheekbones. His sharpened teeth cut into fleshless lips, drawing blood, and his smile turned to laughter. There was a sickness in his laugh, a corruption that reverberated in the skull, like the echo of a rusted bell chiming in Hell. The creature within moved back from the door, warily.

"Tell me, brother..." Tristan put his hand over the keyhole. He closed his eyes and pushed on the door. It swung open. "Do you sense any innocence within me?"

The monk-thing within retreated to a corner and shook its head in the darkness. For the first time in an eon, the creature felt fear.

Tristan stepped within the small cell and extended his hand. "You are twisted," he said. The hunched figure shrank away. "You are broken. You are cursed. These things I understand. My name is Tristan Drogos de Merlon. You fashion more of these for me, and only me," he said, touching the pendant with his other hand, "and I will bring you your innocence."

The monk was motionless.

"Do we have an arrangement?"

The creature hesitated, and then it moved forward, crouching low and looking up at Tristan, sniffing the air. The thing was shrunken, shriveled like a decaying apple, with cheeks puckered and teeth like those of Tristan's—sharp points. Small veins webbed its yellow eyes, and hair sprouted from its ears.

The thing smiled and took Tristan's hand.

"My lord."

4

A View of the Sea

Wearing only an undershirt in the chill beach breeze, William Barding should have been cold, but the girl, Rebecca Occitane, now wrapped in his yellow robes, was giving off an unnatural heat. He wondered if she was ill with fever.

Up ahead, Brynhild Grimsdotter sat astride her white horse, encouraging the beast to ascend a steep path to the clifftop above, toward the still-smoking house, the home Rebecca had shared with her father.

The monk urged his horse onwards, but the animal struggled to make the climb.

"Two leagues farther on," Rebecca said, waking from a half slumber, "you'll find a track the horses can use, then double back along the cliff."

Half an hour later, they arrived at the Occitane family homestead sitting near the cliff's edge, which provided an elevated sea view. They found Robert Occitane lying dead on his back in the yard among the chickens. His amber eyes, like those of his daughter, were open and staring at the scudding clouds above. The corpses of six men, all face down in chickenshit, surrounded him. King Bruwaert's men. Robert had not died alone.

Rebecca slid from the horse and knelt at her father's side. She laid her head on his chest, whispering something to him, something only to be understood by father and daughter.

The warrior and the scholar scanned the carnage.

"He died well," Brynhild said under her breath as she got down from her white horse.

The gaunt monk nodded, taking mental notes concerning the Northern people's attitudes toward death. It seemed a person could attain a more respectable passing if they took a few souls with them. William himself had never considered death as either good or bad but simply something that happened to everyone, sooner or later. It certainly wasn't a cause for celebration or a stiff ale.

The monk dismounted and tried to muster some words of consolation, but none came. He could only watch the girl grieve for her father, his own heart breaking.

Rebecca abruptly stood and went inside the smoking farmhouse. William looked at Brynhild, unsure if they should follow, but the warrior simply waited. The girl returned wearing a shapeless garment of brown hemp, still smoking, though miraculously not too badly fire damaged. She was carrying William's butter-yellow robes in her arms. She offered it to him, and the scholar-monk, now feeling the chill wind on the clifftop, gratefully put the monastic garb back on.

Rebecca picked up a blood-spattered spade lying nearby—Robert Occitane's only weapon it would seem—and began digging a grave near the clifftop to give her father an excellent view of the sea.

"Should we help her?" William asked.

Brynhild shook her head. "Family buries family."

"How about them?" He nodded toward King Bruwaert's soldiers.

The tall Norsewoman snorted and brushed her braided ponytail from her shoulder. "Hah! Twelve armed men come in the still morning to murder an honest farmer and his daughter. Cowards one and all. The fight was unfairly weighted in their favor despite the outcome, which no doubt came as a surprise to them. They are undeserving of burial." She spat on the nearest corpse.

William decided to disregard her advice and help the sniffling girl bury her father. He searched for another digging tool while Brynhild dragged the king's men to the sandy cliff edge and, one by one, rolled them off. When she was done, she dusted her hands and said, "We must keep an honest yard clean. Let the crows and beach dogs have them."

After they had put Robert Occitane in the ground, Rebecca, dirtied and breathing hard, turned to the Norsewoman and the yellow-robed scholar. "He saved my life." She wiped her nose on her forearm. "He was an exceptional father to an ordinary daughter. William, would you say something?"

The scholar-monk was startled but attempted to rise to the occasion. "Oh, yes. Yes, of course." He stood closer to Rebecca and cleared his throat. He stared at the freshly dug grave and clasped his muddied hands together, wondering what in the heavens he might say to console a child who had just witnessed the assassination of her father. "I'm not well versed in this kind of thing. I'm not one of *those* monks, you see." He cleared his throat again. Out of the corner of his eye, he noticed Brynhild watching him intently. God's balls, why was this so hard?

"He died well," William said, feeling his face redden. "It was a good death." He thought the tall woman might be smirking. "He died protecting that which he loved. He died fighting for good, and the Lord, though he does not condone violence, will be having an ale in your father's honor tonight. Rest in peace, Robert Occitane."

Brynhild nodded in approval as she got back on her horse.

"Thank you," Rebecca said.

William smiled. "My dear girl, you are *most* welcome."

"We must leave," Brynhild said.

The girl shook her head, her light brown hair flicking across her face in the sharpening wind. "My home is here."

"More will come. To stay here is to join your father in death."

The girl shrugged, gazing out to sea. "So be it. I'll kill as many as I can. Bury me beside him."

"Is that what your father would want? For you to die now?"

Rebecca looked into the eyes of the tall woman and then to the clifftop grave. "No."

"Then, pack your things."

"Why would Bruwaert do this?" Rebecca said. "My father fought for Bruwaert and Tremain, gone two years in their war, a loyal soldier. Then he is murdered, for what? This?" She held up the small metallic book on the fine chain around her neck as a grim expression shadowed her brow. "I will live to avenge my father, and nothing short of the death of that bastard King Bruwaert will suffice."

Brynhild said nothing and offered the girl her hand. "Come with us and together we will formulate your vengeance."

William glanced sharply at the Norsewoman, wondering what she might be suggesting. "Brynhild, your brothers requested we come before the moon's first quarter, and Abbot Gilbert agreed. We have a book to write, and I would not wish to offend either party by arriving tardily. We can't be running off killing kings."

She did not take her eyes from those of Rebecca Occitane. "My brothers and your abbot can wait. The book can wait."

Rebecca took Brynhild's hand and swung herself up behind the Norse warrior.

William Barding was concerned that he had just become an integral part of a planned regicide and considered the impact on the publication of his book. He sighed. How would the abbot of the Order of Yellow Scholars acclimatize to the news?

5

The stars and stella

Tristan sat in a clearing on the mountainside and counted the stars in the night sky, stars whose light still pierced the distance between but had burned out long ago. He somehow knew which of the heavenly lights were still blazing and which had been extinguished, dead and cold, despite the ghost light. He could feel the heat from distant galaxies radiating downwards toward the trinket strapped around his neck, warming his blood, voiding any need for a fire. Darkness was better anyway. Darkness for dark deeds.

He put his right hand on his chest, over the place where the small metal crown rested against his skin. What kind of thing could give a man the power to see a corpse-star? The thought was almost frightening. And this was just one of the metal carvings. One trinket. What could he do with a few more? A hundred more? He was determined to find out.

Twigs snapped behind him, but he didn't look, for he knew what had made the sound. He shifted his gaze toward the large rural village several leagues below where flames, hastily lit torches, ran wildly in different directions. The alarm had been sounded, but it was too late.

Too late.

Another rustling and crackling.

Tristan traced the scars on his sunken cheek with a skeletal finger. "I got married in that town," he said without turning. "I know everybody who lives in Millington."

There was no reply, only a shuffling of coarse robes and the further popping of dried branches on cold earth.

"What's your name?" Tristan asked.

"I was Jeremiah, once. I am no longer deserving of a name." The voice was husky, still unused to speaking and, something else, overcome with emotion.

Tristan smirked. "How contrite." The frantic lights below swirled like fireflies drowning in a black pool.

He heard a snuffling, a sobbing, and turned around. The creature, Jeremiah, was carrying a child, a boy of no more than eight years of age, limp in his twisted arms. Tristan's brows came together in the cold air.

"Why do you weep?"

Jeremiah laid the pale child gently onto a pyre of twigs and leaves in the gathering darkness. He bowed his head. Tears dripped from his misshapen nose, momentarily reflecting the moon and starlight, and fell onto the motionless boy.

"I've taken the life of an innocent child. I weep for I am not insensible to my crimes." The creature brushed what sunlight would have revealed as golden hair from the dead child's forehead. "Why do you *not* weep?"

Tristan turned away and looked downwards once more. "They are roused to his disappearance and will be here soon. The boy was Ralph Connister's child. The man functions as a mayor of sorts, and so the search will be more thorough."

The gnarled monk glanced around desperately. "We must hide the corpse."

"No, leave it in plain sight. Let the tragedy play out."

A pause.

"Very well." Jeremiah tentatively approached Tristan. "I cannot repay you until—"

Tristan waved a hand. "I understand. The materials are buried deep within Mount Ulfur, the ancestral home of the Monks of Ulfur."

"Yes."

"This was an act of good faith, do you understand? I'll bring you more, you have my word, but you must retrieve what metal remains and fashion more trinkets from it. I must have more. Do you understand, Jeremiah?"

"Yes, yes." A moment's silence passed, within which dead light traveled a million leagues through the eternal darkness. Then, "What is your purpose?" the monk asked.

"War. And to win it."

"To rule all White Cloud?"

"Yes," Tristan said. "And beyond."

"A petty goal."

Tristan sneered and stabbed a finger at the old monk. "Says a man who's just slain and fed on the soul of a child to ease his own suffering."

The monk's face twisted beyond its typical warped aspect. "Damn you, de Merlon. I had no choice."

The flames that pinpricked the darkness below were ascending the mountainside.

"You could have cut your own throat long ago. There's a choice, but one that takes courage in making."

Jeremiah paced the clearing, his filthy brown robes flapping behind him as he walked. "They're coming, they have dogs, I hear them. We must flee!"

"You have good ears, monk, despite the hair sprouting from them." Tristan gazed on Millington below. It would take the better part of an hour to reach them, dogs or no dogs. He had made the climb many times himself. This was not the first time he'd sat in this clearing or the first time he'd admired the stars from this exact vantage point.

Stella had loved this place. She had loved the hills above the town in which she was born.

He looked at the stars once more. Some were dead but burning brightly still. He nodded. Yes, as long as the mind perceived, as long as memory held, the dead still lived.

"I am pregnant," she had said.

Tristan laughed beside her on the blanket in the soft summer grass. "Again?"

Stella rolled onto her side and traced the line of his full, handsome cheekbone. "You sound surprised."

"I've been busy. I don't remember being there for this one."

She pulled her delicate finger away from his face and frowned. "What are you suggesting?"

He laughed harder. "Nothing. You have seen the wise woman? You're not showing."

"I have neither seen nor told a soul, save you, here and now. But I *am* pregnant. A woman knows."

Tristan inhaled the scent of her auburn hair, sweet and heady, like the lilacs that grew on the mountainside. "Well, who am I to doubt the mysterious perceptions of a woman?"

She folded her arms. "This is number five, Trist. I've had plenty of practice carrying a child."

He raised his hands in mock surrender and laughed again. He just couldn't stop laughing around her. "If it's another boy, I think it's time to retire."

"Retire what?"

They both laughed now.

He nudged Stella and asked her, "How many stars do you see?" He counted five in the firmament above.

The early evening skies were suddenly obscured by clouds.

She smiled. "We should return. The boys will be concerned."

"Nonsense. Albert is twelve. He can look after the others. Let's stay a little longer."

"Simon gets scared, you know that. He sees monsters in the darkness."

Tristan moved to kiss her. "A moment longer, Stella love. There are no monsters in the darkness," he whispered.

"We must flee! I hear the dogs!"

Tristan grimaced and stood up, brushing flecks of dried vegetation from his black traveling cloak. He shivered, slapped at his arms. He hadn't felt cold since he put the thing around his neck.

He mounted his black horse and helped the distorted shape of the Monk of Ulfur up behind him.

"Make haste!" screamed the monk.

Tristan smiled without humor or pleasure. "I know this place. They will not catch us. Calm yourself. We are the monsters in the darkness, Jeremiah."

Tristan Drogos de Merlon whirled his horse around and left the clearing of happiness and death behind.

6

The Ghost of Malcolm Dewar

Broadford Higgins kept the key around his neck on a fine chain, a chain that wouldn't choke him to death if pulled hard but merely shatter into a hundred tiny pieces. He wasn't taking any chances. A man would sneak up and kill for a trinket like his, and the Lord knew that Broadford himself had murdered two people to lay his hands on it. He wasn't trusting anybody.

He had ridden a hundred leagues since gaining the key, moving from shitty town to shitty town. In one such rural muckheap by the name of Dunedin, he entered a public establishment called the Prancing Doxy and removed his top hat. He ordered an ale from the barkeep and took a seat in the corner, far from the light of the fire. The trinket warmed his blood; he didn't need additional heat or the light that accompanied it.

The ale tasted fresh though he knew it to be stale. Everything tasted better now—food, sex. The trinket permeating his body, suffusing his spirit, empowered and invigorated him like a shot of whisky.

He looked around at the patrons of the Prancing Doxy. He could murder each one easily or all of them at once if he had to. His strength was growing, and he found himself on the verge of godhood.

But what does a god do of an evening except contemplate murder?

In the mood to get drunk, Broadford quickly finished his ale and grabbed the serving girl by the wrist. She jumped in fright, not having seen him in the darkness of the inn.

"Another ale, girl."

"Yes, sire," she said with downcast eyes.

The redhead's white blouse clung to her breasts with sweat. He could make out her nipples beneath the fabric and became aroused. He decided he would bed the girl. She would never forget him no matter how many men she had been with or would go on to have. His sexual powers had sharpened with the acquisition of the trinket, not that they had been unremarkable to begin with. Oh no, Broadford was among the greatest of sexual swordsmen on his own merits. But now he was extraordinary. A behemoth. A beast. Not even Archibald Kirk could fuck like he could. Not now.

Broadford watched the girl fetch his drink. The Prancing Doxy reeked of drunks and small-town desperation, but at least the serving girls had big breasts. Yes, he had to give the proprietor of the pub a gentlemanly nod for his marketing efforts. Come to the Doxy, get drunk on tits, and forget the pathos of your foul, mindless existence. Clever. The idea would surely take off in a larger town someday.

He laughed, and a small part of him laughed too, but at his own arrogance. That small part, diminishing by the hour, was dying, its voice already lost amid the noise of his new ego.

When the girl came back, he grabbed the handle of the flagon with one hand and the wrist of the girl with the other, then sank the ale in a few gulps. "Another," he said with a grin and released her. He wiped the froth from his manic smile.

"Yes, sire." She curtsied.

She was polite, respectful. He liked that. Appreciated it. Even fell in love with it. He enjoyed fucking those girls most of all, the ones who knelt and paid duty, the ones who adored him formally, the ones who called him sire. Sir. Milord. Master.

"You're a fucking idiot, Higgins."

Broadford leaned back in horror as Malcolm Dewar sat down at the table. The man had no eyes, merely bleeding holes.

The startled toff closed his eyes and breathed. He focused on the heat flowing through his veins, on the serving girl and her flame-red hair. His heart rate slowed. He smiled and opened his eyes.

Malcolm sat there, sneering. "I'm not going anywhere, you prick."

Broadford shook his head, felt his frustration rise. Nearby patrons were deep within their idiotic discussions about fucking their sisters or whatever peasants talked about. He whispered, "What are you doing here? You're dead in a gibbet, swinging in the damned sea breeze somewhere."

The ghost-corpse nodded in agreement, blood oozing down its cheeks. "No thanks to you, bastard."

"Don't blame me." Broadford shrugged. "You should have shared it. I asked you several times to share it. Just a taste, I said. Just give it to me for a while, I said. Practically begged you."

"Why should I have? It was mine as we agreed." Then the spirit leaned forward and grinned. "But do not fret, for my fate will be yours before long. I thank you for freeing me from it before I died. You freed me, Broadie, old mate."

He eyed the corpse warily. "You're welcome."

"I'm here to return the favor," Malcolm said. "Throw that thing away before it destroys you."

Broadford's chest and shoulders shook in restrained laughter. "Not likely, old friend."

The smile disappeared from the face of the ghost. "It's not too late."

"I beg to differ." Broadford pursed his lips and examined a fingernail. "You, I can handle. The little girl, I killed her, a terrible thing I admit it, but that I can handle. All the ghosts and visitations in the world aren't going to change how I feel. This thing"—He grabbed the key trinket and held it before the dead man's sightless eyes—"is worth it all."

"You're a fool."

"Doubtless. I'll die a fool, as you did, but I'll live as a god before that happens, as you did."

"And what of your immortal soul?"

"Fuck it."

The ghost laughed, blood oozing from its eyes, dripping into its mouth, causing the next few words to come out as a gurgle. "It's hard to argue with you when you're in this mood, Broadie. You just won't listen to sense."

"Well, there you have it. Two stubborn old souls going at it, just like we always did." Several of the locals frowned in Broadford's direction. He ignored them and watched as the serving girl turned from the bar and made her way to his table. "If you'll excuse me, I have another ale coming."

Malcolm spat a blood-laced accusation. "You murdered her and told the city guard it was me."

Broadford spread his arms wide. "You promised to kill her, in public too. Naturally, the suspicion fell on you."

"The mother. I promised to kill the mother, not the girl. She had nothing to do with it!"

The fine-clothed toff shrugged. "What does it matter, you made the threat to kill the mother, an oath heard by half the town. It was a small step from there to the daughter, which was an opportunity too fine to pass up. Anyway, couldn't get at the mother, could I? The girl was easier."

The ghost of Malcolm Dewar cast a bloody, sightless scowl. "I never intended on harming either of them. I'm not a murderer of women and children!"

"I know that, but you should have kept your mouth shut." Broadford was becoming thirsty. He looked over the shoulder of the dead man. The smiling serving girl held an ale, resting it between her breasts, but suddenly another patron blocked her from his sight. He turned back to Malcolm. "What I didn't count on was you swallowing the bloody key when they came banging on the door."

"You're damned, Broadie, but you can still walk away."

Broadford scoffed. "I watched as your powers grew. You never talked to me about it, but I knew it was the key. Ever since you took it from the monastery, you were different. When I was in your company, women wouldn't notice me. Me! They fawned all over you, made me sick to watch. We both know that between the two of us, I was the ladies' man, not you. Never you. I swear, you even grew taller. You never had a hangover, and we drank some nights old friend, my lord, how we drank. My suspicions grew, and now I see clearly that you betrayed me."

The corpse laughed, a savage bark. "I betrayed *you*?"

"The key, you could have given it to me. We could have shared it. You kept it to yourself. I call that betrayal, don't you?"

The ghost took a rasping breath. "You murdered the child of my mistress, told them it was me, set me up to be hanged, and then to add insult to injury, you gutted me like a fish while I swung in the salt air. *That* is betrayal!"

He shrugged again. "Necessity drives a man. I'm sure you understand." The serving girl was approaching. "Goodbye, Malcolm."

Then the eyeless thing was gone.

The redhead leaned over, exposing the smooth swellings of her breasts. "Your ale, sire."

Broadford thought of Malcom Dewar's warning, and deep inside his mind, the small figure of the gentleman-toff rose to the surface of a dark, ancient sea and raised his arms, pleading, screaming, *save me*. But the voice was drowned out by a frigid wind, and the tiny figure was swallowed by a massive saw-toothed monster of the ageless deep, top hat and all.

He looked up at the girl, his charming smile returning. "What's a girl like you doing in a place like this?"

"My uncle, he owns this place."

"Really? Well, listen to me. You were meant for better things. You are stunningly beautiful. I mean that."

She looked down and smiled, her coyness igniting Broadford's lust.

"I wager you say that to all the girls."

Broadford looked at his ale and then at the girl, a manic smile frozen on his face. "Yes, yes, I do."

7

Seraphim the Phallus

Dawn would alight from its golden chariot before long, but for now, night suffocated day. The bed chamber was cold and still in the early morning, as cold and still as the frail hand Seraphim held in the darkness.

He had never had an erection like it. The strange metal trinket had infused his body, his blood, with vigor as he penetrated the girl in the dark, filthy little room. He turned her around in his hands as if she were a child's toy—lifted her, threw her in the air, and impaled her. He heard the other customers running in fright and the massive doorman, a grizzled veteran of the war, cloaked in fur and a shaggy beard, banging on the door, growling viciously. "What the hell's going on in there?"

But he didn't enter. Something in the guttural howls of pleasure and pain from within must have stayed his hand from the door. Even large men fear.

It was quiet now. Only one of the two bodies breathed. She had been a girl, once. Now, she was chilled meat. He would have to pay extra, he knew, for lost wages over the next...What was the shelf life of a cheap whore before she died of a common disease? Five years? It would be expensive. Or, he could simply walk out. But he couldn't afford the trouble. His power was growing, but he would pay for now.

He could feel the cool weight of the trinket on his bare chest. One more trinket like this, and he wouldn't be paying for anything ever again. He could take what he wanted with impunity. Money would mean nothing. Not with power like that. God does not pay taxes.

He had strangled the prostitute as he climaxed. He supposed he should feel remorse, but the only thing he felt was his cock. His whole being had inhabited it as he murdered her.

Murdered her with his cock.

He laughed a low chuckle.

Why do you laugh, pig?

Seraphim yawned and feigned disinterest, ignoring the voice in his head, hoping it would go away.

The murder of a poor innocent child, you somehow find that amusing?

Against his own best instincts, Seraphim bit. "Innocent? Come now, we both know her innocence departed long ago. She relinquished it."

Silence, pig. She was God's child. That makes her innocent.

"I, too, am God's child, am I not?"

The voice paused a moment and then spoke, its tone a savage sneer designed to degrade, to debase. *A twisted semblance of such. Malformed, but yes. Yes, you are God's child. Even you.*

Malformed? Seraphim rubbed one hand over his naked body, the other still clasping the girl's fingers. He could see very little of his flesh in the darkness, but he was familiar enough with its proportions. He was lean, muscular, and had long black hair that shone darker than that of any maiden. Hung like a feral horse. Most importantly, he was handsome. So handsome that many a whore had given him a discount to match his charm, some even giving it up for free, and at least one had professed her love for him. At least one. He wasn't about to let the crazed voice scurrying around in his head eat away at him, erode his self-esteem like a rat nibbling at rotten floorboards.

"I may be possessed of many qualities, but malformation is not among them," he said.

The voice continued to scoff, superior, with an affected accent that never failed to irritate Seraphim. *You are diseased,* it said.

Seraphim grew angry. He was a rapist and a murderer, but he wasn't a fake, a pretender, a hypocrite, like the voice. "This conversation grows old and unamusing. I'm basking in the afterglow and need no distractions."

The voice burst into a disturbing cackle that morphed into a hacking cough. *I jest. You have no sense of humor, Seraphim. Smile. Life is good.*

"Yes. Life is good, but would be better without you. Why are you here?"

To make sure you murder your way to your true station.

Seraphim released his hold of the dead girl's hand and rubbed his forehead. The slight ache that accompanied the voice was sharper than usual. "My true station? Well, you should be happy, for today I have ascended to a higher plane."

If he thought his answer would please the voice, he was well mistaken. *Hah! One girl? You think you're going to get your name in the histories over one girl?*

"That's the seventh. Why am I even talking to you? You know how many girls I've done."

One, seven. The occasional cunt-for-sale hardly scratches the surface, now does it? Pathetic. You fancy yourself the devil incarnate? The next Hungry King? You'll have to do better than that.

"Have I not killed enough to satiate you?"

Seraphim immediately regretted the question. He had given the voice the opportunity it had been waiting for. He could almost sense it leaning forward and taking a deep breath.

No. No, you haven't, but I'm glad you asked. I have a valuable piece of advice for you. Listen carefully.

Seraphim bit his lip, closed his eyes, and tried to pretend that he was truly alone.

Stop murdering whores and do in somebody that counts! A king or something, for Christ's sake!

The morning sun was forcing its way through the curtains. Seraphim looked at the girl beside him. The golden light gently rested on her face, her profile glowing softly from within. Faint hairs flowered her cheek, like soft down. A child's face. "Why do you concern yourself so much with numbers?" he said, idly twirling a lock of strawberry-blonde hair around his finger.

Ambition, boy. Something you seem to lack.

"When I'm done, the numbers will take care of themselves. Don't concern yourself with numbers."

It's all in the numbers, pig. I wish you understood that. Immortality is in the numbers!

Seraphim struggled to understand the voice. At times it seemed to reflect his own thoughts, but at others it was as mysterious and as unfathomable as the cold, brutal wind. Immortality is in the numbers? What does that even mean? "I'll murder in my own time," he said. "For now, I wish you to fuck off."

The voice wheezed in indignity, trying to muster a response.

It was old, Seraphim thought, much older than he. It constantly nagged at him. Nothing was ever good enough. Drove him mad. Where had it come from? What did it want?

Pig, it spat. Then it was gone.

He once again clasped the dead girl's hand, trying to find a moment's peace. The hand was cold, and for a moment, Seraphim felt sorry for the girl, even missed her. She hadn't deserved her lot. She was flotsam carried on the current of fate, washed up on his beach. Would have been better off drowned.

Then the moment passed. He let the dead fingers fall, his hand moving to the glowing metal trinket lying on his chest—a pendant in the shape of an erect phallus.

The room lightened further with the unmasking of the morning sun. He let go of the pendant and traced the tattoo across his chest with his index finger. She had asked about the tattoo, traced it too, the girl, the dead one sleeping next to him. Strangely, she hadn't asked about the trinket.

"What is it?" she had asked, eyes all big and innocent.

"It's a tattoo," Seraphim said.

She rolled her eyes. "I know that, silly, what does it mean?"

"It's a dead language. Extinct." *As you shall soon be.* "It's nothing."

She sat up on the bed then, took his hands in hers, and looked at him earnestly. "I'd like to know."

She was sweet, this one.

Seraphim smiled. He took her hand and brushed her fingers over the large flowing script. *Serva Me.* "Save me."

She wore a serious face, her gaze meeting his and not wavering. Then she giggled. "I'll try," she said, looking at his chest once more, her fingers arcing from nipple to nipple and beyond as the tattoo arced. Then she lay down, spread her legs, and giggled again.

The memory made him sad, for just a moment. It wasn't remorse, just a twinge of melancholy.

He laughed. And he didn't stop laughing until the sun flooded the room and bathed him and the corpse in a honeyed glow.

8

The Contract

The King's Balls hostelry was closed to the public in the early hours of morning; nevertheless, it was possessed of three men sitting around a small beer-stained table, two drinking, their breath soured from ale. The third man was outfitted in a light cloak of gray, his features disguised by the shadows within his hood, his face a patch of darkness within the darkness of the room. When he removed the hood, he remained cloaked in mystery. His dark eyes glowed with blackness, absorbing the candlelight from the table in his calm stare, in contrast, his military cropped hair shocking white.

The other two men sat back in their seats and exchanged nervous glances. One man, Alfred Hargreaves, was the owner of the King's Balls and an investor in the local prostitution business in Dysael. He was sweating, his receding hairline glistening in the lamplight. "The freak wears a cock around his neck. I mean, fer God's sake, a cock?" he said to the unusual-looking man opposite him.

Stuart Brody, a thin man with skin hanging from his throat, like that of a turkey, owned two brothels outright. He was breathing heavily with outrage. "He's been scaring off the customers, and we're losing girls. Killed one, you see. He paid handsomely for damages mind, but the other girls are terrified. They're running off, we haven't tracked 'em all down yet. It's just bad for business all round."

"Describe the phallus."

The two businessmen looked at each other and then at the man with the dark eyes, the inscrutable face. Hargreaves said, "It's a cock, like I told you."

"Have you seen it?" The man spoke with no discernible accent, his voice as unreadable as his face.

Hargreaves laughed and snot exploded from his nose. He tried to wipe it off on the table, surreptitiously, and failed. "No, not my thing, but one of the girls saw it. It's a pendant of some kind."

"What's it made of?"

The businessmen exchanged another glance. "A metal, she said it glowed from within. You know, lumin...lumos...what's the word?"

The man pulled the gray hood over his head once more and sat back in his chair. "Luminous. What's this man's name?"

Hargreaves leaned forward and spoke in a spittle-laced murmur. "He calls himself Seraphim. But he sure isn't any angel of light and purity, I can tell you that."

There was silence. The hooded figure seemed to be thinking. "Where is he now?"

Brody leaned forward to join his drinking companion in the center of the small table, whispering in the hushed voice of a conspirator, as if the man in question might be listening outside the door to the tavern, waiting to murder them all. "I don't know, but he's coming to have a girl tonight, it's Wednesday," he said looking at Hargreaves. "He always comes on a Wednesday. In the whorehouse down the end of the street here, the blue building. But for the Lord's sake, don't do him in there. We can't afford to upset more of our regulars. Keep it well away."

The gray-hooded man raised a hand and dipped it into the darkness surrounding his face, whether scratching his chin or picking food from his teeth, the two drinking men couldn't fathom.

"Look here," Alfred Hargreaves said after an inordinate amount of silence had passed. "Are you going to assassinate that bastard or not? We've been informed that you're very good at this sort of thing. Money's not an issue, within reason of course." The sweating man withdrew a bag from his pocket, wiped his forehead with it, and placed it on the table. Eyebrows raised in expectation, he looked at the gray hood.

The mysterious figure pushed back his chair and stood. "I'll find you when it's done." He turned to leave, without taking the bag of coins.

"I want the pendant," Stuart Brody blurted. The turkey-necked man appeared sheepish for a moment. "You know, as a keepsake." He smiled weakly. "If that's all right."

The cloaked figure shook his head. No, it wasn't all right. Then he walked out.

Alfred Hargreaves looked sideways at Stuart Brody, who shrugged and said, "It's well made, or so I hear."

———

OUTSIDE THE KING'S BALLS, the gray-hooded figure crossed the dirt street in the early morning breeze. He mounted a horse of pure black and rode three leagues to a nearby military barracks as the sun broke the horizon and the night winds sought refuge in the still-darkened alleyways of side streets.

Upon entering the barracks, he removed his cloak and threw it at a startled stable boy. The man wore a gray leather vest, layered epaulets, leather leggings of the same color, and two short swords on his hips. He hurried across an empty compound and entered the gloom of a stone hallway leading to a door. He knocked once.

"Enter."

A late-middle aged man with silvering hair at the temples looked up from a large paper-strewn desk. He smiled perfunctorily. "Knight-Captain Lewis. How may I be of service?"

"I believe I've found one of them, Commander."

Commander Lucas Matthewson steepled his fingers and sat back. "Them?"

"A bearer of an artifact, sir. His name is Seraphim."

The commander stared at the ceiling and nodded. "Ah. King Bruwaert will be pleased, more so when the trinket is in his possession, and for that, he'll pay a handsome price. You'll get your cut of course."

"Honor is its own reward," Christopher said. "I'll require men."

"Of course. Jupiter Company is at your disposal. How many do you think would suffice for the job?"

"Ten."

"Ten? For one man? That's most unlike your reputation, Lewis. Everyone here in Dysael says you can handle yourself." He rubbed the growth of his beard, one hand on either side of his jaw. "Do you honestly believe these things bestow supernatural powers on their bearers? I'm genuinely curious as to your opinion."

"I couldn't say, Commander. My opinion counts for little. In any event, he killed a prostitute, upset the local merchants who specialize in that sort of thing, ruffled some feathers. It may just be a crazed patron or . . ."

"Or what, Knight-Captain?"

"There could be something to these trinkets, sir."

Matthewson exhaled a measured breath. "All right. Ten it is. And if he's as dangerous as you're suggesting, make sure you kill this Seraphim character stone-cold dead."

Christopher Lewis saluted, fist on chest, and turned to go.

"Knight-Captain? A moment. There's something you should perhaps know."

The man with midnight-black eyes turned back to the commander. "Sir?"

"Two days ago, several men were killed in the pursuit of"—Matthewson leaned forward to examine a letter in the middle of his desk—"a one Robert Occitane. The man himself is confirmed dead, but the trinket purported to be in his possession is nowhere to be found. A dozen of the most highly skilled of Bruwaert's men were left slaughtered, some most unpleasantly, including members of his Personal Guard. I understand you knew him, this Robert Occitane?"

The knight-captain's face was steady. "Yes, sir. I knew him."

"It's my understanding that King Bruwaert kindly offered you as emissary of sorts, and you fought under this Robert Occitane in the Alliance, I believe?"

"One tour. Yes, sir."

The knight-captain didn't elaborate, and a further moment passed.

Finally, Matthewson said, "Take thirty men."

9

Good Times at the King's Balls

The King's Balls hostelry was crowded but oddly demure. The stern-faced men sitting around the tables in groups had their heads close together, whispering low, seemingly ill at ease. If Seraphim tried hard enough, he could tune in to any of the muted conversations as if he were sitting at their very table. He didn't bother, experience having taught him that all most men talked about were their wives and commanding officers. He had neither any longer and found the discussions petty, unworthy of his attention, a reminder of the feeble creature he had once been.

Pig, do you not find this all rather strange?

Irritation flared. Seraphim hadn't heard the pompous voice for several days, not since the night he murdered the girl, and he was just starting to hope that it might be gone once and for all. He sighed and sipped his ale. "Leave me in peace."

I shall not. You were just thinking how all this was beneath you, and now you spurn the opportunity for more intelligent conversation. I fail to understand you at times. But to return to my point. Is this not odd?

Seraphim looked around the sour-smelling, dimly lit pub. There seemed little out of the ordinary. "Odd? What?"

This disgusting tavern has never been so popular. The patrons are military, can you not see? They're here to kill you for murdering the girl! You must flee! Flee the town, flee Dysael!

Seraphim's long black hair was unbound, and he brushed it behind his ears. "Nonsense, there's a barracks in the town. Even military men need to drink."

"Aye, that they do," said a stranger who sat down at the table, an ale in each hand.

Seraphim had to control the impulse to leap across the table and slice the man's throat—much too public and much too soon after killing the young prostitute. Perhaps the voice was right. Perhaps it was time to get out of Dysael.

The man slid one of the drinks over. "Talking to yourself, Archibald? Or should I call you Seraphim?"

Seraphim caught his breath and smiled mirthlessly. The man was not a stranger after all. "Hello, Christopher. I'd like to thank you for not stabbing me in the back while I was sitting here quietly enjoying my ale."

Knight-Captain Christopher Lewis bowed his head slightly. "I thought about it."

"I'm absolutely positive you did." Seraphim couldn't make out the man's eyes in the gloomy pub, but then again, he never could. Only the faintest glimmer showed from somewhere within the two deep, dark water wells. "What brings the finest assassin in King Bruwaert's army to the King's Balls?"

Christopher ran his hand through his short white hair. "It seems I'm not the only one in the business of assassination these days."

Pig, kill this man, he is dangerous.

"I'm afraid I don't know what you're talking about." Seraphim scanned the pub, the hairs on his arms standing up. Most of the men here tonight were not intent on socializing. They were here for him. The accursed voice was right after all, but he'd be damned if he acknowledged it or the fear growing within his breast.

"You're right. You're quite surrounded," Christopher said.

"Are you here to kill me, Knight-Lieutenant?"

"Those are my orders, but I wouldn't do such a thing here, so publicly. And I'm a knight-captain now."

Seraphim sneered. "Congratulations. All that arse licking and following orders like an obedient dog has certainly paid dividends." He reached behind his neck, collecting his long black hair, and tied a ponytail with a thin cord.

"King Bruwaert wants your pendant. I'm here to collect it."

"Bruwaert?" Seraphim scoffed. "Over my dead body."

Christopher Lewis folded his arms. "Be careful what you wish for. Robert Occitane is dead."

Seraphim glared at the black-eyed assassin. "Is this what you've come to? Hunting down loyal comrades? Robert fought for Bruwaert and Tremain, risked his life for them. Where's your honor? You're pathetic."

"I had nothing to do with Robert's killing."

Seraphim spread his arms. "And yet, here you are."

"For a man who kills prostitutes, you have an odd grasp of honor." The assassin stared at his ale, then looked up. "Do you know why they call this place the King's Balls?"

Seraphim glanced about the room. On the walls of the pub could be seen, if one squinted through the gloom, various memorabilia from the Great War: weapons supposedly wielded by the greatest warriors of the enemy, scraps of clothing reputed to have come from the Hungry King himself, and above the bar, in a place of honor, the prize showpiece in a glass case—two graying lumps of tissue within a shriveling scrotum, the Hungry King's balls, cut from the corpse of the evil lord. Said to have possessed magical properties, his body had been shredded to pieces by various secretive parties, made into keepsakes, and spread to the four winds to be sold on the black market. Bigger than your average set, no doubt, but Seraphim knew they had as little to do with the Hungry King as the bar owner's own sweaty gonads.

"If you think Hargreaves lays claim to the king's true sac, you're a fool," Seraphim said.

"I believe no such thing. Bruwaert's men took them shortly after Hargreaves put them up there, for which the proprietor received compensation." He nodded to the exhibit above the bar. "Those are fakes."

Seraphim laughed. "Then you're doubly a fool, as is Bruwaert. They were never genuine. Sleep with a whore once in a while. It'll save you a lot of time and effort learning things. Hargreaves is a double-dealer. Your fat king's been snorting desiccated goat's balls up his nose, and welcome to it."

Christopher leaned in and whispered, "Well, the point is Bruwaert *does* like his artifacts, and now he wants yours. Come with me, Archibald. Let's talk someplace more private."

A slow smile dripping with venom spread across Seraphim's face. "I'm not going anywhere with you, assassin. That would be the death of me. And call me Seraphim. Archibald Kirk died in the war, as did his honor."

"Very well. Give me the pendant, *Seraphim*, and I'll let you live. I'll tell the commander you escaped. We fought on the same side once. I owe you that. Just make sure you disappear forever. And stop killing whores."

"Hah! Spare me the show of loyalty, Knight-Lieutenant. I think I'll hang on to my cock, if you'll pardon the expression."

"It's Knight-Captain, if you will." Christopher raised his mug. "Here's to old friends, Archibald."

Seraphim hesitated, then raised his ale. "Robert Occitane was the best of us. Here's to Robert."

Both men drank deeply, Seraphim from his own mug, not the one given. He knew better than to drink gifts extended by assassins.

"Three weeks ago," Christopher Lewis said suddenly, "an Ulfurian monk escaped a prison hulk specifically designed to hold him, a ship that sails the world eternally, never stopping long at any port. I say escaped, but it was more likely he was *freed*. Now, Archibald, who would have any reason to do such a thing? And who would know where to find that ship?"

Seraphim found this digression disturbing. Why was he talking about monks and prison ships? Then a thought began to coalesce in his mind, but it remained tantalizingly unrealized.

"The Monks of Ulfur are no more," he said. "Dead more than a hundred years."

"There's a survivor. Perhaps others live in the shadows. We know little of them other than they age slowly, and it seems this one, at least, is a mind reader. They are twisted and poisonous creatures, but extant."

"Hardy little bastards, aren't they?" Seraphim thought a moment, then said, "Who was going to all that effort to hold the monk in the first place?"

Knight-Captain Lewis shrugged, clearly unwilling to divulge that tidbit of information. "When Re'Shan fell, there were rumors of pillaging, theft."

"Pillage is not uncommon whenever a city is sacked. Nor is rape, and murder. Some men specialize in one or the other, but most partake of all three in differing measures." Seraphim raised his mug and winked at Christopher. "We all know where your proclivities lie."

The knight-captain ignored the barb. "While Re'Shan burned, it was rumored that a crew of men indulged in a different kind of pillaging, an abandoned monastery on Mount Ulfur, just outside the fallen city, a monastery long hidden, long thought inaccessible. Sacred relics were taken, or so the rumors say."

"Rumors. Rumors. Why are you telling me this? What are you getting at, Lewis?" Seraphim realized full well what Christopher was getting at. His mind drifted away. He saw the assassin's lips moving but couldn't focus on what he was saying, for he'd just realized who had freed the monk and where they were going. And why. His heart was racing, but he kept his face steady and took another drink.

Christopher leaned forward and Seraphim snapped back to the present conversation.

"You were there," Christopher said. "That's where you got that trinket you currently wear under your shirt. Are you prepared to die for that thing?" He leaned further forward, meeting the eyes of the man opposite him, staring hard, digging, burrowing. "What are they? Why does Bruwaert seek them?"

The man born Archibald Kirk wagged a finger. "You should have been there, instead of somewhere cutting the throats of sleeping men. You would understand then. Understand what we are."

"What are you?"

Seraphim simply slurped another drink.

Christopher pushed harder. "Who was there with you?"

"There were six of us."

"Six? Names. Give me their names."

Seraphim smiled. "Honor, what little I have left, precludes me from saying."

"How many of the trinkets did you find? Where is the monastery?"

"I cannot tell you. He would kill me."

Christopher sat back. "Who would kill you? What are you afraid of?"

"Afraid? Let me tell you about fear. You were a man to be feared. Once. You, with those deep black eyes of yours, those death pits. You used to frighten me, honestly. But I warn you now, you don't know what you're dealing with. Do not cross paths, or swords, with any of the trinket-bearers, not me and especially not him."

"Who? Who are you talking about?"

Pig, you have said enough! Run!

"I run from no man!" Seraphim shouted.

Christopher furrowed his brow and looked around.

Fool, live to fight another day, there are too many!

Seraphim whispered to himself. "He's going for the source."

As you should have done, pig! Silence! This man knows too much already!

Christopher leaned in once more, breathlessly whispering. "Who? The source of what?"

Seraphim flashed his eyes upon those of the assassin and smiled a slow, creeping grin. "The Hungry King is upon you. Doom is upon you all."

"The Hungry King is dead," Christopher said.

"Long live the King!"

The table and drinks erupted, ale spraying slowly through the air, and the assassin tumbled backward off his stool. He regained his feet swiftly, twin daggers in hand. He didn't like surprises. A surprise in his profession rarely augured well for one's survival, better to be the one jumping from the shadows on the unsuspecting.

The man known to him as Archibald Kirk was gone. In a tavern full of soldiers now on their feet, he was gone in an instant. Somehow.

"There!" someone shouted.

On the wall above the tavern bar, beside the mock testicles of the Hungry King, something clinging to the wall like a gecko to a sunburned rock. A crossbow bolt thudded into the wall near Seraphim's head, and he dropped out of sight behind the counter. The barkeep, a mustachioed gentleman of later years, leaped over the bar and onto the main floor with the gusto of a much younger man.

Tables and chairs clattered as every noncombatant headed for the door, leaving only hardened soldiers intent on murder. The room was still packed.

Christopher Lewis signaled for two of his men to move behind the counter, but they hesitated, the hawks clearly spooked by the acrobatics of their quarry. He signaled again with more vehemence and indicated to four others to watch the exit.

He didn't recall seeing Archibald Kirk, or Seraphim, as he now calls himself, carrying a weapon, but he wasn't taking any unnecessary risks. He hadn't lived this long by being careless.

The two men edged their way behind the bar, reluctant to get close to something clearly supernatural. Christopher raised two fingers and pointed at the bar. He and two more men stalked closer, dagger in either hand, reverse gripped. The bar counter was about three yards long of polished red-stained oak. On the silent count of three, all five men rushed in, two flanking either side and Christopher leaping over the counter.

Nobody, nothing, except a trapdoor in the floor.

"Shit." He didn't like this, enclosed spaces with a murderous, and quite possibly mad, trinket-bearer. This day was not going to end well. He knew it would be a brave man to enter the rabbit hole first and so took the initiative himself. He reached down to pull the trapdoor open and almost put his back out. It was locked. He scanned the room for the barkeep, but he was gone.

Was there a key? Was it locked from the inside?

"Get the publican back in here!" he shouted.

Then something strange happened, an oddity beyond any of the evenings offerings thus far. A shimmering haze, like that through which a man walking the distant ridge of a desert might see, crosses the pub. The soldier standing in front of the knight-captain flickered, his chainmail and Jupiter Company eagle insignia phasing out for a moment to be replaced by something else, someone else, then returning again.

He frowned, not understanding what he was seeing.

A lifetime of instinct kicked in, and Christopher threw his head back just in time to avoid the slashing arc of a blade. He lost his balance and fell backward, the man standing directly behind him losing his footing as the knight-captain collapsed on him.

Confusion, then crimson spray.

The two men that had entered the bar from the right side dropped, blood spurting from their throats.

Christopher was on his feet, scanning the room. A figure moved swiftly through the darkened pub toward the exit, a figure closely resembling one of the Jupiter Company soldiers, but it wavered and twisted as if viewed through a thick beer glass.

Damn it, his men were not reacting!

"Stop him!" he shouted, pointing. Once again, he hurled himself over the bar, and ran as fast as he could.

The flexing shadow had almost reached the exit. The knight-captain's men looked at each other in confusion. Two more men blocking the doors dropped to their knees, clutching at their throats.

Then it was gone. Archibald Kirk was gone. Seraphim was gone.

Christopher rushed outside, followed by the remaining men of Jupiter Company. The streets were empty, and he knew now there was no chance of bringing Seraphim to ground.

For a man used to being feared, Knight-Captain Christopher Lewis found that the tables had now turned. Dread seized his heart, a feeling long since removed from his emotional repertoire. It was almost refreshing.

Children's Names

Albert was the oldest. The middle boys were Terence, Geoffrey, and Simon, in that order. Matthew, the youngest.

The rain fell hard outside the tavern, kicking up mud in tiny droplets, and all the while he said their names over and over. It was important to remember their names.

His name was Tristan Drogos de Merlon, and he was determined that the world would remember it. The world would have no choice when all was said and done.

"I don't like it," said the bent figure opposite him, hunched at a filth-stained table. Jeremiah pulled his dirty brown hood further over his head and cupped his hands about the steaming mug of acrid-smelling tea. He wrinkled his nose. "We must avoid people, and yet you drag us through every pissant town in Canterbury and Otago. This is asking for trouble. Neither of us are the type to blend in with idiot farmers and inbred villagers. Why gamble with our lives?" The monk sniffed miserably. "It's cold and damp, which I normally don't mind, but this town and this pub specifically are tainted with something else. What shithole do we find ourselves in now?"

"We're embraced by the hospitality of the Prancing Doxy hostelry in Dunedin, a fine town populated by fine citizens." Tristan had his eyes on a group of four laughing men who had just entered the tavern.

The large bearded man in the center of the group was acting out a particularly amusing tale with his hands, waving them in front of his companions, but took the time to slap a large-breasted serving girl on the rump as she passed by.

"The girls here are pretty." Tristan slid a copper coin across the table toward Jeremiah. "It must be some time since you've felt the ministrations of a woman. Shall we call one over?" A smile played at the edges of his cracked lips.

Jeremiah slid the coin back, nose wrinkled in distaste. "I'm a monk."

"A monk that kills children. I hardly think sleeping with a barmaid is going to push you over the edge of immorality."

The Monk of Ulfur shot his companion a lethal glance and hissed, "We must hide."

"Have you not spent enough time in captivity?" Tristan spoke without taking his eyes from the four sturdy-looking men. "Now that you have your freedom, would you skulk from shadow to shadow like a leper?"

"Fine words de Merlon, but I have no desire to be strung from the nearest tall tree as a warlock. These people are both suspicious and superstitious, a bad combination for one such as I. If you wish to journey to the mountain, we should take the back roads, or better yet, get off them altogether. Somebody will spot us sooner rather than later."

"A man can't rule the world by taking back roads. I do believe you miss your floating prison."

"Bah, no man ever ruled the world by taking unnecessary risks."

"Come, Jeremiah, gird your loins, collect your courage. Can you not smell it?"

The twisted monk scowled. "Smell what?"

Tristan nodded at the four men. The large bearded one was holding something up for the others to see.

Jeremiah turned his shriveled head, and a sharp breath wheezed from the Monk of Ulfur. "He carries the metal?"

"He does. Surely you, of all people, can sense that."

The monk swiveled back to Tristan. "That man's a sheriff, a country fool no doubt, but a sheriff nonetheless. We can't afford a public confrontation until we're stronger."

Tristan continued watching the group from within the depths of his hood, the small metallic crown upon his breast warming to the presence of another of its kind. "This confrontation won't be public."

BEING A SHERIFF was all George Gardener had ever wanted. The position came with respect and no small amount of power, a fact which he used to bed as many women as he could and to drink as much free ale as was given. It also allowed him to kill and take with impunity. He was, after all, the local law. Call it tax. At times, he felt like the Almighty himself, or the Devil, depending on his mood.

Today had been a good day. He'd felt better than ever. Younger, stronger. He'd made love to his mistress, gone to the pub and drunk more beer than he could ever remember drinking, and still had the virility to go home, tell his boys a bedtime story, and make love to his wife—three times.

Yes, it had been a good day. A good day.

But when he awoke with a cold knife at his throat and an even colder hand clamped over his mouth, it was no longer a good day. It was a very bad one.

The dark hooded thing sitting on the bed and leaning over him raised a finger to its mouth.

"Shhh."

George Gardener widened his eyes and glanced to the left where his wife was still sleeping. He prayed that she was sleeping and not dead. He scanned the other way and saw a smaller version of the thing above him sitting on a chair in the corner, cradling one of his boys, looking down at the child with a motherly tenderness. The large bearded man attempted to move but was forced back down.

The thing pulled back its hood, revealing a skeletal face with sunken cheeks, sunken eyes, and thin bloodless lips. Fear threatened to overwhelm the sheriff and drive him mad.

Then the creature removed its hand from George's mouth and whispered, "Where's Malcolm Dewar?"

He didn't understand the question or anything that was happening. His mind had frozen in terror. The creature, keeping the blade tight against the sheriff's throat, reached into a pocket of its traveling cloak and produced a small metallic key. "The man who carried this. Where is he?"

It was the trinket he'd been wearing around his neck of late. How did the thing remove it without waking him?

"Last time." It pressed the blade harder. "Where is he?"

"I don't know no . . . what's his name?"

"Malcolm. Malcolm Dewar."

He looked frantically at his wife and son and tried not to cut his own throat against the blade.

"Do not be concerned," the skeletal thing said. "They sleep and will not wake. We can talk freely, but try to fight or run, and they die."

George nodded, gulped, and licked his dry lips. "I don't know no Malcolm Dewar. I swear."

"Where'd you get this?" The trinket swung on a fine chain in front of George's face.

"S-some toffee-nosed bastard who come into town bold as brass, whoring and drinking the town dry. Putting on airs, can't be having that, not in my district. Fancy prick took my favorite serving girl to bed, the bastard."

"His name?"

He thought for a moment. "Higgins. Higgins it is. Wore a top hat."

The creature removed the knife from George's throat and stood up.

Tall, thought the sheriff. Monstrously tall.

The scarred man spoke quietly. "*Broadford* Higgins?"

"Aye. That's him."

"Where is he?"

"He's locked up down in the cells."

"Give me the keys."

"I don't . . . Gretts has them, in the guardhouse."

The creature gestured to the corner where the other monster cradled the child. "What's your boy's name?"

The sherriff looked over at his son. "I can't . . . It's dark. I think that's Stuart."

Tristan Drogos de Merlon drove his knife into George Gardener's eye socket with the speed of a striking snake. The wife did not wake.

He wiped his knife clean of gore on the dead man's nightshirt. Jeremiah was stroking the face of the sleeping child, a boy of about six.

"I have business at the guardhouse," Tristan said. "Take your time with little Stuart."

The monk-thing began to cry. "Why do you tell me the boy's name? I don't want to know his name."

Tristan's face was a cold mask of contempt. "It's important to remember their names, don't you think? Someone has to remember them."

Jeremiah clenched his sharpened teeth together. Silently, and not for the first time, the aged Monk of Ulfur cursed his liberator. When he next looked up, he was alone with the boy, the boy's sleeping mother, and the corpse of George Gardener.

11

Broken Bones and Top Hats

Where was his top hat? They had taken the key from him. Yes, he knew whose fat raw-knuckled hands held the key, but Broadford had no clue on the whereabouts of his hat.

Blood dripped from his broken nose and onto the straw-covered floor of his cell. He cursed his stupidity. He had flaunted the trinket, drawn attention to himself, and some puffed-up county sheriff caught him off guard in the bed of the red-headed serving wench with the big tits. It took seven men to subdue him. Seven. And despite their numbers, he nearly made it out, but his ale had been tampered with. He was sure of it. He'd probably been dosed with a sedative: perhaps opium, henbane, hemlock, or a mixture of all three.

Did the girl have anything to do with it? What was her name? Had he even asked? Not that it mattered. He'd nearly fought his way out and hurt a few big men in the attempt; they made sure to return the favor after he'd been locked down tight. At least two of his ribs were broken along with his nose. Bastards. Had he broken any laws? None. The charges of soliciting prostitution were absurd.

He snorted painfully, trying to clear his nose, but the blood just kept coming. His wrists were manacled to the walls; he was losing sensation in his arms. If he still had the trinket, he'd be able to tear the shackles from the crumbling stone, but it was gone. His body ached for it. He shifted uncomfortably, peering between the bars into the darkness of the guardhouse, unable to make out anyone patrolling the halls.

"I say, can a fellow get a drink of water?"

Silence.

"I am innocent of any and all charges against me. I demand the right to legal representation. Innocent, you hear me?"

A noise came from the distant guard room. Scuffling, and then a shuffle coming closer. A voice spoke, deep, melodic, alluring like a Venus flytrap or a young serving girl with red hair, big tits, and a shy smile.

"Innocent, you say? Come now, Broadford. You're hardly that. Hardly that."

Broadford tried to make out where the voice was coming from— an oddly familiar voice. A shape was moving, collecting darkness as it approached along the gloomy corridor, expanding, elongating.

"Who's there?" he asked.

"A friend," the voice said.

He was still disorientated from his recent beating, but he was damned sure the figure approaching was no friend. But that voice. He knew that voice.

"Marshal?"

The figure solidified at the bars of the cell and bowed. "Tristan Drogos de Merlon, at your service, though no longer a marshal. How are you, Higgins? Enjoying your stay?"

Broadford looked around the small, filthy cell. "Lodgings are all right, but the service leaves something to be desired. What are you doing here, sir?"

Tristan inserted a key into the rusty lock, and the cell door opened with a grinding click. "Saving you, by the looks of it."

"Marvelous. Bloody marvelous."

A moment passed.

"Why are you just standing there, old friend? Get me out of these things. I can't feel my elbows."

Still obscured by shadows and a black traveling cloak, Tristan moved closer, knelt down, and pulled back his hood.

Broadford jerked back against the cell wall, and his ribs exploded in pain. "God, you . . . oh, you haven't aged well de Merlon."

Tristan smiled a skeleton smile, his sharpened teeth catching the first rays of morning light from the barred cell window.

Broadford tried not to let his disgust show through. "Not well at all. What happened to your face?"

"Well, you were always the handsome one, Broadie. You don't mind if I call you Broadie, do you?"

"No, no . . . not at all." He was trying to compose himself but couldn't help staring at the horrific visage of his former marshal.

"Malcolm used to call you that all the time, as I recall. Malcolm Dewar. You two were as thick as thieves. You remember him?"

"Uh, yes, I remember." He shifted his arse on the straw.

"How'd you get this?" From his pocket, Tristan withdrew and held up the metallic trinket in the shape of a key. Broadford's eyes flashed upon it. "Malcolm was the bearer, not you."

"Ah, we're sharing it, you see? Taking turns, like."

"Is that so? Where is he?" The gaunt ex-marshal never took his eyes from those of Broadford Higgins.

"Ah . . ." The toff blew air from his cheeks and shrugged.

"You want out of here, you tell me."

Broadford manufactured an upset expression and put it on his face. "He's dead."

"How?"

"He got jumped by some . . . you know, jumped just like I did. Some local bandits posing as the law."

"And you ended up with the key?"

"Well, he gave it to me when he knew his time was up."

Tristan traced his scarred jawline with a claw-like finger, a thoughtful expression crossing his hideous face. "Generous to a fault, old Malcolm."

"Yes, good old Malcolm."

Tristan stood abruptly. "You know, I think I'm going to leave you here to be rodgered and rot."

"No, no. Sir. Marshal de Merlon, please." He coughed up mucous and blood, which spattered on the already soiled straw. "Don't leave me here."

"I won't judge you. I simply want the truth, and quickly before we're both discovered." His voice was soothing, unflustered and in control.

Broadford's face became a stage play of sorrow, his tone pleading. "They hung him, put him in chains, gibbeted the poor bastard."

"Why would *they* do such a thing?"

"The trinket drove him mad. He killed his lover's little girl."

Tristan folded his arms. "Drove him mad, and you thought you'd take it for safekeeping? Weren't you afraid it would do the same to you?"

"Well, you know what it's like."

"I do. I very much do." Tristan stood, clearly considering Broadford's tale. "I'm building an army. I want you to help me."

"Certainly. Count me in. Back in the army, back in the saddle, comrades once again."

Tristan gestured around the cell. "Yes, after all, what do you have to lose?"

"Nothing. Nothing."

"And I promise there's much to gain."

Broadford nodded frantically. "I'm in, I'm in, just get me out of here." He hacked up more blood and something else of a gelatinous nature.

Once again, Tristan held out the trinket. "I keep this for now. Agreed?"

"Agreed." Like he had a choice.

Tristan looped the key around his neck. Two trinkets, the crown and the key, rested against each other where de Merlon's traveling cloak was open at the chest. Broadford knew how one trinket could affect a man. What would two relics do together?

He was about to find out.

Tristan squatted down and gripped the chains just above Broadford's manacled wrists.

Broadford looked at his former marshal's blistered, skeletal hands. "What are you doing?"

He didn't answer but grinned with pointed teeth.

Hissing and smoke rose from the chains, and Broadford gaped and gasped as a horrid heat swathed his wrists and hands. "Shit, shit, it's hot!"

Tristan's smile became a grimace of concentration. "Silence!"

Broadford cringed and tried to twist away from the searing heat at his wrists. He could smell burning metal, and a moment later, his hands fell to his sides, still manacled but free of the smoldering chains. His mind raced.

"What are you?" he whispered, staring at the man's pockmarked face, his smoking hands.

"I am your king," Tristan said as he suddenly clasped Broadford's throat. A scream was cut short when Broadford realized de Merlon's hands were cool. "Do not betray me."

The toff shook his head, blood from his nose flicking left and right. "Wouldn't dream of it. Honestly."

"Do as I bid, and this"—Tristan touched the key once more—"shall be yours again. And much more. Much more."

Broadford gazed in wonderment, a smile spreading across his bleeding face. Yes, indeed, here was a man worth following, and for a good cause: personal gain and power, something he could well get behind. He bowed his head. "My lord."

Tristan placed his hand on Broadford's broken ribs. "Be still."

A familiar warmth spread through the toff's body, and he breathed easier, his ribs healing instantaneously. What power was this? He twisted his torso; there was no pain.

"How'd you do that?"

"Magic," Tristan said. "Hold still." He reached up to the man's broken nose and, without warning, straightened it with a loud crack.

Pain shot through Broadford's head and nearly caused him to pass out. "Fuck me! Christ!" he screamed. He felt nauseous.

"That wasn't magic." Tristan smiled.

"Fuck, Jesus."

"It'll heal as good as new. I need your handsome face, old friend, for mine is as hideous as yours is beautiful. Hardly the kind of face that men will flock to and fight for, at least not until they hear what I have to offer. You'll be my face for the time being."

Tristan hauled Broadford to his feet. The newly freed man braced his hands on his knees, fighting back the urge to vomit. As soon as he'd gathered himself, the two tall men exited the cell and made their way to the guardroom.

Broadford spotted his top hat perched on the head of a recently murdered sentry sitting in his chair, staring sightlessly at the wall, blood flowing from his nose and ears. The dead man looked ridiculously affected, he thought. He took the hat and placed it on his own head, where it belonged. After all, not everyone could wear a top hat in style.

12

Homecoming

Jeremiah, the twisted-flesh monk of the Order of Ulfur, slept in the corner of the small room above the Prancing Doxy. The short, hunched man, if it could be called a man, was prune-like, disgusting. He even had hair sprouting from his ears like some nightmarish creature from a fairy tale, those stories that mothers—nasty ones, much like Broadford's own—used to frighten seven kinds of shit out of their children.

"Do you trust it?" Broadford asked, staring at Jeremiah.

Tristan sat gazing into the fireplace. "Trust isn't a necessary life currency."

"Must be a sad life without it."

Tristan kept his eyes on the hungry flames. "Did Malcolm Dewar trust you?"

Broadford decided not to commit himself to an answer. "I'm merely saying, you're putting a lot of faith in it. You believe Jeremiah can show you more of the trinkets, ones we may have missed?"

"That's what I believe. Or at least provide me with access to the raw materials, the metal from which more may be fashioned."

"What if others of his kind await? You'll be outnumbered. Even you, with all your power, might struggle to win out."

Tristan seemed far away. "The monastery has been abandoned for over a hundred years. But if there are others, I'll deal with them when the time comes."

Broadford placed a finger on his nose. It was healing nicely and quickly in the vicinity of the trinkets. It would be a hard thing to leave them, to leave the glow they gave to his blood.

"I felt him, in my mind, probing my thoughts," he said.

"He can read them." Tristan nodded slowly. "You have no secrets from him, or me."

The toff looked at the sleeping monk with a mix of fear and curiosity.

Tristan continued watching the fire, then said, "It's time for you to leave and gather my army."

Broadford got to his feet.

"Bring as many men as you can to Mount Ulfur, near Re'Shan, a place I'm sure you remember. Call the company to arms once more. Meet me there in exactly two weeks. Do not fail me in this. Promise them the metal. Each shall receive his godhood, as shall you."

"Very well, sir. I'll see you on Ulfur."

Tristan turned to look Broadford in the eyes. "Don't think to get the trinkets for yourself." His voice was ladened with threat. "I have the key. This one"—he touched his chest with a sharpened fingernail—"and that one." He pointed to the sleeping Monk of Ulfur. "This world belongs to me, but you shall be rewarded for your loyalty. Or, punished for your betrayal."

The hairs on Broadford's arms stood. "I know on which side my toast is buttered, sir. I am yours to command once more, just like the old days."

Broadford gathered bread and water, placed them in his knapsack, and, with fist on chest, saluted his new king. He placed his top hat on his head and left.

Tristan went back to gazing into the depths of the fire, watching it burn lower.

A rustle of movement came from the corner where the light of the fire no longer penetrated. "Do you trust him?" A dry cracking voice. "This man you've sent to gather your army?"

"He asked me the same of you, as you no doubt overheard. I trust no man. What I trust is a man's desire. *That* is something you can stake your life on."

Jeremiah rolled over and looked at Tristan. "And what does Broadford Higgins desire?"

Tristan shrugged his angular shoulders beneath his black woolen shirt. "I have no idea. Each man creates his own fiction, but the trinkets can deliver it unto him. As soon as I have the trinkets, I have him. All of them." Tristan ran a finger down his ruined face. "Higgins has tasted the powers of the metal and will therefore do as I ask. He can do nothing else. One can never go back."

Jeremiah grunted. "There are some who've been known to forsake the metal. To abandon it."

"They're weak."

"No. Not weak." Jeremiah watched the scarred former marshal as he, in turn, watched the dying fire. "Memories are dangerous things," the twisted monk said. "They can be misleading, a maze one endlessly wanders, a labyrinth that turns, reinventing itself, shapeshifting. Prisons of one's own fevered design. Never trust a memory."

"Mmm. As you say."

"I can see you are lost in yours," the monk said.

Tristan turned his head slightly. "Were you a confessor?"

"Not in the strictest of senses, but of a kind, yes, I suppose. Long ago."

"I do not seek a confessional. Go back to sleep."

Jeremiah rolled onto his back and stared at the dark corners of the ceiling. "I struggle to sleep, another curse of the metal within my blood."

"Then take one of the girls from the floor below."

"I told you, I'm—"

"Yes, yes, a monk. I know. Take one for the companionship. The warmth. It may settle your nerves."

The monk gurgled a laugh full of spite, full of irony. "What need have I for warmth when I have your delightful company?"

Tristan ignored the dig. His thoughts drifted to another time, to the faces in the fire. Then he felt something crawling at the back of his head. "Remove yourself from my mind, monk. Anything I wish you to know, I will tell you."

Jeremiah mumbled something, and a moment later, despite his assertion to the contrary, the Monk of Ulfur was sleeping soundly.

Tristan returned to the fire. Stella was there, dancing in the flames. And the boys. Albert, Terence, Geoffrey, Simon, and Matthew. It was important to remember their names.

He hadn't wanted to leave them, but the war had taken him away. What was a loyal soldier to do when king and country called?

In the progress of war, Tristan Drogos de Merlon had risen in the Alliance forces to command three thousand men in King Tremain's name. They would be proud of him upon his return to Millington. The Great War Hero, the Marshal. But two years away was an eternity. He missed Stella, missed the boys.

"When war comes, there's nowhere to hide," he had said, holding Stella by the shoulders, staring into her beautiful hazel eyes. "Better to meet it head on, stop it there before it reaches here. I go to fight for you, for our boys."

Stella looked down and nodded. "I know, I understand. Don't be gone too long."

"I won't. I promise."

And so, he had done his duty. He had fought for his family, fought for King Tremain, and had even raised the crossed-key insignia banner of King Bruwaert in battle. He had fought for all of White Cloud. After all, it was only the combined might of Tremain and Bruwaert that could stop the spread of death and destruction, the plague of war. The Hungry King was nigh on an unstoppable malignant power, but the two Lesser Kings had done it. The once-enemies, Tremain and Bruwaert, had achieved the impossible. They had defeated the Hungry King, and the land of White Cloud could return to days of peace.

And so, Tristan stepped down after the fall of Re'Shan. No longer the marshal, no longer a commander of men, he was husband and father once more, a much more comfortable fit.

But when he returned to Millington, damnation was waiting for him.

He stood there in confusion. The doors and windows of their modest home were boarded shut. A sign nailed to the door screamed a warning.

Plague. Sealed by the Order of King Bruwaert and King Tremain.

Tristan turned as if in a dream and saw a group of townsfolk gathering, tragedy written large across their familiar faces. This was not to be a happy welcoming party.

The town's unofficial leader, Ralph Connister, stood at their head. He removed his hat and nervously rubbed his bald pate. "We had to seal it. I'm so sorry, Tristan. We were only following regulations."

In a daze, Tristan spoke. "When?"

"Two weeks ago."

Tristan Drogos de Merlon searched for something to pry the boards from the door. Finding nothing, he frantically clawed with his hands.

People, once friends and neighbors, approached him, tried to pull him away. "No, Tristan. No, it's too soon. The plague is still within. It's too soon."

He flung them away.

Too soon? He was too late. What were they talking about, too soon? What was happening? Why were the door and windows boarded up? Where was Stella?

He tore the planks from the door with inhuman strength. The frightened townsfolk scattered and ran. He entered his home, nails torn, hands bleeding.

They lay among flies, bloated and stinking, flesh melting from bones, the youngest lying on the chest of his wife, her arms still holding him, their bodies merging.

What was his name? The youngest? What was her name? His wife? Why was it so hard to remember?

Stella. Matthew. It was important to remember their names, not let the names slip from his grasp. Hold on.

He didn't cry. He kissed each one in turn, a gentle kiss. Then he walked outside to the stream that wound its way near the back garden of his house, removed the crown trinket from around his neck, and let it drop into the water. He returned to his home and lay down beside his wife and youngest son.

They came to set his house on fire then. He saw Ralph Connister through the open door, flaming torch in hand, screaming something, but Tristan couldn't hear for the crackling of the flames. He ignored them all and closed his eyes.

———

TRISTAN AWOKE SOMEWHERE. He sat up and looked around but couldn't understand where he was. Shapes in filthy beds lay on either side, flies buzzing about the still forms, bandages falling from ashen skin, dark-rimmed eyes, twisted skulls. Tristan had seen this before.

Lepers. He was among lepers.

Plague. Wasn't it the plague that had taken his family, infected him? Why was he here? Who had dragged him from his burning house, taken him here? Or, had he walked? Had he been found wandering in a daze?

He couldn't remember.

He lay back down, passed in and out of consciousness. Pain throbbed in his neck, and he was constantly sweating. He felt chilled to the bone. He might be in a leper colony, but he had the plague, he thought. That's all right. Quite all right. He shall join his family.

Then the soldiers came. He could hardly understand what they were saying. They wore masks with long beaks, much like the doctors, but they were no doctors. They would shake him awake with a pointed stick, jabbing at his chest when all he wanted was to forget, to sleep forever.

"Let me die," he whispered.

"The relic, Marshal. Where is it?" said a calm, steady voice.

Tristan tried to speak, but he could only utter the faintest croak. "What relic? Where's Robert? Where's Michael? Soldier, get back to your post."

"You're confused, Marshal. The war is over."

"Where's Stella?"

"Your wife? She's dead, sir."

The agony washed over him anew as he remembered, and something buried deep inside went numb.

"Search him."

Another voice, afraid. "I'm not searching him. You go ahead if you fancy."

"Search him, or Bruwaert will gut us all."

Cool hands passed over Tristan's burning, sweat-slimed flesh.

"He doesn't have it. Oh Gods, got to wash me hands. Wash me hands."

The first voice, the one that seemed in command, spoke to him in a calming tone, as if Tristan were a horse about to bolt. "What happened to your family was a tragedy but no fault of King Bruwaert. Tell us where the trinket is. Just tell us, Marshal, and we'll leave you in peace."

What was the soldier talking about? What trinket?

And then he remembered.

The thing from the hidden monastery. The small metal pendant shaped like a crown.

The soldier spoke again. "King Bruwaert wants the relic. Consider it tax."

A third voice spoke in hushed whispers. "He's too far gone. He doesn't know where he is. We need to search the ruins of the house. Check the bodies of his wife and kids, maybe they have it."

"They were buried by Connister and his men. What was left of them, leastways."

"We dig them up."

Tristan went cold. "Leave my family alone. Leave them be. They do not deserve to be disturbed."

Why could no one see that? Despite all he had given, the sacrifice for king—two kings—and country, after all that, they still hounded him, disrespected his family.

The soldiers left, and Tristan Drogos de Merlon made a decision.

He would not die. He would live to wreak death on Connister, on the town of Millington, on Bruwaert, on Tremain. On those responsible for the death of his family and anybody who stood in his way. He would take from them as he had been taken from—a thousandfold.

War. He would unleash war once again. His would not be the only maggoted family rotting away, buried in the damp earth. This pain he would share, and share gladly.

And so, he staggered from his fly-blown bed, riddled with death, to make his way back home. His face and body were so sunken and scarred that he was unrecognizable to those who passed by him. Villagers who had once called him by friendly terms now avoided the carrier of the Black Death, and of leprosy. They were frightened of him, of his ghastly visage; he was a walking corpse. But they would be truly frightened of him one day. To this, he swore an oath.

He knelt in the cold waters of the stream near the back garden and searched for the trinket. His vision was blurring; he recognized Death's approach. If he couldn't find the metal crown, he'd never leave the creek bed.

But having decided to live, he wouldn't be thwarted. He scrabbled until he felt it; his hand warmed beneath the cool waters. He hung the trinket around his neck and crawled from the stream, his strength spent. He lay there on his back as the sun set, and watched the charred remains of his home turn to silhouette, then melt into darkness.

The sun rose like fire, the pain searing his eyes, burning his brain. Fire.

But the fire was burning low now. Tristan looked at the dark shape of Jeremiah sleeping. He closed his eyes, and let the fire die out. He didn't need it anymore.

Not when the world was ablaze within him.

13

Non-Political, Non-Profit

Abbot Hugh Gilbert looked out over the stone courtyard of the Monastery of the Yellow Scholars and saw order in everything. His quarters were elevated, on the third floor in fact, affording an excellent view of the courtyard, itself a perfectly geometric rectangle. The yellow-robed monks below were all scurrying about in a precise, mechanical manifestation of duty, some sweeping the stone floors near one another yet twirling to avoid each other in graceful pirouettes. Others were reading at long tables, turning their pages in synchrony with their brethren. Directly below the abbot's window, several monks were chanting in orderly rows.

Yes, everything was proceeding as it should on this fine late afternoon, like the springs and dials beneath the timepieces he had worked with when he was apprenticed to a clockmaker as a boy.

It had been years since he was in a city, and he didn't miss it—better the clean air and sedate mind of the rural life, the monastic life. What would that other life have promised if he'd stayed to become a clockmaker in the rat-infested back alleys of supposed high civilization?

The abbot leaned forward on his balcony, careful to avoid the bird shit. Perhaps he was still a clockmaker, but keeping God's time, not that of men. He laughed quietly at the vanity of his own pretensions. Abbot Hugh Gilbert, God's Timekeeper. Still, it did have a certain ring to it, perhaps the title of his memoirs should he ever find the time to write them. Anybody who thought the life of a scholarly monk gave plenty of opportunity for navel gazing had clearly never been an abbot before.

Out on the fields below, farms were divided into further rectangles, each a varying color of green or brown.

Yes, there was an order in everything today, and it pleased the abbot.

What did not please him was the appearance of two—no, three—figures on horseback coming up the winding dirt path encircling a lower hill; one horse was carrying two riders. The abbot's eyes were still sharp despite his sixty years. He grimaced. It wasn't that he didn't appreciate visitors; it was simply that he'd received no forewarning, no letter, no messages of such a visit. The order of things had been disrupted.

Furthermore, and to his growing consternation, at least one rider was clearly a woman. A tall one.

He was not the only one to notice the new arrivals. There was shouting in the courtyard, a cessation in sweeping, a break in the chanting, the clap of books closing. Abbot Hugh Gilbert recognized the dreaded approach of chaos and sighed.

"Brother Marvin!" he shouted.

In the courtyard below, a young initiate looked skywards, blinded by the late-afternoon sunlight.

"Brother Marvin!" the abbot shouted again.

The young man cast a bewildered look into the blue skies, his tonsure reflecting the sun like some organic domed mirror.

The abbot shook his head and tried to control his irritation. "For goodness' sake lad, it isn't God trying to whisper in your ear! It's me, Abbot Gilbert!"

"Oh, Father Abbot. I'm sorry, I was staring into the sun."

"I admire your religious fervor, young man, but I wouldn't recommend it. Tell Brother Kline to open the gates, we have visitors!"

Brother Marvin clapped his hands. "Oh, how exciting. Visitors! Yes, at once."

The abbot watched the young man gird his robes in both hands and scuttle across the courtyard. Exciting? Oh, to be a novice again.

Everything was exciting for the young, even the life of a monk. The boy had much to learn.

Little did Abbot Hugh Gilbert know, as he gingerly descended his bulk down the steps from his humble sleeping quarters to his workstation below, the next few days would prove to be some of the more exciting of his life.

"IT'S BROTHER WILLIAM. Brother William has returned!"

The abbot frowned at Brother Marvin's enthusiastic pronouncement. He searched his desktop as if one of the objects upon it might provide an answer to the confusion that had just washed over him. "But Brother William only left three weeks ago. He's not due back until..."

"December solstice," the initiate offered helpfully.

"Yes, thank you, Brother. December solstice." The abbot placed his dry quill upon the half-written page of an open book. "Where is he?"

"I am here, Father Abbot." William Barding pushed his thin frame past the equally gaunt frame of Brother Marvin, interlocked his fingers, and held them over his heart in the traditional greeting of the Order of the Yellow Scholars.

The abbot returned the greeting, his frown returning. "Brother William, you really should wait to be announced. There's a protocol, an order with which we do things."

"Forgive my haste."

"Well, sit down." Abbot Hugh Gilbert waved Brother Marvin away. "I'm surprised to see you return so soon. My dear boy, the seeds of research germinate slowly. I fear you may be somewhat premature in this effort."

The young monk sat and placed his hands on his robed knees. "Ah, you refer to my book?"

"Indeed, I do. Surely, your manuscript cannot be ready after a mere three weeks?"

William opened a small saddlebag and produced a stack of papers. He laid them gently on the plain desk. The abbot leaned forward and carefully examined several pages.

"It's a little short, William."

"Unfinished, but I can assure you that she is rich in subject matter. I've barely scratched the surface."

"If it's unfinished, why are you here? You should be north, observing her in her element, among her own culture. As the late Sagran Grimsdotter's only daughter, Brynhild Grimsdotter is an important member of the royal family, or what passes for royalty up that way. Her brothers are expecting you, for heaven's sake. Do you understand the opportunity you've been granted? The responsibility? We've been in negotiations for this for years. Look . . ." The abbot left his chair and moved his girth with an odd grace to a bookshelf. He returned with two large volumes.

"This is *The Germania Barbarian,* written by Brother Martin Franks over one hundred years ago and still the premier resource on all things Germanic, a book I'm sure you're familiar with. And this, *The Sultan of Kahlmedia,* a work by the former abbot of the Yellow Abbey, my predecessor no less. We're having to do a fourth copy of it, a *fourth,* mind you. My own book doesn't deserve to be mentioned in such esteemed company, but you, William, I have high hopes for you and your obvious talent."

William frowned. "Impediments, Father Abbot."

Abbot Hugh Gilbert frowned along with the thin monk. "What?"

"There have been certain unforeseen happenstances."

His frown showed no sign of receding, unlike his hairline, which would soon make his tonsure redundant. "What are you talking about?"

"Murder. We came across a girl four days ago. Her father had been slaughtered by a group of men. These men were pursuing her along a beach. We rescued her. I had to . . . I had to kill a man."

The abbot lowered his head and waved his hand. "Righteous acts shall be forgiven. Just a word of advice. In the future, keep certain things to yourself. Consider this a confessional."

The thin monk nodded.

"Go on," the abbot said.

"The young woman, Rebecca Occitane, is in danger. The men were hunting something of value, something passed from the father to the daughter, and these men will not easily give up. Therefore, I have—"

"The young woman was the third rider?"

"Yes, Abbot."

"There are two females in our monastery?"

"Yes, Abbot."

The abbot nervously tapped his fingers on his desk. "I fear some of the younger tyros are in for a wet dream or two."

William scratched his tonsure, his face reddening.

"Who hunts this Rebecca Occitane?"

"King Bruwaert. It was his men on the beach."

"Christ's shit." The abbot froze. "I'm sorry. His name in vain. Penitence later." He looked around in bewilderment. "You said she was carrying something?"

"An amulet."

The fat abbot threw his hands up. "Why would King Bruwaert's men pursue a girl for a mere amulet?"

"I don't know," William said. "There's something else, Father."

"Mmm?"

"Brynhild Grimsdotter plans to aid the girl in the assassination of King Bruwaert."

The abbot sat back on his chair and caught himself just before he fell off—not a single chair in the abbey had a back support; it was considered frivolous. "Assassinate King Bruwaert? We're a non-political organization. If we were found to be harboring assassins . . ." His sentence trailed off.

The young monk waited, but his superior's mind seemed to have exited his portly body. A moment later, the abbot broke out of his daydream.

"As I was saying. Non-political, non-profit." He pressed his hands together. "Basically, we don't get involved. But th-this is madness. Even if they could? I mean, how?"

William shrugged.

The abbot waggled a pudgy finger at the monk. "You must convince them of the inappropriateness of their course of action."

"They are both strong willed, Father. I doubt they would listen to me."

The abbot's round face changed suddenly, disapproval replaced by scholarly curiosity. "What can you tell me about it, the amulet?"

"The object is . . . the girl has it. It's a strange metal. I couldn't tell you just what color it is though I have seen it with my own eyes."

The abbot scratched at his chin. "I need to speak to Rebecca Occitane immediately. I must see this object."

"She's exhausted, Father Abbot, and now sleeps. Her father was dear to her, so you can imagine this has been something of an ordeal."

"Of course, of course. When she awakens, then. In the meantime, where is Sagran Grimsdotter's daughter? You must introduce me. I understand she's quite remarkable."

William nodded. "Oh yes. Remarkable indeed."

———

BRYNHILD GRIMSDOTTER was an outstanding example of a Norse warrior. She was tall, blonde, fearless, and at almost six and a half feet, taller than every one of the five hundred monks in the Yellow Abbey. The butter-robed ascetics gawked as she strode through the hallways of the monastery, their mouths hanging open, eyes staring wildly.

"What's the matter?" She smiled. "Never seen a woman before?"

"As a matter of fact, some of them haven't." Abbot Hugh Gilbert stood in the center of the courtyard with his hands in opposing sleeves, and at his side, Brother William Barding mirrored his pose.

Brynhild came to stand in front of them and folded her bare muscular arms. "What kind of man has never laid eyes on a woman?"

"A monk, I would suggest," the abbot responded.

William made the introductions. "Brynhild Grimsdotter, this is Father Abbot, Abbot Hugh Gilbert."

The Norse warrior looked down at the sturdy administrator. "Father Abbot Abbot Hugh Gilbert. I am pleased to meet you. And I thought we Northerners had long names."

The abbot laughed politely. "You may call me Abbot Gilbert, or simply Hugh if you wish. The Order of Yellow Scholars does not stand on ceremony."

Without warning, the tall Norsewoman grabbed him in a bear hug and kissed his forehead. To his credit, he took the surprise in stride, neither drawing away nor flinching.

The young monk stammered. "Th-that's how Northerners greet each other in the north."

The abbot raised an eyebrow and, able to breathe again, said, "I picked that up, Brother William. I also understand Northerners come from the north. You may remove that redundancy from your book."

William shifted uncomfortably from foot to foot.

The abbot continued: "Mistress Brynhild, have you rested? I understand you've been given rooms."

"I am fine."

"The rooms are not to your satisfaction?"

"The rooms are adequate. I thank you. I need no rest. I'll sleep when in the grave."

The abbot looked at William and back again at the ferociously tall woman. "The stoic reputation of your people sits well with you."

She shrugged her strong shoulders. "It's something my husband used to say."

"Ah, and where is your husband?" The abbot regretted the question as soon as it escaped his lips, remembering too late just where her husband was.

"Sleeping."

The abbot cleared his throat. "Well, I'd like to thank you again for allowing the Order to spend time with you. I personally guarantee that our young scribe here"—the abbot waved his hand toward William—"will portray you and your culture as accurately as we can. It is a great honor for us."

Brynhild nodded and looked around the courtyard, at the monks going about their work but looking at her surreptitiously. "The honor is mine. Your people have produced great works. I've read many. I like your book, Hugh Gilbert. It's titled *The Rise of the Nomad Lords*, is it not?"

The abbot grinned and chuckled, forgetting his earlier moment of embarrassment. "Yes, it is. My, my goodness." His features turned a luminescent rose. Fanning his face with two hands, he looked at William and said, "We should have women in the monastery more often. Absolutely charming. This way, if you please."

William and Brynhild followed him across the courtyard and through an archway. The abbot tried to hide a smile like that of the cat that got all the cream.

"I understand the young woman possesses a trinket of some value to King Bruwaert." The abbot's voice echoed through the stone passageway they were following.

Brynhild glanced at William, who kept his eyes on the back of the abbot's tonsure. "Yes," she said.

"Would you care to speculate why?"

"I have not the first notion."

"Here we are." The abbot rapped at a heavy wooden door, and it creaked noisily open. Brother Marvin peered from behind the door but was briskly knocked aside as the abbot bustled on through, sweeping his arm around.

The library was large, the central space assigned to the copyists and readers, and the walls were lined with thousands of leather-bound books. An unkind soul might have said the library was an ostentatious display of wealth that was unbecoming of the monastic ideology. Abbot Hugh Gilbert would have responded that all knowledge was indeed wealth, but not all wealth was knowledge. So there.

The room was lit by an unadorned, large rectangular window set high in the wall. Sconces around the walls contained torches for night reading, but they weren't required at the moment. Several monks were busy copying manuscripts; so involved were they in their tasks that not one looked up from their lecterns.

The abbot slipped his hands within his sleeves once more. "The girl has suffered a great trauma and must spend a few days in convalescence, during which time you are welcome to sit, read, and reflect. Dinner will be at eight." The abbot made to leave. "Oh, I wonder if you wouldn't mind covering your arms, Brynhild. I hate to ask but . . . some of the boys are jittery."

"Of course, Hugh."

The abbot looked around proudly. "You know, we've had kings in here, but I dare say this is the first time we've had a princess."

Brynhild Grimsdotter smiled. "I am no princess, Hugh. I find the shoes uncomfortable."

14

Hunting Boar

King Shane Bruwaert looked across the unfathomable distance of the royal dining table at his royal wife as she picked bird-like at the vegetables on her royal plate. With a bent wrist and a displeased downturn of her prim mouth, Queen Ainslie Bruwaert pushed peas and potatoes around her plate, selecting an odd item here and there to place in her prudish mouth.

The boy was no better. Lachlan Bruwaert used a spoon to separate the meat from the vegetables, tongue sticking out of his mouth as he concentrated on scooping the vegetables onto his utensil and finally into his mouth.

King Bruwaert watched them both with growing distaste. "Eat your meat, boy. A man needs his meat."

"But I'm only eight, father."

"You'll be a man one day. Eat your meat."

"I don't like it."

King Bruwaert glared accusingly at his wife. "You take after your mother, and not only in that aspect. What's this I hear about you playing with dolls?"

The boy's face froze.

Queen Ainslie Bruwaert came to her son's aid. "Not dolls, dear, rather he's taken an interest in modeling, battlefield reenactments and such. It should please you to know that Captain Haines believes

Lachlan has the potential to master battlefield strategy at the level of a general."

King Bruwaert's grimace betrayed his doubts. "All well and good as long as the soldiers in the mock battles aren't wearing skirts. Eat your meat, a general eats his meat, Lachlan."

At that moment, a rapping echoed around the dining hall of Castle Key, a most unusual occurrence during the evening meal. King Bruwaert placed his silver knife and fork on the table and wiped grease from his gray-black beard. "Enter."

A thin hawk-nosed man took a step into the cavernous room. "I beg pardon for the interruption, my lord, but there's a man to see you on king's business, or so he says."

King Bruwaert checked his beard in a small ornate mirror sitting on the edge of the dining table. He'd missed a spot of grease and rubbed at it with the back of his hand before realizing it was a new growth of gray in his beard. He frowned. "You'd better show him in then."

The king's chamberlain puzzled. "Now, sire? Protocol would stipulate—"

"You've already interrupted me, Grant, so protocol be damned. Bring him." King Bruwaert stared at the unfinished meat and potatoes on his plate. His appetite wasn't what it once was, his hunger paling. He exchanged a swift glance with his wife, and the queen ushered Lachlan out of the room, accompanied by two guards.

A moment later Grant returned, cleared his throat, and said, "Knight-Captain Christopher Lewis."

The man introduced stepped past the chamberlain and bowed.

"Get him something to eat, Grant. He looks hungry."

The chamberlain nodded and disappeared.

King Bruwaert indicated an empty chair to his left.

Christopher, with a glance at the four armed knights, two on either side of the king, took the proffered place on the bench.

"What news from Dysael, Knight-Captain? Whatever it is, you've come quite some way to Castle Key to tell me."

Christopher bowed his head slightly. "I'm honored you remember me and my current posting, sire."

"You've done good work for me in the past, Lewis. I always make a point of remembering those who've shown loyalty, and I repay it in kind. What's your business here?"

"I have news of the relics of Ulfur."

King Bruwaert took a drink from his wine flagon, resisting the urge to lean forward and blurt out a succession of questions. He mustn't sound overeager. "What news?" he asked as casually as he could muster.

"I spoke with a bearer of a trinket three days ago."

King Bruwaert's facade of control broke. "Spoke with? I have given express orders for—" At that moment, Grant returned with meat, bread, and wine. The king attempted to control his breathing. "Go ahead, relieve your hunger and thirst. We all have needs that must be met before civility has its day."

He watched as the knight-captain ate, the king's curiosity threatening to burn a hole in his gut. He considered dismissing the guards, but the thought of being left alone with an assassin dissuaded him. A king trusts no one, despite what he'd just said about loyalty.

The man was voracious. There was something about him, something primal, something that reminded the king of himself before he was buried by age and lard.

"Do you know what you're eating?" King Bruwaert asked.

The knight-captain swallowed a bloody chunk of meat. "Wild boar, I believe."

"Yes. Do you see that?" The king waved a fat ringed finger toward a wall.

"That's your family's ancestral coat of arms, sire."

King Bruwaert screwed his brows together. "Not that. Haven't looked at that in years. Next to it."

Christopher looked again. "The boar's head?"

The mounted animal was a truly massive example of the species, its ferocity not dimmed by death, a rigor mortis snarl forever caught on the beast's features.

"I hunted that down in the forests of Dysael when I was about your age. All I had was a scrawny dog, a blunt blade, and my own wits."

"Very impressive, my lord. Your strength is renowned."

"Don't be obsequious, Knight-Captain, it's only a wild pig. However, I *was* quite the hunter in my youth. Look at me now." He patted his rotund belly. "I've grown fat. And worse, I've lost the impetuousness of youth, the arrogance that lets the young believe they can do anything they set their mind to." The king sighed. "Let's just say the animal you're eating did not meet its end at my hands. I sat here on my fat arse and watched it served up to me. Where's the dignity in that? For either the animal or me? I miss the man I was, Lewis." He looked closely at the darkness within the knight-captain's eyes. "The relics are rumored to restore a man's vitality, to regenerate his vigor. No man knows vanity as a king knows vanity. I want those trinkets. This man you spoke to, did he have it on his person? Did you get it?"

"He escaped with the amulet."

King Bruwaert slammed his fist onto the table, causing his plate to clatter noisily to the floor. The assassin didn't flinch but kept right on eating. The king smiled and attempted a relaxed laugh, failing, at least to his own ears. "Honestly, I don't know why I'm so upset," he said. "Follow me."

The king gained his feet with surprising alacrity and stalked from the room. The guards followed, two ahead of him and two behind Christopher, who was still chewing on wild boar. They walked through a series of stone hallways that split and twisted within the massive Castle Key until they came to a corridor of painted and sculpted deceased kings, and then finally, to a large side room.

"Here," King Bruwaert said. A gesture of his hand encompassed a room replete with glass cases and carefully balanced objects on wooden stands. "Artifacts of religious or occult power. I collected them all." He rubbed his graying beard. He picked up a glossy white horn of some animal and turned it in his hands. "Each promised eternal youth and strength. But still I grow fat. Still I grow old. It's superstition, you see. All of it." He stood there, ignoring his guards, ignoring Christopher, just gazing at the horn, lost in thought.

The assassin interrupted the king's reverie. "The man I spoke to showed . . . unusual abilities."

King Bruwaert swung on him. "What do you mean?"

"He seemed to shimmer, to become translucent like a crystal. In this way, he made his escape from a room of thirty men. He slaughtered four heavily armed soldiers before they had even noted his presence."

The king's eyes lit up with renewed hope. "Gods! Then, it's true! They contain power!"

"It would seem so."

King Bruwaert couldn't understand why the assassin was just standing there, immobile. "Find him. Find the others, the other bearers!"

"I need more information, my lord, if I'm to do my duty." The man's black eyes seemed to hunt down those of the king.

King Bruwaert balked at the nerve of the man, feeling as if he were on the sharp end of an interrogation. "What do you wish to know?"

"How many are there? The relics. How many men carry them?"

"How do I know? I know only of two."

"Robert Occitane?"

"Yes." The king raised an eyebrow. "You seem rather well informed on this whole matter."

"I am so in order to serve you, my lord. And the other?"

"Tristan Drogos de Merlon."

"Where is de Merlon now?" Christopher asked.

"Dead."

"How?"

"The plague. He and his entire family, no sign of any artifact. His was the first name presented to me, but the plague got to him before my men could."

"Was he confirmed dead?"

"He had the plague, man. Covered in boils and sores on his deathbed. He is no longer breathing, of that there can be no doubt."

King Bruwaert looked at Christopher closely. "Unless you are suggesting . . . ?"

"The metal has regenerative powers, as you have touched upon."

King Bruwaert scratched his beard. "Could he . . . ? No, he didn't have it with him. No, no, he's dead. Surely."

"As you say. And what of Robert Occitane?"

"I only discovered his whereabouts a week ago. Turns out he was living barely fifty leagues from here, on the coast. I sent, and lost, some good men, but again, there was no trinket on the body. A disturbing trend. Someone must have taken it."

"Do you have any idea who?"

"He has a daughter. All indications point to her. She was, after all, not accounted for among the dead, and Occitane didn't bury himself."

"Where is she now?"

"A foolish question. If I knew, I'd be in possession of one of the artifacts and no doubt off hunting or fucking somewhere." King Bruwaert studied the assassin's face, hoping to find something, anything to suggest he knew more than he was saying, but the knight-captain's eyes were impenetrable pools of darkness. "It's of paramount importance that you find this man you spoke to, what was his name?"

"Archibald Kirk."

"Find him. Find the names of the others who carry the metal. Torture him, them, torture everyone if you have to."

"Archibald Kirk was King Tremain's man. He fought for Tremain, and by extension you, against the Hungry King in accordance with the Alliance, as did Robert Occitane. I'm not comfortable hunting down former comrades."

King Bruwaert's rage boiled at the man's audacity. "Damn you! You'll do as you're told!"

Uncowed, the knight-captain said, "There's such a thing as loyalty to comrades, Your Highness."

"And what about your loyalty to your king? Not to mention *their* loyalty? These men possess items of tremendous power. As their king, I hold divine right to these objects, objects which should be offered freely."

"You are not, strictly speaking, *their* king. Tremain commands them."

King Bruwaert waved a fat hand. "Details. Under the Alliance, both kings retain power over the two kingdoms and its peoples."

"You twist the Alliance to suit your purposes."

The man's impudence was breathtaking. "Yes, I do." The king let his anger fade and sighed. "In my defense, I had no wish for Occitane to die. I'm not in the habit of murdering war heroes. Something clearly went terribly wrong. He killed twelve of my men. Twelve mind you! With a garden spade! Blood all up and down the beach, for God's sake. He must have had help. Must have."

The dark-eyed man with stark white hair interlocked his fingers and glanced around the gallery. "If Tremain finds out you're hunting down his men, the Alliance will be in jeopardy."

"Tremain's a fool! The war's end has seen him become soft and doddering, tending only to his plants in the gardens of Canterbury Castle. The Alliance will not last forever, and I'm determined that Castle Key will be in a position of power when the inevitable happens. Besides, Robert Occitane lived within my kingdom proper and is therefore subject to my law, my whim. Find this Archibald Kirk, question the man, find the others. I must have the trinkets. All of them!"

"A final question, sire. From whence did it come, this immortal metal?"

"From within a monastery on Mount Ulfur, or so the speculation runs, and the metal is rumored to contain power. That's all I know." The king shrugged.

"Why don't you simply search the mountain for the metal?"

"Do you think I'm a fool? I've had my men all over Mount Ulfur for a year now, ever since Re'Shan fell and the rumors arose. The monastery is hidden, if it even exists. Distinguishing legend from fact, well, good luck with that. That's why I need a trinket-bearer. I need someone who's been there, do you understand? To show me the way, to show me the truth." King Bruwaert looked at his fat wrinkled hands holding the ivory horn. "I grow old. I grow old and feeble. I'm terrified of pissing my bed at night, of losing my ability to bed a woman. If this metal is indeed the fountain of youth in fractured pieces, I want as many of them as can be found. Do you hear me?"

"I hear you, sire."

"Find out what you can. Research everything, go everywhere. You shall be rewarded for your loyalty."

"Loyalty is its own reward, Your Highness."

Loyalty is its own reward? King Bruwaert suppressed a condescending laugh; he couldn't afford to mock the only man in his kingdom potentially capable of tracking down the metal he so desired. "Of course. Commendable, Knight-Captain. Its own reward. As you so eloquently say."

Christopher Lewis bowed and began to make his exit.

"Knight-Captain?"

The assassin stopped and turned around.

The king was looking down at the horn in his hands. His voice was far away. "Do you still dream?"

Christopher glanced at the horn, then back to his king. "Yes, sire. Occasionally."

"I dream of running in the forest, always the same dream. I am a predator. I am strong, virile. I *will* hunt boar again. You're the only man in my service who has spoken with a trinket-bearer and lived. It all depends on you. Don't let me down."

The assassin bowed again and was on the hunt once more. But his hunt was a much more dangerous game than wild boar.

15

Tremain and the Gardener

H is beard, once flaxen, was now streaked with silver, but King Tremain didn't mind. Silver wasn't gold, but it was more beautiful in a way, had a certain gravitas, a kind of honor. While some might clamber for gold, those who seek silver have their pick, don't have to jostle each other at the table. Silver was a more civilized color on balance.

King Tremain sat on the garden bench, stroking his silvered beard, and watched Canterbury Castle ease its granite shadow across the manicured lawn and gardens. The castle was an awe-inspiring feat of technology, a marvel widely recognized as the finest structure ever built in White Cloud. The central keep was almost one hundred feet high, and the curtain walls enclosing the bailey had never been scaled or fallen to a siege engine. Turrets of whimsical design set atop each of the four battlements sent the children of visiting dignitaries into breathless flights of fancy concerning princesses and dragons.

But King Tremain, though he admired it, did not love Canterbury Castle. No, he loved the gardens outside its walls, gardens replete with memories of his youth, of better times, of his family—particularly the boy. It was always the boy he remembered most when he sat here. He could picture the white-haired child now, ineffectually hacking and slashing with the trowel, eager to weed out the offending thistles.

"Easy boy, you have to get under them, at their roots, or they shall return to spoil the splendor of the rose garden." The king smiled and tugged at his flaxen beard. "Look about you. This is the result of time and patience."

The earnest child looked up from his task and admired the magnificence of the sprawling estate with its pinks, reds, and yellows. He closed his eyes and breathed in.

King Tremain studied the frail boy's face, watched as the child enjoyed a moment of wind-touched peace, took in the piquant scent of intermingled flowers. The king knelt next to the boy and patted him on the shoulder. He showed the child the dirt under his own fingernails.

"These hands have held swords of great reputation, have signed great declarations, but never have they been happier than digging in these flowerbeds." The king's face became serious. He swept his hand to encompass the gardens. "All of this I now entrust to you. No title shall you have, no wages. You'll come when the gardens are empty at the end of each day, and none shall know of the favor you do your king." Then he winked and smiled. "But your duty here is important, and honor is its own reward, wouldn't you agree?"

The wide-eyed boy nodded.

Several men were making their way down the manicured garden path in the distance.

"Good lad. Off with you now, you mustn't be seen here." King Tremain gestured at a young woman standing next to a yellow-green bay laurel. She came forward and ushered the child through a gate at the back of the garden, toward the darkening green grove outside.

"Boy," the king said, moving toward the child.

The child turned with large eyes.

The king's face was grave as he knelt again, bringing his eyes level with those of the child. "I'm sorry. You deserve more than a life in the shadows."

The child smiled for the first time and whispered shyly, "Honor is its own reward, father."

And now, almost three decades later, the king, stroking his silvered beard, sat among the fragrant roses–their pinks, reds, and yellows still piquant after all this time.

King Tremain indicated for his patiently waiting chamberlain to come forward. "Sit, Simmons," he said and patted the garden bench beside him. "I apologize. I was lost in reminiscence."

"A servant may not sit with a king," responded the tall, knobble-kneed Simmons.

"Sit."

The chamberlain placed his elongated frame awkwardly on the bench and rubbed his lower back.

"What news of the children?" the king asked.

"You are to be a grandfather again. Patrick has successfully passed his seed, and the child is expected in—"

"God, man. There's a woman involved, what of Margret?"

"Your daughter-by-union is healthy, and the unborn child is healthy, as far as the doctors can ascertain."

A smile. "Good. My own flesh-daughter?"

"She is well. Her daughters are blossoming. Both have shown improvements in literature and music and will be accepted into the Academy of Fine Arts."

"At five and seven?"

"Your granddaughters are precocious, sire."

"Clearly." The king closed his eyes and inhaled the scent of flowers as the wind played across his face. "And my other son?"

Simmons withdrew an envelope from his waistcoat pocket and held it out. King Tremain took it and stared at it. He let out a long breath and opened the missive.

Simmons waited patiently.

The king folded the letter and returned it to his chamberlain. "Destroy that."

"Yes, sire. What news, sire?"

King Tremain put on an affronted expression. "And does a king tell his chamberlain secrets of state?"

"A king does not invite his chamberlain to sit and enjoy his garden, sire."

The king laughed. He looked at Simmons, his smile dying. "War. The threat of war."

"So soon, sire?"

"The weeds return with vigor immediately after the garden's been cleared." The king sighed. "This is the way of things. We must pull up the roots. I want all our forces in the Freelands to move to Re'Shan within a week."

"King Bruwaert will want to know why."

"A training exercise. The Alliance still holds, and while it does, the fat bastard is powerless to intervene. Send orders for Apollo Company to be at the ready."

"Yes, sire. And your son?"

King Tremain glanced at the letter, then at the beauty of the royal estate, the flowers the boy had so loved. "He is digging deep and is in much danger, but he's patient. A fine gardener, I would say. A fine gardener indeed."

16

Michael the Hand

The young man lay in the weight of his battered armor, near the battered fountain, in the dusty, battered town of Shae. Bodies lay scattered everywhere, men sprawled, all dead, except one.

Amal Muna could see his chest rising and falling, shallowly, almost imperceptibly. His head lay in the sun, blood matting his blond hair and seeping into the thirsty dirt-sand of the town square. It was late autumn but brutally hot in the Great Southern Sands. It was always brutally hot in the Great Southern Sands.

She peered at the midday sun through splayed fingers. If the young man's life didn't bleed from his head, it would be burned from his body by the unforgiving red orb in the bright blue sky. So, she attempted to drag him into the shade of the circular fountain at the center of the town square, only a few yards from where he lay on his back. She was sixteen, and he was older and considerably heavier.

Amal's rippling black hair fell over the knight. The strands swept the small shield insignia of his silver chest plate, and his handsome, bloodied face. The knight. That's what they were called, wasn't it? Knights? She stopped, breathing heavily with effort. She had to remove his armor, or she could never shift the man. There had to be a strap or buckle, something to indicate where she might unclasp the heavier sections of his metal plates and chainmail vest, but she found nothing and so tried rolling the man onto his side.

The lack of apparent fastenings was frustrating. This was more complicated than her sister Fiona's wedding garments, which had taken four hours to put on with the assistance of several brides-maids. A wedding gown was a simple thing when measured against this young man's armor.

She sighed. Men. How did they ever get into these things? How did they survive in the desert with such impractical clothing?

Finally, she found a spring, a clip. Compressed, one section of shoulder armor fell to the dust. She felt along edges and nooks, pushing hard, removing the armor section by section. After removing the torso armor, she grabbed the chainmail vest and pulled like a carthorse, the young man's arms flopping above his head as she peeled off the intricately woven vest. His undershirt had collected under his chin, exposing his stomach and chest.

He wore a silver necklace with a small pendant, of a color Amal couldn't name, fashioned in the shape of a hand and immaculately detailed. She wondered at it, then pulled the shirt down to protect the man's modesty. She hauled the unconscious, near-naked young knight into the shade of the fountain, splashed some water on his face, in his hair, trying to find the source of the bleeding.

When she found the gash within the mass of his blond hair, she nearly emptied her stomach. The wound was deep. It would need to be closed and soon.

She ran for home.

The streets were empty save for the bodies of the dead soldiers and the equally dead townsfolk caught up in the conflict—many she knew by name. She didn't look at their dead faces. Looking would make it all real. Only two people yet lived in Shae, and one of them was dying.

She returned with her mother's sewing kit and bathed the man's head in water from the fountain, cupping the cool liquid and smearing it through the man's hair. She couldn't see the wound now. The blood flowed too freely, his life rapidly exiting his body.

Amal looked to the skies. God, what should she do? She didn't know what to do.

A little of something is a great deal better than a lot of nothing, her father used to say.

Yes, papa. That it is.

She stood and cleaned her hands in the fountain. For the first time in years, she noticed the statue of mother clasping child rising from the pool. She stared at the waters now streaked with crimson. Shae was a city built in the Great Southern Sands, and yet here was life-giving water in the middle of great swathes of killing sand. The townsfolk had been rightly proud of the fountain, their showpiece for friends and family visiting from distant cities. Even statesmen from far lands had stopped to admire and comment. Yes, the towns-folk of Shae were rightly proud of the fountain in their town square. Now, the townsfolk who hadn't fled were dead and would never again taste those waters or be rightly proud of them. Or be anything ever again.

Amal Muna squeezed her eyes shut and focused on the task at hand.

She returned to the side of the dying man. The blood had stopped flowing. The magenta liquid had turned into a gelatinous texture, like soft rubber. How odd. She cleaned it away and inserted the needle into the bruised skin of the young knight's skull. Her fingers trembled. She wanted to stop for fear she might kill him.

A little of something is a great deal better than a lot of nothing.

The man was going to die anyway. Nothing she did would change that. But even if he lives here today, he'll die some place else, at another time. Why should she bother?

Because a little of something is a great deal better than—

Yes, papa. Quiet now.

She pushed, poked, and punctured. The needle and thread were quality. Mother might have complained about father, endlessly, about how she'd had her choice of men, about how she would never understand why she'd married him, but she would never have her husband walk the streets of Shae without the finest clothes other people's money could buy and her skills could manufacture. Amal pictured them now, arm in arm walking, he smiling at the beautiful woman on his finely clothed arm, she brushing that arm and admiring her own handiwork.

Amal was done stitching, thankful that her mind had drifted away to happier times. She tied the thread off and wondered how to get the man inside into bed. She wondered how she could feed him.

She wondered a lot of things.

She wondered why war had come to Shae. She wondered which side she was supposed to be on, having little idea who the dead warriors in her town represented. They all looked the same: shining steel, chainmail, arriving within hours of each other. As far as she could tell, there were few distinguishing features to any of the dozens of corpses lying in chaotic symmetry in the dust.

She looked at the young man and wiped his blood on her pale blue dress. He didn't look like the enemy. But about that, she could be wrong.

A little of something—

Shut up, papa.

Her house was too far to drag a full-grown man, but the Frees family home was on the verge of the town square. She could make it there.

Amal Muna hauled the soldier across the dust. Her back ached, but the man seemed to grow lighter the more she pulled him, death lightening her load. His soul, perhaps, leaving his body? How much did a soul weigh?

The Frees house was not far now. A house on the edge of the square was an expensive affair, as befitting the wealthiest of wealthy families in Shae. Perhaps that was why they had chosen not to run—they were the elite. The two-story house she was slowly approaching was a glorious testament to the Frees family wealth and history, but a history that had reached a sudden and shocking end, an end no riches could circumvent.

Perhaps they thought they were above war. Above death. The hacked corpses littered throughout their home testified otherwise.

Amal dragged the young man into the foyer of the Frees house and cursed her stupidity. The bedrooms were upstairs. She should know that, having been here as a girl, as a friend of Nessiah, the youngest Frees daughter, a friend before the politics of age and social standing had separated them.

Upstairs, she thought. She had to get him upstairs. Or bring the bed downstairs.

Of course the Frees family had heavy beds. Heavy was expensive, and no expense was spared for the Lords of the Sands, the Kings of Nowhere.

Amal ignored the two corpses in the kitchen downstairs, and she ignored the corpse of her childhood friend on the stairs as she hauled the knight upwards. She had to nudge Nessiah aside with her foot to make room for the young man. Nessiah's long black hair draped the steps. She tried not to stand on it; Nessie loved her hair clean. Amal felt ill.

"I'm sorry, Ness."

She heaved the limp soldier to the top of the stairs, sweating with exertion, and into Nessiah's bedroom. With a final effort, she straddled the man and hauled him onto her dead friend's bed, his body collapsing on top of her, taking all her strength to push him off. She laid out his feet and put his head on a pillow.

She searched the Frees family home for bandages, but finding none, tore strips from her childhood friend's white dress, strips without blood on them, while trying to avoid looking at Nessiah's face.

The man was now stitched and bandaged, but blood was soaking through the dressing. Amal shook her head as she looked down at the dying man, for dying he was. She had done all she could do, but she knew it wasn't enough. The wound was too grievous.

She pulled up a small wooden seat next to the orange clay bed and sat down, taking a moment to breathe, to look closely at the young man. She leaned over and peeled an eyelid upwards. He had blue eyes, in contrast to Amal's brown. Then she studied the alabaster porcelain of his throat and face. She had seen white men like this before, but he was still a rarity, an exotic in this part of the world. She removed the hand pendant from under the man's shirt and stared at the intricate details, puzzled at the strange luminous metal from which it had been made. It seemed to subtly change colors in her hand. She let the pendant fall from her fingers back to the man's hairless chest, then sat back and waited.

She waited for the townsfolk of Shae to rise from the dead, for the heavily armed invaders from both sides to walk backward out of the city gates, for Nessiah to awaken and pointedly ignore her when they passed in the streets. For the waters in the Fountain of Shae to run bloodless once more.

17

Leaving Shae

Amal's elder sister, Fiona, had outshone the desert sun in her glorious wedding gown of sapphire, her parents both crying and smiling. The entire town of Shae had turned out to celebrate. Even Amal's oldest friend Nessiah was among the throng of guests and well-wishers in the square. She came forward from the shade of the statue within the fountain, holding her shoes in one hand and taking Amal's hand in the other.

"Come on," Nessie said. "Let's run barefoot like we used to."

Amal felt sad. "I haven't seen you for so long, Nessie. Why did you stop being my friend?"

Nessiah waved her away with that pretty lop-sided grin. "That doesn't matter. I'm here now, when it truly counts."

Amal gasped, holding back tears. "But you're dead. You're outside on the steps, so much blood."

"No, no." Nessiah laughed. "Listen to me. All we have to do is run, like when we were young."

"We're still young."

"Just run, Amal."

"Nessie, I miss you, I do."

"Run, Amal."

Amal awoke and saw the knight looking at her, the dead man on Nessie's orange clay bed. But he wasn't dead. Nessie was dead. As pig-headed as she was, Nessie couldn't deny being dead any longer, but this man was clearly alive. He breathed deeply and stared with pale blue eyes, grasping the small metallic hand, the one she had seen when stripping him of his armor in the venomous heat of the town square. She leaned forward in the chair and examined his bandages. She ought to change them, that's what a healer would do, she thought.

So as not to startle him, she said gently, "I'm going to take off these bandages and clean the wound. Do you understand?" She pointed at her head and mimed an unwrapping motion. "Change the bandages?"

He just stared.

She reached to take the dressing from his head, and as swift as a desert scorpion's sting, he clasped her wrist, his strength overpowering. "Ow, you're hurting me. I just want to help you. Please, let me go."

He released her, and she rubbed her arm. She sat back, unsure of what to do as the knight pushed himself up and looked around. His blue eyes returned to Amal's face. He nodded and pointed at his head, apparently granting her permission to unwrap the bandages.

Amal fumbled with the bloodied wrappings, peeling them off as gently as she could. She gasped when she saw his exposed head. His blond hair was matted with crusted blood, but the wound had closed and seemed to be healing. How long had she been asleep?

The man didn't flinch as she cleaned his scalp with a wet rag and peered closer. The gash in his head appeared six weeks healed, the stitches she had sewn now redundant and already falling out like sunburned skin. She sat back and shook her head, looking at the man's fist still closed over the amulet about his chest.

He let the trinket fall from his fingers, the small metal hand glowing a color somewhere between blue, red, and gold. How could it be so many colors at once? He threw aside the coverlet and made to gain his feet.

"No, stay in bed." Amal put her hand out, palm facing the man. "You need to rest."

He got to his feet, immediately losing his balance and collapsing back. He breathed heavily, head bowed.

She thought he was about to empty his guts. "Wait here," she said.

Amal went outside to the Frees family yard and found some soup heating over the stone oven. It had almost evaporated, but there was enough for a single small meal. She returned to the man and watched as he took the proffered bowl, eyeing it as if he didn't understand the purpose of the contents. She mimed an eating action, the soldier understood. He slurped the soup slowly, as if he were fighting the urge to vomit with every mouthful.

Finally, when he had eaten and placed the bowl on the bed, the man rose to his feet again. Amal moved under his right arm to support him. He gave her a puzzled expression but allowed her to come in close. Together, they staggered to the door. The man rested against the frame. His heart beat frantically; she could feel it fluttering under his ribcage. Amal and the soldier moved toward the top of the stairs and gingerly eased their way downwards, the young knight hobbling sideways like an old man without his walking stick.

"That's Nessie," Amal said as they passed the corpse of the youngest daughter of the House of Frees. "We used to be best friends."

The knight glanced at Amal, then at the raven-haired girl on the steps, his brow furrowed. When they came to the bottom of the stairs, the knight pushed Amal away.

"You don't talk much. Are you the enemy?"

The knight moved outside toward the town square. She watched as he made his way through the dead warriors, each one occupying his own idiosyncratic death-pose, no two cadavers alike. The young man stopped at one particular corpse and knelt, laying his hand on the dead man's chest, bowing his head.

He must have been a friend.

Amal didn't know why, but suddenly she felt a pang of jealousy. She shouted from the doorway of the Frees family home. "I saved your life, by the way! You'd be dead like them, like him, if not for me!"

The man stood and looked around at everything except Amal. He approached the fountain in the middle of the square and drank from it.

"There's blood in there!" Amal shouted. "Everyone is dead!"

The young soldier ignored her and drank. He knelt beside his armor baking in the heat of the midday sun, but he didn't take it. Instead, he pulled a leather vest from another of the dead warriors and picked up a discarded saddlebag. From within, he took a bread roll and began to eat it.

"What's your name? I'm Amal," she said, shouting.

He continued walking the town square and gathering supplies. The young man seemed to grow in strength with every bite of bread.

"You should be dead. It's unnatural."

He looked at her then, and she shrank back from his piercing blue eyes. Panic welled up from within at the man's preparations. "Are you leaving?"

No response from the fellow.

She walked outside into the direct late-afternoon sunshine. "I'm a good cook," she said. "And I can sew."

He took another drink from the fountain, then filled a bottle and strapped it to his belt by some arcane military magic.

"There are no horses left alive," she said, approaching the man. "You can't leave. The desert will kill you."

The man continued to ignore her.

She frantically scanned the square. All dead. Everyone here is dead. She turned back to the knight. "Take me with you," she said. Fiona's wedding day came back to her mind once more; the reception had been held in this very square.

The young man was walking toward the city gate.

"Take me with you," she said again. She looked around desperately. Was he really leaving? Was there no one else?

The young warrior was beginning to shimmer in the midday heat.

He's mad. From death's door to walking the desert alone, *completely mad.*

She followed him, nonetheless.

"Wait," she said. Amal realized absentmindedly that she wasn't wearing sandals. "Wait, take me with you."

Something called to her. *Stay*, it said. *Your family is here. Your life is here in Shae.*

No, Amal thought. No, there was nothing here for her. Not any longer.

Your family is here, the voice said again. She tried to ignore it, as the young soldier was ignoring her. She padded across the mix of dirt and sand, following the man. "Please," she said, "wait for me."

He just walked away, and she followed through the dead streets of Shae.

The sun approached its zenith, but the man paid it no heed. He was out of the gate now, walking the road to . . . Amal wasn't sure where the road led. She'd never walked it before.

"Wait, please wait."

He didn't wait.

"How can you be so cruel? I saved your life."

Her feet hurt. Small stones paved the road, no great burden for a pack animal or leather-shod foot soldier, but for a perfumed, pampered, and beloved daughter of Shae, the surface sent pain shooting upwards from the soles of her feet.

Had she been pampered? Had she been mistaken all this time? She thought she was strong. Papa taught her to be strong. She was sorry. She was weak.

The voice. *Your father was weak too. He couldn't hold them off.*

Shut up.

You have to understand, the voice said.

Shut up. "Please wait, Sir Knight!"

The voice wouldn't remain silent. *Your father —*

Shut up.

The young man had made a ridgeline a half league outside of the city. He was scanning the land beyond, shielding his eyes from the sun. Amal was trying to catch up with him, but her feet were cut now, bleeding. It hurt. She couldn't keep up.

Your father couldn't protect your mother.

Shut up!

But it was too late. She remembered. Amal was back in the closet now, watching as the soldiers raped her mother. She could see through the crack in the doors. Her father was lifeless on the floor, dead eyes looking at Amal through the crack. *Don't make a sound*, he seemed to say.

Mother was looking at her too, on the bed, on her hands and knees. *Don't make a sound*, her eyes said, face twisted in pain.

So, she had bitten her tongue as Fiona screamed from the next room, bitten her tongue as she watched her mother dissipate before her eyes, watched as half a dozen men took her spirit with sexual violence before they murdered her.

Shock overwhelmed Amal, crushed her. "Everyone is dead. Please, wait." She slumped to the stinging heat of the dirt, her feet bloodied. She looked back toward Shae. She had failed Papa, Mama, Fiona. She was sorry. She cried, quietly.

The invaders hadn't opened the door to the closet, and because of that, she was still alive. She sobbed, her tears falling to the uncaring dirt-sand, forming damp beads that rolled slowly downhill. She took a breath and tried to summon the strength to walk back to Shae, back to her home, to lay down with her family, lay down with Mama, Papa, and Fiona, lay down with their bodies as she had neatly arranged them, lay down and die. There was no one left alive who cared for her, and the thought broke her heart, shattered her soul.

She had been foolish to think she could go on. She simply didn't possess the strength. Living or dead, she belonged with her family.

Something blocked out the sun.

She looked up, and he was there, looking down at her. He squatted and lifted her feet gently in his hands, examining them. The young knight then stood, lifted Amal by her arms, and swung her around and upon his back.

She clasped him tightly as they made the ridge and descended the other side into the Great Southern Sands.

18

Oasis

The young knight carried Amal across the burning desert sands on his back, and as he did so, she peered down the front of his leather jerkin, watching the finely detailed hand-shaped trinket sway on his chest.

Why had he and the other soldiers suddenly materialized from the desert haze to fight and fall? The Great War was over, or so she had thought, and even at its peak, no bloodshed had ever come to the small desert town of Shae. Why now, more than a year after the fact? Everything she loved was gone. Shae was dead, and she could never go back, nor would she ever want to.

"What's your name?" she asked the knight.

He ignored her.

Did he even speak the common language of the Great Southern Sands? Amal looked at the sky from beneath her mother's keffiyeh. It would be evening soon. The heat was stifling. How did the knight keep going, step after sinking step through the sand, stumbling over rocks?

"Michael," he said finally. "My name is Michael Alaine."

Amal's heart jumped. His voice sounded like a much older man's—deep, laden with experience, melancholy. "Oh, you can speak the desert tongue?"

"A little," he responded.

"I'm Amal. Amal Muna. Why did you come to Shae? Who were you fighting? Are you fighting for the good side? Where are we going?"

He didn't respond. The only sound meeting Amal's ears was the soft crackling and sucking of desert stones and sand under the soldier's trudging boots.

She bit back on the flow of inquiries and took a quiet breath. "Michael, have I asked too many questions?"

He nodded.

"I'm sorry. Mother always said I was excitable. I *am* excitable, but that's not a crime, is it?" She thought a moment and decided to press her luck. "Michael Alaine, would you answer *one* question?"

"Yes."

A surge of panic rose as she struggled to choose a single question. There was so much she wanted to know. Her confusion stifled her. She had to choose carefully.

"Why do you wear a hand-shaped pendant around your neck?" She was horrified at the question the moment she had uttered it, and equally surprised; she hadn't realized she even wanted to know. Of all the questions, why this one?

He didn't answer her immediately, but she could feel that this time he wasn't doing so to ignore her. He was simply working himself up to a reply.

"It contains a magic, a magic that has saved my life on many occasions. I wear it for protection," he said in broken common desert tongue.

And there it was. A magic amulet. She wasn't sure she liked the answer but knew she'd have to make do with it. Some people, after all, were very superstitious, but father used to say there are many types of people in this world, and we must remain tolerant, for tolerance is the key to peace. Amal wondered if she should bequeath this item of her father's wisdom to the soldier but decided to keep it for herself. She didn't want to come across loquacious or even, heaven forbid, annoying. That wouldn't do. Instead, she said, "It's getting dark. You should rest, you're still hurt."

He shook his head, his shoulder-length blond hair caressing her brown cheeks. "We walk during the night, rest during the day. Isn't that the way with the desert people?"

He was right, for the nomadic tribes at least. She, however, had grown up in the most beautiful oasis-town in a hundred square leagues. She'd gone to bed and risen with the sun her entire life, living in the cool shade and among running water all that time.

They walked on into the evening and the bitter cool of night. Amal looked up and said, "The stars are more beautiful when viewed from the desert, did you know that? There's nothing to take away from their beauty. No lights, no noise. Aren't they incredible?"

Michael raised his pale blue eyes to the diamond encrusted firmament. "Yes," he said.

She wrapped her arms a little tighter around his chest and whispered in his ear. "On particularly fine evenings you can even see Orion the Hunter."

"I see it."

"You do?" Amal stared again at the twinkling vault of heaven. "No. You're mistaken. It's not visible tonight."

He didn't reply.

"You're so quiet," she said. "I'm sure it's not good for you. Mother always said stoic men bottle everything and explode in madness when the time comes." She yawned and clung tighter for fear of falling off Michael's back. She felt drowsiness envelop her. "I think my feet are better. I can walk."

"Walk tomorrow."

"All right, Michael Alaine," she said. "You're so warm. I'll just nap for a bit."

Amal fell asleep on the man's back, but he kept right on moving.

———◆———

AMAL WOKE UP ALONE on a bedroll, the first rays of the morning sun suffusing the horizon with red and pink. She thought the knight had abandoned her, then she breathed easier when she saw he had erected a makeshift tent nearby, laid out his supplies and clothes. But where was the pale knight with the pale blue eyes? And where had he found the tent?

She heard splashing and followed the sound up to a ridge peppered with palm trees. She lay on her stomach and peered over the lip. He had his back to her, bathing in a pool. This man had a talent for finding water in the desert, no doubt. She watched briefly before turning away, giving the man his modesty. Something inside of her made her turn back, and when she did, the pain of her loss eased but for a moment. Here was life in the desert, movement and warmth, something human that breathed and laughed and loved. This was better than death, this young man, his muscles fluid beneath his skin. This was love. Or the promise of it.

He looked at her, and she froze. His eyes met hers for a moment but shifted to a new sight—four riders in desert garb of flowing tunics, their curved scimitars drawn, the figures calmly making the ridge, two on either side of Amal. They paid her little heed as they descended to the edge of the water in the brightening morning.

Michael Alaine raised his hands to show he had no weapons.

A rider spoke, his face hidden, his voice unemotional. "You bathe in water meant for drinking, a capital offense."

Amal stood. She understood the language; it was not the common tongue but a nomadic dialect. She feared Michael didn't understand what the man had said and couldn't explain himself or escape sanction. She spoke up in their language. "He didn't know, forgive him."

Another of the riders removed part of a headscarf to reveal a feminine face, hawkish nose, fiercely brown eyes. "Who are you?"

"I am Amal Muna, a daughter of Shae."

The woman looked from Amal to Michael and back again. "You must warn your people. The hunters come."

Sorrow resurfaced in Amal's heart. "It's too late. Shae is dead. My family is dead."

The four riders turned to the naked knight. He still wore the amulet, if nothing else.

She went on, knowing that Michael's life now hung by a thread as thin and fragile as any to be found in her mother's sewing kit. "He saved me," she said, pointing to the soldier in the pool. "He didn't abandon me when I needed help. I owe him my life, such as it is. Please do not harm him."

The riders looked unconvinced, exchanging concerned glances.

"He's a good man."

The woman smiled sadly, shaking her head. "Child, I fear all such distinctions of good and evil are about to be swept away."

"It's not too late," Amal said. "I can save him in return. I can. I have nothing, only him. Please. Let me save him."

The riders murmured among themselves. The woman got off her horse and offered the reins to Amal. "You can save no one, least of all yourself, without a way out of the desert. I hope you know what you're doing, child."

She took the reins and bowed her head. "Thank you."

The man who had first spoken put his arm down and pulled the dusky-skinned woman onto the back of his horse. She studied Amal's face and reached down for her hand. "Come with us, for the Northern men bring only death."

She shook her head.

"So be it. I wish you well, Amal Muna, daughter of Shae."

After watching the riders disappear into the distance, Amal walked the horse back to the campsite and tethered it in the shade of a palm tree.

Michael joined her, and she averted her eyes as he dried and dressed. He sat down cross-legged and looked at the horse. "This will hasten our journey. It is good." He cleared his throat gently. "I could not understand what they were saying, but I have the feeling you just saved my life. Again."

"Perhaps." Amal smiled with pleasure. "Where are we going?"

"To Re'Shan. The force I serve is based there." He paused and brushed water from his hair. The air was still cold, but the oncoming day would be brutally hot.

"I'm sorry, Michael. I know you dislike questions, but I must ask. Why did your army come to Shae?"

"I'm a soldier. I go where I'm told. Do you understand?"

"I understand."

Amal was surprised when Michael asked a question of his own. "Do you know of the Hungry King?"

"Of course. Everyone knows of him. A cannibal. He was defeated in the war to end all wars. The kings to the north, Tremain and Bruwaert, stopped him with assistance from the Nomadic Lords and the Freelanders."

Michael ran his hand back through his damp blond hair. "But the Hungry King's army was not entirely wiped out. When Re'Shan fell and the war ended, his soldiers fled to the Great Southern Sands. Some of them were living among you. I stayed on after the war. It was my job, my comrades' job in Achilles Company, to clean up the remnants of the Hungry King's army in the desert."

Amal furrowed her brow. "I know everyone in Shae. There were no outsiders among us."

"Yet we found them and fought them."

She shook her head. "I was born in Shae. There was no foreign army among us. I would know."

"It's possible they had been living among you for some time." He looked at the sun making its ferocious ascent at the far end of the desert. "The killing heat comes. We have far to travel. But now, I am tired and must sleep."

Amal nodded. "Of course."

"You too."

"I have slept," she said.

"Sleep beside me."

She arched her eyebrows in surprise. "What are you asking?"

"For you to sleep beside me, in the tent. You'll burn in the sun otherwise. Don't think too much, girl."

"I wasn't thinking anything."

"Nor I." Michael looked embarrassed. "How are your feet?"

Amal realized with a start that she had given no thought to the state of her feet. She ran her hands over them. "They're better, thank you for asking."

"Sleep beside me, and they'll be fully healed come sundown."

She stared at the knight quizzically. "How do you know this?"

He sighed. "Questions, always questions. I'm tired from carrying you halfway across the Great Southern Sands. Do as you wish." He got up and disappeared within the small tent.

Amal Muna looked once more at her feet and then at the encroaching sun. She followed Michael inside the cool tent and lay down beside the soldier from Achilles Company. She listened as his breathing became steady and deep, and stole a glance at his profile when she was certain he was no longer awake. He couldn't have been older than twenty-three. He had the face of an innocent, a cherub-faced boy.

She laughed silently at her own idiocy. This man was a soldier, a knight, a killer of men, and perhaps women for all she knew. He wasn't innocent. But for now, he was all she had.

19

Wild strawberries

Rebecca Occitane had slipped in and out of consciousness over the three days it had taken to reach the sanctuary of the Yellow Abbey, the shock of her father's death setting in. Brynhild had supported Rebecca on her white steed, but it was William who rode beside the girl, talked to her in comforting whispers, related his life in the Abbey, chatted airily of his fellow monks, of the fat Abbot Hugh Gilbert, of how the leader of the abbey was a harsh but fair man, of William's desire to be a writer. It was all nonsensical ramblings, trivia, but Rebecca listened, found his voice comforting, and silently thanked the monastic scholar a hundred times.

She had a vague recollection of the horses climbing a winding road in the bright wind-blown afternoon, and of seeing the Abbey there, squatting in the hillside like some massive stone toad.

Brynhild carried her to a dark room and gently placed her on a bed. Then Rebecca slept and remembered nothing. And everything.

It was a dream, she knew, when she saw her father in the yard sawing timber. She held a basket of wild strawberries on her arm, their aromatic breath vivid in her nostrils.

No, not a dream, a memory disguised as a dream, a memory she tried to cling to.

"Are you all right, father?"

Robert Occitane stopped cutting wood. "I'm fine, Rebecca. Why do you ask?"

She looked at the farmhouse, where the chickens were clucking peacefully in the yard, and then farther out over the cliffs to the sea, toward the horizon where two shades of blue merged. "I was worried."

Robert laid down his saw, his amber eyes smiling. "Do you think you're ready to beat me?"

She sighed.

"Oh, father, not now. I'm tired from picking strawberries."

"I see. Too tired to beat an old man."

Their eyes met, then Rebecca laughed, dropped her basket, and sprinted.

Robert was a yard in front of her when he reached the earthen track zig-zagging down to the beach below. "Run!" he shouted into the salt air.

They had run this race many times before, and he'd always been the winner. But not this time. This time it would be her turn, of that Rebecca was determined. She picked her spot, a bend in the path that could be skirted by a strategic leap and slide—this she did, coming farther down onto the track and overtaking her father. Robert laughed.

The track was three leagues from end to end, narrow and steep, impossible for horses to negotiate. This was why her father had worked so hard to carve it out of the cliffside.

"It'll be a footrace girl, and then you'll have a chance," her father had said upon first taking her down the track.

She had felt the flutter of fear's wings in her heart. "Do you think they'll come one day?"

He gazed far out to sea. "I don't know. But if they do, you run."

And she ran.

She ran all the way to the beach and turned back to see her father making his arrival a few seconds later. He was beaming from ear to ear, exhausted, breathing so hard with effort and mirth that he couldn't speak. He grabbed her by both shoulders, and when he'd collected himself, he stopped smiling, looking into her eyes.

"Well done," he breathed. "Never, never be second to the bottom of this track ever again. Do you hear me?"

Her own smile faded. "Yes, father. I hear you."

Rebecca turned at the whinnying of a horse. When she looked back, her father was lying dead in the yard, his eyes closed. There were soldiers around him, some dead, some still standing. And horses, they all had horses. The men had their hard eyes on her and cackled bearded, callous, guttural laughs.

"Where is it, pretty?" said the man with a patchy red beard.

Rebecca looked down at the basket on her arm. She felt the heat of something resting on her chest, something almost visible under the light fabric of her tunic. The men were standing between her and the path leading to the beach. She placed the strawberries on the ground and stepped away, edging toward the cliff and the path.

"In there," she said, pointing to the basket.

They took the bait.

Her father opened his dead amber eyes and whispered one word.

"Run."

And she ran.

She awoke in a dim room, tears streaming down her face. William Barding was there, sitting and holding her as she screamed in pain and anger. He said nothing, did not hush her, did not tell her she was safe, did not tell her that everything would be all right.

He simply held her while she emptied her soul.

He smelled like wild strawberries.

20

The Researcher

"She's been asleep for two days," Abbot Hugh Gilbert said. "I think we should send for a healer."

"Rebecca awoke this morning, Abbot," Brynhild Grimsdotter said, leafing through the pages of a book in the library. She held a small reading glass in her hand, holding it over the fine script on the pages.

The abbot noted the oddity of the contrast between the fragile reading device in the woman's hand and the woman herself, who was nothing short of a giant, and certainly nothing approaching fragile.

He looked around. The library was bustling. Friday was reading day at the Yellow Abbey; all scholars were free from their duties for a day, and barely a reading seat could be had on the long wooden benches, save for the immediate spaces available on either side of the intimidating Norsewoman.

"She did? I wasn't notified. What's she doing?"

"Eating."

"But it's late afternoon. You said she woke this morning."

Brynhild gently turned a brittle, crackling page. "She did. She has something of an appetite."

"Goodness. Take me to her, if you would be so kind, Princess Grimsdotter."

The Norsewoman frowned. "You may call me Brynhild. In fact, I insist."

"Very well, Brynhild. Please, lead the way."

OUTSIDE THE ENTRANCE OF THE ABBEY, William Barding and Rebecca Occitane were sitting on a bench, gazing at the patchwork fields below, Rebecca absentmindedly chewing a piece of bread. William rose at the sight of his superior and Brynhild, and the girl followed his lead, wiping her mouth clean of crumbs.

The abbot swept the girl's hands up in his. "Rebecca Occitane, I am Abbot Hugh Gilbert. I understand you've suffered tremendously, and I'd like to offer the condolences of the Order of the Yellow Scholars. The Abbey is yours for as long as you wish to stay."

Rebecca simply stared at the abbot's pudgy hands. "Thank you, Father. I'm feeling better. I won't burden you for much longer." She looked up.

Her bright amber eyes were startling, the pupils large like circular insects trapped in diaphanous stone. "My dear girl, you are no burden, none whatsoever." He glanced from the girl to the Norsewoman and back again. "However, I would not recommend a plan of action involving the attempted assassination of King Bruwaert. We here at the Abbey are a non-political, non-profit organization. In short, we don't advocate for murder."

"Bruwaert holds no such scruples," Rebecca said calmly.

The abbot pouted. "That may be so—"

"I believe now is not the time to discuss such matters. Rebecca is not fully healed," Brynhild said.

He released the girl's hands and put his own within the sleeves of his robes. "Of course, of course."

"You are expecting another visitor?" Brynhild nodded to the winding dirt road below, upon which was a single horse and rider.

"Actually, we are. A researcher."

The warrior watched the black horse and gray-robed rider approaching. "Researcher? Of what kind?"

"I didn't ask. Our library is open to any who make a formal request to read."

"Anybody?"

The abbot threw his palms to the heavens. "We are a non-political, non—"

"Profit organization. I understand." Brynhild turned to William. "Get Rebecca inside. Now, please."

"What danger is a researcher, a fellow scholar?"

"None," Brynhild said, "but this man is military."

The abbot swiveled his plump head on his shoulders for a clearer look. "How on earth can you tell that from here? He's robed, riding a horse two leagues away. And even if he is military, we're a non-political . . ." He found himself alone, staring curiously at the new arrival wending toward the Abbey. He shielded his eyes from the sun. At this distance, he could identify nothing to distinguish the gray-robed rider as male or female, military or otherwise. But then again, he wasn't a battle-hardened warrior princess with experience in these things.

As it turned out, Brynhild Grimsdotter had overreacted. The new arrival was a simple researcher after all, having visited the Abbey in the past. He pulled back his gray hood, and Abbot Hugh Gilbert recognized his distinctive features. Christopher was his name, if his memory served correctly.

"Welcome, Christopher. You're listed as anonymous in the visitor's book. Why all the secrecy?"

The man got down from his horse and handed the reins over to young Brother Marvin. "Well, I'm on a secret mission, and secrets beget secrets, as they say," he said and ran his hands through his close-cropped white hair.

Both men clasped their fingers over their hearts.

"Well, welcome. The library is yours. If you find any secrets hidden within, do let me know."

Christopher smiled, but the abbot could see in the man's midnight-black eyes, the second pair of unusually colored eyes he'd gazed into this afternoon, that the mirth fell short.

IN THE LATE AFTERNOON on the following day, the library was mostly occupied by busily transcribing butter-robed scholars. Only two readers sat in the library: Brynhild Grimsdotter and the newly arrived researcher. Of the two, only one was actually reading.

The blonde ponytailed Norsewoman had a book open on the table but was watching the newcomer sitting with his gray hood over his bowed head, perfectly still. He didn't move for an hour, not one rustle of robes, nothing except for the intermittent turning of a silent page. She didn't like him. There was something about the lack of motion in the man that troubled her. Whether the stranger noticed her occasional glances in his direction, she couldn't say, but her instinct told her that he was fully aware.

When the first sconces were lit against the accruing darkness, the man closed his book and left it on the table. An acolyte swiftly gathered up the tome and disappeared through a door between two pillars. Brynhild knew there was an extension to the library, an archive containing older, more delicate works. She pretended to read her own book as the man calling himself Christopher Lewis—his name squeezed from an uncomfortable Hugh Gilbert—glided past her to the exit.

When she was sure he was gone, Brynhild waved the young librarian over.

"The book that man was reading. I'd like to see it."

The round-faced fellow bowed and returned to the archives.

As she sat waiting, Brynhild looked around the reading room at the hard-working copyists, all wearing the same expressions of concentration. She inhaled the scent of paper and ink and, for a moment, allowed herself to think that the world was more than blood and death, violence and greed, that there were good people doing good things, albeit mostly cloistered away, ignored by society as a whole. But as long as the world had the word, everything would be all right in the end.

The attendant returned and placed the book on the table. Brynhild smiled and nodded her thanks. She opened the book to the introduction.

Though containing archaic terminology, the book was written in the common tongue. *The Fall of the Order of Ulfur*, by Tobias Waterstone. The tome was eighty years old, its pages fragile, but the print was large enough to read comfortably in the fading light of the reading torches. She whispered thanks to the copyist all those years ago who had taken pity on readers with less than perfect vision.

Brynhild was a skilled reader. World Literature had been part of her royal education and perhaps the reason for her deteriorating eyesight at close range. For her, reading had never been an arduous task. From the very first tales of high adventure, she'd been hooked, entranced, taken to the word like a bird to the sky.

She delved into the old book. The honorable Tobias Waterstone's prose was hard going, a little flowery and self-important, but there was no denying that the man had a passion for his subject. His book was organized. A table of contents and page numbers—a rarity in the older books—assisted the reader in their educational expedition.

Not long after nightfall, before the torches in their sconces had burned halfway down, Brynhild Grimsdotter had gathered the seeds of the book, and they germinated rapidly in her mind. She scrambled to her feet and ran for the door, startling a librarian who had to leap out of her path.

Rebecca Occitane was in terrible danger.

21

The Buried Monastery

From high on Mount Ulfur, Robert Occitane watched the city of Re'Shan burn below. Lush green vegetation grew on the mountainside in stark contrast to the arid city of domes and spires that marked the beginning of the Great Southern Sands. The desert was shrouded in a haze of smoke and heat, and for some odd reason, the view reminded him of his home on the cliff overlooking the sea. He thought of his beloved Rebecca. The war was over. She'd be safe now, and he'd be home soon.

The air at three and a half thousand feet entered his lungs but didn't satiate his desire for oxygen. He was breathing heavily from the climb, the screams of terror and delight seeming to follow him from the sacked, smoking city below. How much farther would he have to climb before the sounds of rape and murder, the shrieks of men, women, and children, would cease to torment him?

Robert suspected he'd be climbing for the rest of his life, until the air became so rarified that nothing could possibly survive, until Death cupped his hands over his ears.

A voice suddenly came from above. "Commander Occitane, hurry! They've found it! We're here!"

Broadford Higgins was standing on a large rock a few yards up the narrow goat track. He was grinning from ear to ear, his excitement palpable.

"You're out of uniform, Higgins. War is no place for frippery," Robert said.

The tall man looked down at his flowing sleeves and delicate lace cuffs, his smile undiminished. "One man's frippery is another's finery, sir. Besides, the war is over."

"You still represent Tremain and the Alliance, not to mention the boys of Prometheus Company. We're not done here yet."

"The clothes are clean, Commander. No blood, no shit stains. I made the man remove the accoutrements before I cut his throat."

"We're not in the business of murdering civilians, Higgins!"

Broadford stopped smiling and looked at the destroyed city three thousand feet below. "As you say, Commander, as you say."

The path they were climbing leveled out onto a mossy plateau, turning away from the cliff's edge and heading into dense vegetation. Robert could hear running water and followed Broadford into a clearing. A small waterfall fed by the ever-present ice caps far above cascaded over a rocky outcrop and disappeared into an opening in the ground. Around the pit kneeled three men, all in the uniform of Prometheus Company, their voices lost within the sounds of the crashing water. One of the men, a younger soldier, was pointing down into the opening.

Broadford approached and slapped the blond-haired youth on the shoulder. "How'd you find it?"

Michael Alaine looked up with pale blue eyes and said, "I was climbing to clear my head. I stumbled upon it."

"Well, this is some climb, lad, some climb. You must've had a lot on your mind."

"Who's going first, then?" said a man with sand-colored hair.

"Are you volunteering?"

Malcolm Dewar laughed. "After you, Broadie. Toffs before dross."

Another man kneeling at the lip of the pit stood up and revealed himself to be even taller than Broadford Higgins. He spoke in a dark, mellifluous voice. "Michael, you've been down there?"

"Aye, Marshal de Merlon. I have."

"Would you be a brave lad and repeat your deed?"

"Yes, sir." The young soldier stood and looked around.

"Malcolm, the rope, if you will. Broadford, the torches," Tristan said.

Malcolm knelt and removed a rope from a pack while Broadford Higgins busied himself with a leather saddlebag.

"Here." Michael held back a mass of ferns covering an iron rung embedded in a large boulder about ten feet from the opening. "Thread the rope through here, that's how they must have secured passage in and out."

"Where's Archibald?" Robert asked.

The group of men scanned the clearing. "Probably off sticking his cock in a mountain goat," Broadford said.

Malcolm laughed. "Always horny like one."

At that moment, a clean-cut man appeared through the fern leaves. His black hair was tied back in a ponytail. He too wore the outfit of Prometheus Company, complete with a flame emblem on the arm of his surcoat. He smiled and said, "Just taking a piss, gents, but it's nice to know my codge occupies your thoughts when I'm not around. I'm touched, really."

Broadford scoffed. "Touched in the head."

Archibald Kirk watched Michael Alaine wrapping the rope around himself. "So, we're going in then?" He exhaled deeply. "Never been one for the deep, dark places of the earth, except vaginas of course, but all right."

Robert approached Tristan and spoke softly. "What are we doing?"

"Having one last adventure."

"I'm too old to be clambering around the underside of a mountain. This seems wrong."

Tristan glanced sideways. "Come on. Aren't you curious? Don't you want to know?"

"What I want is to return home to my daughter."

Tristan folded his arms and watched the young soldier preparing to step over the edge. "We all have family waiting for us. This I understand well. The war is over. It won't be long now. Consider this a final opportunity to secure your family's future."

Robert frowned. "How? By pillaging some mythical priory? To what end? We don't know if the monastery is even in there."

"Michael is an earnest fellow. He says it's there, and I trust him as far as I trust any man."

Robert Occitane closed his amber eyes. "I can't stand the screams anymore, Tristan."

The tall man put his hand on Robert's shoulder. "Perhaps we'll find peace inside," he said, nodding to the dark hole.

"What are we hoping to find?"

Tristan Drogos de Merlon ran a finger down his powerful, full jaw. "Hard to say. But we've all heard the stories of lost treasure. Something's down there. I can feel it."

"Rope is secure at this end," Malcolm said.

Michael wound the free end of the rope around his waist and under his arms. "There's a landing about six feet down, only big enough for one man at a time. Don't miss it, long fall if you do. Give me a moment to light the torch, I'll shout when the next man can come."

"Good luck to you, son," Tristan said.

"Keep these dry, lad." Broadford handed the young man a saddlebag containing torches.

Michael strapped the bag to his back and took a deep breath.

"The heaviest man belays," Tristan said. "Broadford, that's you."

"Aye, Marshal."

Michael stepped to the edge. "The rock wall is slippery. Lean well back, spread your weight. Like this." The five men watched the youngest soldier brace himself against the vertical pit wall, ease his weight backward, and then lower himself into the streaming water. Their faces were momentarily misted by the clear water splashing off Michael Alaine's body.

Every man stood peering below, listening intently, but they could only hear the rushing slap of water on rock.

"Where is he?" Malcolm asked.

"Steady on, mate. He's only just gone in. Give the boy a chance," Archibald said softly.

"Quiet," Robert said. "We listen."

And they listened. After a minute or two, the rope became slack, and a light glowed eerily from below, flickering on the smooth, wet walls of the cavern within.

"I think I see him," Malcolm said.

And then an echoing shout from below. "Next bloke down!"

Each man eyed the other in turn. Tristan said, "Come on, the boy did it. Move your arses. Kirk, you're next."

"Aye, sir." The handsome soldier pulled on the rope, and it came to the surface. He wrapped it around himself as Michael had done and tried to imitate the boy's climbing stance.

"Don't bump your pretty face on the way down, Archie," Broadford said, bracing his foot against a rock.

"And end up looking like you? I'll fucking top myself first."

A minute later, the ponytailed man was gone beneath the falling water.

Robert Occitane went next. He gasped as the frigid water squeezed the breath out of his body, the power of the icy flow nearly causing him to lose his footing from the rock wall. Below he saw Michael Alaine's young face peering up, his body hidden within an alcove. Robert slipped and swung above the abyss for a moment, then Michael grabbed his ankle and steadied him.

"Down, sir, let yourself down."

Robert's feet touched a narrow landing, and when there was enough slack, he crawled into a small opening in the sheer rock wall. The space wasn't an alcove but a tunnel not high enough to stand in, with arched walls made of some kind of copper brick glowing in the torchlight. Robert removed himself from the rope and squeezed past Michael, joining a crouching Archibald who was holding the torch further down the passage.

"Next man down!" Michael shouted, his voice bouncing around the enclosed space.

"Bloody freezing down here," Archibald said.

"Dry yourself as well as you can," Robert responded. "It's the water that makes you chill."

Both men got as close to the flame of the torch as they dared, blocking its light.

"Sorry sirs, I need that light to see the next man coming," Michael said.

"Of course, son." Robert stood back, allowing the blaze to outline the shape of the tunnel. He noticed steps leading down into the darkness ahead. "What do you think is down there?"

Archibald shrugged. "Your guess is on a higher pay rate than mine, Commander. It's only young Michael been here, and not too far down, so he says."

A panting Tristan Drogos de Merlon joined them. "This passage is getting a little crowded for comfort."

"Only two more, sir," Michael said. "Broadford's got the hardest of it."

The chill of the dank air floated over each man, and when Malcolm and Broadford joined them, the group made way for Michael to assume the lead position.

Taking the torch from Archibald, the blue-eyed soldier said, "Righto sirs, this way."

The group had to walk in a squatting position, and Robert's legs burned, his knees threatening to crack.

The steps came to a small landing, turned at right angles and continued on. At the next landing, the arched ceiling of the tunnel elongated, allowing the men to walk upright. Robert rubbed at his lower back and breathed a sigh of relief.

They came to another landing and a rectangular opening much too low for comfortable ingress but wide enough to allow four men to enter abreast, if they ducked.

"Is this the main entrance?" Malcolm asked.

"Yes," Michael said.

Malcolm spat out a laugh. "The monks must have been dwarves. Oddest door I've ever seen."

"It's not a door. It's a window."

"A window? Who would bother with windows down here?"

"The monastery wasn't built down here. It fell from a higher position, as far as I can tell. You'll understand when you get inside."

"Fell?" Broadford said. "Just how safe is this thing?"

"I'm not a structural engineer, Captain. Are we going in, or aren't we?"

"How far have you been in?" Tristan asked.

"A floor up and one down."

"And your opinion, son?"

"It's stable."

Tristan nodded. "Light another torch, one in front, one behind. Broadford, you take the torch at the back. Keep together."

They entered the opening and dropped down to a hallway thick with dust. The columns that supported the ceiling were punctuated by thin web-like cracks. The torchlight evaporated into the ether at a far shorter distance than was normal, as if the darkness were absorbing the light from the flame. Any doubt whether the six men were indeed walking through a monastery was expelled when the torchlight fell upon a massive wooden cross embedded in the wall of what was clearly a refectory.

"Where's the brewery?" Broadford said. "Monks make beer, don't they? And wine?"

"Quiet," Tristan said. "Keep moving. Michael, where are the internal stairs?"

"This way."

The men came to an archway, within which was a stairwell leading up and down.

"Where now?" Robert asked.

"The next floor up is the top floor," Michael said. "Not much there. Down, I don't know how far it goes. I've descended one floor, but there are others."

Tristan looked at Robert. "Down?"

He nodded. "Down."

On the lower levels, the floor leaned as if the structure had been elevated with blocks on one side. The six struggled to gather their balance.

"When it fell, it didn't settle level, you see?" Michael's voice bounced off unseen surfaces just beyond the flickering light.

"The monastery was once on the mountain side?" Robert asked.

"I believe so, sir."

They traveled down two more floors, coming across broken vases, ruined books, tattered robes, melted candles, discolored patches of dark on the cold stone floor. Nothing of any secular value.

Malcolm pointed. "Here!"

The crew gathered around a perfectly square crack in the floor.

"It's a trapdoor, but no handle or pulley," Robert whispered.

"Pry it open," Tristan said.

Each man produced a knife at the same time from within jacket pockets, boots, and other hidden places, and inserted the blade vertically into the crack.

"On the count of three. One, two . . ."

They pushed down and in, the trapdoor lifted, and they discarded their knives, scrabbling to get their fingers under the stone slab.

"Damn. It's heavy!" Archibald shouted.

"Don't drop it now," Robert said. "Some of us will lose our bloody fingers. Get your hands under, all the way! Heave!"

The slab of stone left its cavity.

"All right, over here. Now drop it!"

The slab clattered to the stone floor, a ringing echo circled the room. Each man peered into the darkness below, and there, hanging over blackness was a rope ladder.

One of the torches began to splutter. "Light another torch," Robert said. "Throw the dying one down."

Malcolm offered an observation. "Is that wise? The risk of fire?"

Robert shook his head. "Unlikely. Anyway, we have to see what's down there. Just make sure you don't ignite the rope ladder."

"Or Archibald's pretty hair." Broadford snickered.

Michael crawled to the edge of the black hole. He dropped the torch, and it hit the floor below and sparked to life briefly, then died.

"How far down?" Robert asked.

"Ten feet, Commander. The fall wouldn't kill you. Break an ankle but wouldn't kill you." The young soldier pulled at the rope ladder. "It seems stable."

"See anything else down there?"

"A giant spider."

Archibald Kirk gasped. "What?"

There was a moment's silence, then Michael chuckled softly.

"You little shit, Alaine." The ponytailed sergeant scowled, and the chamber echoed with laughter.

And then the six men from Prometheus Company delved deeper into the mysteries of the long-lost monastery of the Monks of Ulfur.

22

The Trinkets

Young Michael Alaine descended through the trapdoor first. Marshal Tristan Drogos de Merlon followed. Then came Sergeants Archibald Kirk and Malcolm Dewar, and then Captain Broadford Higgins. Commander Robert Occitane was the last to climb down the swinging rope ladder into darkness.

He wondered again at the madness that had overtaken the group. They were proud men, proud to wear the flame insignia of Prometheus Company, proud and fiercely loyal to King Tremain. But what had drawn them to crawl through a hole in the side of Ulfur? To scrabble in the damp depths, among the ruins of a precariously balanced priory? He wasn't sure, but the sense of unease within him continued to grow.

Michael held a freshly lit torch that cast light upon the stone walls and pillars erupting from a leaning stone floor. The cavernous room was musty, not a breath of air circulated to caress the face.

"Anybody else notice something odd about that rope ladder?" Malcolm asked, dusting off his hands.

"No, it was steady enough," Broadford said.

"That's just it. It's near new. Not a fray on it."

"Let's move on. We seem to be in some kind of narrow hall," Robert said. "Michael, Malcolm, Broadford, head that way." The commander pointed slightly uphill where flaking support columns darkened and diminished in the distance. "Tristan, Archibald, and I will head down there." He gestured the other way. "Broadford, give us your torch, and a spare please, Michael."

The young man reached into his saddlebag and handed over an unlit torch. "Shout if you find anything."

"Is it the best to split up, sir?"

"Scared of those spiders, Archie?" Broadford snickered.

"No, I'm just saying we don't know what's down here." The eerily lit faces of Archibald's comrades stared back at him. He shrugged. "All right then. Wiser heads than I, obviously."

And then six became two groups of three.

———

"CHRIST," MALCOLM SAID, holding the torch up to something on the wall.

"What is it?" Broadford asked, coming to the torchbearer's shoulder.

"Told you. Christ," the sandy-haired sergeant said.

There on the wall hung a picture of the baby Jesus cradled in his earthly mother's arms.

"Bloody idiot," Broadford murmured, disappointed. "Thought you'd found something."

Malcolm laughed. "It's a nice picture mate, might fetch a coin or two down the hill."

"We're not here for paintings, bedswerver."

Malcolm smiled and looked around. "Where's Michael?"

"Right here," said a voice at the edge of darkness.

Malcolm jumped and had to take a deep breath. "Don't lurk in the shadows, lad, make yourself known, would you? You're quieter than a ghost, give me the bloody fidgets worse than this place."

"Come on, down here," Broadford said. "I see something shining."

An altar, a candelabra, flashed in the torchlight.

"Is that silver?" Malcolm asked.

Broadford picked up the three-armed candle tree from the darkened corner. "It is. Pure silver."

"And here," Michael said. On the floor, several small dust-coated crosses dully shimmered.

They gathered the objects and cleaned them on their trousers.

Broadford gasped. "Lord. These are gold without a shadow. We've struck the cornucopia boys." He gave a shout of joyous laughter that reverberated through the ancient crypt-like monastery.

No sooner had the laugh faded than another laugh came, a foul, cackling simulation.

"What was that?" Malcolm swung his torch around, illuminating only aged, disintegrating pews. Michael and Broadford swiftly unsheathed their knives.

"An echo, wasn't it?" Broadford asked.

"That was no echo," Michael said.

Broadford continued to hold his knife out. "I outrank you, and I'm telling you that was an echo."

"Put the candle tree and crosses in the saddlebag," Malcolm said. "We check other rooms. Under no circumstances do we lose touch with each other."

"Maybe we should get out, find the others," Michael said.

"No, we finish it. We clear everything. I'm not coming back here."

Michael and Broadford didn't put their knives away as they stuffed the candelabra and crosses into the saddlebag. Malcolm kept watch, peering into the blackness.

When the loot had been safely tucked within the bag, the three men edged their way toward another archway leading off into yet another room. The labyrinthine darkness was oppressive, and the men's nerves were on edge, each man listening for a return of the fiendish, echoing laughter.

The next room was smaller, devoid of pews or any furniture save another altar, upon which stood a chalice possibly constructed of gold and something more—tiny, brilliantly sparkling gems encrusted in the metal.

"Oh, yes indeed," Broadford said, stepping toward the altar. He stopped at the sound of creaking. "What was that?"

"The floor," Michael said. "Look at the floor."

All three men looked at the old, warped, rotting wood.

Malcolm spoke softly. "Don't move, Broadie, that floor looks a little dodgy."

Michael and Malcolm watched as the boards under Broadford Higgins's feet groaned and sagged. "Shit," the tall, well-dressed rake said.

The floor gave way with a damp, muffled crack, and both man and altar disappeared.

"Broadie!" Malcolm Dewar leaped forward on his stomach and lost his torch within the newly opened mouth. He watched from the precipice as the flame spun slowly in the tar-like darkness, briefly illuminating a sheer rock wall from which water plummeted into the abyss below, and just before the torch was swallowed, flashing upon steps carved into that same rock wall at an impossible angle, leading seemingly nowhere.

Then darkness.

TRISTAN DROGOS DE MERLON, Robert Occitane, and Archibald Kirk entered a circular chamber off the long column-lined hallway. Around the chamber, on plinths, were strange clay miniatures: dragons, twisting serpents, bat-like creatures with fine veins in their outstretched wings. Some models had fallen from their pedestals and were unrecognizably fractured on the dust-laden floor. In the center of the room on a raised platform was something that resembled a coffin made of natural glass. The men tentatively approached the quartz-like sarcophagus.

The large box was too small to be a coffin; rather, it was some sort of thick, cloudy, rectangular display case. Within, something glowed in golds, reds, and purples.

Robert held the torch closer, and the objects inside disappeared in the reflected torchlight. Holding the flame further away from the crystal case, he could make out the luminous objects once more.

"What are they?" he asked.

"We have to open it," Tristan said.

They searched for a hinge or locking mechanism but could find no apparent way to unseal the glass box.

"We smash it," Archibald said.

Tristan frowned. "That's rock crystal, there's no smashing that."

"Worth a try, ain't it?"

"Go ahead," Tristan said. "Mind your toes, Archibald."

The ponytailed sergeant lifted the case with some effort and hurled it at the stone floor. A whipcrack echoed through the chamber, the case bouncing across the floor and hitting a plinth, causing it and a clay fork-tongued snake to crash to the ground. The display case was intact; the stone floor, however, had a large piece missing.

Silence struggled to overcome the resonating clang of crystal on stone. And just as the reverberating echoes were dying, a scratching, skittering sound came from outside the chamber, as if clawed feet were scrambling for purchase on smooth stone.

Three knives gave voice to a singular metallic whisper as they left their sheaths at the same instant. Tristan pointed at the open archway and put his finger over his lips. The men moved forward in unison. They gained the archway and edged into the column-lined hallway. The sound of flapping wings came from somewhere, impossible to locate in the disorientating dark-filled space. Then nothing. The men listened, barely breathing. It was gone, whatever it was.

"Bats," Tristan said.

"Big ones from the sound of it," Archibald said.

Then a chilling screech from far away.

No man voiced what they were all thinking. The scream belonged to no bat.

"Least it's not bloody spiders," Archibald said. "Can't stand spiders."

They waited, but the blood-curdling shriek didn't return. Robert exhaled slowly. "Bats, spiders. Nothing to fear, lads, we're all big, strong men. Come on, let's get this done."

Approaching the quartz case once more, the men put away their daggers. They turned the box on end, searching.

"Here," Tristan said. "A groove cut in the back, if I can just get my fingers . . ." Suddenly a popping sound, and one side of the case slid away. The box was open, revealing five objects embedded in a sticky, malleable material.

Robert picked up the case and returned it to its platform.

The three men gazed at the pulsing artifacts, each trinket changing color from moment to moment, carved in fine detail from a metal unlike anything any of them had seen before.

"What is it? I mean, what are *they*?" Archibald asked.

"I believe you're looking at the rarest metal on earth, Sergeant," Tristan said.

"Rarer than gold?"

"Oh, much."

"Marshal! Commander!" Michael Alaine, Malcolm Dewar, and Broadford Higgins entered the chamber.

"What happened to you, Higgins?" Robert asked. Broadford's jaw was dripping blood from a cut.

"Fell through the floor, sir. Barely held on above the chasm. Was done for if Malcolm and Michael hadn't been there to pull me up."

Robert nodded. "Well done, Dewar, Alaine. Citations all around when we get out of here."

"We found silver and gold, sirs," Malcolm said.

Neither Robert nor Tristan responded. They were again staring at the objects within the open crystal case.

"What have you found, sirs?" Broadford said, moving forward to look, as did Michael and Malcolm.

The six men stood transfixed at the beauty of the ethereal, unworldly metal lighting each man's face a subtly different color.

Suddenly, Archibald Kirk took the finely carved figure of an erect penis. "This one's made for me, wouldn't you say, gentlemen?"

Laughter. "Aye, the biggest dickhead in the room. It's yours all right," Broadford said, reaching out to take a trinket.

His hand was slapped away by Malcolm. "Hang on, mate. Michael and I saved your life. We go first. Fair, yes?"

Michael demurred, but Malcolm was having none of it.

"No, mate, you got us down here, without you we wouldn't have nothing. Take it, if the sirs don't mind?"

Tristan and Robert shook their heads. "Not at all," Tristan said.

Malcolm gave a small intricate hand to Michael and took the key for himself.

Broadford's face flushed with a sickly smile as he looked at the two ranking officers. "Well, sirs, go ahead. At least there's the gold."

Robert took the book.

Tristan, the crown.

And it was over.

The six men retraced their steps to the surface. As they made their way back to the rope ladder, Archibald sidled up to the marshal. "Sir," he said. "You say this metal is matchless in our world?"

Tristan nodded. "You'll never find its like anywhere else."

"That would make it worth a pretty penny."

"Should you ever wish to part with it."

"That's good, sir, very good."

"Indeed," Tristan said. "I believe I can reliably say that your life will never be the same."

23

The Battle of the Yellow Abbey

The Order of the Yellow Scholars was less a monastic association than it was a private educational enterprise. But there were still rules. Sexual relations were forbidden, though Abbot Hugh Gilbert well understood that boys would be boys and had had to, on more than one occasion, sit down and have a serious discussion with some of the younger, more unbridled members of the abbey.

Fighting, however, was strictly outlawed—no ifs, buts, or second chances. The Yellow Scholars were, in fact, trained in short swords and throwing knives, but any violence perpetrated toward a brother monk on abbey grounds would result in immediate dismissal. Fortunately, the abbot had never had to deal with that particular problem.

Until today.

"They're fighting on the walls!"

The abbot lifted his head from his desk with a start, having just nodded off, and wondered if he were having a lucid dream.

Brother Marvin stood there, scrawny hands wringing, sweat breaking out on the young man's tonsure. "The tall woman and the researcher!"—the acolyte scurried out of the room, the abbot rushing after him, up a flight of stairs to the courtyard—"Up there!" Brother Marvin pointed.

The abbot gasped at the sight. On the second-floor walk-way, under a waxing gibbous moon, Brynhild Grimsdotter and

Christopher Lewis were at war, she with a long curving sword and he with a pair of shorter blades.

The abbot hiked his robes and sprinted for the stairs as fast as his bulk would allow. He thought he had given express orders for all weapons to be securely locked away. He hadn't counted on such a blatant violation of abbey policy and cursed his own lack of preparedness.

Upon the walkway, Brynhild stalked forward, taking advantage of the favorable reach of her katana, striking left and right, forcing the gray-robed researcher back.

The way Christopher deflected the katana strikes with his two shorter blades testified to an experienced combatant. If he was a researcher, he was an academic of some martial prowess and knew how to handle himself.

Brynhild sliced again and Christopher blocked.

"Stop this at once! We are a house of peace!" The abbot had barely uttered his puffing protest when the gray-robed man leaped on top of the parapet and somersaulted over the head of the tall Norsewoman, who ducked and barely avoided having her blonde braid sliced off.

"Good lord," the abbot whispered. It was like watching some kind of deadly, graceful dance limned by moonlight—blades arced, sliced, flashed silver, sparked metal on metal. He stood transfixed, clueless how to put an end to the battle.

Brynhild spun low and lashed out with her blade. Christopher backed away, then lunged as soon as the woman's blade arced past his navel. He, in turn, missed his countershot as Brynhild sprung cat-like out of range.

Rebecca and William had arrived and now stood beside the abbot, and for a moment, neither combatant swung at the other. The moon shone down on the five figures on the walkway and a dozen terrified monks in the courtyard below.

"Brynhild, what's happening?" William asked.

The warrior had her back to the fragile-bodied scholar and spoke cautiously over her shoulder, eyes never leaving her opponent. "This man is an assassin come to kill Rebecca."

The girl had now also produced a knife from somewhere, blade glinting as hard as her drawn brow. She moved in, crouching low, ready and willing to join the fight.

Things were getting out of control, thought the abbot. Everyone had a concealed weapon, and the abbey had rules. Order must be maintained. Why was that so difficult?

Watching Rebecca carefully, Christopher Lewis backed up as the girl slunk in. "You're mad," he said, addressing Brynhild. "I am here to harm no one. First, you blatantly observe me in the library, and now you attack me unannounced as I take the night air."

William stepped forward and pulled the girl out of the fray. She twisted and turned, but the thin monk showed surprising strength and determination. "No, Rebecca, calm down. Brynhild may have misjudged the situation."

The Norsewoman snorted. "I have misjudged nothing. The book. I saw the book. He's here for Rebecca, for the amulet. He mustn't be allowed to leave, or he'll bring Bruwaert's forces down on us, on the abbey."

Knight-Captain Christopher Lewis raised an eyebrow and looked at Rebecca.

The abbot was almost at the end of his monastic tether. "For goodness' sake. What book?"

"Tobias Waterstone. *The Fall of the Monks of Ulfur*," Brynhild said.

The abbot raised his arms to the moon in exasperation. "I've read it. What does the book have to do with anything?"

Brynhild pointed to the assassin with the tip of her katana. "Ask him, ask him why he's here."

Christopher Lewis cocked his head. Moments passed within which the man didn't seem to breathe, despite the exertions of his encounter with the Norsewoman. "You're Robert Occitane's daughter? Yes, there's a resemblance."

A stunned silence encompassed the group beneath a watching moon.

"You see? How could he know this?"

"We're a non-political organization, Miss Brynhild, Master Lewis." The abbot spoke as soothingly as he could. "I would ask that you put away your pointers. Those are the abbey rules, and you'll abide by them while you have been extended a welcome here."

Christopher Lewis immediately bowed, laid his twin blades down, and raised his hands. He smiled at Brynhild, who stood statuesque, all color leaving her already pale face. Finally, she grimaced and let her katana fall clattering to the walkway.

The abbot nodded at William. "Take their weapons, Brother, and this time lock them up tight," he said and held out his upturned palm. "Yours too, young lady."

Rebecca glowered and placed the knife handle in the abbot's fat hand.

"Ladies and gentlemen, I think we all need to take a breath and retire somewhere a little more private. The library will stay open later than usual tonight. We have a book to discuss. And mind you, the first person to resume hostilities shall face the wrath of the Abbot of Yellow Scholars. Am I understood?"

"Yes, Abbot," Christopher said, still smiling.

The tall Norsewoman spoke through clenched teeth. "Yes, Abbot."

Abbot Hugh Gilbert turned to the captivated audience of monks below and shouted, "Stop gawking and get back to your duties, an abbey doesn't run itself!"

Butter-colored robes flapped and scattered in all directions, like a startled flock of yellow warblers.

The abbot, still sweating, led the way downstairs to the library, wondering when he'd ever again have cause to chastise an assassin and a warrior princess.

BRYNHILD AND CHRISTOPHER stared each other down from opposite sides of a circular table in the library. William fully expected them to leap across the table and throttle one another. Rebecca nestled between him and the abbot, who had asked all copyists to leave. The book in question, *The Fall of the Monks of Ulfur*, lay on the table between the group, the eerie tome reflecting the flickering light of the wall torches. It was just a book, thought William. Why had violence erupted over a simple book? Still, he knew words contained power. Yes, this he knew well.

Brynhild snarled. "Why does Bruwaert send you here, assassin?"

"Knight-Captain, not assassin, if you please."

"Hah! Knight-Captain sounds a pretty title, but you move like an assassin."

The abbot sighed. "Let's not rush in and bludgeon any potential for civil conversation before we've even started."

Brynhild began checking her braided ponytail for signs of damage from her encounter on the walkway. "I apologize, Abbot."

"Yes, well. It's a fair question, I suppose. Knight-Captain Lewis?"

"I do not serve Bruwaert."

Brynhild scoffed as she flicked her ponytail back over her shoulder. "Robert Occitane was murdered by Bruwaert's men for an amulet, and a week later you arrive here looking for the same amulet. That cannot be a coincidence."

"Who says he's looking for an amulet?"

"The book," Brynhild said, as if the answer should have been obvious to everyone.

"This mysterious book again. First question is first. Who *do* you serve, Master Lewis?"

The knight-captain looked at the book in the center of the table and then off into the mid-distance. He said nothing.

"Out with it, sir," the abbot said.

Christopher hesitated. Then he said, "I am Tremain's man."

Abbot Hugh Gilbert puzzled. "Tremain seeks the amulet also?"

"No, he does not."

"Then, why are you here?"

The man cleared his throat and shifted in his seat, but the abbot pursued his line of questioning. "Speak, sir. No more secrets."

"Ostensibly, I follow King Bruwaert's commands. I seek the trinkets, but not for his benefit. My employer, King Tremain, wishes a close eye kept on Bruwaert. He doesn't trust the man."

"That we can all agree on," the abbot said. "So, you're *a spy* for Tremain?"

The gray-robed man shrugged slightly. "In effect."

"An unlikely story," Brynhild said.

Anger broke the man's composure for the first time. "Believe what you will. I risk my life in telling you the truth."

The abbot rubbed his tonsure. "You said trinkets in the plural form. More of these things exist? What do you know of them, of the Occitane pendant?"

Christopher Lewis looked at Rebecca. "May I see it?"

Rebecca glanced around and slowly removed the trinket from within her tunic, letting it hang in full view. All eyes were drawn to the glowing miniature book, ingeniously sculpted from a transcendent metal.

"What can you tell us about it, Knight-Captain?" William asked.

Taking a deep breath, Christopher patted the volume on the table. "I've been reading the Yellow Scholars' account of their brethren, the ancient Order of Ulfur, but my understanding is fragmented, the pieces of a puzzle I can't seem to fit together."

The abbot nodded. "You're not the only one who finds themselves confused. Tell us your story. Perhaps we can help each other."

"Very well. Bear with me, for the tale I'm about to tell is outlandish at best." The knight-captain picked up the book.

"Tobias Waterstone recounts how, more than a century ago, something fell from the sky with a blinding flash and the sound of a thousand thunder strikes. This celestial object crashed into the great mountain overlooking Re'Shan, a mountain we know as Ulfur. It caused a chain reaction which destroyed the monastery built high on the cliffside. Some say the mountain swallowed the monastery, but whatever happened, the structure belonging to the Ulfurian monks vanished on that same day. Nevertheless, this didn't spell the end of that order. They survived, even flourished.

"The melted sky metal was discovered all over the mountain, including a lode buried deep within Ulfur, an ore from which they fashioned strange glowing trinkets, sold them, even exported them. But the metal they worked with poisoned them all. The Monks of Ulfur sank into corruption, began to destroy each other, to murder innocents in the night, trying to satiate some insatiable hunger, bloodlust. The metal became an addiction. When the order finally fell into depravity and cannibalism, they scattered and disappeared, never to be heard from again."

Christopher Lewis fell silent.

To William, the tale sounded like nothing more than a demented nightmare, but from the looks of his enraptured companions around the table, it was a nightmare they were all beginning to believe real.

The man with the close-cropped white hair and unnaturally dark eyes went on: "I said the Monks of Ulfur disappeared. That was true . . . until King Tremain came upon and captured one of them a few years ago. His name is Jeremiah." The knight-captain paused. "Somebody killed a jailor and broke Jeremiah out of his prison a month ago."

A murmur rumbled among the group.

"Who would wish to release such a diseased creature?" William asked. "King Bruwaert?"

"King Bruwaert doesn't know of the existence of Jeremiah, never has. Of this I'm sure from my discussions with the fat king."

"Then, who?"

Christopher took a deep breath and continued: "At the end of the war, when Re'Shan fell, a group of men discovered the hidden Monastery of the Ulfur Monks deep within the mountain itself. These men, I believe, also discovered the metal in the form of trinkets within. One of these men was Robert Occitane."

Rebecca gasped and widened her eyes.

"I know the names of two more. Archibald Kirk, who now calls himself Seraphim, the other, Tristan Drogos de Merlon, ex-marshal in Tremain's army and purportedly dead."

William looked at the trinket resting on Rebecca's chest. "Are you saying this thing is . . . it's one of the trinkets from Ulfur? Made of the sky metal?"

"That's a possibility."

Brynhild frowned. "Bruwaert knows of these men. He wants the metal, so he's hunting them down."

"This explains the murder of Robert Occitane," William said, then addressed Christopher. "But you say Bruwaert didn't release Jeremiah?"

"As I said, he has no knowledge of the monk."

"Again, who would want to release a vile Monk of Ulfur?" William asked.

Christopher Lewis rubbed his chin. "My guess is that one of the men that discovered the monastery after the fall of Re'Shan is returning to the mountain and needs the monk."

"Needs? Why?" the abbot asked.

"A hound to sniff out the metal, to manufacture more wearable artifacts, thereby increasing the power of whoever released him."

"Power? But it leads to corruption and depravity."

Christopher placed the book on the table. "This man, whoever he is, doesn't seem to understand, or perhaps he doesn't care. 'The Hungry King is coming.' Those are the words of Archibald Kirk, a trinket-bearer himself and a man who shows all the signs of blood corruption."

Brynhild scowled. "Is it Kirk? Did he release the monk?"

"The new Hungry King, as he puts it, is not Archibald Kirk, but he knows who it is. I saw it in his eyes."

"What's the intention of this madman?" Abbot Hugh Gilbert asked.

"To raise an army. To bring war once again. A war to end all wars."

The abbot shook his head, seemingly unable to process the information. "Madness, utter madness."

"Yes, madness." The knight-captain's eyes fixed on the beautifully carved book—now gold in hue, now blue, now red.

"How long have you known this?"

Christopher Lewis looked up as if waking from a dream. "This is speculation, a theory. I *know* nothing."

"Rebecca, I think you should remove the trinket." William spoke softly.

"My father gifted it to me. I will not let it go."

"I don't think your father quite understood the danger, dear girl," the abbot said.

"Please, you need to remove it," William said.

Rebecca slowly placed the trinket beside Tobias Waterstone's book.

The abbot stared at it in horror. "What are we to do with this accursed thing? And how are we going to stop this fool, whoever he is, from releasing a new evil on our world?"

"Rebecca," Christopher said, "do the names I've mentioned, Tristan Drogos de Merlon and Archibald Kirk, mean anything to you?"

"No. Should they?"

"Did your father ever talk of the amulet, where he found it and with whom?"

She shook her head. "He never spoke of the war. He wanted to forget and I . . . I respect my father's wishes and didn't ask."

"I must go to Mount Ulfur," Christopher said firmly. "There it began, and there events will quicken, but I fear it's already too late."

"This is a dangerous task upon which all our fates rest. You need heroes to accompany you."

William glanced at the abbot and wondered who, apart from Brynhild, could be the heroes to which the abbot referred.

"We have a fat king to kill," Brynhild said.

Christopher shook his head. "That would be unwise, even if you could. You'd risk war between the Kingdom of Otago and your people."

"The girl needs vengeance."

"I understand, but there are more important events unfolding than personal vengeance."

With eyes narrowed, Brynhild looked intently at Christopher Lewis. "Nothing is more important than personal vengeance."

William wondered just how much of Brynhild's desire for revenge could be attributed to the death of her own father. He desperately wished he had a pen to scribble notes for his book.

The Norse warrior's eyes widened again, an idea written on her face. "*You* could do it," she said to Christopher Lewis. "You can get close to the fat bastard, as his personal assassin after all."

The knight-captain crossed his arms. "That would cost me my life, even were I successful."

"Then, it must be me." Brynhild nodded. "I promised Rebecca, and I keep my oaths."

"Noble, but foolish," Christopher said.

The abbot shook his head vigorously. "I cannot sit here and be party to a plot to assassinate the king, as dislikable as the man is."

"And I cannot sit here at all. I leave for Ulfur tomorrow morning," Christopher Lewis said.

"I'll go with you to aid you however I can, but in return, you must get me close to Bruwaert when it is over."

The assassin looked at the tall Norsewoman in surprise. "I can make no such promise."

Rebecca spoke, her voice quivering with emotion. "Bruwaert is responsible for the death of my father. I seek justice. But perhaps justice for family is not something an assassin would ever understand." Her translucent amber eyes met midnight-black and did not flinch.

Time seemed to elongate. Christopher uncrossed his arms, letting out a slow, controlled breath. "Very well. If Brynhild wishes to come, I will not refuse her offer of assistance. She possesses skills I could use. If we return, I'll see to it that you have the opportunity to avenge your father. The journey to Ulfur, however, will be dangerous. You, Rebecca, stay here."

The girl leaned forward, her gaze still locked on the assassin. "I'm going with you."

The man shrugged, realizing the futility of argument. "Then, gather your things. We leave in the morning."

"Meanwhile, what do we do with that?" the abbot said, staring with distaste at the amulet.

"Destroy it. Bury it," Christopher Lewis said.

Rebecca snatched the small book-shaped trinket and clutched it to her chest. "My father gave it to me. It's not evil, my father wasn't evil, he showed no ill-effects. It's mine."

Brynhild and William exchanged glances. The abbot eyed the girl, obvious disquiet on his puffy features.

"It's not corrupting me, if that's what you think. I know my own mind, I am fine."

Christopher pulled the hood over his head, and his face disappeared in shadow. "Very well. If you'll excuse me, I must retire. Tomorrow the journey begins."

Brynhild watched the knight-captain withdraw from the room. When he had gone, she rose to her full height and said, "Thank you for allowing me access to your library, Hugh. I very much enjoyed reading the books."

Rebecca got to her feet. "Thank you for your kindness, Father."

The abbot stood and clasped his fingers over his heart. "You are both welcome."

When the two women left, the abbot sat once more and said to William, "I think you'll have quite enough material for your book when this is all over, Brother. Should you survive."

"To clarify . . ." Brother William said, "I'm to join forces with an assassin in the service of King Tremain, a Norse princess, and a vengeful child to save the world from a madman, and then assist in the murder of King Bruwaert?"

"I know nothing about that last part," the abbot said, shrugging his shoulders.

"I thought we were a non-political organization."

The heavy-set abbot got to his feet with a grunt of effort and rubbed his tonsure. Walking away, he sighed and said, "Non-profit, lad. We're still non-profit."

24

Brittsdale

The stars were beginning to disappear, to smudge, the most distant pinpricks of light gone altogether, the nearer stars wavering in and out of view. The night sky was almost empty now. Without the trinket, Broadford's vision was returning to that of a mere mortal, the secrets of the universe retreating from him, excluding him from its conclave.

But at least he could breathe through his nostrils again. He ran his fingers down both sides of his nose. His hands were shaking, and his armpits and back were soaked with sweat. He needed the metal. De Merlon would give him what he needed, but only if he completed the task assigned to him.

I require men, de Merlon had said. *Bring me more men for my army.* Hah. Be a good dog and fetch. That was the truth of it.

Resentment flowed through Broadford, heating his blood in lieu of the trinket. He had even contemplated beating de Merlon to the mountain to gain the metal still embedded deep within Ulfur—an act explicitly forbidden, punishable by death, or worse. He could do it. De Merlon's progress would be slowed by the ancient monk. He could get there first. If he could just lay his hands on enough of the metal, he wouldn't fear de Merlon.

No, no, he didn't know where the metal was. De Merlon had the key in the physical form of the old Monk of Ulfur; the old wreck knew where to find it. Broadford stood no chance of getting his hands on the metal before the marshal and the monk.

And so, for now, he must be a good dog and fetch.

He was riding north to Brittsdale. The wrong direction. Re'Shan and the mountain that loomed over it were to the south, but he had little choice. He knew men in Brittsdale, men once loyal to Prometheus Company, men he could trust. No, not trust. That was no longer possible. Trust, loyalty, honor. Just words now. No, he needed angry, bitter men who had served in the Great War and were no doubt struggling to adjust back into society, as he had done. What he needed was a lack of hope within an angry breast, and the mines of Brittsdale would provide that.

Promise a man a better life for himself and his family, make him believe you, and he'll listen. Promise him power, and he'll follow. Promise him something where he has nothing, and you have him. He has little other choice.

Yes, Brittsdale. In the mines, in the alehouses, in the stockades. There he would find them.

Broadford looked at his shaking hands. Soon. He had to have his key soon. And when he had it back, when his blood was pumping fire again, then *he* would be king. No more would he play fetch. No more the lapdog.

The road to Brittsdale meandered across the plains of North Otago, eventually entering the rolling hills and valleys of South Canterbury, leaving Bruwaert's Kingdom and entering Tremain's. Brittsdale was near the now unpatrolled border. Not since the formation of the Alliance had there been guards manning the roads at the join between Otago and Canterbury. Two kingdoms, one country, that had been the catch call. One nation to stare down the Hungry King. For the most part, it had worked. Former enemies had buried their grudges and fought and died side by side in a common cause. Travel between the two states was open and free. For now.

Brittsdale was close. Broadford recognized the gentle waves of rustic patchwork farms—each tree, hedgerow, windbreak—the grass, plants, and trees a different shade of laurel, mint, fern, pine, moss. It was early evening. In a few more hours, the flatlands would become a mysterious mist-laden blanket of shadowed-green dreams, and the hills would rise with rich mineral-laden peaks. Then the rustic beauty would give way to industrial smoke and nightmare, become a barren land hollowed from the sweat and toil of man's muscle.

There, he would find them.

———

BROADFORD STOOD IN THE MUD outside the Three-Breasted Frog and tried to control his shaking hands and his gnawing guts. He checked the buttons on his fancy waistcoat, adjusted his top hat at a rakish angle, took a deep breath, and entered the tavern with a breezy air.

He took in the bar at a glance: no attempt at any kind of themed decoration, nothing adorning the walls, no flowers, no paintings, just bare wooden benches, populated by bare wooden patrons and their bare wooden faces. This was what desperation looked like. This was what the bottom of the barrel looked like. The pure, unadulterated practicality of getting drunk, the need for oblivion. Not even one serving wench. Not a brunette, blonde, or redhead, especially not one with big tits. No one to spike your drink and take you to bed. What was her name? The girl in the Prancing Doxy?

Broadford strutted to the bar, sat casually, and smiled. He clicked his fingers at the scowling publican, who was all jowls and sharp-browed frown.

"Whisky, good sir. What's your selection?" Broadford made sure to speak with more of a plum in his mouth than usual, and loud enough to be heard by the entire alehouse.

The barman pointed to a single bottle on the shelf, cobwebs anchoring the glass container in place.

"Ah, Apothecary Whisky," Broadford said, grinning. "Excellent. I love the monks, don't you? I'll have the bottle. A popular choice with the locals, I take it?"

By this time, every patron in the Three-Breasted Frog had noticed the toff's presence among them.

"We can't afford it, you upper-crust bastard!" shouted a card from somewhere close by.

And so, it begins, thought Broadford, swinging himself around to face the drinking miners, farmers, slop shovelers, and thieves. He'd either leave with an army or get the shit beaten out of him. Again. Gods, he wished he had the key around his neck.

He conspicuously raised and dropped a copper coin on the counter; it clanked and rolled in a circle. In response, the publican begrudgingly gave him the bottle and filled a small smeared glass, then slid the coin into his grubby apron. Broadford took a gulp of whisky, and it flowed through him, warming him, steadying his nerves. Without the metal, the whisky would have to do. He removed his top hat with great care and placed it on the bar.

There was silence, the collected crew awaiting his reply.

Broadford licked his fingers and smoothed back his dark oiled hair. "Why did Prometheus cross the road?" he asked.

The silence continued, but deeper for the genuine puzzlement affecting the gathered drinkers.

He smiled. "To give mankind fire, you ignorant cocksuckers!" He swallowed another whisky and, in an instant of complete quietude, wiped his mouth on the back of his hand.

Scattered laughter broke out, several men having recognized him.

"Prometheus Company!" shouted a large man standing unsteadily and emptying his ale into his massive mouth.

Broadford raised an eyebrow and his own empty glass. "Big Ted! Whisky, my friend?"

And what man bereft of hope, living in squalor, having lived through the horrors of war, simmering with resentment, and already drunk, would ever say no to a freely given glass of Apothecary Whisky?

Not a single one, and especially not one named Big Ted.

"TREMAIN BETRAYED US!" Big Ted slammed down his whisky in an emotional but thoughtless moment, spilling a few precious drops of brown liquid. In a panic, he leaned down to slurp it from the table before it dripped to the floor.

"Shhh, shut your mouth," Cracker Jackson hissed. "You'll get us locked up or beheaded." He swung his protruding eyes, set too wide apart, wildly around the room, looking like the amphibian gracing the tavern sign above the door of the Three-Breasted Frog.

Big Ted pulled his cow-sized tongue away from the table and sat upright. "I was born under Tremain's rule, d'you know that?" He had no hair on the top of his head, only straw-like twigs around the back and sides, as if a bird had set up a nest on his skull.

Cracker lifted his arms and looked around. "As was I and all of us here. It don't give you no right to spout treason."

"It ain't treason. It's an opinion. It entitles me to an opinion, don't it? The Alliance ain't worth the paper it's signed on."

Broadford nodded sympathetically and patted Big Ted on the back.

Spade Johnson folded his hairy arms. "Well, there you walk on more solid ice. Not many 'round here will disagree, but what was Tremain supposed to do? The Hungry King was killing everything in sight, eating people I hear. Can you believe that? Eating people! Better the devil you know. I'll take Bruwaert over that animal any day." He scratched his bushy walnut-brown beard.

Broadford clapped Spade's shoulder sympathetically.

"Bullshit," Big Ted said. "Where are we now?"

Cracker jumped in, bulbous eyes looking in different directions. "We're not dead! Or enslaved! That's where we are now."

"Not enslaved?" Big Ted looked at his gnarled, filth-stained hands. "Twelve hours every day down in the pits. Me hands are bark."

Broadford topped up each man's whiskey glass, sympathetically.

Spade snorted into his impressive beard. "Yeah, well at least we can enjoy an ale at the end of the day, and you can piss and moan to your heart's content. Can't imagine the Hungry King letting you off the chain for a wee tipple, can you?"

"Maybe we would have been better off," Big Ted said.

Broadford ingratiated himself into the conversation, like a snake injecting deadly venom into an unsuspecting rabbit. "Marshal Tristan Drogos de Merlon agrees on all counts, gentlemen. He concurs. That's why he's sent me to find you. He wants you to return. You, specifically. 'Get Big Ted and Cracker, and Spade,' he said, 'and bring them to me'."

The three men looked at Broadford incredulously, which they were justified in doing as de Merlon had said no such thing.

"Marshal de Merlon wants us?" Big Ted said.

A serene nod. "He does"

"What for?" Cracker Jackson asked, eyes goggling.

"He's raising an army of his own."

"The war is over," Spade Johnson said, spit catching in his massive beard.

"He has coin, coin for everyone."

"Grand," Cracker said. "But why? Who we fighting?"

Broadford realized with horror that in his zealousness to escape his recent incarceration, he had tied his colors to de Merlon's flag without knowing the man's true intentions. Not that it mattered. Broadford's own cause was all he cared about. He wanted the key resting on his chest once more. Frantically, he searched for a convincing lie.

"He believes Bruwaert is about to betray Tremain. He'll take the fight to the fat bastard before that happens." He was pleased with his choice of falsehood, as he recognized the potential grain of truth in it, and it was this grain that sprouted the best lies.

The three men shared glances. "The Alliance is over?"

"Soon."

"Not soon enough," Big Ted said. "And he's got money?"

"Gold, silver, whisky. And something more."

The men leaned forward with eager stares. Broadford prepared to deliver the coup de grâce, then hesitated, and once again realized he hadn't thought this through. How could he tell them of the sky metal, what was he to say? It sounded like superstitious nonsense if one hadn't experienced it firsthand. *Lads, he has in his possession several artifacts that invigorate your mind and body, and gift you with what I call a universal vision, oh and it makes your cock hard as soon as you touch it.* He'd sound mad. These men were on the cusp of diving in, and they'd practically put their own heads in the noose. He mustn't frighten them off now.

"Well, what does he have?" Big Ted asked, scratching his bird's nest, searching for eggs.

"Women," Broadford blurted.

"Eh?"

"He, uh, he's come across a harem of women, three hundred of them, young, beautiful. Imprisoned during the war, out in the Great Southern Sands. So, he let them out, you see, freed them. Poor dears haven't had a proper meal or seen a man in years. Very hungry and grateful to de Merlon and any man that serves him, if you take my meaning."

The men looked at each other, and Broadford wondered if they'd see through the fantastical tale. He needn't have worried. They started laughing, slapping each other on the back.

Idiots. Absolute idiots. Broadford knew the absence of women wouldn't bother them once they had the metal secured around their necks; the nooses would be too tight by then. At any event, the metal was better than sex, or at least made sex better.

THE EARLY MORNING SUN was just beginning to creep over the shoulder of the smoking mountains; the mines never ceased spewing ash into the sky. The hell-pits would be short a few men today.

Broadford let out a slow breath, trying not to spew. He had a magnificent hangover; he'd almost forgotten what one felt like. He sat on his horse on the outskirts of Brittsdale, at the appointed place under the blasted oak tree, and watched the beginnings of de Merlon's army ride by. They totalled fifteen scrawny, scraggly, or conversely overweight but malnourished, peasants, convicts, and hopeless misfits. Most of them had been through the Great War and were battle hardened. He nodded at Big Ted, Cracker Jackson, and Spade Johnson clip-clopping by.

Broken men. Spittle at the bottom of an ale glass.

But it was a start.

25

Re'Shan

Amal Muna gazed in wonderment at the city that was Re'Shan. Though the city lay at the edge of the Great Southern Sands, sand itself was in short supply within the city walls; many of the streets were constructed of stone tiles, the first such streets she had ever walked upon.

Re'Shan was a hodgepodge of seemingly random domes, turrets, and minarets crowding in on each other, some buildings eight stories high, blocking out the sun; Amal had never dreamed of the architectural madness man was capable of. Busy teams of turbaned plasterers crawling over bamboo scaffolding testified to the ravages of the Great War that had ended over a year ago, but Re'Shan was well on the mend, the patient out of the sickbed and in full health once again, if walking with a noticeable limp.

The streets were cooler than those of Shae. The narrow alleyways birthed by the tall, closely spaced buildings funneled a breeze around the urban structures, a remarkable achievement that Amal knew instinctively was no accident. Here was grandeur, a real city of intelligent design, populated with different races of equally intelligent peoples: some black skinned, some so white they appeared albino, and every shade between. Children chased each other through the dust, hawkers shouted out prices, customers haggled, preachers sermonized, people pushed, bustled, laughed, talked, drank charcoal-colored teas and coffees. Here were soldiers, merchants, beggars, civil servants, and exponents of a myriad different religions in their multicolored robes—a truly cosmopolitan megalopolis.

It was overwhelming, vibrant, joyous. But it stunk of camel dung.

Michael Alaine stepped down from the horse and grabbed Amal by the waist, helping her dismount. They appeared to be in some kind of public square containing a series of covered stalls and shops offering goods of incomprehensible origin.

The young soldier looked unsure, glancing everywhere but at Amal. He spoke over the noise of the city. "I must return to my unit. I can go no further with you, nor you with me."

Amal had been dreading this moment. She had known it was coming but had hoped that he would . . . what? What had she dared hope? That he would change his mind?

She looked around at the industrious goings-on in the square. "I'm not sure which path awaits me. I . . . I feel a little lost."

Michael pointed to a civic building with columns in white stone. "Do you see those two women wearing purple veils, there sitting on the steps? They are members of the Lavandula Femella." He gently placed the cool leather reins in Amal's trembling hands. "Give them the horse as subscription into their congregation. They'll provide for you, see to it that you find employment."

She ventured a question, sick in her stomach at the inevitable answer. "Will we meet again?"

With a pained expression on his youthful face, he said, "I'm a soldier. I . . . I'm sorry for the loss of your family. I wish you all the best."

All the best? That was it? Amal swallowed her protest, swallowed the tears threatening to drown what dignity she had left. He had made up his mind, so she must simply accept what she could not change. "I understand. I thank you for helping me."

Michael turned his eyes to the ground. "I have helped no one. You saved my life. It is I who thank you, Amal Muna."

Despite her breaking heart, she smiled. "Will you be all right?"

He looked up. "I'm not sure."

"Good things come to good people, Michael Alaine. You are blessed."

His face registered an odd expression that she could not read. The young soldier simply shook his head and walked away through the thronging crowd, leaving her holding the reins of a thirsty horse. When he disappeared, she let out a breath and stroked the animal's neck. "We must be brave, my friend. Life goes on."

Amal walked over to the two purple-veiled women sitting on the steps, a begging bowl holding several dusty copper coins at their feet. She could tell that beneath their veils they were old, shriveled like dried grapes in the desert sun, but the two were holding an animated discussion in the common tongue. They seemed to be in mid-argument when they noticed her standing there. They stopped their bickering and stared up at her.

"I am Amal Muna, daughter of Shae."

They continued to stare.

For want of something better to say, Amal said, "I have nowhere to go." She held out the reins of the horse.

One of the women stood with some effort, looked Amal up and down, and accepted the offered reins. "My name is Andromeda," the old crone said, switching to the desert tongue. She lifted her purple veil and smiled, revealing a gapped grin that could have easily been bettered in beauty by a toothless horse. She eyed Amal once more and said, "Welcome to the Lavandula Femella."

———

COMMANDER ANTON FRANKS leaned forward on his desk and watched the battalion doctor scrounging around Michael's scalp. The commander spoke in barely concealed irritation. "You should be dead, Alaine. The survivors of Achilles Company arrived back three days ago, and I have it from Captain Jasper that there was no one left alive on the field."

"Jasper got it wrong, Commander. I'm not dead." Michael sat stock-still on his chair and waited for the doctor to complete his examination.

"Apparently not." Commander Franks looked over his sharp-edged spectacles at the ongoing inspection. "Well?"

The doctor scratched around his widow's peak. "He's . . . fully healed. A vicious scar remains, however."

"Healed? From what?" The commander frowned.

"The wound he sustained in Shae."

"A battle that took place a matter of days ago? Are you telling me he's already healed, from a wound so grievous that Captain Jasper, a seasoned veteran keep in mind, decided to leave him on the battlefield as a lost cause?"

The doctor's bottom lip protruded as he shrugged. "Perhaps it's an older wound."

Commander Franks wrinkled his forehead. "Is it an older wound, Alaine?"

"I was knocked unconscious, but this"—he pointed to his head—"this is an older wound."

The commander scowled, clearly unconvinced. "Mmm. I'll have a word with Jasper. That was most . . . careless of him to leave one of our best young men behind." He sat back in his chair and folded his arms. "You were also blindingly lucky finding that horse in the desert. Long walk back without it."

"Fortunate, sir."

The commander leaned forward again and clasped his fingers together. "I'll be honest with you, Sergeant. I find some parts of your story hard to fathom. Still, I mustn't focus on the negative." Franks eyed his man. "You may be surprised to know that you were to be posthumously promoted for sterling service in the field."

Michael's face remained carved from stone. "A great honor, Commander."

"Posthumously, mind you, but now that you're miraculously alive, we'll have to make that a living, breathing advancement in the ranks as befits a living, breathing soldier." The commander looked at the doctor. "Are you done?"

The doctor's bottom lip extended slug-like once more. "Uh . . . There seems little wrong with the man."

"Then, you're dismissed."

The doctor took one last look at his patient and left the room, shaking his head.

Commander Franks stared at his sergeant. "Michael, what are your intentions?"

The young soldier stood at attention, only to be waved back to his seat. "I don't understand the question, sir."

"You play your cards close to your chest. I like that. You let your actions do the talking on the battlefield. I like that even more." Commander Franks lowered his voice. "I've overheard some of the men calling you the Silent Knight."

"I'm aware of the name, sir." Michael's face remained impassive.

"Silly, isn't it?" Franks sighed. "Let me be blunt. You, Alaine, are officer material, but you have to be a little more self-confident, gregarious. You have to let go of this . . . brooding side of yourself. A commander of men must be heard, do you take my meaning?"

Michael nodded. "Yes, sir."

"Your intentions, Alaine? How far do you want to go in the Alliance military?"

He stood again with his hands behind his back and his eyes focused on the wall behind Commander Franks's head. "As far as I can, sir. I'm a career man."

"Good lad, we've too many mercenaries running around for my liking. We need men like you. Blood honest and steel straight." Commander Franks's demeanor changed, and he looked uncomfortable. He picked up a paperweight from his desk, a model of Canterbury Castle complete with central tower and four artfully designed battlements, and turned it over in his hands, studying it. "Take a week off to recover."

"I am well, sir. I don't need to rest."

The commander slammed the model down on his desk with a crash, then removed and folded his spectacles. "Listen to me. If you wander straight out of the Great Southern Sands looking as fresh as a mountain lily, with no apparent wounds, there'll be murmurings amongst the men, some of whom are superstitious, as you well know. I'll have the doctor sign it off. Keep your head down for seven days. Spend some time in the hospital gardens, but you are not to return to barracks. That's an order and very much for your benefit, Sergeant."

"Yes, sir."

"Get out, Alaine."

———

THE COMMON ROOM BROILED with the body heat of three hundred women. Dinner of soup and bread had just been consumed, and the collective stomach of both young and old was full, giving a sense of well-being and creating a comfortable, if not jocular, sororal atmosphere. Plates had been removed, and the sisters of the Lavandula Femella were amusing themselves with chat, games, and gambling.

The organization was dedicated to the betterment of women in the Freelands. Their goal was to pass on skills that would allow even the most unemployable woman to make a wage. To this end, the society taught the lost and disillusioned women of the dry lands how to read and write, which Amal could already do better than the most capable tutors; how to cook and sew, skills which again she was already comfortable with; and how to please a man in bed, addict him to sexual pleasures and keep him coming back for more. This, Amal Muna knew little about.

"Listen, whoring is the oldest profession, and some might say the most noble a woman could have," Andromeda said in the desert tongue, her wrinkled face looking up sternly from where she was knitting.

"I'm sixteen years old." Amal protested.

Andromeda rolled her sunken eyes. "We've all got to make a living. You're pretty. It's a no-brainer, unless you want to be cooking, sewing, slaving the rest of your life. I'd bloody jump at the chance if anybody would jump at me, but I'm long past it. Begging and cleaning dishes all me life, look at me hands, ruined they are." She stopped her knitting to examine the back of her skeletal, worm-veined hands.

Amal took a long breath. "I can read and write, surely there are more suitable opportunities for—"

Andromeda raised a palm. "Listen, love, we're not saints here, we all have to pull our weight. The Mothers have decided that spreading your legs is the fastest and most profitable way for you to contribute, and who am I to argue?"

Anger bedded down with exasperation. "If I refuse?" Amal pouted.

The old crone sighed and resumed her knitting, squinting at an unwanted double loop. "Out on your ear, doing the same thing before long but for far worse n'cruel masters."

Amal crossed her arms. "I'd rather die. It is *not* a noble profession."

"Nobility be damned. Look at Prunella over there," Andromeda said, nodding toward a nearby woman reading a book. "Whored for twenty years she did, though you'd never think to look at her." She chuckled maliciously. "Didn't hurt her none." The woman in question looked up from her historical romance and turned toward Andromeda, who went on. "Think she even misses it, don't you Prunella? You miss all those young bucks tearing away at you privates, eh? No one wants to touch your wrinkled body now do they? Eh? Do you miss it? Tell us, do."

Prunella closed her book with a soft clap and glanced from the hag to the daughter of Shae. Smiling, she spoke to Amal. "Love, if it's a choice between doing what I did, and having your fruits shrivel up and fall from the tree like Andromeda here, never having had a man, *ever*, climb up in her bits looking for sweets, well, you can take that path, sad and lonely though it may be. I regret nothing that I've done."

Andromeda's features almost disappeared within a puckered whirlpool of annoyance in the center of her face. Prunella continued: "Do you have family? Knight in shining armor waiting to deliver you off to a fancy castle?"

Amal thought of Michael, and her heart sank. "No."

"Me neither. Life's not fair, love. Least you have friends, old and ugly as they may be, and steady meals. It ain't so bad."

Andromeda nodded and patted Amal on the knee, the long-standing war with Prunella forgotten in their shared sympathy for the black-haired desert girl. "You'll get used to it, dear. We all have to survive."

CAPTAIN FELIX JASPER shook Michael's hand and stepped back two paces. He studied his recently returned comrade. "Your brains lay all over the sand, Michael. You can't blame me for riding out and leaving you. I'd never seen a man more dead."

"I'm not blaming anybody, Captain." Michael looked at the piled clothes in his hammock. "Who's in my bed?"

"Sorry," Royce said, scurrying forward, half bowing. "I'm sorry, sir. Your mosquito netting had no holes, and I thought since you were . . . I mean since you were gone so long . . ."

"It's all right, Royce. I can help you mend your netting."

Several soldiers passed by and patted Michael on the shoulder. He shook their hands in turn. They were milling around the barracks, preparing to bed down for the night. Since the battle at Shae, several of the hammocks had remained empty.

The small soldier, Royce, grinned, his overbite showing like that of a large rodent. "I'd appreciate that, sir. I'm not much for sewing. Welcome back to Achilles Company, by the way, sir. The lads shed a few tears when they thought you was done for."

Michael nodded his appreciation. "I'm not that easily killed, Royce."

"I'll say." Jasper stroked his jet-black moustache and twirled the ends until they were fine needle points. "I can see the hospital patched you up right as rain." He stepped forward, almost face-to-face, looking closely at Michael's head. He frowned. "Right as rain. Not a scratch on you."

Michael busied himself with unpacking his knapsack and reclaiming his hammock. "The medics are skilled."

"Those medics are fucking Jesus from what I can tell." Jasper sniffed. "I heard you're getting a promotion on top of everything."

"It would seem so."

"Second in a year and a bit, isn't it?"

Michael nodded. "I was made a sergeant in Prometheus after the fall of Re'Shan."

"You'll be a marshal in no time at this rate." Captain Jasper reached under his nearby hammock and produced a bottle from a small trunk. The bottle was covered by a thin brown papyrus jacket upon which a scorpion was painted in gold relief. "Let's celebrate. Got this from Shae. Genuine desert wine, made from oasis berries. I've heard it's good. I was saving it for a special occasion, and I believe a surprise return from the grave qualifies."

Royce dutifully supplied three pewter cups, and Jasper filled each to the brim. "To the conquerors the spoils." Jasper smiled.

"We weren't conquering Shae," Michael said casually. "We were liberating it." He sipped the wine, whereas the other two inhaled the contents of their cups.

Jasper laughed long and hard, spraying wine into the face of Royce. He then slapped the stunned soldier on his spindly shoulder. "Royce, me boy, what's the difference between conquer and liberate?"

The small man opened his mouth and looked from captain to sergeant.

"You see, that's why you've never been promoted, shit with semantics."

Michael began to feel the trinket burn against his chest. He drank the wine down in one savage gulp. The metal still burned.

Royce looked nervously with rodent eyes between his two senior officers. "Let's have another drink."

"I'm done," Michael said. He pushed the cup against Royce's chest and stalked away.

Captain Felix Jasper watched the blond-haired soldier go, and continued to twist away at the fine points of his moustache.

───────

AMAL MUNA sat on the windowsill on the fourth floor, clothed in a long flowing cotton dress of white tied at the waist with a gold sash, typical attire of the nomad tribes. She'd never worn one like it before, not being a daughter of the nomad tribes, but Andromeda and Prunella had thought it alluring, something the customers might like, so she had gone along with it as they fussed and argued how to arrange it on her. Prunella had even cut the sleeves away. *Titillation*, she had said, winking. Amal wasn't quite sure she understood.

The window was open, and the evening sky was a newborn infant sprinkled with effervescent stardust. Re'Shan ran away from Amal to the edge of the desert, but she wasn't looking down at the city. She was looking upwards.

"The stars look beautiful, don't they?" she said.

The man was sitting on the bed, unbuttoning his shirt. "They are lovely."

"Oh, you speak the desert tongue, sir." Her fear subsided at the familiar language, a commonality between her and the man. "Out there in the desert, they're startling, believe me, there's no noise or lights to take away from their beauty. You should see them from out there."

"Is that where you're from? Out there?" His voice was dark, sweet, sticky like honey.

Amal kept gazing on the stars. "I was born in Shae. Do you know it?"

"I can't say I do."

Amal clasped her arms tightly around herself and continued to stare at the night sky.

"Are you cold?" he asked, not unkindly.

"No. I'm . . . I'm not cold."

"Is this your first time?"

She thought of her family. For them, she must survive, at any cost. She braced herself. "Yes."

The room was dim, lit only by a small lavender-scented candle, which sent wispy black shadow-fingers clasping at Amal's neck and shoulders.

"You are beautiful," the man said.

She bowed her head. "I do not think so."

He layered on the honey. "Whatever else I may say, this I speak in earnest. You are beautiful. Your skin is impeccable."

Amal looked at the stars again, rubbing her bare arms. "This isn't how I imagined my life."

"Life is so rarely what we hope for." His voice had a smile caught in it, like a fly in the same cloying honey. "Look at me."

She couldn't bring herself to turn around. "I'm sorry. I don't think I can do this."

"Am I so unattractive?"

"No, sir."

"How do you know? You haven't looked at me yet. Look at me. Please."

Amal's hands were shaking. She turned her eyes toward the man, and in the smoky, pale flicker of candlelight, he released his raven-black hair from its bondage. He was handsome, in a cold way. He sat shirtless on the bed, the candle flame etching out his long black hair, fine nose, and tattoo curving across his chest.

The tattoo read *serva me* in a flowery, antiquated script.

Save me, she thought.

Save me.

26

Bearer's Blood

Seraphim threw Amal onto the bed. "Take your clothes off," he said.

Amal sat up and scrambled backward. "Sir, I offer you my most humble apologies, but I've decided this is an inappropriate use of my resources."

He frowned. "What are you talking about, girl?"

"I've changed my mind."

"I've already paid. If it's money you want, I can offer you further remuneration for your services. I understand a large percentage of the fee goes to your handlers, so this coin is to be exchanged between you and me. It shall be our secret." He winked.

"Oh no, sir, I couldn't take your money. That's just it, you see, I'm not a . . . a . . ."

"A whore?"

"Not that there's anything wrong with that, sir, I mean Prunella is a good person, and I'm not judging or saying I'm better than her. The gist of it is, I just don't think my heart and soul are in it."

Shut her up! She's driving me mad!

"Take your clothes off."

"I have to go, sir."

Seraphim waggled a finger. "You amuse me. I like you. Stay." He removed the phallus trinket from around his neck and held it out. "Give me your hand. Go on. Hold it out!"

Amal closed her eyes and stretched out her hand. Seraphim let the trinket fall into her palm. She opened her eyes and stared at the pendant, her brows coming together.

"There. I dare say that's the first time you've held a prick in your hand. Not so bad is it? Now, let's graduate to the real thing."

Amal dropped the amulet onto the bed. "I must go."

Suddenly, he was on her, pushing her back, his jet-black hair covering her face, mingling with her own black hair, suffocating her.

The door exploded inwards. Michael Alaine stood there. "Get off her!"

"Leave or die!" Seraphim shouted and jumped lithely from the bed. He stopped, staring hard in recognition and puzzlement. "Alaine? What are you doing here?"

"Sergeant Kirk?" Michael looked at Amal. "Are you all right?" He held out his hand. "Come. Let's go."

Pig, the metal, get it!

Seraphim eyed his amulet on the bed and lunged, but Michael had him by the hair before he could lay hands on it and threw him across the room. "Leave her alone!"

Seraphim got to his feet and raised his hands in a gesture of non-confrontation, his scalp stinging. "I was simply reaching for my necklace." He cocked his head and frowned at the intruder. "What's happened to you, Michael? Have you gone mad?"

"And you, Archibald? Are you now just another rapist and murderer?"

He knows! He knows!

"I'm simply engaging the services of a prostitute. Hardly a criminal offense."

"You're a killer. I can see it in your eyes. Just like the others." Michael looked around the room, his fists clenched. "This is my fault," he mumbled. He stared at Seraphim, with eyes wide, almost pleading. "It's the trinkets, can't you see?"

"I don't know what you're talking about."

"They're rotting us from the inside out!"

They all know! This is the second one hunting you down! You should have killed Lewis! You bring them all down on us!

Seraphim silently cursed the voice in his head. He had enough on his plate trying to calm an unusually agitated Alaine. This man was not the Silent Knight he knew. He had to focus, ignore the voice, focus on the distressed soldier. Michael was a good fighter, his skills now complemented by a trinket of his own; Seraphim could feel the sky metal, could smell ozone coming off the young man like the aftermath of a lightning strike, an energy passing between the two trinkets. He smiled as calmly as he could. "Give me yours, then. I'm quite happy to take the burden for both of us."

Michael scowled and turned to the girl. "I'm sorry. I had no intention . . . This was not what I thought . . ."

Amal was standing by the bed, confused. "Michael, why are you here?"

The young knight looked almost embarrassed when he said, "To save you."

Seraphim narrowed his eyes, looking from Alaine to the girl, who smiled and moved toward the blond soldier. She hugged him, and Seraphim took his opportunity. He grabbed the phallus from the coverlet and hung it around his neck.

Rage filled him. Jealousy and envy set fire to his ego. This girl was his. They *all* were. All of them. All the whores and bitches, the angels and mothers, all of them, every cunt that had ever been born or ever would be. The totality of *woman* belonged to him. He would not share.

Amal Muna continued to embrace Michael and whispered, "Prunella asked me if I had a knight waiting for me. You . . . you came for me."

Then, a soft slicing thunk of metal through flesh, Seraphim stabbed Michael Alaine in the back.

Amal screamed as the knight, with a pained expression on his face, fell to one knee.

Seraphim raised the dagger high and plunged it downwards once again, but Michael reached upwards, the blade piercing his upturned palm, coming to a halt above his head. With his free arm, he smashed his elbow into the self-styled shrine of Seraphim's groin, causing the raven-haired man to grunt and fold to his knees.

Michael pivoted to face Seraphim, the knife gouging a hole in his palm, breaking bones as his hand rotated one hundred and eighty degrees around the blade. The Silent Knight didn't make a sound as Amal watched in horror and shouted for help.

Now both men faced each other, both on one knee, eye to eye. They rose as one, Michael clasping the fingers of his bloody hand over the pommel of the knife and Seraphim's fist. Blood was pouring from Michael's upper back, inches from the base of his neck. He kicked at Seraphim's balls again, but Seraphim was ready and twisted his hips to avoid a direct blow.

The sound of running feet clattered on the stairs and hallway outside.

Flee pig!

Seraphim gritted his teeth, let go of the dagger, and disappeared.

Amal stopped screaming, staring open mouthed. Michael grappled nothing but smoke and shadow. Seraphim had vanished.

But Michael Alaine could see his foe, could make out his outline. The hand-shaped trinket at his chest gave him sight, gave away his enemy, betrayed the secrets of the other. Seraphim would not escape so easily.

Michael punched him in the mouth, caving in several teeth and knocking him backward.

Seraphim rolled, gained his feet, screaming, "Not my fucking face!"

The man born Archibald Kirk felt a wave of heat boil up from his stomach and balls like an oncoming orgasm, and then something ignited, like a flame to a gas-filled mine shaft. A pulse exploded outwards from his body with stabbing pain and energy, sending Michael flying against the wall and knocking Amal from her feet.

Seraphim had no idea what he'd just done.

Visible once again, he looked down at himself in astonishment, his trousers blown clean off, the skin on his chest smoking, the trinket glowing a strange color, one he'd never seen before. The flowing script of his tattoo felt freshly inked, stinging, bleeding, raw. Then his body faded from sight once more.

The candle had been knocked from the table, the room now lit by nothing but a quarter moon and the stars through the window.

Michael got back up. "Amal?"

"I'm all right." Her dress was sprinkled with a dark smoking pattern, like ash from a fireplace.

"Amal, get out."

Before she could gather herself to make a run for the door, the brothel bouncer arrived, blocking it. He was carrying a hand-held lamp which swung wildly, casting crazed shadows that elongated and twisted around the room. The man was bald, eyebrows shaved, his entire face lightly tattooed as a death's head skull, as if his bones were rising from the depths of his flesh to the surface of his skin. He raised a meat cleaver.

"Fuck off, now!" Death's Head said.

Michael didn't respond to the man. He was watching Seraphim stalking closer, invisible to any eye but his own. He raised his hand, the blade still skewered his palm, and calmly pulled the dagger out and gripped it.

The bouncer lost a little of his aggression. "What the fuck?"

"Get her out, now," Michael said, pointing at Amal but focusing on Seraphim.

The hair on the back of Death's Head's neck was prickling. He held out his hand to Amal. "Come on!"

"Help him!" she screamed.

The bouncer looked around. "I can't see nothing."

She then picked up a porcelain bottle of powder that had fallen from the bedside table. With all her strength, she threw the bottle at the floor, where it hit and broke, sending a fine pale dust into the air and settling on the stalking figure.

"Christ almighty," Death's Head said, seeing the shadow of a phantom crouched low.

"Get her out!" Michael shouted.

At the sight of this powdered apparition, Death's Head grabbed the girl by the hand and pulled her toward the door.

The candle had set fire to the dry skirting boards, flames adding light to the nightmarish scene in shades of crimson. The bouncer and Amal were gone, only Seraphim and Michael remained.

He can see you! It's the metal, it's in his blood!

The voice was right, the trick of bending light was useless against the blue-eyed soldier. Seraphim flicked a switch in his head and became visible once again.

The voice was manic in its desperation. *Run!*

But it was too late. Seraphim's ego wouldn't allow for another retreat, couldn't accept the dishonor of defeat at the hands of a junior officer, or any man in single combat. Besides, Alaine had stolen his girl, and *that* he couldn't tolerate. The young man had lost a lot of blood from wounds in both shoulder and hand. He was weakening. He could take him, Seraphim thought, but he was now without the blade. Michael held it in his blood-slick fingers. To Seraphim's surprise, the wounded knight dropped the knife to the floor.

What is he doing? screamed the voice.

Michael was staring at his hand. The blood had stopped flowing, hardening in a long strip like tanned leather, hanging a yard long.

Pig, I do not like this, I tell you again, you must escape!

Michael looked at Seraphim and whirled the newly formed blood whip at his opponent's head with a loud crack; Seraphim's nose disappeared in a spray of blood, cartilage, and bone.

Seraphim shrieked in agony and horror and rage.

Behind the intense flash of excruciating pain, he instinctively knew he must close the distance, or the fight was over. Ignoring the searing anguish, he rolled forward under Michael's next strike, going for the knife on the floor, but Alaine kicked the blade away a split-second before he could put fingers on it.

Another lash of the blood whip scoured the flesh off Seraphim's back, cutting nerves and dropping him flat on his stomach. He couldn't feel his right arm.

He pushed himself over and put his hand up, "No more, Michael, no more. I give up, lad." Seraphim heard his own voice as if he were outside of his body. Without his nose and several teeth, his voice was unrecognizable, a garish, ghastly gurgle. His face, no doubt, was worse. Who would love him now? He coughed blood.

Michael hesitated, and Seraphim kicked him in the balls, returning the earlier favor. The young man doubled over, and Seraphim kicked out again, collecting Michael in the throat and breaking something within. He gasped for air. With one hand, Seraphim ripped off a piece of loose skirting on fire at one end and smashed him over the head with it, gratified to see his shirt catch fire. Seraphim ran for the open window, the door no longer accessible through the now furious blaze, and jumped.

He watched the ground come to meet him from four floors below and curled into a ball, waiting for the sickening impact, deciding to take the brunt on his right side as that arm was already gone.

Leading with his right shoulder, Seraphim crashed to the ground, blacking out for a fraction of a second.

"Wake up, wake up, sleepyhead."

A voice as familiar as his own. "Mother?"

"Darling, you're late for the academy. First day. Out of bed."

"Mother, you have to leave."

"Why, darling?"

"Father, he's not well. You're not safe here. He's a spider. Please, ma, you have to get out."

High tinkling laughter. "Don't be silly, Archie. Your father's not a spider."

Get up, pig! Get up! He comes!

A crowd of faces in Seraphim's bedroom looked down at him. No, not his bedroom, the street outside a whorehouse in Re'Shan. Shit, where was Michael?

A flaming star came spiraling to earth in the night sky—screams, the crowd backing away, Michael Alaine, clothes on fire, falling through the air, flames along the length of the blood whip, an unholy sight.

The voice in Seraphim's head screamed, *No, no! Why won't he leave us alone? We are brethren, tied together, allies!*

Seraphim dragged his naked, broken body to its feet.

Michael landed heavily, something snapping in his knee, and rolled. He stood on one leg, fire now extinguished, and limped forward, clothes still smoking.

"What are you?" Seraphim rasped.

Michael spoke through pain, through clenched teeth, through bubbling blood in his mouth. "It was a mistake, Archibald. We should never have gone in there. It was my fault. I found it. I have to undo it."

Seraphim glanced around him, soldiers, about a dozen in full armor and long swords approaching in formation, well drilled. He didn't have the strength, he thought. One last chance. He turned to Michael and tried to make him understand. "We are brothers now. Cursed, together. We must run."

"You're not my brother."

Seraphim lunged at a girl foolishly close in the gathering crowd and hauled her in front of himself. She screamed as he put his one good arm around her neck, using her as a shield. There were moments left now, a last throw of the dice. He sniffed her hair before remembering his nose was gone, only succeeding in choking himself on his own blood. He grabbed her breast. One last squeeze, one last titty, he thought, and moved toward Michael.

The voice. *No, no! Run!*

Michael tried to back up, there were people behind him, his broken knee buckled, limiting his mobility. Seraphim was upon him before he could maneuver, the panicked girl between them. He retracted his blood whip and braced himself.

The three of them tumbled to the ground. In the melee, Michael threw the girl to safety and Seraphim went for his eyes, scrabbling to dig his fingers in the sockets. The young knight twisted his head away and clasped Seraphim's throat, rolling on top, and squeezing.

Flee!

No, thought Seraphim. Too late for that.

His stomach boiled once more. He felt the explosion coming slowly, but when it erupted, the blast was much weaker, his strength fading, unable to dislodge Michael's death grip on his neck. Though a paler version of the earlier blast, at close range it still stunned the young soldier, tearing skin from his face and threatening to send him into oblivion. The first man to pass out would be the first to die.

Seraphim scratched and clawed at Michael with his one good hand.

"Get off that man!" The soldiers had arrived, screams and shouts as men ran to get water, the whole six-story whorehouse on fire casting a hellish light on the scene.

Bloodlust was upon Michael, and he didn't feel the blows to the back of his head as he crushed Seraphim's windpipe. More blows fell, and the world turned upside down. Before losing consciousness, he saw Seraphim's limp body lifting off the ground, trembling, as if invisible puppet strings were jerking at affixed points in his flesh.

The metal within Seraphim's blood raised him upwards in its eager attempt to return to the stars, and then it issued from his body in fine, tiny droplets, leaking blue, magenta, silver, and gold, like an upside-down rain shower on a summer's day. When the metal had fully departed his body, Seraphim fell back to the dirt with a thud.

The man born Archibald Kirk was dead.

Michael thought he heard Amal calling his name from somewhere up high. He looked at the stars, they blurred and went out, one by one.

27

Drowning

Michael Alaine woke with a gasp, above him no longer stars but two curving support beams that formed a large cross against a grubby alabaster ceiling. Disoriented, it took him a few moments to understand he was lying in a bed in a military hospital. He had burns on his back and chest, three broken ribs, a dislocated knee, a hole in his hand, a fractured shoulder blade, damaged cartilage in his neck, and he had lost an inordinate amount of blood.

What he didn't have was the trinket.

He was, however, healing all the same, his blood having absorbed microscopic amounts of the metal over the previous year, the metal now working furiously to save its host.

But he hurt like he had never hurt before.

To his surprise, a young woman sat holding his hand. The lower part of her face was covered by a fine silk scarf, but he knew who she was. She wore a long flowing dress of light green and a hijab of the same color, though a shade darker. Amal Muna was the only thing that made sense or seemed familiar.

"You're making a habit of being there when I wake up," Michael mumbled through dry lips.

"You're making a habit of almost getting yourself killed." Amal leaned in close with a cup of water and put it to his lips. "The doctor says you have nerve damage. Can you feel my hand?"

Michael squeezed. "No. It's numb."

"Can you feel anything?"

"Pain. Everywhere else."

She lowered her voice. "Michael, what's happening? Why are you under arrest?"

Memory returned, brutal, uncomfortable images forcing themselves upon his waking mind. "I killed a man."

"But you were only defending me and yourself."

"It may not have looked that way."

Amal spoke hurriedly, the words spilling out. "There are a dozen heavily armed men outside this door. I overheard them talking. You're to be accused of sorcery, of the dark magics."

Michael nodded, and a flash of pain shot through his neck and head. "You'd better get far away from me."

"You saved me. I won't abandon you."

"I was returning the kindness. You owe me nothing."

The door creaked open, and Captain Jasper walked in. He stopped and took in the scene. Bringing up a chair next to Michael's bed, he glanced at Amal, who turned her head away. Contempt written large across his face, Jasper said, "You're finished, Alaine. Whatever you picked up out in the desert"—the mustachioed captain shifted his eyes to Amal—"is going to get you hanged for murder and witchcraft. I can't say I didn't see it coming. You're an odd one. And you keep odd company."

Michael said nothing, staring at the crossbeams above him, but his heart was racing.

"It was me that knocked you out, Alaine, me that got you off that poor unfortunate soul you did for. I'm to be commended and given a new rank." He smiled, reaching into his pocket, and pulled out Michael's hand-shaped trinket, letting it swing on the end of the chain.

Michael resisted the urge to grasp for it, eyes fixed on the cross beams, breathing steadily.

"I guess there was a spare promotion lying around." Jasper pocketed the amulet, twisted the ends of his black mustache, and left the room.

As soon as the door closed, Michael whispered urgently, "Amal, you have to get out of here. They'll accuse you of witchcraft, of being involved. Now, you must go now."

Amal's eyes were disturbed, her brow furrowed. "That man..."

The dread that filled Michael's heart began to overflow, threatening to overwhelm him. Instinctively, he knew what she was going to say. A last shred of loyalty and honor raised its hand in a dark prehistoric sea, protesting, drowning. He spoke softly before Amal could finish her sentence. "Achilles company...we were sent to...help...to..."

Amal took a deep breath. "He, along with several others...that man killed my father and raped my mother and sister, murdered them all."

Michael felt sorrow, anger, and shame in equal measures, all sense of obligation to his unit, his army, his commanding officers, dissipating forever. There was nothing left, nothing but this girl, this girl who needed him like nobody else had ever needed him or would ever need him. Loyalty had been superseded by something else, a feeling, an idea, yet intangible.

Quietly the door opened, and two young soldiers entered. They stood behind Amal. One of them, pimples on his cheeks, said, "Miss, you are to come with us."

"Leave her alone."

"Now, miss."

Blood rushed to Michael's head, stabbing him in the temples. "She has nothing to do with this. She is innocent."

Amal had picked up enough of the common tongue to know what the pimpled soldier was saying. She said, "It's all right, Michael. You rest. Please rest."

The two men grabbed Amal, one soldier on each frail arm. Michael sat up, pain tearing through him, tearing stitches. "Leave her be!"

The other soldier, with bulbous nose and crooked teeth, savagely backhanded Michael. In his weakened state, he never saw the blow coming. Once again, the blackness overwhelmed him.

28

Temptation

Brynhild Grimsdotter watched the man riding a few yards ahead on a mount as charcoal black as the rider's extraordinary eyes. Christopher Lewis was a complex puzzle: apparent knight-captain in Bruwaert's army, actual spy in the service of Tremain, an assassin—despite his protestations to the contrary—and most definitely a liar.

He rode beside William, conversing, Christopher now dressed in the butter-robes of a yellow scholar—yet another guise he had so casually assumed as simply as slipping the cloth over his shoulders. He had maintained it a good ruse for the road, two Yellow Scholars on a pilgrimage to Re'Shan, accompanied by a bodyguard. Just how Rebecca Occitane, now riding her own small gray mare at the rear of the group, played a role in this little narrative, he hadn't explained.

He hadn't explained a lot of things. Brynhild trusted the man less than she had trusted her late husband to abstain from drinking, fighting, and fucking. The man's story had holes wide enough to put his arse through.

Brynhild still wasn't sure how she had found herself woven into his oddly colored, bizarre tapestry. He had told an intriguing tale, admittedly, but far-fetched. A madman heading for Ulfur to claim magical amulets that gifted supernatural powers to each bearer? The rebirth of the Hungry King? A new war? Ancient monks, secret monasteries?

Far-fetched, undeniably.

But she needed him. Rebecca needed him. He could get them close to Bruwaert, give the girl a chance for revenge. And so, for now, she would tag along, albeit keeping a watchful eye on the man.

It was a beautiful day, the dull breeze neither chilled bones nor chapped lips, and the road between the Yellow Monastery and Balclutha, sixty leagues to the south, promised an unimpeded journey. Brynhild estimated a week would see them in Re'Shan, if her theoretical knowledge of the southern geography held fast. The truth was she had never crossed these lands, but she knew distance, knew what a good horse was capable of. Yes, a week. Perhaps eight days.

William Barding dropped back from where he was riding with Christopher, and the yellow scholar's brown mare soon fell into step with Brynhild's white courser.

"I've just been chatting with Christopher," he said brightly.

"I see that," Brynhild said, her tone dark to William's light.

"He's a fascinating fellow, quite a career to date. Was there at the fall of Re'Shan when the Hungry King was brought to ground, had quite a hand in it, apparently."

"Perhaps you should be writing *his* biography."

William looked sideways, surprised. "Are you jealous, *Kita No Ki?*"

A grimace clouded Brynhild's features. "Only the Easterners call me that. It sounds odd coming from your mouth. No, I'm not jealous. I'm wary."

"Wary, of Christopher?"

"Yes."

William raised two diaphanous eyebrows. "You don't trust the man?"

Brynhild snorted. "He shows up specifically to read books about supposed occult amulets, and this just after Bruwaert's men kill Robert Occitane for such an amulet. Doesn't that seem odd to you?"

The monk extended his bottom lip in thought. "He explained that all quite rationally, as far as I could tell. Anyway, why would you volunteer for this mission if you suspect him of dubious motives?"

"Your jolly abbot volunteered me." She paused. "I'm here to watch over Rebecca, that is all."

William shielded his eyes and looked at the blue sky in which a single hawk circled, looking for prey. "Um, we have time, and it's a beautiful day. I was hoping I could ask you some questions about your people, your culture."

"For your book?"

"Well, *your* book. A book about you. But yes, it's my book."

"Mmm. Nothing is freely given, not unless you're a monk. I have a question of my own which I insist you answer before I talk."

"Of course."

"Why are your people called the Yellow Monks?"

"Scholars, we are, officially, the Yellow Scholars."

"Very well. Why not the Red Scholars, or the Blue Scholars?"

"Because those colors were already taken," William said matter-of-factly.

Brynhild stopped her horse, a smile playing at the edges of her mouth. "Is that a joke?"

William stopped his horse in turn and looked back, his face serious. "No, why would it be?"

Brynhild's laughter startled the hawk and caused Christopher Lewis to turn around in his saddle. She laughed for a long time, clearing the skies, the hawk now gone to a place where it could hunt and think undisturbed. She finally gathered some self-control and wiped tears from her eyes. "In that case, William Barding, I find your answer very funny, very funny indeed."

———

THE COASTAL CITY of Balclutha was still twenty leagues away. At a push, they could have made the city walls by mid-morning, but the chances of finding lodgings at that hour would be slim. The early autumn night was gentle, clear, so they decided to camp on the road. They even dared start a fire, bandits not being a common occurrence in Otago. Many say what they will about Bruwaert, but he kept law

and order in his state. Things would be different when they entered
the lawless Freelands and the dangerous Forest of Thieves.

William sat beside Rebecca as the fire crackled and sparked. She
hadn't said a word on the day's ride; in fact, she'd been quiet since
the monk and the warrior princess first encountered her. He wondered if the girl was too badly broken to ever be put together again.
That would be a shame. She was possessed of a passionate spirit and
had much to offer the world.

The fire cast good warmth against the mild chill of the night, the
planets brilliant against a velvet firmament.

"I've never seen the stars look so beautiful," William said, moving
a little closer to the girl and patting her on the shoulder. Rebecca
only stared at the fire. The amulet hanging on the outside of her
tunic shined in the firelight. The monk's skin began to tingle.

Christopher Lewis was already asleep, lying on his side at the edge
of the firelight. The man liked to get an early night, that was certain.
Assassins, if Brynhild was to be believed, kept a regular lifestyle.

William marveled at the skies; a million stars sprinkled the heavens. It was breathtaking.

Dry twigs cracked under the weight of the six-and-a-half-foot
Norse warrior as she entered the circle of firelight, her hair wet
and unbound; she'd been bathing in a nearby creek. She sat, tilted
her head, and began drying her hair by the fire, the golden strands
thickly falling, intertwined over the milky white skin of the woman's
face. She now only wore her underwear.

The monk was mesmerized by her wet cleavage and the hon-
ey-colored triangle of pubic hair beneath the thin fabric of her cut-
off stockings. Blood rushed to his penis, and he tried to stop his
erection by force of will, silently admonishing himself for his complete failure and lack of willpower. This was not the first time he'd
witnessed Brynhild near naked. The Norsewoman cared little about
propriety, comfortable in her own skin whether clothed or not.
She had told him that men and women bathed together in the hot
springs in her homeland, that shame at one's own body was a cul-
tural nonentity. William had found the notion refreshing, but now
he found it distinctly arousing, and completely disturbing.

Brynhild caught him looking at her. He hurriedly averted his eyes, but she did not avert hers. He could feel her stare, as if her eyes invited his own to find their courage and return to the fray. *I am not ashamed*, they seemed to say. *Gaze on me.*

He looked back. She was drying her ears and smiling. His face reddened. Suddenly, it was infernally hot. William rose to his feet, robes gathered over his groin as Brynhild continued to observe him and smile.

"I will bathe in the river, if you don't mind," he said.

Brynhild shrugged, her breasts rising and falling subtly with the gesture. "Why would I mind?" She watched him scurry away. "The water's cold," she warned after him.

"Good," William muttered as he left the firelight.

Brynhild's smile faded when she saw Rebecca staring into the fire. "Child, you must stop moping."

"I'm not moping. I'm thinking."

"Then, stop thinking."

"I have lost somebody."

"We all have," Brynhild said.

"There is nobody else I care about, and no one to care for me."

"Then, make more people you care about."

"How?"

"It's not for me to tell you how, but I can tell you there's nothing more important." Brynhild admired the stars in the night sky, their cold, callous beauty. "I lost my own father many years ago."

Rebecca saw the Norsewoman with fresh eyes. "I'm sorry. How old were you?"

"Seven."

"How did he die?"

"Ale, lies, lust. What usually kills a man?" Brynhild noted Rebecca's confusion. "Murdered," she explained. "Stabbed in the back by a trusted ally."

"Why?"

"For wealth, power. I'm not sure. It doesn't matter."

"It seems so foolish. To die for such petty things."

"Yes."

Rebecca turned her bright amber eyes from the fire. Brynhild had to make a conscious effort not to look away from her piercing gaze. "Is that why you're helping me? Because you lost your father too?"

Brynhild thought for a moment. Then she said, "I don't examine my own feelings in that way. I have no idea why I'm helping you other than it feels the right thing to do. I cannot explain further than that." She smiled. "If you desire a meticulous analysis of one's motivations, talk to William. The writer within him may offer you insights on that front that I cannot."

"You shouldn't tease William."

Brynhild was startled at the abrupt change in the conversation. "I have done no such thing."

"You display yourself before him. William is shy."

Brynhild snorted, more forcefully than she had intended. "Shy? He's a monk." She paused. "Forgive me, William is a *scholar*. His mind is full of words and dusty pages, not women and certainly not me."

"He's still a man."

"And how do you know so much of these things, or what William feels?"

"Some things are innate, especially when it comes to men and women, do you not think so? William is a good man, a gentle man, but even good men struggle with temptation."

Brynhild looked off toward the creek. "You are wise for a country girl. Let me add to your vast wisdom—"

"Your tone doesn't need to be so condescending."

Brynhild found herself brought up short once again but conceded the girl was right. She *was* growing peevish. Perhaps Rebecca had touched a nerve. Perhaps she should apply a little of William's self-contemplation to discover why. She would attempt to do so at a later time. "I apologize."

Rebecca nodded. "Accepted. Please, add to my vast wisdom."

Brynhild looked at the trinket hanging from Rebecca's neck. "It's not only men that face temptation."

29

Return to Ulfur

Mount Ulfur had a life of its own. It was a living thing, an over-seer, a titan at the edge of the desert, gifting crystal-clear water to the city of Re'Shan below. It thrust from the desert floor, its subterranean roots anchored deep in Hell, and penetrated the Heavens. It was maleficent. It was angelic. It was death, destruction, and rebirth.

"We are approaching," de Merlon said. "We make the climb tonight."

Tristan and the shriveled monk rode the same tired horse, both looking up at the mountain and the dark shadows of clouds moving stealthily across a sky of cobalt blue.

"Perhaps we should rest tonight, climb tomorrow. It'll be dark soon," Jeremiah said.

Tristan couldn't hide the irritation in his voice. "One would think you're reticent about returning home. What is darkness to one such as you? Your night vision is the equal of mine, or better."

"We have traveled far, and the climb is steep. I'm not as young as I once was."

Tristan eyed the snow-headed giant once more. "You haven't been as young as you once were for a hundred years. We make the climb tonight."

"You aren't the only one seeking the metal. There'll be soldiers upon the mountainside."

"Another reason to make the climb under cover of darkness," Tristan said, anger settling on the former marshal's brow. "What's wrong, Jeremiah? We've come all this way, and you seem unwilling to take the last few steps."

"What if they've found it? What if the metal's gone?" The gnarled monk spoke with an edge of concern, fear.

Tristan didn't reply, he only spurred his horse forward, thinking.

I didn't release you from the Gorgon for the pleasure of your company. It had better be there, for your sake. These thoughts you are welcome to read.

The city at the edge of the Great Southern Sands slowly made itself known. The warmth of the encroaching desert was like a wave despite the early evening and the absence of the sun. Within the space of one league, the temperature soared. Above the rebuilt walls of Re'Shan, only the tallest spires, domes, and cathedrals poked their heads out, but the city was vibrant even outside the walls: traders gathered and bartered at the gates, children rode horses in circular pens for the amusement of their parents, and lovers strolled the manicured grass and gardens on the west side of the road near the eternal rivulet originating seven thousand feet above. The atmosphere was festive. But over it all, loomed Ulfur.

Tristan and Jeremiah headed half a league east before they came upon the city gates, taking a smaller road meandering toward the foot of the mountain. This would be the most dangerous part of the journey. Once upon the mountain, Jeremiah would be in his element and would know every track up and down the giant. But getting there, now that would be a different tale.

Sure enough, as they made their way along the road, soldiers were walking toward them in scattered groups, weary, clearly returning from a day's hard climb.

"This road's closed," one soldier said, walking past with a drooping ginger moustache to match his drooping shoulders and defeated gait.

Tristan didn't remove his hood or have to utter a word; the exhausted soldier didn't stop. When he had disappeared in the shadows of the silver birch trees lining the road, Tristan and Jeremiah trotted onwards.

"A rather lackluster display of commitment," Tristan said. "The man should be court-martialed."

"Fortunate for us he didn't stop. But we won't always be so lucky."

"Do you remember the way?"

Jeremiah cackled. "Twenty years I lived on that mountain, and another forty years, yes forty years did I live within it. I know the mountain. I remember the way."

"Are there others of your kind still within?"

The monk made no reply.

Tristan's patience burned away like paper in a blazing hearth. "Answer me, old one."

Jeremiah sighed. "When I left, I . . ." The old monk seemed unable or unwilling to finish the thought.

Ash in the fireplace. "Answer me!"

"When I finally left, and I don't recall exactly when I left, you must understand, I was less than human." He stretched a sickly smile across his withered jaw. "Not that I'm a saint now, but we . . . we were in a bad state."

"What are you trying to tell me, Jeremiah?"

"If there's anybody still within, they'd be indescribably devolved. A demon without saving grace."

Tristan looked up at the looming giant. "That doesn't sound good."

"No, not good at all. I'd like to remind you, de Merlon, that if you're determined to pursue your course of action—the metal and domination of White Cloud—you'll fare no better."

"I am strong."

Jeremiah nodded, smiling behind his master's back. "Mmm. Yes, strong. You will not fall foul of the metal."

"I will not fall foul. I warn you, if you attempt to betray me, if there's some kind of trap waiting for me, it will not end well for you."

Jeremiah cackled and clenched his sharpened teeth. "End well? Things ended badly for me a century ago. Nothing has changed since that time, nor will it. I'm in Hell, you see? An endless cycle, doomed am I to repeat the same mistakes again and again. You're merely the latest incarnation of this Hell, a twist on the same horrid, repetitive story. I will not betray you, what need have I for that when you have sealed your own fate."

Tristan allowed the gnarled monk to rant. The mountain awaited. The metal was up there somewhere, buried deep, and the only one who could find and forge it sat behind him. Let Jeremiah rave. When de Merlon had what he wanted, then Stella would be avenged. Stella and the boys, Albert, Terence . . .

They came upon a small wooden guardhouse manned by two young soldiers carrying pikes and bearing the wing insignia of Mercury Company. Under the rules of the Alliance, the two Lesser Kings had chosen the names of different deities to distinguish between their respective armies. Tremain had selected the Greek gods, and Bruwaert the Roman. These men belonged to Bruwaert's forces.

One man with a fat face and thin body left the guardhouse, flaming torch in hand. "Halt! No one's allowed upon the mountain."

"It's a free country, boy, *that's* what we fought and died for under the Alliance, is it not?"

The young man held the torch out, trying to peer into the early evening darkness of de Merlon's hood. "Show your face."

"Hold your tongue and stand to attention! I am Marshal Oliver Burrell, formerly of Icarus Company. Who's in charge up there?" Tristan pointed at Ulfur.

The man, believing he was standing before a superior officer, albeit one from the other side of the Alliance, stood straighter. "I'll need some identification, sir. Or I can't let you pass. King Bruwaert's orders."

"Neither you nor Bruwaert has authority over me, boy, with or without the Alliance. I'm Tremain's man. Stand down, or you'll be flogged! I ask again, who's in charge on the mountainside?"

"Ah, Commander Forbury, sir."

"How many men are with him? What company?"

The other soldier in the guardhouse had by now come to stand beside the first. The second man, bizarrely, was possessed of a long, lean face on a rotund body. The guards looked as if they had somehow swapped heads in the guardhouse. Both men shifted from foot to foot and cast awkward glances at the other's mismatching features.

"I'm not privileged to give out that information, sir," Fat Head said.

De Merlon kicked his horse forward, almost collecting the two startled soldiers, who, not wishing to cause a fracas among Alliance partners, could only watch the two cloaked riders pass by. Once out of earshot, de Merlon asked, "How many was the boy thinking?"

Jeremiah opened his eyes. "One hundred men from Vulcan Company, stationed at two thousand feet. They're bedding down for the night to search anew at daybreak."

"They haven't found it, then."

"No, but our presence will have been reported by daybreak tomorrow."

"Too late. They will not find us. All is well."

But all was not well.

Tristan Drogos de Merlon could not recall his youngest child's name. Albert, Terence, Geoffrey, Simon . . . What was the youngest's name?

He roared silently with horror and rage but let no manifestation of his grief make itself known to the ancient monk. He couldn't let Jeremiah sense his weakness, and so he had to grieve for the death of his smallest child somewhere deep inside, somewhere the monk couldn't reach, grieve all over again for the loss of the child, for the loss of the memory of his name. He couldn't understand why. Why would he forget?

More soldiers meandered past, looking at the odd sight of the tall and short figures on single horseback. Tristan saw nothing. In his mind he was screaming and desperately clawing at the door of his home once again, but this time he couldn't get in as his wife and children burned within.

He apologized to Stella. He apologized to his children. He should have been there.

Tristan Drogos de Merlon swore revenge on the world, vehemently, again and again. He'd let nothing stand in his way, not now, not when he was so close to the source of the sky metal, the source of his growing power.

30

The Forest of Thieves

Rebecca fumbled the assassin's blade, and it pierced the dirt road, standing upright like a makeshift tomb marker.

Christopher Lewis leapt from his horse, yellow monastic raiment flowing, plucked the knife, and bounced back onto the saddle in one fluid motion. He handed the hilt of the knife to Rebecca as their horses trotted side by side on a dirt path between tall leafy eucalyptus trees.

"Try again," he said, watching the girl replace the dagger in the concealed forearm wrap in her tunic sleeve. "Remember, you're not reaching for the hilt, you're going for the clip. Simply release it with your longest finger and gravity does the rest."

The assassin demonstrated once again, curling his hand dexterously inwards, and with a small plucking motion of his middle finger, the hidden blade dropped hilt first into his hand, giving him his favored reverse grip. "Most importantly, if you miss the hilt, don't grasp for the blade as it sails past. It's too late, you'll lose your fingers. I'll teach you the pinch-catch later, for now just keep working on the release."

Rebecca took a breath of the minty pine and honey scented air coming off the darkening eucalyptus leaves, relaxed, and curled her hand inwards as Christopher had done. "I can't reach, my fingers aren't as long as yours."

He nodded for her to persevere.

A moment later, the knife dropped silently, and she caught it expertly in her palm.

"Well done."

She looked at Christopher and smiled.

A few yards behind, William Barding leaned over and whispered conspiratorially to Brynhild. "I can hardly approve of this. Rebecca doesn't need to learn the ways of... killing."

The warrior raised an eyebrow. "I do not like nor trust the man, and assassins are the least honorable exponents of the martial arts, but in this case, I cannot agree with you. She needs to learn to protect herself."

William's voice grew louder. "She's fifteen years of age. Abstinence from violence is the best approach."

"You saw how she dispatched Bruwaert's men on the beach. She's good with a knife. More than that, she's gifted. The girl has taken to it naturally, it's too late for abstinence."

He bridled. "I believe that was a reaction to the death of her father and not her natural character. Or, perhaps it's the amulet she wears, perhaps it's...." His voice trailed off, and a look of growing distaste appeared on his features. He clearly suspected that the relic of Ulfur was the driving force behind the feral violence in the child's heart.

"You worry too much," Brynhild said. "Did you see her face when she caught the dagger? She was smiling. Did you see?"

The monk shifted uncomfortably in his saddle. "What of it?"

"She hasn't smiled, not since I've known her. Let her forget for a while. This is good for her."

"The arts of warfare are not suitable for—"

"Come now, even the Yellow Scholars are trained in using knives. You, yourself, have killed men. She's a natural warrior, she needs to learn how to kill, and kill efficiently."

He jerked his head away from Brynhild, as if her words were an oncoming sword blow. "Kill efficiently? What does that even mean? She's a young woman. This isn't a wholesome activity for a girl."

Christopher Lewis had turned his horse about and was casually riding back to join William and Brynhild. Rebecca was continuing to practice her new skill.

"She should be learning to knit, sew, cook, and clean? Set the hearth to fire and rub the feet of a dominant male?"

The monk waggled a finger. "That's not what I'm saying, as you well know."

"Then, what *are* you saying?"

"She's too young. That's all."

"She's old enough. I was thirteen my first time."

A quizzical expression played across Christopher's face. He had been in earshot only for the last part of the conversation. "What are you two talking about?"

The tall Norsewoman and thin scholar-monk looked at each other.

"Well," Christopher said, "whatever it was, I'll leave the parenting to mother and father."

Brynhild and William now cast horrified glances at the knight-captain.

"We're being followed," he said.

"Do you mean the riders three leagues back?" Brynhild asked.

"Eh?" William twisted his head around and peered back along the path to where it disappeared among the trees. There was no sign of riders.

"What do those dark eyes of yours tell you?"

Christopher rubbed his hand over his short white hair. "We're in the Freelands and have just entered the Forest of Thieves. The riders comprise five men and one woman, well armed. Two crossbows, four short swords. My eyes tell me this is trouble."

The tall warrior nodded in appreciation of the assassin's sharpened senses. "What's your suggested course of action?"

"We set an ambush for them before they do the same for us."

"I like this plan," Brynhild said.

William didn't like the plan and said so. He was roundly ignored.

—————

"WHY DON'T WE just let them ride by?" William whispered from where he lay below the lip of a small grassy embankment at the edge of the dense woods. He peeked across at a similar embankment on the other side of the road where Christopher and Rebecca were hiding.

"Because," Brynhild hissed, pushing the monk's head down below the line of sight from the road, "when they realize we're not ahead of them, they'll return to find us. We cannot avoid this conflict. If they are so inclined to attack us, it *will* happen. The assassin is right. We do this on our terms."

"Why does everything have to end in bloodshed?"

The tall woman patted the thin man on the shoulder. "You don't get out of the Yellow Abbey much, do you, William? Now, silence."

The monk grasped a dagger in each hand. He hoped the assassin and the warrior princess were wrong, that their instincts had, just this once, engaged themselves prematurely. This hope, he knew, was pathetically frail, outrageously flimsy. But he clung to it all the same.

The riders all wore boiled leather jerkins of black or tan and rode in ambling formation, unhurried and loose, but a formation nonetheless—one crossbow in the lead, one at the rear, the four short swords forming a square between the long-range weapons. The lead crossbow rider had a tattoo covering her chin in flowing swirls. She looked left, right, and raised her hand. The five behind her stopped, weapons raised.

The dark-skinned female lifted her head and shouted, "Perfect place for an ambush!"

William's heart pounded. Brynhild put her finger over her lips.

And then words from the other embankment. It was the assassin's voice. "*He tawhiti atu koe i te kuini o te whare.*"

The tattooed woman looked surprised. She waved away a question from one of the men behind her and said into the air, "*Ko wai koe?*"

"What's he doing?" William asked. Brynhild shook her head and listened.

"*Kei te hiahia au ki te korero*," Christopher said.

Suddenly, William recognized the language as that of the Nomad Lords of the Deep South.

"*Tino*," the dark woman said. She then switched to the common tongue. "Come out and we'll talk. We shall not strike first. You have my word."

Brynhild peeked over the lip of the grassy hillock, then ducked her head back and whispered, "Christopher is going out there."

"What should we do?"

"I can't let him walk alone. We are companions now, for better or worse."

The monk grasped Brynhild's forearm with more force than he had intended. "Sorry," he said, looking at his hand on her arm and removing it, "but maybe just let him talk first. You have a habit of charging in and making things worse."

She scowled. "I do not." Her frown was replaced by a look of genuine concern. "Do I?"

"My dear woman, you do."

Brynhild felt embarrassed, a feeling which threatened to morph into anger, but she wouldn't let her quick temper have its way. She respected William Barding, and sometimes even a princess must listen to well-intentioned criticism, as stinging as it may be. And one could hardly rebuke a monk, or a scholar, or a knife-wielding warrior-monk-scholar, or whatever William was turning out to be. So, Brynhild bit her tongue, waited, and listened.

Knight-Captain Christopher Lewis walked down to the road and pulled back his yellow hood. He raised his chin and let his voice ring out through the shedding trees. "Since when do the lords and ladies of the Deep South resort to banditry?"

The tattooed woman smiled, half-grin, half-grimace. "Hah! Since they found themselves squeezed from their own land, almost driven to the sea!" The woman's dark curly hair bounced along with the words of righteous indignation.

Christopher outstretched his arms. "That was the Hungry King, not the Alliance. We are all free peoples again."

"Free? Hmmm. A bird, once caged, is never again free." She peered closer at the man in the monk's garb. "To whom do I speak?"

"I am Christopher."

"I am Mahuika. From whence do your people come, Christopher?"

The assassin hesitated, and Mahuika smiled.

"Come now. Either your mother or father is Maori, any fool could see that. The other, is clearly not."

"My mother was of the Southern Tribes, yes."

"Well, brother, you also are far from home. I apologize if you thought my friends and I meant you any harm."

"And did you? Mean us harm?"

The Maori woman laughed. "Where are your companions?"

"Waiting until the threat is gone."

"The threat is gone, brother. I give you my *fafau*. My word."

"*Tino*," Christopher said. "Friends, come! We are in no danger!"

Mahuika watched with interest as Rebecca, William, and Brynhild rose from their hiding places and walked to the road, fallen eucalyptus leaves acting as a carpet for their cautious tread. The Maori woman stared at Brynhild. "A Northerner?"

Christopher nodded.

"The stories are true. Are all her people so large? She is impressive." Mahuika looked the Norsewoman up and down, making appreciative comments as to the size and health of the Northern specimen.

Brynhild bristled. "I speak the common language and am no farmyard cattle."

Mahuika raised one hand. "If any offense has been issued, I apologize. I propose we share a campfire tonight. Strength in numbers is a powerful deterrent to those with evil on their mind. The Forest of Thieves can be a dangerous place after dark, brother."

She got down from her horse and approached Christopher. They grasped each other by the shoulders, bringing their heads together to gently touch noses. When the greeting was over, he stepped back and acceded with a nod.

———

THE LIGHT OF THE FIRE fell on the slope of the deep dell within which the ten figures sat. They had set up camp a league from the road and wouldn't be seen unless stumbled over.

Brynhild wouldn't sleep tonight, for she trusted neither the assassin masquerading as a yellow scholar nor the Maori woman with the *moko* chin tattoo. The woman's motley band of men hardly inspired confidence either.

Mahuika inquired of their destination, and when Christopher murmured something about a pilgrimage to Re'Shan and more specifically Mount Ulfur, the woman frowned. "That's an angry hive," she said. "You had best avoid both Ulfur and the city at the edge of the Great Southern Sands should you wish not to be stung."

Christopher raised a curious look. "Explain, sister."

Mahuika seemed to weigh up the consequences of her next words. She turned to one of her men sitting in the circle and said, "Ricard, tell them what you know of Re'Shan."

Ricard was tall and lean, his face even leaner, with sideburns dyed green, oddly mismatching his natural red hair, like an oversized imp from a children's story. He held his hands out to the fire and said, "The city is in lockdown. Several men have disappeared upon Mount Ulfur, and even soldiers stationed at garrisons within the walls of Re'Shan itself are vanishing. The senators are spooked, they've instituted martial law. It's as if the Great War never ended. Innocent people dragged from their homes, rounded up and questioned in a hunt for witches and warlocks. It's a dangerous place for both soldier and civilian."

Brynhild watched Christopher closely, waiting for some kind of reaction. She noticed Mahuika watching the assassin's face with equal interest. So far, the man sat quietly, his face merely registering polite attention.

Ricard sniffed, pulled his fur-lined cloak tighter about himself, and stared at the fire. "Most recently, two men possessed of supernatural strength fought in the streets of the city. Gods among men, they were. One of them murdered the other and is now imprisoned, badly injured, near death himself."

A faint reaction glinted on the cold blade of the assassin's face. He asked, "Did these men carry anything upon their persons, anything unusual?"

An impish nod. "Aye. Amulets. Some say the fountain of their power. Some say fashioned from a magic metal found on Ulfur. That's why the soldiers search the mountain daily, they seek the metal. Hearsay is connecting the confrontation in Re'Shan with events unfolding on the mountain, the disappearances of the soldiers."

William looked at Rebecca.

No, William, thought Brynhild. *Don't draw attention to her.*

Rebecca put her hand to her tunic.

Keep your hand still, girl!

The warrior crept her hand immeasurably closer to the katana resting on the ground beside her. Christopher didn't take his eyes from the tall imp; the assassin, at least, understood the danger. But the moment passed, the Maori woman and her men seemingly unaware that a trinket of power lay in their midst, within their very grasp. Brynhild let out a long silent breath.

"When did this battle take place?" Christopher asked.

The wind picked up, blowing sparks like fireflies flitting into the cool darkness. "Three days ago."

"And what is to become of the survivor?"

Ricard the Imp scratched a green sideburn. "He's to be hung, most likely. Men do not take kindly to...other men with unusual abilities. Bruwaert's soldiers are sniffing around the man, but he's heavily guarded by Achilles Company, which serves Tremain and is keeping the fat king's men at bay. But the man is doomed come what may."

"Do you know his name?" Christopher asked, but Ricard simply shook his head.

Silence enveloped the group for several moments, and Mahuika's attention meandered over William's and Christopher's robes. "For monks on a pilgrimage, you seem overly excited by news of a military nature," she said.

The assassin smiled. "I'm interested in current affairs. I'm writing a book on life in the southern cities after the war."

"A book? Hmm. Outstanding." Mahuika nodded appreciatively. "That must be your quill and ink you have strapped inside your sleeves, then." She laughed, and was startled when Brynhild Grimsdotter laughed along with her.

———

WILLIAM BARDING PACED around the ashes of the cold campfire, clearly agitated, as the first rays of the sun sent dull shards of light into the dell. "You heard her last night, the Maori woman. Re'Shan is dangerous, certainly no place for Rebecca. Everyone's hunting for the amulets! I won't allow Rebecca to be accused of witchcraft, or worse."

"Keep your voice down." Christopher raised his hand in farewell as Mahuika waved from her horse in the distance, then turned and disappeared with her men into the early morning mist back to the north—the opposite direction to which they'd been traveling the previous day. Christopher furrowed his brow. "What could be worse than being accused of witchcraft?"

The scholar-monk threw his hands up. "I don't know, does it matter?"

"You knew this road would be hazardous. You're welcome to turn around. Take the girl with you."

Rebecca spoke up. "No, we go on. I'll talk with the man Ricard spoke of, the one who carried an amulet. Perhaps he knew my father."

William's index finger had taken on a life of its own; it seemed to wave and wiggle the man attached to it. "Or he could be the madman himself, this, what does he call himself...the next Hungry King? Absolutely forbidden. We must turn around. We must go back."

"No!" Rebecca shouted, her amber eyes wide with rage. "I won't go back. I want to know what's happening, what happened to my father, the reasons for it. I'll learn what I can and have my revenge on the fat king."

William's mouth dropped open.

Rebecca softened her tone. Going on, she said, "William . . . I thank you for all you've done for me. Without you and Brynhild, I'd be dead like my father. But I must seek the truth, and if Christopher's right, if a madman seeks to bring war to White Cloud again, I'll help in any way I can to stop it. Whatever small part I can play, I'm willing to do so. When it's over, and if I'm still alive, I'll kill Bruwaert and avenge my father."

Watching the remains of the campfire, William slid his hands into his sleeves and said, "Are you still set upon the path of vengeance?"

Rebecca looked pleadingly into his eyes, but he wouldn't meet her gaze. "What other path do I have?"

The monk nodded and walked away.

"I've upset William. I didn't mean to," she whispered low.

Brynhild patted her on the shoulder. "He's hardier than he looks. You need not concern yourself."

Mounting his horse, Christopher Lewis said, "You're right, Rebecca. We need to talk to this man. If he is indeed a trinket bearer, he may be able to enlighten us on many things. Perhaps we might finally have a name for the Hungry King."

"William is a worrier," Brynhild said, "but he may have a point. What if this *god among men* is corrupted by the metal?"

The black-eyed assassin wheeled around his charcoal-black horse and said over his shoulder, "Then, we must be very, very careful."

31

The Sky Metal

Cracker Jackson's eyes had spent their entire lives avoiding each other, the left and right drifting further into different hemispheres of the man's head. The truth be told, neither eye enjoyed living on his head at all and had been working for several years to pop themselves right out of their sockets and make a run for freedom.

Because of his wayward eyeballs, Cracker had been called all kinds of names as a child; the least imaginative among them were, in no particular order, frog face, frog eyes, frog fart, or just froggy. None of the names had bothered him. He knew most of the teasing was rooted in insecurity and turned the torments back on his tormenters. He was called Cracker because when he found the cracks in his foes' armor, he would crack them open, physically or mentally.

One boy had attempted to cut at him with a standard amphibian comparison, but Cracker noted the boy was left-handed, the only sinistral in the entire village. He struck mercilessly, teasing the boy viciously about his *dung* handedness. He didn't do it with any malice but simply to deter any future attacks on himself, and it worked. Pretty soon everybody cut the frog jokes.

Cracker was also a natural skeptic. He hadn't thrown himself into the righteous cause presented to him by Broadford Higgins as eagerly as had Big Ted and Spade Johnson.

He didn't have kids, and the wife he did have would hardly notice his absence. He sure as hell wouldn't miss the mines. Indeed, when he looked back at his life, it would be fair to say it hadn't worked out as he'd hoped, but that didn't mean he had nothing to lose or that he would jump overboard into the sea of folly for the promise of a golden fish.

Something didn't gel with Higgins's story. If war was brewing between Bruwaert and Tremain, then why did no one except Broadford Higgins seem to know about it? And as far as Marshal Tristan Drogos de Merlon sending the toff to collect them for his new army? It was flattering, and part of Cracker's ego, any man's ego, would take this as affirmation of his worth, confirmation in the face of a lifetime of internal self-doubt and external naysayers. See, he was worthy, for a worthy man had chosen him.

He wished he could believe it wholeheartedly, but Cracker was hanging on to his restraint. Something wasn't right.

On the journey from Brittsdale to Re'Shan, Broadford had gathered an army of dross, of drunks, of human detritus, of misbegotten losers, Cracker included. But perhaps it didn't matter. A cause to fight for, any cause, was preferable to rotting away in the mines, especially if there was reward in it. Money. Women. Whisky. Whatever.

Still, he watched the gentleman toff carefully. Broadford's hands started to shake the closer the men got to Mount Ulfur, his top hat never sitting comfortably on his head, the man forever adjusting it at a different angle.

Higgins was shitting his fancy pants, that Cracker Jackson could see as plainly as the cursed eyes on his own face.

He looked at the giant mountain piercing the clouds. It had brooded above them all during the Great War as the six-month siege of Re'Shan raged on below. It was impassionate, uncaring, like Zeus watching the battles, toils, and deaths of men, laughing all the while. He admired Ulfur's snowy head. It hadn't changed. It was as ominous as ever, seeming to say, *Welcome back, old friend, haven't had enough of me?*

Broadford Higgins rode ahead as the walls of Re'Shan materialized a few leagues in the distance. When he returned, he called a halt to the march of the ragged band of approximately eighty men—if they could be called men—picked up like shit on boots through Otago and the Freelands. Cracker Jackson, Spade Johnson, and Big Ted could safely be counted among the best in quality of the ragtag bunch of ex-soldiers approaching Re'Shan, and that was saying something.

"The city is blockaded," Broadford said, "as is the road to the mountain." A mumbling passed among the men. "Remember, when we encounter Bruwaert's soldiers, you are not to attack. The Alliance still stands. We must speak to Marshal de Merlon before we lift a finger in anger. Is that understood?" There was a general murmuring of assent, not that anybody in the group was willing or able to take on anyone, for the time being. "Big Ted, Cracker, Spade, with me. The rest of you set up camp here."

The four men rode away, leaving a bewildered company of drunks and thieves to sprawl out on dried grass under silver birch trees, not knowing what was happening, or even what day it was, but enjoying the warmth of the southern climes, letting it ease the pain of their aged and diseased limbs.

"What's the plan, sir?" Big Ted asked as his horse trotted beside that of the gentleman toff. "Where's the marshal?"

Broadford simply pointed to the mountain.

Several questions were forthcoming, but Broadford only muttered that for now every man needed to save his breath for the climb ahead.

And so, after much ducking and weaving and hiding behind trees on the approach, they attained the base of the mountain and began to climb Mount Ulfur. Only once on the ascent did they encounter a half-dozen soldiers lurking in the undergrowth, coming forth shouting, "Halt! Who goes there?" But Broadford hadn't lost the gift of the gab and bluffed his way onwards.

They climbed, and as they did so, Re'Shan came into view over the city walls below, the Great Southern Sands sprawling beyond the city. Onwards and upwards they crawled, each man's lungs tested and found wanting, blowing out the cobwebs of a civilian life that had offered them nothing but empty promises, frustration, and hardships.

They came upon the cascading water, the small opening through which it rushed, and once again Broadford Higgins made preparations to enter the hidden monastery of the Monks of Ulfur

Cracker Jackson, Spade Johnson, and Big Ted exchanged glances. "What? In there?" Spade pointed to the opening. "Nobody said anything about climbing into yawning holes in the mountainside."

Broadford put his hands to his hips. "The monastery is inside, boys. The monks found it, don't you see? Everything you've ever dreamed of is waiting for you. Down there."

Big Ted backed away. "Nothing about monks or long-forgotten places either. Are you sure about this, Captain Higgins?"

"Never more. I've tasted it. Power beyond anything you could dream. The marshal's in there. He'll explain everything, trust me, lads. Only a few yards down, might get a bit wet, but that's all. Come on, you've journeyed all this way, don't give up now." Broadford took a torch and rope from his shoulder bag. "Look, I'll go first just to show you it's safe. I'll call you when it's time."

Big Ted slowly approached the opening once more, leaned over cautiously, and peered inside. "All right. All right, Captain. I'm in."

Spade scratched at his beard and nodded in agreement.

Cracker Jackson's heart was beating, his instincts screaming, this place reeked of a trap, he and the others flies to Broadford's spider. He wanted to grab Big Ted and Spade, tell them to turn around and get out before it was too late, but they seemed intent on forging onward, apparently unaware of the danger.

Broadford fitted the rope around his waist and his shoulders. A moment later, he disappeared into the chilling rush of mountain water.

Cracker felt his life had come to a crossroads, and he tried to formulate a warning. He felt as if he were watching someone he cared about mounting a wild stallion with flames shooting from its nostrils, his loved one smiling, careless of the danger.

Don't get on it. It's going to throw you, break your neck, can't you see?

But he realized in a startling instant that he didn't really care for anybody, didn't, in fact, have loved ones to warn.

Maybe he should have had children.

A sickly light wavered in the darkness below. Cracker swallowed his fear and, when it was his turn, braced himself against the lip of the abyss, took a deep breath, and plunged downwards through the wet, icy maw in the side of Mount Ulfur.

"MARSHAL DE MERLON!"

Nothing but an echo in the darkness.

"Marshal de Merlon!" Broadford shouted again. "He's got to be in here somewhere. Stay close to the light."

Just then, a scratching, scraping sound cut its way through the air. The sound reverberated down the hallway toward them, passed through each body and continued on, bouncing off ancient, cracked support columns.

"Oh shit, what was that?" Big Ted asked.

"Damn it, I don't know. Just shut up for a second."

Cracker, Spade, and Big Ted huddled closer to Broadford.

Footsteps padded through the darkness. A voice, old, as dry as the desert below, said, "What are you doing, Higgins? Are you trying to wake the dead?"

Broadford held the torch at arm's length, trying to peer into the darkness. "Jeremiah?"

The hunched figure of the ancient monk congealed in patches of solid gloom. "Who were you expecting? The Pope?"

"Where's the marshal?"

"He sent me to collect you." Jeremiah looked around the chamber, scanning above into the arching shadows. "For Christ's sake, keep your voice down, there's something in here we don't wish to disturb."

Big Ted's voice tightened in fear. "What? What's in here?"

"Follow. Keep quiet," the gnarled monk said.

Big Ted and Spade Johnson flicked concerned glances about themselves, sporadically looking upwards as if a giant bat were about to tear their scalps from their skulls. Cracker Jackson didn't look up. He was far more disquieted by the gnarled figure now acting as their guide. The sense of dread gripped him tighter, threatening to suffocate him. What was the hunched thing? Where the hell were they going? What had he gotten himself into?

He stayed close to Broadford, who stayed close to the twisted monk as they went down through secret counterweight doors hidden within alcoves, down through the bottom of the monastery, downwards on twisting steps carved into the inside of the mountain itself, allowing only one man at a time to delicately step a hair's breadth from a sheer fall into blackness.

Cracker looked behind him and upwards. He could make out the dim outline of the monastery nestled between two massive crags. Parts of the ancient structure seemed to float in the darkness within the mountain.

Eventually, they came to a large semi-circular platform lit by torches. Tristan Drogos de Merlon sat at an altar formed of basalt, on a simple chair formed of the same igneous rock. He wore no traveling cloak, no shirt, no shoes, only black leather trousers. Water fell somewhere in the emptiness, its rushing echo slapping around the cavern. It was warm in the belly of the churning, boiling giant.

Tristan stood and smiled, arms outstretched, a grinning crucified messiah-devil on an invisible cross. Cracker felt his bowels loosening.

"Welcome gentlemen," Tristan said. "Welcome my soldiers!" The man was beaming as if he'd just been brought the army of the Kingdom of Macedon rather than three tired and broken men. He gestured for Broadford to come forward.

The marshal seemed to possess no body fat, his extreme musculature like that of a skinned buck or an anatomist's model. He clasped Broadford in a powerful embrace. On his striated chest, Tristan Drogos de Merlon wore his crown-shaped amulet along with the key. Broadford stared at the trinket, eyes hungry.

"Here, my friend," de Merlon said. He removed the key from around his neck and slipped it over Broadford's head. The gentleman toff seemed to stand taller, his chest expanding right along with a smile across his face. De Merlon ran a sharpened finger down Broadford's nose. "I see your face is as beautiful as ever, Broadie."

Broadford nodded, his grin spreading.

Tristan turned his attention to the other men. "And who have you brought? Ah, Big Ted, Spade Johnson, and Cracker Jackson, the finest men I've had the honor to serve with. Welcome to Mount Ulfur, gentlemen!"

Cracker wanted to run, but something made him stay. He saw the marshal, or what had once been the marshal—now a macabre, animated corpse—nod to Jeremiah. From within his robes, the monk produced several items and handed them to Tristan, who in turn hung the objects, small necklaces made of a leather strap and glowing metal, around the necks of Spade and Big Ted.

Each amulet was amorphous, a sliver of the sky metal mixed with more base metals, each without recognizable shape.

Then it was Cracker's turn.

As the amulet was placed around his neck, Cracker's disgust at de Merlon's horrifying appearance faded, replaced by a glowing warmth in his blood, a sense of well-being, trust and loyalty, love and honor, all the finer emotions, all the nobler emotions, all the better things a man is capable of.

Spade Johnson and Big Ted were clearly sharing his feelings, judging by their grins.

Cracker smiled. Everything was going to be all right.

Tristan grabbed him by the shoulders and looked down into the man's frog-like eyes. "Can I trust you, Cracker?" the skeletal messiah asked.

"Aye, Marshal de Merlon. You can."

"Good man." He let go and moved to the basalt table. He opened a saddlebag and presented it to the gathered men. "How many soldiers do we have?"

The men stepped forward to look inside the bag. "Us four and eighty more down below," Broadford said.

Tristan nodded. "Good, that's a good start."

Within the bag, slivers and chunks of otherworldly metal winked and glinted, a leather strap tied through miniscule holes within each. "Here, Cracker. You and the others take the bag below, share them among the men. More are forthcoming, oh yes, more."

"Yes, sir," Cracker said.

"Broadford, stay a moment."

Broadford watched Cracker Jackson, Spade Johnson, and Big Ted follow the twisted Monk of Ulfur upwards through the darkness. Then he turned to the marshal.

"Eighty men, well done, Broadie." Tristan patted him on the arm.

Broadford was surprised by the enthusiastic response of the marshal. Eighty was less than he'd hoped for, and Tristan hadn't seen the rubbish quality of the men, yet. Still, with the trinkets, eighty might prove to be enough.

"I want to show you something."

Broadford followed de Merlon to the sheer rock wall at the back of the platform, and Tristan took a flaming torch from a sconce and held it up to the wall. "Look closely, Captain. What do you see?"

He peered closer, only observing the wavelike patterns in the gray rock, the occasional glittering of hidden insects within crevices. Then he saw it. A ripple of silver, or gold, now purple, thin veins of metal shooting through the rock, leaving trails like the tails of shooting stars in the midnight sky.

"It's embedded all through the mountain but almost impossible to access without teams of men and the most modern of digging tools. But that doesn't matter, we have enough now. Enough to move forward. Jeremiah and I have been busy in the forge, very busy."

Broadford couldn't take his eyes from the metal. It reminded him of blood splatter on the faces of the battlefield dead.

Tristan put his arm around him, leaning in. "I know what it is," he whispered.

Broadford didn't understand. "What it *is*?"

Tristan nodded. "It's *alive*." He exposed his sharpened teeth in a ghoulish smile. "It's not of this world. It bonds with the one who carries it, entering the host's blood."

"Like a parasite? Like a leech?"

"Parasites only take. This both gives *and* takes." Tristan held the torch closer to the veins of sky-metal ore. "It's a symbiote. A companion." He glanced at the key, the toff unaware. "Individual pieces of this creature will fight to survive, even against others of its kind. This is why they gift the bearer abilities. It's survival, not altruism, you see?"

The gentleman rake tried to comprehend. "What do they take in exchange for their gifts?"

Tristan laughed and moved away. "We leave the day after tomorrow. There's one more thing I must do before we claim Re'Shan and move north."

Broadford was still staring at the sky metal that had impacted with such force on Ulfur long ago, piercing the giant's side.

The metal was alive?

32

Bedside Manners

Rebecca Occitane wore a dirty white frock emblazoned with a red cross and carried a ceramic tray of fruits through the military hospital in Re'Shan. Brynhild, William, and Christopher had decided, after much debate and stabbing of fingers, that Rebecca had the best chance of getting to the prisoner unmolested while they waited outside in the shadows.

The hospital was a three-story structure, and the man she sought was under heavy guard on the top floor. Entering the city of Re'Shan had proven to be an easier exercise than reaching the prisoner. On every floor, she was stopped, searched, and questioned, but she maintained the same story: she had just been transferred in from Sil'Raka to the east, she was a trainee, she'd been told to deliver fruit to the prisoner's room, she had her duties to carry out as she was sure they had theirs. Commander Franks would be along any moment, and if they'd like to explain to the commander why the fruit had not been placed at the patient's bedside, then they were entirely welcome to explain that to him in person, but she wouldn't want to be in their shoes when they did.

The grim-faced men allowed her to pass. Fortunately, not one of the soldiers noticed the green tinge of the grapes and desert melon, marking them as unripe and practically inedible to anyone other than a camel.

She could see the early evening moon through the barred window of the prisoner's small room as she entered. The man lay asleep on his bed, and another figure sat at the patient-prisoner's bedside.

Rebecca had not expected someone to be sitting there. A concerned relative, perhaps? The figure was cloaked in a robe or traveling cloak, black or blue depending on how it moved in the moonlight, with the hood pulled over, the profile obscured. What should she do?

"He's sedated," the seated man said, for it was a man's voice, deep and melodic.

"I'm sorry. I didn't know there was anyone else in here."

"I'm not here," the man said. "Go about your business."

Rebecca looked around for a place to set the fruit. For want of a better location, she placed the tray at the foot of the sleeping man's bed. The prisoner was young, his blond hair matted in sweat. He didn't look like a madman.

"His name is Michael Alaine," the hooded figure said.

"Are you here to deliver last rites? Is he dying?"

"Despite his injuries, he is well, and I am no priest. As I said, he's simply sedated."

Rebecca stepped closer and looked down at Michael. "Why is he sedated?"

The hood turned in her direction, but she couldn't make out the man's features. "He is dangerous, or so they believe. They have smothered the poor boy in opium, bryony, and henbane, enough to kill any other man."

"Can he be woken?"

"I'm attempting to do so now, but that's our secret, don't tell the guards." The man added, "We both have secrets, yes?"

"Secrets?"

"Come now. You are no nurse."

Rebecca thought of denying the accusation but knew, somehow, that would be fruitless. She gazed upon Michael Alaine and took a chance. "They say he's a god among men. A man who can't die."

"I wouldn't go so far," the man said. "Certainly, he has abilities above those of most men, but he is yet mortal."

Rebecca looked closer at the sleeping Michael Alaine.

"They've taken it," the man said.

"Who are you?" she asked the hooded figure. "Why are you here?"

"I'll tell you my truth if you tell me yours." A smile flavored his voice.

The amulet on her skin shivered, sending sparks through her chest. *This man has answers*, it seemed to say. *This man can help you*, it whispered. She took a deep breath and exhaled. "I agree," she said.

"Splendid. I wish to wake Michael to discover who's taken his amulet, and I wish to return it to him."

"Why?"

"I'm not entirely selfless. I believe he can help me."

"How?"

"Dear girl, it's my turn."

"All right," she said.

"I'm afraid my questions are hardly original, for they closely resemble your own. Who are you? Why are you here?"

Rebecca took another deep inhalation, hesitated, and decided to risk everything. "It's possible this man knew my father. I want to know of my father's last days in Re'Shan. I seek to understand his death. And I want to know who the Hungry King is. I believe this man, Michael Alaine, as you have named him, can shed light on all these matters, and perhaps more."

The cloaked man remained motionless. After what seemed an age, he rose and walked to the barred window, gazing out at the silver half-moon in a zaffre sky. "You didn't tell me your name, my dear."

"Nor did you tell me yours."

Another pause, a decision made. "I am Tristan Drogos de Merlon."

Rebecca gasped. Christopher had mentioned this man at the Yellow Abbey, the name of a man supposedly dead. She stared at the back of the man's hood. "I am Rebecca Occitane. My father was Robert Occitane."

The obscured head turned slightly. "Robert is dead?"

"Yes. You knew my father?"

"I knew him." The man's voice changed, quivering with some emotion beyond Rebecca's understanding. "He was a good man. What happened to him?"

"King Bruwaert sent his men to kill him."

De Merlon lowered his hooded head to his chest. "For the amulet? For the book?"

"Yes."

He looked back up at the moon. "I was there with your father when he found them, the trinkets. Your father was my friend." The man's fists were curled into tight balls. "He was my friend, as far as any man has ever been a friend. I have so few, so few I can trust. Just one more thing they have taken from me."

"And this man? Michael Alaine?"

"He too was there. He knew your father. We are all bonded together, you see."

"You carry the sky metal? You have one of them?"

Tristan turned around and removed his hood. Rebecca caught her breath at his sunken, scarred face. He pulled out the crown-shaped amulet of glowing metal, holding it up to reflect the moonlight. "Bruwaert did this to me," he said, running his fingers down his pockmarked cheek. "And Tremain. The metal saved my life, but I lost my family. I've lost everything. They are to blame, the Lesser Kings." The charred skin on the man's face stretched in a grimace of rage.

"It's not fair," she said. "The injustice of it all is overwhelming."

His angry expression faded slowly, and he studied her as if finding his way on a map. He nodded and let the amulet fall beneath his cloak, obscured. "I feel your pain," he said, "and your anger. The anger I feel most of all."

"*You* are the Hungry King." Rebecca's amber eyes were as full as the hunter's moon.

The man did not reply. In a smoky whisper he said, "You carry your father's pendant. What is it you want, Rebecca Occitane?"

She put her hand to her chest. "Vengeance."

Tristan nodded again. He looked at Michael Alaine and said, "Bruwaert will pay for Robert's death, that I promise you. For their persecution of the bearers, they will *all* pay. For all the loved ones they took, they will pay. For every attempt on our lives they will pay."

Bloodlust boiled in Rebecca's stomach, rising through her chest, constricting her throat, forcing fumes into her skull. The metallic tang of gore coated her mouth. "What must I do?"

"Oh, it's quite simple. Merely open your heart, open the flood-gates of hatred within your breast. Can you do that?"

"Yes."

"Of course you can." He reached out. "Take my hand."

Rebecca hesitated, but only for a moment. She clasped his cold clawed fingers. He had answers, this man had all the answers. This man understood. This man would be the vehicle through which she would gut the fat king.

Tristan smiled down at her, and she no longer found his visage repulsive. She saw the fully fleshed man he had once been, a father and a husband. She saw all the potential within his soul. She saw the goodness in him.

He stepped closer to her, taking her other hand. "I came seek-ing an old friend, and now, I've found a new one. Come, Rebecca. Honest, wholesome retribution awaits. In the name of your father, Robert Occitane."

33

The Silent Knight Awakens

Michael Alaine awoke to see a lonely cloud gently drifting through an azure sky. For a moment he thought he was back in Shae, lying in the town square, the fountain bubbling nearby, the dead and dying bleeding and burning in the sun.

Where was Amal? She was supposed to be here . . . to save him like she always did. Where was she? And the thing, the thing around his neck. What was it? An amulet in the shape of . . .

A hand? Yes, it was a hand.

So tired.

"Wake up, Michael. You have to wake up."

A man's voice. Not one he recognized. No, wait, he did recognize it. He did, but he couldn't place it.

"Michael. Where's Rebecca? Where's Rebecca Occitane?"

Occitane? Michael rolled over and tried to pull the coverlet over his shoulders. Was the war still on? Was he still in Prometheus Company? No, that didn't make any sense. The war was over. Where was the coverlet? He reached for it only to find it absent. With a start, he realized he was lying on grass.

He sat up and the world spun. A tall, pale woman with her hair tied back from her scalp looked down at him. Her visage revolved across the horizon and back. Gods, she was taller than the mountain. What was its name? Ulfur? Who was this mountain-sized woman?

He remembered something. He was in Re'Shan. Archibald Kirk. They had fought. Kirk was dead. Amal was taken by that bastard Jasper.

He squeezed his eyes shut and breathed hard. He staggered to his feet and swayed, before strong hands gripped him by his shoulders and arms, steadying him.

"Michael. It's me, Christopher Lewis. Do you remember me?"

Michael stood taller, brushing the hands away. He squinted at the man. Lewis? He was well known in Re'Shan, the man with the short white hair and the black eyes. The assassin. Bruwaert's man. Why was *he* here? "I remember you. Where's Amal?"

"My name is Brynhild Grimsdotter," the tall woman said. "We seek a young woman of fifteen. Her name is Rebecca Occitane. I'm given to understand you knew her father, Robert."

Michael rubbed his hands over his face. "Commander Occitane? Yes, I knew him. But where's Amal?" He looked around. They stood on short well-tended grass. Flowers grew nearby. A park of some kind.

A gaunt-faced monk stepped forward. No, not a monk, one of the yellow scholars. The assassin was wearing the same color robes.

The scholar, the real one, not the assassin, spoke in a concerned tone. "I apologize, young man, but we don't know about Amal. Please, do you recall Rebecca coming to see you? Light brown hair, bright amber eyes."

Amber eyes? Like her father, then. Michael struggled to stitch together a coherent narrative. Nothing made sense. Who were these people? He felt for his trinket, and then he remembered the prick Jasper had it.

"Your amulet's gone," Christopher Lewis said. "I have many questions, but events have accelerated. We need to get out of here."

For the first time, Michael became aware of shouting, saw men running, heard a horn blaring somewhere, a call to arms.

"What's happening?" he asked.

"Re'Shan is under attack. The Hungry King has returned."

RE'SHAN WAS INDEED UNDER ATTACK. Men from both Bruwaert's and Tremain's forces scattered in all directions, many of them pointing to the mountain from whence smoke rose in wisps. Battle was raging on the mountainside.

Ulfur spewed forth insurrection, a deluge of rebellion appearing from nowhere, like rainwater gushing and gathering strength as it descended to be met by another surge of soldiers at the foot of the mountain, and like two tributaries crashing together, a more powerful force smashed in waves upon the dam that was the city gates.

Men were shouting, children were screaming. No one here had forgotten the Great War, and none had thought to see its return so soon. Horror, fear, and panic swept through the streets.

Michael Alaine had been ignored by the guards in the mad scramble to arms, which allowed Brynhild and Christopher to carry him unmolested from the hospital and lay him on the manicured lawn of the public gardens.

Now, the group followed Christopher as he hurried through the streets toward the city gates. "Tremain's forces in the Freelands are gathering to the north," he said. "Apollo Company. But they'll get here too late. We must ride to reach them before the main tide of war. They must be alerted."

"We can't leave without Rebecca," Brynhild said.

Christopher stopped. "I'm sorry, but I don't have time for a search."

William almost jumped on the knight-captain. "We're not leaving without her!"

"Very well. You two stay. Michael will come with me."

"I'm not going anywhere without Amal."

Christopher sighed, his frustration evident. He looked at Michael. "Who's the Hungry King? Who are we dealing with?"

"What are you talking about? The Hungry King is dead."

A group of men suddenly appeared from a side alley. Christopher instantly drew his twin short-swords from beneath his yellow robes and spaced his feet slightly wider than his shoulders, ready for battle, but the men merely sprinted past them toward the city gates.

Christopher secreted the blades away in the wink of an eye. His attention returned to Michael. "Listen carefully. One of the men that entered the monastery on Mount Ulfur a year ago, one of the original bearers of the trinkets found therein, has returned. He's using the sky metal to build an army. It has begun. You know who this man is."

"Why would any man wish to do such a thing?"

Christopher shrugged out of the yellow robes, revealing a set of gray leather armor beneath. "The why does not matter. I spoke to Seraphim. He was also there. He hinted at the identity of this man, but the prick escaped before I could gain more information." He cast aside the butter-colored robes.

"No one named Seraphim was there that day."

"You would know him as Archibald Kirk."

Realization froze Michael's blood, stunned him. The growing dread within his breast, the creeping fear that he had opened a tomb of horrors never to be closed, crushed down on him like Ulfur falling on his head. He looked up at the mountain, the smoke of battle curling into the sky. "It's my fault," he whispered. "I showed them the way. *I* was the one that found the monastery. You say one of them, one of *us*, brings war to White Cloud again?"

"That's exactly what I'm saying. You must tell me who it is."

"I don't know. How could I?"

"Who was there with you? Tell me!"

Michael bowed his head, thinking. "Commander Robert Occitane."

"Dead."

The young soldier digested the news, shaking his head in disbelief. "Archibald of course, but he's dead. I killed him."

It was now the assassin's turn to show surprise. "All right. Go on."

"Marshal de Merlon."

"Also dead," Christopher said. His voice colored with irritation gave way to one laced with growing panic. "If everyone's dead, who's leading the army that attacks Re'Shan as we speak?"

Michael shrugged and turned up his palms. "I don't know. The only other two were Malcolm Dewar and Broadford Higgins."

"I'm familiar with both men. One a drunk and a womanizer, the other a fop, drunk, and womanizer. Neither seem the type to lead men anywhere other than a whorehouse."

"That's all. Those were the men." He felt an ache in his head. "How did Commander Occitane and Marshal de Merlon die?"

The siren call was increasing in pitch, in desperation, and steel clashed from somewhere up ahead. The assassin ran his hands through his hair and sank to his haunches. "It doesn't matter. I'm too late. All is lost. I have failed my king."

"Are you sure they're both dead?" Michael asked.

Brynhild spoke up. "I saw Robert Occitane's corpse. He's dead."

"And de Merlon?"

Everyone looked at Christopher, who stood once more and sighed in exasperation. "King Bruwaert believes he fell victim to the plague. I have no reason to doubt him."

"Marshal de Merlon isn't dead." All eyes turned now to Michael, who went on, "I . . . I think I heard him."

"What? When?" Christopher moved closer to the young knight.

Michael hesitated, his eyes losing focus, as if trying to pin down a memory. "Last night, I think. He was in my room in the hospital."

Stunned silence blanketed the group. "Dear God," William whispered.

"And now I recall another voice." Michael glanced around at the horrified faces staring back at him.

"No, no, no." The monk shook his head.

"A girl." The memory of the voices solidified in his waking brain. "Yes. They spoke together."

William put his hands to his face, sinking to his knees. "He's taken her! The Hungry King has taken Rebecca!"

34

Forgiveness

Running footsteps echoed down the hallway, and Amal Muna peered out of her cell. The small bony soldier called Royce stood there, chewing at his bottom lip with his overbite, a concerned look on his long rattish face.

She sensed something was terribly wrong. Something other than losing her family to violence, other than losing the one man who had offered her hope, other than being imprisoned for witchcraft, other than having to listen to the guards whisper between the bars with gap-toothed, foul-smelling smiles that she would be hanged soon, oh so very soon. Or drowned. Hanged and drowned, drowned and hanged, in which order they hadn't decided yet.

Yes, other than all that, something was terribly wrong.

The horn of alarm sounded. Metal clinked on metal, hastily grabbed weapons clattered from racks and whispered into sheaths, and leather-shod footsteps pounded on stone. Then there was nothing except the lone horn sounding in the distance.

Royce jerked his head left and right, sniffing the air like a whiskered rodent. After a few minutes, the taller soldier with the sharpened mustache came into the hallway and whispered in Royce's twitching ear. The small man nodded and left.

The mustachioed captain approached Amal's cell and pressed his narrow head through the gray iron bars, the tips of his wide black mustache, momentarily held back by the metal grille, springing forward a few seconds later to join the rest of his lean, cruel face within the cell.

"You have beautiful skin," Captain Felix Jasper said. "Can you understand me, witch? I speak so little of the desert language. Do you understand?"

Amal drew her knees up under her chin. Her long cotton dress of green was soiled where men had thrown ale at her, and her long black hair flowed freely around her shoulders, her hijab having been confiscated, grown men having wrapped it around their heads and paraded before her like children.

"I love the desert people. The girls are clean. Your people are savages, but you keep your bodies clean. I like that."

Amal could make out only too well what the mustachioed man was saying, his message an echo of what the other man had said, the one with the tattoo, the man now dead. Why did they obsess over her skin?

Jasper took out a key and held it up to his face, smiling and winking. "It looks like we're under siege. Who knows? I might end up dead before dusk. It's going to be a busy day, but I think I have a moment to spare for you, beautiful witch of the desert."

He opened the cell door, and Amal looked for a place to hide. Perhaps she had overlooked a hidden nook in the small room.

She hadn't.

He moved inside, twisting the ends of his mustache into sharp points. "You can't save him, you can't save Alaine. You're always hanging around the man, but you can't save him. Poor little brown desert girl, you can't even save yourself, forget about saving the world." The man's face grew ugly with desire. "Did you fuck Alaine? Did you bewitch him? Is that where he got his freakish powers from? Do it to me. Give me your gifts." He reached for his belt buckle and dropped his trousers.

Amal closed her eyes. She had avoided death long enough. It was time. She opened her eyes.

Jasper lapped at his mustache with his tongue. "Succubus. Yes, Succubus of the Great Southern Sands. I give myself to you." He removed his shirt; his chest was bare.

Hadn't he had the amulet?

Suddenly, the rat-soldier, Royce, came flying through the air and hit the straw-covered cell floor, his face a bloodied map of bruises and swelling.

Michael Alaine stood there. She smiled at the sight of him, and Jasper jerked around in panic, his trousers still around his ankles.

The knight was not alone.

Beside him, a tall blonde female wielded a lethal-looking curved blade; a man in gray leather armor, with black eyes like a starless sky, gripped twin short swords in hand; and a thin man clothed in yellow robes, clutched daggers, fierce determination on his lean face.

This was a band of heroes, Amal thought. Heroes, if ever she had seen them.

Royce crawled backward into a corner.

Jasper looked down at his thin hairless legs, and his knees started to tremble. He looked back at Michael, who had cold hatred written all over his youthful face. Jasper attempted to pull his trousers up, but the young knight shook his head, and the captain let his breeches fall around his ankles once again.

Michael pushed Jasper to his knees and helped Amal to her feet.

He put a knife in her hands, kissed her on the forehead, then stepped back. Captain Jasper had pissed all over himself and the cell floor.

Amal held the knife in confusion.

Then she understood.

She stared at Felix Jasper and then at the battered Royce cowering in the filthy corner. Had there been a mouse hole to crawl in, the rat-man would have squeezed himself through it.

"After everything these men have done, you would be justified in cutting their throats," Michael whispered.

Amal's thoughts returned to Shae, to her family. Nobody could deny that she deserved retribution. She knew Michael wouldn't think any less of her.

She had failed her family, but she could even the scales, if only slightly, here and now.

"Mother said when death comes, we all learn to forgive. The trick is to get forgiveness in first." She returned the knife to the young knight. "My life has meaning. I've been chosen for a reason but not this." she said. "Not this."

Michael remained silent, nodded and took her hand. As he was leading her from the cell, she stopped and leaned over to look Jasper in the eyes. With a clear space between each word, she pointed at herself and then at Jasper, and said, "I save you."

Felix Jasper blubbered his thanks but stopped when Christopher Lewis entered the holding cell. A brief interview played out between the two men, the interview consisting of the gray assassin's knife pressing against the throat of the trouserless kneeling captain, and one whispered question.

"Where are the amulets?"

Jasper stammered that the hand pendant had been stolen from his very person while sleeping, and the other, the phallus, taken from a heavily guarded Commander Franks's office. Not a trace of either. Who could have done such a thing was a mystery to one and all.

Christopher Lewis knew all too well who could have achieved such a feat. He had a name now.

Tristan Drogos de Merlon.

Then the band of heroes disappeared, leaving Jasper kneeling in his own piss.

35

The Metal Army

Broadford Higgins couldn't believe his eyes when two hundred men came down the mountain under the banner of Tristan Drogos de Merlon, a banner proclaiming a red mountain on a white background, Mount Ulfur imposed upon the Heavens. Broadford and his men hoisted their own banner of the same imagery at the sight of the newcomers. He could make out the hammer and forge insignia of Vulcan Company on the surcoats of many of the approaching men.

Bruwaert's once-loyal soldiers now riding under de Merlon's banner? How had he done it? How had he turned them? And how was Broadford to explain this to his men? All notion of sides had just been swept away. Who was on whose side? Who was the enemy?

Broadford looked behind him. Cracker Jackson, Spade Johnson, and Big Ted were waiting on their horses under the silver birch trees, and beyond them, his men, or more accurately, de Merlon's men. They had numbered eighty when they arrived in Re'Shan, but in a little over a day and a half, those numbers doubled as word of the metal spread. Soldiers had handed out the shapeless metal necklaces, and tired old men cracked their backs and stood upright. Men with grievous war wounds to knees and other joints climbed trees and played with each other like children. The sick recovered their health, the old became young again, the weak became strong, lives with no promise or hope became full of promise once more. Each man was as strong as a stallion and ready to fight.

"Broadford Higgins!" a man shouted, riding at the head of the battalion coming down the mountain. The man was middle aged, bloated at the belly, a slug-like nose on a square head. He pulled up and saluted, fist on chest.

"I am Higgins," Broadford said. "*Marshal* Broadford Higgins." The gentleman toff laughed inwardly with pleasure at the sound of his new title. Yes, it sounded right. *Marshal Higgins.* "Who are you?"

The slug nose spoke. "I am Commander Roger Forbury of Vulcan Company."

Broadford eyed the man suspiciously. "Vulcan Company serves Bruwaert."

"No longer," Forbury said. "King de Merlon now commands us."

Heat radiated beneath Broadford's shirt, the key at his chest warming his skin. He wondered . . . On an impulse, he pulled out the key-shaped trinket, which at first Forbury merely looked at, his square face impassive. Broadford continued to hold the key in the early morning air between them, saying nothing, egging the man on silently.

Dead light traveled millions of leagues through the universe before Forbury reached beneath his own shirt and revealed the small, lovingly carved phallus.

A myriad number of potential narratives ran through Broadford's head, all of them ending with one undeniable outcome. Archibald Kirk was dead. Evidently, Tristan Drogos De Merlon was proving very adept at shuffling around trinkets, stroking egos, making promises, and generally manipulating his constituents. It was clever, but Broadford saw through it all. Whatever promises de Merlon had made, Forbury could forget about them. He was already a dead man.

Broadford smiled, put away his trinket, adjusted his top hat and said, "Brother, welcome to the holy cause."

"All wrongs will be righted," Forbury said, putting away his cock and saluting again.

Lard-arsed fool.

Broadford returned the salute, trying not to laugh in the man's face. "All wrongs," he said and turned to look at the city gates. "With our combined forces, we have approximately three hundred and fifty men, each one the equal of five within the city walls. That makes the numbers about even. We have to get inside, and soon. We need food. We can't afford another six-month siege."

The block-headed commander revealed a haughty, irritating smile. "Do not fear Higgins, the master has men on the inside. The doors will open for us before midday."

Broadford was disturbed by two things. First, Forbury was now referring to de Merlon as *master*, which didn't bother him nearly so much as the second thing, the fact that he hadn't been made privy to the information of the city gates opening before noon.

Playing favorites, master? That won't do.

"Excellent." Broadford smiled confidently. "If you'll excuse me, I'll inform my men."

Forbury sniffed and looked down his nose at Broadford. "Battle commences shortly, Higgins. Be ready."

Broadford would kill the slug himself, trinket or no. He was marshal here. De Merlon had given that title to him. Broadford turned his horse and trotted up to his three Brittsdale Generals.

"What's happening, sir?" Cracker Jackson asked.

"De Merlon has been busy. We now fight with Vulcan Company."

Cracker screwed his face in disbelief. "But that's Bruwaert's lot, sir."

Broadford put a beatific smile on his face. "They've seen the wisdom of the crusade and turned against their king to join us. It's a righteous choice they must be applauded for."

"Can we trust them?" Spade scratched at his award-winning beard.

The truth was, he didn't trust anyone. This whole war was a farce, but he couldn't get out now, even if he wanted to. The metal around his neck was speaking to him, whispering. It said, *when this is all over, you'll find a quiet corner of the country, a good tavern, and you'll drink and fuck until the Heralds signal the End. But for now, you have to do this, for us. Just get through this, and we can run away.*

Broadford looked at his broken-down generals and beamed. "Yes, we can trust them. They wear the metal, like you. What's not to trust?"

———

SURE ENOUGH, BEFORE MIDDAY, soldiers loyal to Bruwaert and Tremain were savagely murdered within the city, and the gates opened. Several darkly garbed hooded figures walked the streets of Re'Shan at the forefront of the invasion, throwing out necklaces and pendants, brooches and bracelets from buckets, like flowers on Rosalia, infecting the city. "Put them on," the dark figures called. "Put them on."

"Put them on or die."

Many soldiers loyal to the Alliance fell. Some put on the trinkets in desperation and felt the surge of power that came along with them. Many of the new bearers felt so alive, so real and enriched, that they weren't prepared to die, seeing that life was beautiful and precious under any reign. They instantly changed allegiances and fought for de Merlon under the banner of the red mountain of Ulfur.

Others, a much lower number, wore the trinkets and fought for the Alliance anyway, using their new found strength to stave off the horde surging through the streets. These were the men who believed in loyalty and honor. But these men, for all their strength, were overwhelmed by sheer numbers.

A few threw the trinkets away from themselves, unwilling to accept the bargain, unwilling to sacrifice a part of their souls for power in the here and now.

Better to die clean, they thought.

And so, they died clean, and the trinkets they had cast aside found their way to new hands and hearts, gifting power and taking humanity as they went.

36

Restarting the Forge of Vengeance

Jeremiah walked the precarious steps within the walls of the ancient monastery of the Monks of Ulfur. The cavern was pitch black, and one false step would send his hunched form plummeting to its destruction, dashed on the bludgeoning rocks far below in the innards of Mount Ulfur, the belly of the beast.

He thought about stepping into one of the many death traps in the floor.

But he didn't.

Jeremiah's sunken yellow eyes pierced the blackness with ease for he had spent years in this darkness; it was the sun he couldn't stand, and the dry heat. Give him the dank pits and the moist stone walls and rocks of the depths. Give him the inside of Ulfur, and you could take the open air, the skies, and the desert. The hollowed places of the world, yes, that was his cradle and would be his coffin—probably before long, the way things were going.

Jeremiah screamed furiously into nothingness. Not even an echo deigned to respond. Tristan Drogos de Merlon had broken his promise. His word, the man had given his word—a word now shattered, twisted, and deformed, much like himself, like them both.

The metal for the innocence. That had been the arrangement.

True, the marshal had allowed Jeremiah several opportunities to . . . satiate his needs, his desires, on the journey to Ulfur. But it was hardly a fair exchange after risking his very life crossing what had seemed like the entirety of White Cloud with all its pitchfork and torch-wielding village idiots. Jeremiah had taken him to the deep places within the mountain. He had shown de Merlon the metal, the very source, in fact. The motherlode.

And how had the master thanked him? Forced him down on his knees, forced him down to scrape the glowing metal from the rocks, forced him to restart the ancient forge, forced him to make trinkets, but not *too* powerful, oh, not too powerful. Combined with pig iron, the trinkets would be one-tenth, only one-tenth the potency of the originals. Those were the instructions. De Merlon would not share power so freely.

Tristan had stood there, looking down at the metal embedded in the shining floor; the metal *was* the floor, it was so abundant. His skeletal, sunken face gawked like a schoolboy at his first pair of tits. There was enough there to make him a god.

"I need five thousand within a week," the Hungry King said in the forge room deep within Mount Ulfur. The cold oven, the hammers, the tongs, and anvils were coated in a century of metal dust.

Jeremiah stared at Tristan as if he were mad, which he most likely was. "That's impossible. At best, I could forge a hundred a day, but they'd be shapeless, lacking in any art whatsoever."

"You need not concern yourself with the art of it. I want industrial production."

"We don't have enough hands."

But he was wrong.

Tristan Drogos de Merlon fully intended on getting his own hands dirty.

And so, they both worked tirelessly, without sleep for days. The waterwheel-powered blast furnace, so long dormant, turned and hissed once again.

De Merlon accelerated the manufacturing process by sheer force of will. His output astonished the twisted Monk of Ulfur. The tall man worked like the Devil. Within days, shapeless shards of worthless pig iron imbued with sky metal piled up in mounds on the floor of the forge room. The monk was exhausted, but the crazed marshal wouldn't stop, nor could he.

But for all Jeremiah's sweat and toil, his loyalty, what was his reward? He would be her attendant. Her *attendant*? Cruel. Like putting a feast in front of a starving man and telling him he couldn't eat. Not even a grape. He had done it to spite him, to keep him under the thumb. It was manifestly unreasonable.

Don't touch Rebecca Occitane? He thought it might have been a joke. And don't frighten her? That was the salt in the wound. How could he not frighten her? He was well aware of his physical appearance; he couldn't help but send the hounds of hell yelping with their tails between their legs.

Preposterous! Jeremiah was inclined to suckle on the girl just to return the ungracious favor. He was to nursemaid a young woman? He had nothing personal against the girl, but de Merlon was insane if he thought he could control himself. It didn't make any sense. Why put a wolf in charge of a lamb?

Silently fuming, Jeremiah followed the steps as they wound downwards, curving back on themselves. Suddenly, his ears picked up a sound from above, something flapping about in the darkness of the long-abandoned priory. He could see the outline of a distant shape, could make out its wings. It looked like a bat, perched on a ledge somewhere above.

Jeremiah hesitated, then decided to reach out with his mind. He found the thing and inserted smoke-like tendrils of his own consciousness into the creature, probing for a recognizable thought.

He found one.

Startled, the ancient monk broke off his inquest and quickly withdrew his thoughts. The creature was no bat. A moment later, he felt the thing return the examination, the being's mind searching for his, waves of thought coming in pulses.

You are come home, the winged thing said within Jeremiah's very mind.

Who are you? Jeremiah thought in return.

You are not know me?

His heart sank. You were once a Monk of Ulfur?

I am still, Brother.

Jeremiah shivered. What's your name?

I was Hosea.

He remembered the name. Hosea. He had been one of the more recent acolytes, among the last batch of initiates entering the monastery all those years ago, before everything had descended into horror.

Unbidden recollections assaulted Jeremiah: fragments of hungry faces, naked male bodies, young and old, squirming among each other, tongues lapping sweat and other juices from taut, loose skin, smiles turning to manic grins, biting, blood, screaming in the darkness.

He shook his head. The young man he remembered bore no resemblance to the winged creature above. While it was true that Jeremiah had also changed, and not for the better, this thing that perched above him, *this* was something other altogether. *This* was the result of never having left the mountain.

Are there others? Jeremiah said in his mind.

Yes, deeper. I am do not go there. They are changed.

Changed? In what way?

Changed. They are no longer human, like us. Do not go there.

Jeremiah felt ill. This thing claimed to be human, yet it flew on bat-like wings. What lurked deeper? What could be less human than this?

You bring danger, Hosea said.

Danger? What danger?

The man whom you are come with.

Jeremiah nodded. I'm aware of that.

And she.

Who?

The girl who is come.

The thing flew away into the shadows. Wait, Jeremiah thought, but the thing that had once been Hosea, acolyte of the Order of Ulfur, was gone.

A SINGLE CANDLE BURNED in the large anchorite cell. Only one of the rusting beds was possessed of an occupant. The fumes from the candle curled up and were sucked from the room by a vacuum somewhere above. Rebecca Occitane looked like a child as she slept. She was fifteen years of age. Was that even considered a child these days? Jeremiah wasn't sure. Girls of the same age had married and borne children, had become Queens and ruled over the lives of thousands of people.

Well, he didn't know what she was.

How does he wake a girl of fifteen? How does one wake a wife, mother, or queen? Weren't they all the same?

Jeremiah was old, having lived through dynasties, through scientific advancements unimagined at the beginning of his lifetime. He had seen the birth of wonders such as gunpowder, vertical windmills, and mechanical clocks. One might think he had accrued some wisdom in that time, but when it came to females, he knew as little now about women as he did when King Groubert had been Lord of the Freelands over a century ago.

No, he hadn't the least idea how to wake a slumbering woman-child. So, for want of a more imaginative idea, he kicked her.

She sprang up with a knife in her hand and a feral snarl on her face, faster than Jeremiah could fart. The old monk's eyes widened. Perhaps Hosea was right. Suddenly, Jeremiah had the sensation that he was less a nursemaid than he was a whetstone for a freshly forged blade.

"Who are you?" Rebecca asked.

Hands raised. "I am Jeremiah, I'm to be your . . . I'm to assist you in . . . I am your guide."

"Jeremiah? Tristan told me about you. He told me you were disfigured."

"Well, yes. I am."

"It's dark. I can't really make you out."

"Well, don't be in any rush to do so. I am, in fact, hideous."

The girl rubbed one eye with the back of her fist. "My name is Rebecca Occitane."

The Monk of Ulfur noted that although the introductions had been made, she hadn't lowered her knife. Apparently, she didn't trust him. The feeling was mutual.

"Where are we?" she asked.

"High on Ulfur, though it may not seem so. You had quite the climb yesterday. I'm not surprised you've been sleeping like a baby." He attempted a smile, but his face resisted. "Come," Jeremiah said. "Re'Shan has fallen, again. We ride for Otago and King Bruwaert."

"My friends? Are my friends all right? They mustn't be harmed."

He picked up the candle, which had almost melted down into its small silver tray. "There's a war on, in case you hadn't noticed. People get hurt."

"Not my friends. They are left out of this."

"You should have thought of that before you decided to take sides with a bloodthirsty—" Jeremiah stopped. He wasn't sure what he was supposed to be doing for this girl, but he was sure it wasn't bad-mouthing the master. "In any event, if it's revenge you seek, and it seems everyone and their camel seeks revenge these days, we must leave, now."

"I don't remember getting here."

"Come, come," Jeremiah said. "Retribution awaits. Justice and vengeance await, and all of those other frilly things girls like."

Rebecca finally put her knife away. She looked around and, finding nothing of personal value, moved to join the twisted monk with hair sprouting from his ears.

Together, they left the long-abandoned sleeping quarters of the Monks of Ulfur and ascended to the world outside. He listened for the flapping of wings but heard nothing.

Jeremiah held Rebecca's hand to guide her through the darkness, but he had the clear impression that she didn't need his assistance; her steps were confident and steady on the lethal walkway. He tried to imagine what particular skills the pendant at her neck gifted the young girl. Night vision seemed to be among them.

He felt the warmth of her fingers and wondered just how long it had been since he'd touched one so young and not allowed his darker instincts to reign. He tried to ignore the feelings of hunger that continually repulsed him, tried to repress them. He must not anger the master. He must hold out.

"Is vengeance such a bad thing?" Rebecca asked as they climbed the stone steps in the gloom.

Jeremiah raised his wispy eyebrows in surprise. "I've never had need for it, personally. I couldn't say." They puffed on in silence, and then he said, "Killed your father, did he? Bruwaert?"

"He'd never dare attempt so in person. The coward sent men, many men to kill him."

"Mmm. That is a tragedy. However, war is a—"

"It wasn't war. The war was over."

"The war is never over. It's simply on hiatus. The Sumerians still fight the Elamites, only the names and places have changed."

They ascended through the collapsed monastery of the Ulfur Monks, upwards to the steps leading to the outside world. Smoke was rising in patches from the city of Re'Shan far below.

Rebecca sighed.

Was she about to balk and change her mind? He'd have to hurt her if she tried to run.

"When do we get to Otago? When can we assail the Castle Key?" she asked.

The girl's eyes in the clear light of morning were luminous amber, and for a moment, Jeremiah thought they were carved from the sky metal. "The Castle Key is not easily assailed. Patience. Patience."

"It has to be soon," she said. "I've waited long enough. I *will* have my revenge."

As she angrily stalked off down the mountain path, an uneasy feeling crept up Jeremiah's spine, the uneasy feeling that he may now have two masters, both blinded by the lust for retribution. He scuttled after Rebecca and tried to keep up.

37

The Soul of a Trinket

Commander Roger Forbury was forty-five years old, liked a drink, liked his food, and he'd recently taken up smoking cannabis imported from the groves on the outskirts of Sil'Raka. He would smoke the drug in the calabash water pipes and terra cotta bowls of the desert people. While he hadn't taken to all aspects of the desert dwellers' culture, they made a good pipe, that couldn't be denied.

As a result of his predispositions, the commander of Vulcan Company was understandably out of shape, his waistline and head growing blockier by the day, his lung capacity shrinking in equal amounts. Climbing Mount Ulfur every third day had been a nightmare. If they'd just stationed him on the mountainside, that would have been satisfactory, but no. Reports. He had to come down to give King Bruwaert's advisors their accursed reports, always the same report: *there was no sign of any monastery on the mountainside.*

He could have sent a lackey, a subordinate officer, but they insisted he do it personally. Bastards. And so, he was sent back up and came back down to report the latest findings in the fruitless search. Up and down, up and down.

It was a tumultuous two weeks, no doubt. First, men from Vulcan Company started to disappear, perhaps deserting, or falling to their deaths somewhere. Nobody knew. Then stories came up the mountain of a battle between two inhumanly powerful men in a whorehouse in the city, each a bearer of a strange, glowing talisman.

So, as it eventuated, the trinkets proved no myth; therefore, the monastery must also be within the realms of reality. The orders came up, heavier than usual in their wording. *No more failures. Find it or be demoted, or worse. You have one week*, they said. *Bruwaert is watching*, they said.

Then the Hungry King paid Forbury a visit.

The commander had been preparing a report in his tent halfway up Mount Ulfur, a single candle the only light. It was quiet, like most evenings, the constant buzzing of mosquitoes and other clamorous insects in the desert city far below absent on the mountainside, only the whisper of the wind in the sycamore trees and junipers. Every man had been accounted for, which marked the first time in three days that a man, or men, had not vanished. He was alone with his ink, quill, and papers, a one-man guard stationed outside.

At first Forbury thought the guard had come in to ask a question. He couldn't understand why the man was just standing there.

"Speak up, lad," the commander said without looking up.

The man said nothing, so Forbury raised his head, an angry question about to fly from his lips. Tristan Drogos de Merlon stood there looming over him, staring down with that horrid face, burning eyes set in a cadaverous skull. Forbury tried to scream, but he couldn't force the air from his lungs; he *had* no air in his lungs. He felt like a weight was crushing down on his chest. If only he could squeeze out a single word, a whine, anything. He had to alert somebody.

But he was powerless.

De Merlon smiled a ghastly, hellish grin. The man had pointed fangs like the baiting dogs bred for fighting bears or bulls. Forbury tried to stand, but the tall skeletal figure waved him back into his seat, almost kindly. *Don't bother yourself*, he seemed to say. Forbury sat. He had no choice.

The tall man leisurely flipped through the reports on the commander's desk, scanning papers, nodding to himself. Then, with sunken, piercing eyes, he looked at Forbury once more, and curled a sharpened fingernail. "Follow me," he said.

Forbury, in a dreamlike trance, rose from his desk and followed the man. The guard had disappeared from outside the tent. De

Merlon glided through the soft-barked sycamore fig trees, the fluted trunks glowing dark yellow in the moonlight. They climbed the mountain, on several occasions de Merlon turning and waiting for Forbury, who was more than ever painfully aware of his stumpy legs and bloated midriff. They came to a clearing, and there in a circle sat the disappeared, the thirty men Forbury had officially reported as missing in action over the last two weeks.

De Merlon stood in the middle of the circle and turned to Forbury. The tall man shrugged his traveling cloak from his shoulders and stood naked among the junipers, his skin drawn tight over muscled skelature, three amulets resting on his vascular chest, each glowing, the trinkets among the circle of men responding.

The men had turned, had gone over to Tristan Drogos de Merlon, his to command now. The strange, skeletal man had found the metal within the mountain. It was too late.

Forbury must go over to de Merlon's command, too. But would he turn? Would he resist? Would he stay loyal to Bruwaert?

He couldn't help but stare at de Merlon's nude body pulsating with strength, health, power, despite the drawn skin, ruined face. He'd never seen anything like it. The man was a furnace; Forbury could feel the heat radiating from him over five yards away.

De Merlon looked up, raising his arms to the night sky with its peppering of stars. His body began to burn, flames licking his fingers, around his abdomen, his penis aflame. Forbury couldn't look away. He wanted to scream, *the Devil is among us!* He sank to his knees and cried.

A swirling haze of fluid-like flame encased the form of de Merlon, his body now entombed in a womb of fire. The tall man touched the head of the soldier seated nearest him.

Flinching, the beginnings of a scream on his lips, the young soldier found his own body surrounded by a ghostly licking flame. He marveled at the conflagration that swirled about his clothes and flesh, a smile spreading across his face as he realized that this heat healed but would not harm. He touched the man seated next to him, passing the flame along to his comrade, and as each man caught fire, the stars above brightened, the Southern Cross aflame as the men in the circle were aflame.

Roger Forbury was not aware of the blazing asterism in the endless night sky; he was only aware of his body, now on fire. The potency of a deity surged within him.

Then it ended, the fire snuffed out. The cool mountainside winds bathed the circle of men once more.

The flames on de Merlon's body subsided more slowly, dying, extinguishing. Tristan removed one of the trinkets from his neck and walked toward a kneeling Forbury, holding it out. He said, "You are with me now. All wrongs done to you shall be righted. You must convince every man on this mountain. We kill the Lesser Kings."

Forbury nodded. Better to live enslaved than die free, he thought. At least there'd be no more climbing the accursed mountain.

He took the pendant, a small, finely carved penis, and put it around his neck. With it came a rush of power, energy; he instantly felt like a virile buck leaping through an ancient green forest.

So now, Forbury rode on his gray mare just behind the master, a position of great honor, as de Merlon led his army north to Otago, toward Castle Key and the first of the Lesser Kings, King Bruwaert. But alongside him was that prat, Higgins, in his outlandish top hat, jockeying for the best seat at the master's table, trying to get ahead. The commander made sure to keep the nose of his horse in front of that of the fop's. *He* was the king's second in command. That was the agreement, the promise when de Merlon came to him like a ghost in a child's nightmare made corporeal.

Behind him rode men once loyal to the Lesser Kings. A mismatched army, true, sewed together like a court jester's garish outfit, but the needlework was of a fine quality—stitched with sky metal. The seams would not split or disintegrate easily. This army was a stronger union than the Alliance had ever been.

Forbury watched De Merlon riding his black stallion at the head of five thousand soldiers, trotting casually out of the city gates of Re'Shan, resplendent in a cuirass and plackart of thinly beaten sky metal. The armor throbbed, pulsed otherworldly colors. It was magnificent. De Merlon looked like a born king; even his devastated face with its pocked, sunken, and scarred flesh took nothing away from his grandeur. *The scars of war*, the men had whispered. Here was a man who had sacrificed everything. Here was a man to follow, a Lean King, a Hungry King, not the fat, self-serving Bruwaert, or the distant, uncaring Tremain.

Forbury desperately needed to masturbate. This pleased him. He'd been masturbating like a monk for days now, ever since he'd put the thing around his neck. He had rediscovered the libido of his nineteen-year-old self. It was the talisman, he knew, but Lord, it made him ache with lust. He smiled. The drink, food, and smoke had been slowly robbing him of his manhood for years, but no more.

THE CITY AT THE EDGE OF THE DESERT belonged to de Merlon now. Those men who hadn't turned lay dead, loaded in carts and dumped outside the city walls, victuals for the vultures. Rebecca Occitane was upset, naturally. Death was always upsetting. Still, she rode at the tail of his army, Jeremiah at her side, the Monk of Ulfur still heavily cloaked.

The chess game of war had started remarkably well for Tristan, his first incursion swift and surgical. Re'Shan had fallen with greater speed than he could have hoped, but he wasn't yet willing to reveal his bishop for fear it would upset his pawns. No, Jeremiah would remain as indiscreetly positioned on the board as possible. The ancient monk's true nature, if revealed, would test the resolve of even his most loyal, sky-metal drunk soldiers.

Tristan was King on the board. And his Queen? The gods of war had gifted him with the most powerful piece in the game. Rebecca Occitane, daughter of Robert Occitane. She was the most potent force in his army. She was the key. To everything.

Tristan laughed quietly. Beneath his shirt, two trinkets softly jingled, one against the other—his own crown and Michael Alaine's hand.

Of the two, the hand radiated more power. This had struck Tristan as odd when he first held them in his hands, studying the

metal and how the amulets reacted to one another. He had thought
each trinket roughly equal in power. This was not the case. Through
careful observation, Tristan unraveled their mysteries.

He had gifted the dead Seraphim's phallus talisman to the turd,
Forbury, in exchange for his loyalty, but there was a brief time when
Tristan held four, four trinkets in his possession! The crown, the
hand, the phallus, and the key were all his momentarily. He had held
each one, touched them to his scarred face, put them in his mouth
and tasted the metallic tang of each as he sat in the darkened monastery on Mount Ulfur.

Why? Why would one contain more power than the other?

And then he realized. Like the first sight of the moon to a baby,
the shock of understanding went through him.

The victor absorbed the vanquished. Alaine had defeated Kirk
in battle; the hand had taken the cock, so to speak. Tristan laughed.
The energy of the bearer, the pure emotion mixed in with the sky
metal, was absorbed by the pendant. In his fight to the death, Alaine
had gone through a barrage of emotions, each one fueling the trinket, infusing it, supercharging it.

Rebecca Occitane wanted vengeance. Right now, she was priming
the book trinket, readying it, and when she kills the fat king, the
book will be ready. Ready for him to pluck like fruit from a tree.

Yes, without a human soul, the sky metal was worthless. He knew
it when they scraped it from the walls within Ulfur. The metal was
dormant. No matter how much he wore around his neck or on his
arms, it would give him nothing, imbue him with no additional
power. The sky metal needed the soul of the bearer to spark it into
life, and Tristan only had one soul. He was limited. He needed the
metal as worn by others, others of exceptional spirit.

Rebecca Occitane possessed a soul of pure fire; he sensed it. She
was an engine fine-tuned for destruction, an engine of hate, much
like himself. The girl will provide him the most powerful object on
earth once she kills the fat king. Then it will be ready. Then he'll kill
her and take the book. Then he'll absorb the trinket's power, absorb
the girl's soul. And become a God.

38

Honor Is Its Own Reward

Christopher Lewis sat in a forest clearing within a circle of desert ash trees, their leaves mostly fallen, creating a carpet of golden brown. Tristan Drogos de Merlon's army was at this very moment riding north on the north-south road only four leagues away, its goal to pierce the Freelands and then onwards to capture Otago, King Bruwaert, and after that, Canterbury Castle and its king, Laurence Tremain.

The knight-captain looked at the sky between the bare branches of the trees, the unmoving clouds seemingly trapped, impaled upon the very tips of the desert ash. A noise of cracking twigs brought his attention back to earthly matters.

Three riders eased their horses down the gentle slope to the forest clearing, glancing left and right as they came, each man armored in hard-boiled leather, swords drawn, their breath and that of their horses churning out a wall of steam. Even this close to the Great Southern Sands, the oncoming winter was laying her icy foundations.

Christopher stood and watched the riders warily approach. One of the men, teeth protruding like those of the horse he rode, called a halt about three yards from the knight-captain. Each of the riders bore a spear emblem upon their epaulets, announcing them as soldiers of Mars Company, once loyal to Bruwaert. Were they still so?

Christopher saluted, fist snapping to chest, and the man with the horse's mouth gave a return salute, though his performed with much less enthusiasm, a perfunctory effort.

Leaning forward in his saddle, the man scanned the clearing, his eyes finally settling on the knight-captain. "We risk our lives coming here," he said, his voice rough, like bootstep on gravel. "You ask much."

Christopher bowed his head slightly. "Your bravery is commendable, Sergeant Holt. It's gratifying to find men still loyal to their king."

The sergeant exchanged glances with the other two riders, both young with dirty, blackened faces as if they'd leaned too close to the forge fires. He said, "Loyalty is a fluid concept. One must be prepared to . . . adhere to less rigid ideas in the current climate. One's life depends upon it."

"No one understands that more than I."

"Do you have the coin?" one of the younger soot-faced men said, his breath sending vapor into the air.

Holt shot a silencing look and cleared his throat. "I apologize for the boy's manners, but now that he's broached the subject . . ."

With his eyes still on the three riders, Christopher reached into a saddlebag among the chilled dying leaves and brought forth a small bag. The sound of clinking coins sparkled through the clearing, bouncing off the frosted branches. Three pairs of eyes gazed hungrily.

"Where's the girl?" Christopher asked.

Sergeant Holt snapped out of his daze and said, "She rides with de Merlon."

"*King* de Merlon," the soot-faced youth said.

Holt's face flickered with distaste and fear. "Aye, King de Merlon. She's accompanied by a monk who's always cloaked. Some say he's Ulfurian, one of the ancients from the mountain itself. Nobody knows, but both of them ride at the rear of the army, both heavily guarded. Who is she?"

Christopher didn't answer. He said, "Can you get me close to her? Or close to de Merlon?"

Holt shook his head. "That I cannot do. The monk reads minds, or so it's said. Any threat approaching, and he'll sniff it out."

"What's your plan?" the soot-faced boy asked.

Again, Christopher didn't answer.

"The gold," the boy said with a sneer. "We want it."

The knight-captain hesitated, then threw the small bag to Holt, who fumbled it and watched as it clinked to the forest floor. He and the boy jumped from their horses, scrambling for the bag. The sergeant grabbed it and elbowed the youth away. "Get off, Stanton, We'll divvy it up later. Blimey boy, one might think you don't trust me."

The third rider, the other dirty-faced fellow, sat with his hands on his pommel, face frowning, disturbed by something.

Holt and Stanton remounted their horses.

"You got any more?" the boy asked, a contemptuous grin on his face.

"If you take me to her, perhaps."

"Let's just kill him," Stanton said to Holt. "Let's kill him and take it all."

"Temper your arrogance. This here is Chris Lewis. Killed more men than you've had shits."

Stanton eyed Christopher. "But he doesn't have one of them." The young man took a small shapeless amulet from within his vest. "Doesn't have one of these, does he? Ain't so tough now. We can take him. Easy. How come you ain't got one? Not in favor with the king?"

"I prefer to stay clear headed," Christopher said. "Nothing gets you killed faster than too much confidence, *boy*."

"Who are you calling a boy?"

"Steady on," Holt said, a warning in his graveled voice. "Don't make me regret bringing you along, Stanton."

The third rider, the quiet one, spoke. "He's not alone. There are others. Up there." The boy, fingering his shapeless amulet in one hand, pointed with his other at the trees on the rise.

The youth called Stanton instantly leapt from his horse, teeth bared, drawing a sword in mid-air, and Christopher rolled into a low defensive stance, his two short blades in his hands. Holt's horse reared, the sergeant fell from the back of it but somehow landed on his feet. The other young rider turned his horse, preparing to run.

Brynhild bounded from the cover of the trees, katana in hand

Christopher could barely hold off Stanton; the young fellow swinging and hacking like a man possessed forced the assassin back.

A crossbow quarrel slammed into the shoulder of the boy fleeing on the horse. Such was the velocity of the bolt that it pierced his leather armor, but he paid it no heed, digging his heels into his horse's flanks, moving away. Another bolt sliced through the air and hit him in the neck, piercing his throat, the bolt passing right through, ripping a hole in flesh and cartilage as it went. He dropped from his horse but immediately got to his feet, trying to stem the flow of blood with his hands.

Holt had removed his sword from its scabbard, scanning the treeline for another bolt, and hid behind his rearing horse, holding onto its reins.

Stanton was screaming and slashing from all angles, leaving himself open. Christopher kicked up mud and frozen leaves, but the young man shrugged off the soil, completely unaffected by the tactic. Just then, the assassin spotted the opening he'd been waiting for, the boy lunging too far and losing his balance. The knight-captain stepped in and went for his heart, missed, but punctured a lung, and stepped back out.

Stanton didn't slow down; one lung was all he apparently required.

Holt was screaming for everyone to calm down, that this was a misunderstanding, but it was too late; Stanton seemed intent on taking Christopher's life or losing his own.

The other young man staggered around the forest with a gaping hole in his neck, his life bleeding out between his fingers, his horse and only means of escape gone. He dropped to his knees and fell forward on his face among the crisp golden leaves. Amal, William, and Michael, who carried the crossbow, appeared from the treeline and moved down to the clearing.

"Wait, wait," Holt said. "This is a mistake."

Stanton screamed, and bubbles of blood from his punctured lung popped between his lips. He hurled his sword at Christopher, who dodged it. The foolish boy was now defenseless. Then, suddenly, a fallen branch lying nearby, of its own volition, flew from the cold ground into Stanton's hand. He swung the branch at Christopher, collecting the assassin in the jaw and knocking him senseless to the cold ground, twin blades falling out of reach.

Brynhild raised her Katana and sliced Stanton's branch in two, and the boy discarded his makeshift weapon. He leapt onto the prone assassin, and the Norse warrior put her katana in its scabbard and tried to pull the bloodied young man off Christopher. His strength was unnatural. The boy had his fingers grasped around the assassin's neck, slowly throttling him.

Brynhild withdrew her katana once more and placed the blade against the boy's throat. "One chance. Let him go."

Stanton didn't listen, and she cut the boy's throat, blood spurting over the assassin's face. Still, he didn't die. Brynhild cut deeper, nearly beheading the boy, and his grip around Christopher's throat loosened.

Gasping for breath, the knight-captain rolled away and staggered to his feet as Stanton collapsed face down on the frosted earth.

Holt threw his sword aside and put his hands in the air, his horse running through the trees, back toward the north-south road.

Christopher spat the metallic-tasting blood from his mouth, snorted it from his nose.

William pointed and said, disbelievingly. "Look."

The second young man had reclaimed his feet, hands still clamping down on the holes in his neck, the entry and exit wounds of the crossbow bolt. He was walking around aimlessly, looking at the trees as if out on a morning walk. He approached Christopher and Brynhild, trying to say something but only uttering a rasping series of vowels.

William stared in horror as the boy turned to him, gurgling another meaningless message. The boy risked removing one hand from his neck, pointed at the wound and placed his hand back over his torn flesh to stem the spurting blood.

"I think he wants us to bandage his neck," William said.

Nobody moved.

Then Amal Muna gestured for the man to be seated on a log. She reached within her bag and retrieved a roll of white cloth. The boy sat, wide eyes. She didn't bother cleaning the wound or trying to stop the bleeding, experience having taught her that, as far as the men who wore the amulets were concerned, their bodies had a way of taking care of themselves. She simply wrapped the bandage around his neck as tightly as she could without strangling him.

His arms still reaching skyward, Holt said, "I had no idea he was going to attack. I swear." He looked from the assassin to the Norse warrior and back again. "Don't hurt me, for old loyalty's sake, Lewis."

A collective breath steamed its way into the frigid air, weapons disappeared in differing scabbards.

The knight-captain massaged his jaw and spat out a bloodied tooth. He then casually retrieved the bag of coins from Holt's pouch-belt, staring at the man. "Tell me everything you know about de Merlon." He knelt over Stanton's corpse, ripped the shapeless amulet free, and then held the crimson-stained metal in front of Holt's face. "Tell me about this. How many men possess them?"

Holt still had his hands up, swiveling his head from Christopher to Brynhild to Michael holding the crossbow. "Everyone. Every man in the army has one. You saw what it did to him." He nodded at Stanton. "And him." He looked at the other young man with his throat wrapped about with bandage. "Stanton controls wood, and Greg there can sense things, that's how he knew your friends were hiding behind the trees. Every man has a different . . . gift. They bring out different skills, you see? Some, they drive mad with bloodlust. You saw how hard it was to kill the boy. De Merlon has an army of them, young and old, all cock-a-hoop and ready to die."

Christopher removed the trinkets from around the necks of Holt and the injured boy. He clasped them together with the amulet that once hung on Stanton's chest. He looked at his companions, his midnight-black eyes settling on Michael Alaine. He held out the three trinkets.

Michael stared at them for a long minute, face impassive but his eyes hungry. Amal came to stand beside him and touched his shoulder gently as they exchanged a momentary glance. The young knight looked at Christopher and shook his head.

Christopher then offered them to William.

The monk put his hands within his sleeves. "No, I do not wish to wear the accursed metal around my neck, nor keep them anywhere on my person."

The knight-captain turned to Brynhild. She also declined.

"You can't stop him," Holt said. "Join us, or run."

Christopher walked away, leaving Michael Alaine to stand over Holt, crossbow at the ready. Brynhild joined the assassin at the edge of the clearing, out of earshot of the others.

"What are you thinking?" Brynhild asked.

Christopher looked at the three misshapen amulets in his hand. "We have to stop him."

"How do you suggest we do that? I have little experience with the sky metal, but I've seen things today that frighten me, supernatural things. This will not be a conventional war."

"I don't know how we stop it, but we must."

"Who's to say that this isn't for the best?"

Christopher looked askance at the tall Norsewoman.

"De Merlon seeks to run Bruwaert to ground," she said. "He takes Rebecca with him. Perhaps he can do what I cannot and provide the vengeance she seeks."

"And then?"

The Norse warrior shrugged.

"De Merlon will not stop there," he said.

"Perhaps this is the lesser of two evils."

"You don't believe that. You've seen what the sky metal does." The knight-captain held up the trinkets. "De Merlon has killed good men. He uses this sky metal to poison his followers, twist them to his bidding. He makes something inhuman out of them. That can't be the lesser of two evils. It simply can't be."

"So, what's the plan?" Brynhild asked.

"We ride north, we warn Bruwaert's forces, Tremain's forces. We warn them of the dangers of accepting the metal. We prepare them against it."

"What of Rebecca?"

"She has chosen."

Brynhild shook her head, her braided ponytail twisting across her shoulders. "You can't be sure of that. She may have been taken against her will."

"She's unharmed for now. If I can, I'll infiltrate de Merlon's army to find out more. But first we ride north. Apollo Company is nearby, and find them we must, before de Merlon's army does."

Brynhild exhaled heavily, her breath like smoke in the cooling air. "Is it not odd that we now aid Bruwaert rather than seek his demise?"

Christopher stuffed the three trinkets into the pockets of his gray leather breeches. "We aid the free peoples of White Cloud. Bruwaert be damned. This has little to do with him."

"And those two?" Brynhild indicated Holt and the boy.

"We tie them to a tree. By the time they free themselves, we'll be gone."

Brynhild folded her arms. "They'll warn de Merlon sooner or later. We must kill them."

Christopher knelt at a small shrub, ice melting on its finely serrated leaves, turning to cool drips. He wiped the plant across his cheeks, attempting to clean Stanton's blood from his face. "No. They didn't attack us."

"Do you trust them to say nothing when they eventually escape their bonds?"

"I don't know!" Christpher snapped. "But I won't kill two unarmed men. There's no honor in that."

A snort from the blonde ponytailed woman. "Honor? How far do you think honor will get you in these most dishonorable of times? Honor is the Achilles heel that will see you dead, for your enemy fights with none."

Christopher stood up. "Perhaps, but without honor, what is there?"

"It'll cost you in the end, Christopher. Dearly."

"Then, I'll pay. At any rate, honor is its own reward. I ask for nothing more."

A slow smile played about the edges of Brynhild's mouth. "*Honor is its own reward.* Many would scoff at that, but I like it." Suddenly, she reached out her hand. He stared at her, then grasped the offered hand. "You know, assassin," she said, "I think I'm beginning to change my mind about you."

"That's a relief. Now I can die happy." He looked skyward. "We must ride north as fast as our horses can carry us. We must warn the Lesser Kings that death comes for them." Christopher turned and, as he walked back to the others, said, "Just to clarify, I'm a knight-captain, not an assassin."

39

The Last Monk

Jeremiah, monk of the ancient Order of Ulfur, was disturbed. Looking into the campfire, he was thinking that he may well be the very last of his kind. In the flames, he saw the foul bat-winged creature within Ulfur. Hosea was his name, the thing that had flitted in the darkness, that had screeched, the naked thing with claws. As disgusting as Jeremiah now was, and he knew only too well just how twisted and repugnant he appeared to the casual observer, he was, at least, a man. Of a kind. He was haunted by the idea that none remained remotely human but him, that he held the torch for all that had once been good and bright about the Order of Ulfur. Oh, the irony.

The Monks of Ulfur hadn't always been defiled and decayed, morally corrupted cannibals and killers of children. No, there had been a time when the Order benefited humanity, spread kindness and hope.

But that was long ago. More than a century had passed since their fall into darkness.

But Jeremiah still lived. He still carried the memory of what once had been holy, yet all the while committing unholy deeds that disgusted him, deeds that he couldn't help thinking about committing all over again. He loathed himself, but that self-hatred was not potent enough to stop him. Nothing could stop him.

Jeremiah looked around the campsite with its newly lit fires, hundreds of them spreading across the Freelands on either side of the north-south road, and was disturbed. The last two-day march north had been met with resistance. Men bearing the lyre insignia of Apollo Company, loyal to Tremain, had harried de Merlon's army throughout the Forest of Thieves. De Merlon's men had scattered the last of the trinkets in the forest, went into the trees and hung them from branches, inviting the attackers to come pluck them at their leisure. But Apollo Company proved very disciplined, not one man hiding among the undergrowth availed themselves of the opportunity to gain godhood. Jeremiah suspected Apollo Company had been forewarned, that somebody had told them of the addictive, mind-altering powers of the metal.

Somebody.

And so, progress north to Castle Key had been slowed, brought to a virtual standstill while the forces of de Merlon's army went hunting by day and night through the forest.

Tonight, however, was peaceful. The fires burned and men chatted nearby.

Jeremiah knew that if de Merlon failed in his venomous crusade against the Lesser Kings, the monk would face extermination. Despite his hellish circumstances, the horror of the last one hundred years, he yet hoped to live. He yet hoped for something better, though what that was he couldn't say.

Jeremiah was disturbed. Rebecca Occitane had been spending more time with de Merlon. The Hungry King had taken her under his wing as some kind of surrogate daughter. It was pathetic.

He was disturbed. He was disturbed by a thousand thoughts flitting through his head like a thousand black bats in a massive cavern, bats with tiny human faces. But at least now de Merlon's army had passed through the accursed Forest of Thieves, and Apollo Company couldn't hinder their progress without exposing themselves to fletched arrows and metal-tipped bolts. On the plains, Tristan Drogos de Merlon and his men had the advantage. Soon, they'd leave the Freelands and enter Otago. Soon, they'd be within sight of Castle Key.

Jeremiah looked again at the campfires spread about the plains, threatening to rival in number the stars in the sky. Six thousand men now, a thousand mercenaries from the Freelands had joined the holy crusade, for money and profit, if not the honor of the cause. The Freelanders had never held love in their hearts for the Lesser Kings, particularly Bruwaert. If the fat king had any sense, he'd flee, flee north to Canterbury and his old nemesis-ally, King Tremain.

The old monk shivered at the recollection of the flaxen-bearded king Tremain, the king that had incarcerated him within the prison hulk Gorgon long before. How long ago? Jeremiah had no idea. The years had fused together like barnacles to the hull of a sunken ship so that he no longer knew how old he was. But he did know that if Tremain were to have a second opportunity, he would show the old monk no mercy. The further north they marched, the closer to danger Jeremiah came. However, de Merlon, and now the girl, had their hearts set on revenge, and that was that. North they would go. Jeremiah could not run away, de Merlon would find him. He was mad and growing more insane by the day.

It was de Merlon that Jeremiah truly feared.

That stupid girl couldn't see it, but she would soon. When it was too late.

Jeremiah knew of the madman's plans for Rebecca, knew that he intended to kill her and take the amulet to feed his growing power. Yes, he knew, had taken a great risk in probing the madman's mind. Tristan Drogos de Merlon would kill Rebecca as soon as *she* had killed Bruwaert.

But if he failed, if de Merlon was somehow defeated, and if the chance came, Jeremiah would claim Rebecca for himself and satiate his hunger one last time before it was all over. The girl was doomed, either at de Merlon's hands or his own.

"Why do you stare at me, Jeremiah?"

Because he wanted to kill her and feed on the innocence that still resided in her, dwindling though it might be. "I apologize. I was lost in thought."

Rebecca, clothed in a basic white tunic clasped at her waist with a simple belt and copper buckle, sat on the other side of the campfire. She looked at the licking flames and said, "Have you seen him today?"

"King de Merlon? No."

Rebecca continued to stare at the fire. "Why does he hate Bruwaert and Tremain?"

The old monk ran his tongue across his sharpened teeth and watched her watch the fire. "For the same reasons you do. He blames them for his loss."

She threw a twig absentmindedly into the blaze. "I spoke with him. He told me of his family. His children."

"Did he tell you their names?"

"No. Do *you* know them?"

Jeremiah was disturbed again, this time by her eyes, eyes of golden sky metal it seemed. He thought carefully before answering, wondering how it might work to his advantage. "Yes. He used to recite them in his sleep. But he doesn't do so of late."

"Why not of late?"

Careful. "He rarely sleeps now." And he was forgetting them, a sure sign of his ever-growing madness.

"Tell me their names."

Jeremiah recoiled at the question, bile rising to his throat. He didn't like the names of dead children, had always buried them along with their little bodies. This was a distasteful exercise, but Jeremiah could sense the girl was not about to let the sleeping ghosts of the young lie. Slowly, Jeremiah exhumed the names from the dirt of his memory, de Merlon's memory. "Albert. Terence. Geoffrey. Simon. The youngest was Matthew." Jeremiah felt sick.

"To lose them all. That's so sad."

"Yes."

"And you? Have you lost somebody you loved? Did you have a family?"

Jeremiah shifted uncomfortably. Not in a hundred years had anybody asked him such a question, not in a hundred years had anybody cared to ask him. Jeremiah looked up at the stars in the night sky. "I was a Monk of Ulfur. A monk. Therefore, I had no family as you would understand it, but the brotherhood itself, well, we loved each other as family."

Rebecca nodded, staring at the fire once again. "That's nice."

Jeremiah recalled a glimpse of naked male flesh in the darkness within Mount Ulfur, fingers scratching, teeth biting at first pleasurably, then rending and tearing, blood, his or that of someone else? He couldn't remember. "Yes, it was . . . nice."

"But it's all gone."

"All gone."

She looked at him again with those peculiar eyes. Lord, such sweet, innocent, brutal, uncompromising eyes.

"Perhaps you can start again," she said.

Jeremiah coughed up a laugh and was surprised to feel tears building in the back of his yellowed eyes. "Domestically speaking? Yes, of course, a hideous witch might take pity on me. Do you know of any that perhaps you could introduce me to?"

"Women are not only interested in looks. It's what's in your heart that counts."

Then, he was doubly damned. Jeremiah shook his head. "I fear it's the celibate life for me. A bachelor until the end."

Jeremiah became irritated at the girl's unusual ability to pry him open, especially when he'd spent a century remaining very guarded against such social interactions.

Suddenly, there was the rustle of movement nearby, men moving quickly. Jeremiah and Rebecca turned as one. A horse and rider thundered through the encampment, knocking soldiers aside and setting up sparks from careless hoof fall. Men started murmuring as the rider dismounted and headed for the Hungry King's tent. Rebecca got to her feet and walked toward de Merlon's pavilion, Jeremiah following, staying close behind.

The pretentious oaf, Higgins, was standing outside the master's tent, talking to the slug-nosed Forbury. Two idiot generals in de Merlon's idiot army. Surely, not even a force of sky-metal crazed warriors could hope for victory when commanded by buffoons such as these. The two men looked to be in a heated argument when suddenly they left off their discourse and disappeared within the tent on the heels of the rider.

Three other men guarded the tent entrance: the frog-eyed soldier known to Jeremiah as Cracker Jackson, along with the man with a giant bird's nest for a head, Big Ted, and the one with the massive beard, Spade Johnson. They each shook their heads as Rebecca made to enter de Merlon's tent.

"Not now, miss. His majesty is busy," Cracker Jackson said, folding his arms.

Shortly thereafter, Commander Forbury exited the tent. His face was pale, disquieted. He scurried off into the darkness.

Broadford Higgins pushed his way out of the canvas door. He stood to his full height and stared down at Jeremiah, his mouth turning down at one edge in disgust.

"What's happening, Mr. Higgins?" Rebecca asked.

He shrugged. "Nothing. Nothing. You two go back to the fire. Get some sleep. We're two days' ride from Castle Key. You must prepare yourselves."

Jeremiah and Rebecca slowly returned to their seats by the campfire. The girl, who seemed lost in thought, said, "What do you think that was all about?"

The twisted monk looked innocently at her, eyebrows raised. "Oh, I'm sure it's just boring old reports, you know, numbers of enemy soldiers, horses, equipment and so on. Nothing to bother yourself about."

Rebecca lay down beside the fire, her light brown hair falling over her face. Her sleep would be fitful again tonight, he knew. It had been fitful every night that Jeremiah sat watching her, delving into her dreams and hopes and fears.

He'd been reading her thoughts, smelling them, savoring them.

He'd read Higgins's thoughts too, outside the Hungry King's tent. When their eyes had met, Higgins had unwittingly revealed all: a group of Freelanders newly loyal to King de Merlon had prepared a gift for the new Hungry King. They had found the woman and boy, Ainslie and Lachlan Bruwaert, wife and son to King Shane Bruwaert, fleeing north to Castle Key with a small entourage. The rising surge of war had caught them short on a royal tour of the Freelands.

Jeremiah, ancient Monk of Ulfur, hoped and prayed that King de Merlon would show a little mercy.

And give him Bruwaert's boy to eat.

40

Crossroads

Broadford Higgins rode his horse forward through the spooked soldiers milling about and pointing down the north-south road. Something had halted the northward advance, and the Hungry King wouldn't be happy with the delay, for on the morrow they'd reach Castle Key and the fat King Bruwaert. He scanned left and right for any signs of a trap, the murmurings of disconcerted soldiers fading behind him as his horse trotted down the road under brooding afternoon clouds. What could hold up the march of six thousand soldiers, each supercharged with the sky metal?

There, on a white horse in the middle of the carriageway, sat a man leaning forward with hands on pommel, waiting, like a guardian of the road, a toll collector, menacing in some unknowable way. The man seemed to be casting an invisible barrier, keeping de Merlon's army at bay. Behind him the road blossomed into a crossroads, left to Dunedin, right to Balclutha, straight on to Castle Key.

Broadford looked back. The main force of Tristan Drogos de Merlon's army would be upon them in minutes. This man, whoever he was, was placing himself in the path of great danger. This man stood in the path of vengeance.

"Nice top hat, Captain Higgins." The man on the white horse was young, blue eyed, with blond shoulder-length hair.

Looking around, still suspecting a potential trap, Broadford said, "Hello, Michael. I must admit to being a little surprised to see you here. And I'm officially *Marshal* Higgins now."

The boy raised his eyebrows.

"Yes, I know, it's been a rather lightning rise up the ranks. Still, that's what loyalty buys you, I suppose."

Michael nodded and repeated the single word. "Loyalty." He said it with an expression Broadford recognized as disappointment.

"You need to get your arse gone, Michael. Or join us. Just don't sit there with a disapproving look on your face. He's coming."

"He must listen to reason."

Broadford almost laughed. "Oh, what reason is that?"

"This war's futile. It will achieve nothing but bring death to more innocent people."

The toff raised a mirthless smile. "You haven't spoken to Marshal de Merlon for a while, have you? *King* de Merlon, as it is now. He's too far gone, trust me. There's no reasoning with him. Get out of here, Sergeant Alaine. While you still can. That's an order."

Michael's blue eyes searched Broadford's face. "And you, sir? Why do you serve a madman?"

Broadford felt the metal on his chest, felt the warmth in his blood. He looked up at the broiling clouds, different shades of gray upon gray. "He's got his hooks in, lad. The metal has its hooks in. It's too late for me." Broadford looked closely at Michael, trying to read the Silent Knight's face. "Did you kill Archibald Kirk?"

Confusion flashed on the boy's face, emotions born and dying in fleeting moments. "He . . . I had to. He wasn't in his right mind. He tried to kill me, and a friend."

Broadford shrugged. "I'm not judging. Not me."

"He's coming," Michael said, looking over Broadford's shoulder.

The toff didn't have to turn around to know the boy was speaking the truth. He could feel the master closing in, could feel the heat growing at the nape of his neck. "Run, Michael," he whispered, but the boy was too stubborn.

Broadford watched Michael track the approach of the Hungry King and hoped the boy's eyes didn't spontaneously burst into flames and burn from his sockets.

A crunching of heavy horse hoof.

It was too late.

TRISTAN DROGOS DE MERLON, armored in the ethereal, luminescent sky metal, came nearer. His chest plate and gauntlets shone brilliantly, but the man's face, in contrast, was ravaged, destroyed by war and disease, and something else which lurked in his decayed visage, something not physical: the man's scars ran deeper than any injury done to his flesh. Michael could see that de Merlon's soul had undergone a frightening transformation.

The Hungry King smiled, his cheeks sucked inwards, creating deep pockets in the man's face.

"Michael Alaine. Welcome," Tristan said.

"You must stop this mad crusade."

The smile faded. "You're disappointed in me. I see it in your face."

The young man was close to tears. "We fought to stop the Hungry King. We all fought side by side. Now, you *become* him? I don't understand."

Tristan said nothing. He scanned the horizon ahead where the north-south road cut the darkening plains in half. He said, "We were wrong. We fought for nothing. Every man was in it for himself." He turned in the saddle. "Is that not so, Broadford?"

The toff didn't meet his lord's eyes. "That is so," he murmured.

"But this"—De Merlon swung his arm to take in his encroaching army—"look at these men, how they've come together within days. It's beautiful. They all see the nobility, the righteousness of the cause."

"The metal binds them, for now. But it will drive them all mad. Nothing will come of this but death. There's no honor in this." The clouds above darkened, reflecting the despair in Michael Alaine's voice, the skies threatening rain, promising tears. "I started it. It was me that found them. But I can stop it."

Tristan shook his head. "You can't stop this. It's not yours to stop."

Rain drops pattered on Michael's black leather jerkin. His eyes widened, pleading. "There's no good in it, sir. The Marshal de Merlon that I knew would never do this, would never lose his honor in such a way."

The Hungry King's expression changed from sympathy to indignity, his scarred face twisting in anger. "Honor? Look at us, we three." Tristan waved a hand, encompassing Broadford, Michael, and himself. "We're the last of the six men who entered the mountain that fateful day, and I believe of the three men here, right now, I, *I* am the only one not to take the life of a brother, for brothers we are, united in what we found that day, bonded forever in life and in death. Speak to me of honor, Michael, look me in the eye and speak to me of honor after you've murdered a brother."

"Archibald was insane. I had no choice."

"There's always a choice! By your reckoning, all men who carry the metal are insane. Malcolm Dewar is dead." De Merlon glanced pointedly at Broadford Higgins, who kept his eyes averted, then looked back at Michael. "Archibald Kirk is dead at *your* hands. And Robert, dear friend Robert Occitane, murdered, slaughtered by the very king he aided in war, killed by the fat king Bruwaert. Did Tremain come to his aid? No! But I come to his aid, even after his death."

Michael's fine brows drew together, rain flattening his blond hair to his head. "The girl, his daughter, Rebecca. You have her."

"*Have* her? I have nothing. She came of her own volition, determined to see this through. She wants vengeance as much as I do. And you? Running around killing people who cross you, you're a hypocrite. The metal is still in your blood, I can smell it. You may not wear the amulet any longer, but you are one of us all the same."

Michael could only shake his head.

"They intended to hang you for the power you showed. How can you defend them?" De Merlon went on, the rain hissing and spitting from the top of his hairless skull. "They would have killed you for your difference. Men are so small minded, but I have saved you, *I* have changed everything. Now you are the norm," Tristan swept his hand behind him again at his gathering army on the road. "Now they're *all* like you. Brothers, one and all. Join us."

Blue eyes in the rain. "I'll never join your hollow cause."

Tristan Drogos de Merlon sighed sadly. Without enmity, he said, "Fool." He reached to his neck and pulled out two amulets, the crown and the hand. "Join us, and I shall return this to you," he said, separating the hand from the crown and holding it up.

Michael's body trembled, his guts churned. He could taste a metallic tang in his mouth. He felt his lust rise.

Tristan smiled, brought his horse a step closer to Michael. "I didn't see it, but I heard, oh yes, I heard that your blood congealed to form a weapon, a whip, is that not so?" Tristan's face was hungry, eager for details. "Tell me."

Michael felt sickened. "Yes."

A nod. "Fascinating." Tristan raised an open palm to the sky, and a small flame grew and flickered in his hand, steaming among the raindrops. He smiled as he watched it run up and down his skeletal fingers. Then he closed his hand, and the flame was gone, snuffed out without even a wisp of smoke. "I can use it to heal or to hurt." The Hungry King leered at Broadford, who was shifting uneasily in his saddle. "Marshal Higgins, what's your power?"

"I'm immune to hangovers, sire."

The Hungry King laughed and brought his sunken eyes to bear on the young soldier. "I always thought of you as a son, Michael. Join us." Tristan took the amulet from around his neck and held it out, smiling.

Michael stared at the hand-shaped trinket. He desperately wanted to reach out and take it, knowing the warmth within would make everything better. His blood craved it, called for it. He thought of Felix Jasper. He felt the rain pelt against his face, closed his eyes, and tried to focus on the stinging droplets.

The young knight thought of the destruction of Shae, the rape and murder of the innocent, the horrific loss of Amal Muna's family at the hands of Achilles Company, a company he had believed in, a cause he had believed in, a war he had believed in. He opened his eyes, meeting those of the Hungry King. "You're right about one thing, sir. Every single man is in it for himself. There is no honor. There never was."

Silence hung between the three men.

Tristan stopped smiling and withdrew the amulet. He said, "Tell Bruwaert that I'm coming for him." The Hungry King's face slowly became a feral snarl. "Tell the fat king I will roast him over a spit, put his head on my wall. He is my boar. Tell him he's going to burn. Tell Tremain his death will follow." Tristan trembled, heat emanating from him like a sunrise.

Michael's horse snorted, and Broadford's horse flinched and stepped sideways.

"They will all burn, do you hear me? Leave now, Michael Alaine. Our bond is broken. The next time I see you, I'll kill you." Flames hissed and flickered across Tristan's face. "They will all burn!"

Broadford's horse reared, the toff's hat falling to the dirt road, the rider barely hanging on.

Michael backed his horse away and turned around.

"I thought of you as a son, Michael. A son."

Michael Alaine rode away in the clattering rain as fast as he could while the Hungry King swore death upon the world.

41

The Fat King

King Shane Bruwaert stood at the top of the central keep in Castle Key and watched an ashen haze materialize in the distance, like purple-gray storm clouds broiling on the horizon.

"Your Highness, we must flee now."

Bruwaert's chamberlain, Grant, was standing behind him, staring anxiously across the fields, wringing his thin hands. The man's hawk-like nose twitched. Smoke. Bruwaert could smell it now too. His kingdom was on fire; Otago was under siege.

"How? How did this happen so fast? Where is General Roberts? I need a report!"

"He hasn't returned from the field, sire. I believe we should flee."

Bruwaert raised an eyebrow and looked at the ominous smoke clouds. "And leave the safety of Castle Key? Take our chances out there, to be harried down like a rabbit before the hounds? At least within the walls, we can hold out until Tremain gets here, if he ever decides to get off his arse and come to the aid of the Alliance."

"Very good, sire." The chamberlain's voice resonated with uncertainty. "I shall inform the men to make preparations to shut the gates."

The fretful footfall of Bruwaert's chamberlain echoed and disappeared within the spiral staircase in the center of the keep. The king's attention was caught by something in his gray-streaked beard. Was that a fleck of ash? God, what was happening out there?

His thoughts returned to the previous day when the tall Norsewoman had ridden up to the gates and started braying like a donkey pushing out a foal. "King Bruwaert! I demand to speak to the King!"

Demand? Even from the council chambers he had heard her voice, and that through a closed portcullis. This woman possessed healthy, aggravating lungs—to this he would forever avow. He'd had a good mind to leave her waiting just to counter her pomposity, teach her a lesson in manners. But then she shouted, "War, war comes!"

Bruwaert sighed and looked at his advisors. Among them were two lesser nobles from the Tasman, far to the north, here to build diplomatic relations, and a minister from Dysael recently arrived to discuss the possible accession of Dysael to the Kingdom of Otago, a great coup and one Bruwaert had long worked for. This was an important meeting. This was an important day. A day turning out to be thoroughly embarrassing. "Excuse me, gentlemen."

The king made his way to the courtyard, noting with discomfort that his former audience followed at his purple-feathered cape tails. This was to be a public confrontation, and Bruwaert would be damned if he was going to be shouted down in his own castle by some *woman*.

The banshee shrieked again, her voice tinged with a Norse accent. "Open the gates!"

The king eyed his advisors, foreign ministers, and expectant soldiers, took a deep breath and boomed in his best royal timbre. "I give the orders here! You shall make a formal request for an audience like everyone else! Now begone from my gates before I have your head disintroduced from your shoulders!"

"Open the gates! Are you and your men afraid of one woman on horseback?"

The king furrowed his brows. This barbaric Northerner had failed to be awed by his commanding tone. "Who are you?"

"Brynhild Grimsdotter, daughter of Sagran Grimsdotter."

Something about the name of the father was familiar, sounded important. Bruwaert cursed under his breath. "Open the gates."

The portcullis raised, the internal gates opened, and the largest woman he had ever seen rode forward on a brilliant white charger. The King's Guard moved in close, swords and spears at the ready. Bruwaert waved them back. "Put your weapons away." Turning to the woman, the king said, "Well, I hope you have good cause to be shouting down my gates."

The woman was even larger when she dismounted and stood before the King, his advisors, and one hundred gathered sentries. She said nothing, just looked at him as if she were contemplating strangling him right then and there. And from the look of her bare arms exploding from her sleeveless brown leather jerkin, she was quite capable of doing so.

The silence was bizarre. The king cleared his throat and said with as much royal pomp as he could muster, "Why are you here?"

"An army marches north to kill you." She said it like she was informing the king that he had a gravy stain on his doublet.

"And?"

The woman's brows furrowed. "This doesn't concern you?"

Bruwaert smiled, feeling he now had the upper hand in the current conversation. "I am aware of the army. Four thousand rag-tag mercenaries badly organized. Old men and foolish boys. I have a force of ten thousand well-trained soldiers at my disposal, not to mention the safety of a fortified Castle Key. We will cut them down."

"You've been misinformed. They number five, possibly six thousand now, and most of them wear the sky metal."

Bruwaert's face lost some of its cheer. The sky metal? He looked down. Why had this not been made known to him? He looked up and flashed a different kind of smile, one meant to instill confidence. "Still, we outnumber them, we outnumber them." Bruwaert had used this smile to bed several chambermaids since his succession to the throne; of course, he wasn't stupid enough to believe it was the smile alone that got them naked. He was, after all, a king and serving girls don't say no to kings, but he always thought his smile was charming, even disarming, but it had no apparent effect on the Norsewoman.

If anything, she looked more inclined to stab him through the eye than before.

"Apollo Company offers its services. They are noble men, loyal to Tremain and willing to fight and die for the Alliance," she said.

Bruwaert suffered a horrible moment of uncertainty. To accept the offer would mean a loss of honor, would show a weakness here, now, when his men and gathered dignitaries were watching. To accept the offer would make him less of a king, and more importantly, less of a man to those he commanded.

Surely, ten thousand men could take five thousand, or did she say six?

"Who commands this upstart army out of Re'Shan?" he asked.

"A man by the name of de Merlon. Tristan Drogos de Merlon."

With a shock, Bruwaert recognized the name. He stared at Brynhild Grimsdotter. "De Merlon is dead, a victim of the plague, a year ago."

"Then, a dead man leads an army a day from Castle Key. A dead man seeks your head."

The king's anger flared at the woman's flippancy and also a growing fear. "I know this man, de Merlon. A marshal in Tremain's army." He puffed out his chest. "So, Tremain seeks to stab me in the back?"

Brynhild shook her head, her braided blonde ponytail coming to rest over her breast. "This man is a renegade. Tremain has nothing to do with it. De Merlon seeks Tremain's downfall along with yours."

Bruwaert became acutely aware that the gathered dignitaries were measuring him and his response to the situation, waiting for a sign of weakness, a loss of face, not to mention this conceited Northern harpy looking down her high and mighty nose at him. He wouldn't give them, or her, the pleasure of backing down. "Harumph! Are we supposed to believe that Tremain knew nothing of this? Perhaps you are his spy, or perhaps you work with de Merlon to undermine me."

"I come here alone. I give you this information at my own risk. Apollo Company will assist you where they can. You may take or refuse this offer. Personally, I don't care what happens to you." Brynhild Grimsdotter placed her hand on the pommel of her sword.

Whether this was to punctuate her last point or was simply force of habit, Bruwaert wasn't sure, but several of his men reached for their weapons in response. She said, "You could die here today, and many would count it a blessing."

The minister from Dysael gasped, and the king felt his face redden. This woman had practically no sense of self-preservation, but Bruwaert could tell by her vicious sneer that she had meant exactly what she had said. His fury rose, threatened to overcome his kingly restraint and dignity. "Get you gone! Tell Apollo Company King Bruwaert does not require its services." Bruwaert raised his arms and swept them around the courtyard. "I have honorable men of my own, loyal to their king. We will defeat this fool who marches north!" There was a hurrahing among the assembled men.

And without a further word, without even a nod of her fierce Northern head, the woman leaped back onto her horse, gave a final scornful glance at the king, and rode away.

She had been contemptuous, she had been arrogant, she had been scathing. Had she stayed a moment longer, Bruwaert would have ordered her tied down and lashed for her flagrant and public disrespect to the mighty King of Castle Key.

But now as the smoke thickened on the horizon, as Bruwaert tasted the acrid ash of the fall of his empire in the air, he wished she would return. Yes, he would accept the offer of help from Apollo Company.

Was it too late?

42

The Defeated King

King Bruwaert sat tied to his broken throne with a rope, his face flickering with pain at each movement against the rough hemp. His generals had been impaled and roasted over open fires—skinned hares at a village feast—and some of his finest soldiers had turned and joined the other side. Smoke rolled across the sky, smoke from burning corpses, the smoke of defeat and death, pungent in his mouth and nostrils, bringing him to a hacking cough.

The gates to Castle Key were open, and the enemy was inside, running about and screaming in delight, looting anything they could find. But the metal-crazed mercenaries didn't touch the king. They just walked by him, some laughing, others casting sympathetic glances in his direction. *Those* glances disturbed Bruwaert the most.

The mercenaries had dragged his throne into the courtyard, set it on a makeshift dais at the top of several marble steps facing the massive open portcullis a hundred yards away, for the grand entrance of the conqueror.

The men stopped running. They lined up facing each other in the center of the courtyard, creating a carriageway, an avenue of triumph leading from the gates of Castle Key to the defeated king.

A flag flapped in the wind, a red mountain against a white sky. Bruwaert gazed disinterestedly, not knowing what it represented.

Two hundred men knelt as the Hungry King appeared at the gates. He was resplendent in his sky-metal armor—a tall, magnificently glittering titan. Bruwaert, hopelessly alone, watched the serpentine gait of the Hungry King as he approached, helmetless, hairless, his smile stretching paper-thin flesh across sharpened teeth.

The Hungry King climbed six steps from the courtyard floor to the raised platform and stopped in front of the defeated king. He raised his arms and slowly turned to encompass Castle Key and the battlefield outside, wordlessly inviting appreciation. His smile widened even further, cutting open the very mouth of the Hungry King, and dark blood dripped from his lips to his chin.

"And when the victor is vanquished, who then will sing his song?" the creature said, removing his leather gloves.

To Bruwaert's surprise, Tristan Drogos de Merlon brought his tall frame down to one knee and bowed before him. A hush washed over two hundred men, a vacuum sucking all thought into a vortex. He stood again and looked down at Bruwaert.

"What do you want?" the defeated king asked.

The Hungry King shook his head, seemingly disappointed in the question. "Your lands, your wealth. What does it matter?"

Bruwaert snarled. "You're a plague, spreading death and destruction."

"Yes, yes I am."

"If you're here to taunt me before you kill me, spare yourself the effort. I will not beg for my life."

The Hungry King put his hands on the armrests of the throne and leaned forward to stare into Bruwaert's eyes. "No. I don't suppose you will." He gestured for a chair, and one was brought to him. He eased his angular skeletal frame into it as if settling before a blazing fire in the hearth. "Father," he said, "let us talk."

Bruwaert laughed, a scoffing snort, the laugh of a man who was condemned and had nothing left but pride, a man who had accepted death and no longer feared it. "I'm not your father. You're the son of a whore, and I've never bedded a whore."

De Merlon laughed. "You're a murderer and a rapist."

"Lies!"

The Hungry King wagged a finger as if at an errant schoolboy. "Not lies, as you well know. I've heard stories of when you first came to power many years ago. They say there wasn't a family in Otago that didn't lose a son to the stake or a daughter to your royal *scepter*. You rule by fear, and violence. As you have lived, so shall you die."

"Then, what are you waiting for?"

"Guidance. Teach me how to rule, father, as you did."

With the speed of a much younger man, Bruwaert withdrew a dagger from within the folds of his robes, having wiggled free of the rope, and slashed at the throat of his tormentor, but the dagger only caught Tristan a glancing blow on the forearm as he somehow evaded the venomous strike of the old, fat king. Bruwaert lost his balance and toppled forwards.

Tristan ripped the blade from Bruwaert's hands and waved away his men as they sought to come to his defense, albeit too late. He cast aside the knife with a clatter and helped Bruwaert back onto his throne. The Hungry King's forearm was bleeding, but de Merlon merely laughed, licked at the wound, and then waved his hand over the cut, flames dancing from his fingers, cauterizing the flesh, the bleeding stopping instantaneously.

"I do not fear you," Bruwaert whispered.

"Where are your wife and son?"

"Somewhere you'll never find them." Bruwaert gulped and tried to read de Merlon's face.

Without braggadocio, de Merlon said, "I am Death. In time, my shadow will devour theirs."

"You're nothing but a leper."

Tristan ran his skeletal, clawed finger down his scarred jawline. "I am not beautiful, true, but a leper? That is uncharitable. I *was* a leper. And riddled with the plague. But I lived. I lived to see this day. And now here we sit, father."

"I do not fear you."

Tristan paused and leaned closer. He whispered, "It is not me you should fear." He turned to look back at the gates, Bruwaert following his line of sight.

Walking through the gates came a tall man in a gentleman's coat and top hat; a shorter man hidden within filthy brown robes, his back hunched, twisted as if racked one time too many on the torture table; and between them, a young girl wearing a white, knee-length tunic fastened at the waist, oddly disparate to the other two who were oddly disparate to each other. A more unlikely trio one could not hope to see.

"Clear the castle," Tristan said.

Two hundred men scurried for the portcullis, the three figures cutting through them like sharks through the surf.

Within minutes, Bruwaert found himself sitting and staring from the Hungry King to the man in the top hat, to the decaying monk, to the girl. She gazed at him, those striking amber eyes fixed on his own, unnerving, drilling through him like those of the Norsewoman from the previous day but even more disturbing if that were possible.

Nobody spoke. Then Tristan Drogos de Merlon said, "This is Rebecca Occitane."

"Am I supposed to know who this child is?"

"You killed my father," she said. "For this." Rebecca pulled an object from under her tunic—a small book fashioned from the luminous, ethereal sky metal.

The defeated king stared open mouthed. For more than a year he'd been seeking it, spending all his time thinking about it, spending all his resources to find it, and finally, here it was. It was beautiful.

What did the girl say? Killed her father? Occitane? Rebecca Occitane? Bruwaert remembered. Robert, her father was Robert Occitane. His skin prickled, the hairs on his arms standing erect, his heart hammering in his chest. This child was his death.

"I killed no one!" Bruwaert blustered. "My men made an error in judgment. I never sent them explicitly to kill your father."

"Liar!" The girl's amber eyes flared.

"Broadford, bring them in," Tristan said.

The man in the top hat bowed and left.

"If you're going to kill me, just be done with it!" Bruwaert said.

"Not yet. Not until you have suffered. As I have suffered."

"I didn't order Robert Occitane's death," Bruwaert whined, looking at Rebecca.

"Liar. Did you order *my* death?"

"Of course not! What possible reason could I have for wanting you dead?"

"Because I carried this." Again, she thrust the trinket in Bruwaert's face.

He could almost taste it. His gray-flecked beard was moist with sweat. "My . . . my men, they were out of control."

"*Your* men! *Your* men! Under *your* control, under *your* command!"

She had a point. If he could just touch the trinket, just once before he died.

"Shane!" a woman screamed.

Bruwaert's heart froze in horror. The big toff, Broadford, had one hand twisting Ainslie's arm behind her back and the other hand around Lachlan's neck. The boy grimaced in fear and pain.

No. Not his family.

43

The Fall

"**I**'m sorry about him. I'm sorry about everything. You must believe me."

Rebecca Occitane had been staring absent-mindedly at something on the floor of the courtyard. "Hmm? What did you say?" The man speaking to her was fat and old, his beard streaked with flecks of gray. He was a king. King Bruwaert was his name. This was the man who had murdered her father—had him murdered.

She tried to focus her thoughts, eager as they were to flit away like butterflies at the end of a summer's day. What had she been looking at? A knife. Serrated like dragon's teeth. Where had it come from? Blood coated the blade, yet it sparkled in the dying sunlight, seeming pure somehow, uncorrupted.

"I said I'm sorry about your father. His death."

Rebecca slowly took in her surroundings. She was in Castle Key, the ancestral home of the Bruwaerts, standing in the courtyard. Behind her was Broadford Higgins, Jeremiah, and Tristan Drogos de Merlon. There was a weeping woman and a boy about eight years of age. Bruwaert's wife and son. Up half a dozen steps in front of her was the fat king, Shane Bruwaert.

"You're sorry?"

He nodded, sweat flicking in droplets from his graying beard. "I am deeply sorry."

Smoke was rising outside the castle walls. What did it signify?

"Why are you sorry?"

Bruwaert looked about him and then back at the girl. "Because he's dead."

"He's dead? *Who* is dead?" Rebecca began to climb the steps to the throne.

The king cast another flustered glance about the collected figures, his face puzzled. "Your father. That's why you're here isn't it?"

Tristan approached Rebecca, who now stood directly in front of Bruwaert, and put a clawed hand on her shoulder. She looked at him and then returned to Bruwaert. "Tell me again. Why am I here?"

Bruwaert gulped. "I don't—"

"Why?"

"To avenge his death," Bruwaert blurted.

"*Why* am I here to avenge his death?"

The king was breathing hard, his chest rising and falling rapidly. "You think it my fault he is dead."

She bored her gaze into his head. "And is it *your* fault?"

"Listen—" Bruwaert stopped speaking when he saw de Merlon pick up the blade from the courtyard floor, the same blade he had tried to assassinate de Merlon with a few moments earlier.

The skeletal king gave the knife to Rebecca and whispered in her ear, "For your father."

Rebecca gripped the blade. "I've been waiting for this."

From outside Castle Key, a horn blasted.

Tristan scanned the skies and then returned his attention to Rebecca. "Kill him."

Ainslie and Lachlan Bruwaert screamed and pleaded for the life of the fat king, the woman's husband, the boy's father. At a glance from de Merlon, Broadford Higgins clasped his strong hands over their mouths, muffling their cries for mercy.

Rebecca felt the weight of the knife in her hands. Something was wrong. This wasn't how she thought it would be. She turned to look at the woman and her child. "What will happen to them?"

"They too shall die."

She shook her head. "My rage does not encompass them." Her voice was steady, unemotional.

Tristan's face changed, his confident smile faltering. "Mine does. As he took my family, so shall I take his."

"But they are innocent, they have nothing to do with . . ." Rebecca stared at the bloodied knife again.

"I see that perhaps you never loved your father at all."

Rebecca's eyes became savage, and she thrust the knife toward de Merlon. "Don't say that!"

Tristan smiled, his face a garish skull. "You see? That's the girl I know. They will all burn for what they've done to us. Make them watch as you kill the fat king!"

She gazed at the blade in her hand. She couldn't think. The world was shifting beneath her feet. "I . . ."

"For your father!"

A horn blasted again.

Through the gates rode Commander Roger Forbury on his gray mare. He came to a clattering halt before Tristan. Seeing his former king strapped to a broken throne, Forbury looked away, trying not to meet the defeated king's eyes. "Tremain's army is bearing down on us!" the slug-nosed commander said.

Tristan snarled. "How many men?"

"At least ten thousand! They cover the plains. After our losses, we are now outnumbered three to one."

"Tremain's men are no overconfident fools. They are well armed and well trained. They've been forewarned. We've lost the element of surprise. Shut the gates! Bring everyone inside!"

"Sire, we don't have food for a siege."

Tristan waved him off. "Bring them in! We just need to hold out . . ." He trailed off and looked at Rebecca. "Just a little longer."

"Aye, sire." Forbury clattered off toward the portcullis.

"Kill him," Tristan Drogos de Merlon said.

"Him." Rebecca nodded toward Bruwaert. "But not his family. Give me your word that they'll remain unharmed."

The Hungry King wore a murderous expression on his cracked, ravaged face, a face contorting for several moments before relaxing. He breathed out evenly. "You have my word," he said. "No hurt shall come to the woman or child. I will release them when it's done."

"No!" Jeremiah shrieked.

Rebecca turned, startled.

"I have been faithful!" the gnarled Monk of Ulfur screamed. "I have done your bidding, de Merlon! But you promised me I would have innocence, innocence for the power of the metal. You promised me I would feed on more children! I want this boy as per our agreement!"

"What did you say?" Rebecca asked.

The old monk glanced about himself. "Me? I said nothing."

"Yes, you did. You said something about an agreement. Innocence for the power of the metal? What does that mean?"

The monk's eyes grew wide in horror, and he put his fingers to his temples. "She reads my mind! She's in my mind!"

Rebecca, suddenly understanding, said, "You...you give him children?"

Tristan cocked his head. "I...it was a necessary price to pay."

"He feeds on them? How can that be? How can you let him hurt children?"

Tristan's face was a mask of skeletal steel, impassive, withdrawn, far away. "When my children lay dying, where was mercy? When they hammered the boards over the doors and windows, according to *his* law"—Tristan thrust a talon toward Bruwaert—"did he or his men spare a thought for *my* children? When my family truly needed their king, their village, their friends, when they truly needed mercy, they were afforded none."

"Two evils cannot undo an evil."

"Spare me your platitudes! I thought we *both* sought vengeance!"

"This is not vengeance. This is something other. They're right about you. You're truly a monster. You can't be saved."

"No. No, how can I make you understand? This is for my family. For my boys."

Rebecca softened her face, let her scowl fall away. "I understand your grief, Tristan. But you...you've let madness into your heart. You've let tragedy destroy the goodness in you."

The skin on Tristan's face crawled, expressing a range of emotions—surprise, contrition, sadness, but mostly anger.

"You can't do this. It's wrong. It's evil," Rebecca said.

"No! I'm not evil. This fat turd is evil! Tremain is evil! They make us fight and die for them and give nothing back. This is divine retribution, surely *you* understand this."

"My desire for vengeance is every bit as strong as yours, but there are other ways. There must be other ways." She cast the knife aside, and the blade clattered across the courtyard floor.

Tristan followed the bouncing blade as it came to rest. "Very well. You win, Rebecca Occitane. I give you my word. I will not harm the woman or child, nor shall Jeremiah." He knelt and picked up the knife again. "But you *must* kill the fat king." He held out the blade.

A horn blared again, and a thousand men crammed through the creaking castle doors as the gates began to close. The heavy metal portcullis shrieked as it descended.

"You lied to me," Rebecca said with a mix of anger and sadness. "I thought my father was your friend. I don't trust you."

"Your father was my friend, I swear. I grieve for him. I grieve for my family." Tristan sank to his knees. "I'm not evil. I'm empty. Can't you see? I'm a dry, desiccated corpse both without and within. I don't even have tears left to cry." He looked down at his hands, the right still clasping the bloodied blade, and whispered, "I can't remember their names." His mouth gaped like a fish without air. He tried to speak but only a hoarse whisper issued from his cracked lips. "I can't remember my children's names. One by one they have been taken from me, all over again. All over again."

Tristan Drogos de Merlon trembled. Rebecca knelt with him and took his hands. She met his eyes, tried to hold them in her gaze. She softly said, "Albert . . . he is the oldest. Then Terence, Geoffrey, Simon. The little one is named Matthew. Matthew."

He screamed a hoarse shriek of agony into the smoky skies. "My wife, I can't remember her name!" Tristan shook his head violently, as if trying to twist free of bonding ropes. "Gods, I can't remember her name!"

Rebecca held on to his hands and said, "Try, you can remember, if you try."

"They've taken everything from me. Everything."

She grasped his ruined hands tighter. "No, remember. What did she look like?"

"They will all burn!"

"No. Listen to me. Look at me. Your wife's name. You just have to remember."

"I can't remember!" he howled like a dog at a dying moon.

"What did she look like?"

Tristan's voice calmed slightly. "She was beautiful."

"Tell me. What did she look like?"

"I can't . . ."

"What did she smell like?"

He closed his scarred eyelids. He was there on the mountainside once again above Millington, gazing up at the stars, Matthew growing within her belly. He reached over to kiss her, to smell her hair, to breathe in the scent. There it was, on the edge of his memory, sweet and heady like. . .

Lilacs.

Like lilacs on the mountainside. Tristan opened his eyes. "Her name was Stella. Stella. My wife." Tears streamed from his sunken eyes, running down his ruined, scarred, pockmarked face, and his body heaved, the floodgates broken.

She hugged him, whispering, "You see? You can cry. You can cry."

Tristan sighed, seeming to empty, to deflate.

Rebecca went on soothingly. "You can remember. Everything will be well, everything will be all right. You must not fret." She rubbed his hairless head, like a mother caressing a child woken from a nightmare. "You must not fret. You have them back now."

Then, as she clasped him, Tristan, crying like a baby, dug the blade into Rebecca's chest and twisted.

"They will all burn," he said, sobbing quietly into her ear.

44

A Band of Heroes

"Tell me about Rebecca."

William turned and looked into Amal's brown eyes as she came to stand beside him. He saw something of Rebecca Occitane in the desert girl's face. They were of similar age, both of proud bearing, but more than that, each seemed to contain a power born from unimaginable pain. The young soldier, Michael Alaine, had spoken of the vile fate that befell the desert city of Shae and Amal's family. The monk was unable to hold back his tears at the tragic tale. Even the normally staunch Brynhild walked away shaking her head, keeping her emotions close to her chest as usual, but not before William saw the flash of horror and sadness on the tall Norsewoman's face.

The yellow scholar's gaze drifted back to the battlefield below. The patchwork plains were alternately burning, sending plumes of choking smoke into the roiling sky, or drowning in blood as men fought desperately for their lives, ant-like figures slashing and hacking at one another, the violence of the conflict undimmed by the haze of distance. Several leagues from the hill, upon which William and the others had made their camp, stood the royal war tent of Tremain, above it the family crest—the four towering battlements of Canterbury Castle, red on a black background, vibrant, unbowed—flapping in the growing winds.

Castle Key, by contrast, looked dead, grayed-out in the distance. No flags flew from her battlements. No insignia rose to meet the overcast skies. Rebecca was in there, somewhere behind the sealed gates.

Though Amal had used the common language of White Cloud, William swallowed hard and attempted to speak in the desert tongue. He thought he should be sensitive, under the circumstances.

Amal, smiling, pointed to her ear. "I thank you, but please speak your own language. I understand."

The monk nodded, cleared his throat, and began again. "Rebecca...she is a child. She has suffered, as you have suffered, though not...well...everyone has suffered. I do not mean to compare one's pain to another." He shook his head at the stupidity coming from his mouth. "Goodness me. What I mean to say is that Rebecca is a good person in bad times, if that makes sense."

"I do understand. Please say more."

William took Amal by the arm, and together they walked away from the scenes of war below. He noticed Brynhild and Christopher conversing on the other side of the encampment, standing near their horses. The tall woman in her sleeveless brown leather jerkin and the man in his gray leather vest and epaulets had, oddly, exchanged weapons. The warrior princess was turning over the assassin's twin short swords, and the assassin was running his finger along the glinting blade of the warrior princess's katana. For a moment, all the previous enmity between the two seemingly dissipated, and they almost appeared, dare he say it, friends?

Then tempers sparked, and terse indistinct words passed between them, a returning of weapons to familiar hands, and the woman turned angrily to her white coarser; the man, shrugging, inserted his twin swords into the scabbard attached to the flanks of his black steed.

Well, thought William, at least they hadn't cut each other's throat with each other's weapons. There's progress.

William and Amal walked arm in arm toward the center of the encampment, where they sat under a pohutukawa tree, the only tree adorning the small hill. The scholar-monk fished through his saddlebag and pulled out a purple woolen shawl he had found in the streets of Re'Shan. He had intended it for Rebecca but didn't know when or if he would see her again, so he offered it to Amal, who wrapped it about her shoulders against the cooling breeze.

William went on: "Rebecca has a good heart, a passionate heart, but she's become blinded by hate. She wants to kill the man who killed her father. I tried to convince her that . . . that whatever has been done . . ." He stopped, unsure how to go on. "Goodness, I'm ineffectual with my words today." He sighed. "You see, vengeance is a perpetual engine of destruction, like a game of dominoes, nothing remains standing. Nothing until new pieces are set, only to fall again. Does that make sense?"

Amal nodded. "Yes. I understand."

"I failed her. I failed in my duty to look after her." Tears streamed down the monk's face, onto his butter-colored robes.

Amal put a hand on William's shoulder. She pointed to Michael Alaine; the blond soldier stood silently with arms folded, looking down on the battle below. "He saved me. And now he wishes for us to leave this place, to ride far away so that I will live, and his efforts are not wasted."

"That would be wise."

"I will not go." Her words had a forceful air about them. "I choose to stay."

The scholar smiled. "It seems young people these days are nothing if not willful."

The young desert woman nodded. "Willful, yes. He cannot control me, nor I him. Therefore, we abide by each other. We accept and act in accordance. There is no blame."

William wiped his face free of tears and took a deep breath.

Leading their horses, Brynhild and Christopher approached the two sitting under the pohutakawa tree. The assassin said, "We go to speak with King Tremain. We must tell him what we know and join the fray."

William and Amal stood, still arm in arm. The thin scholar said, "I'll ready my horse."

Brynhild waved him away. "No, you stay with Amal. This idiotic war is for . . ." Turning to Christopher, she said, "Well, idiots."

"I wouldn't be much of a biographer if I were to hide away and miss witnessing your majestic deeds in battle. Besides, I'm not very good at looking after young women."

"That duty is mine," Michael said, joining the group.

"You should fight for Tremain on the fields," Christopher said to the blond soldier. "Your king has need of every able man."

"I have no king."

"Every man has a king. As every man is honor bound to fight for him," Christopher responded curtly.

Michael's face reflected the dark scowling sky above, his reply like a flash of lightning cutting through the atmosphere. "Honor? Hah! I fought for Tremain in the war, fought for Prometheus Company and Achilles under the red and black insignia of Canterbury Castle. And under those same colors did my comrades slaughter the innocent in Shae." He looked at Amal. "I fight for no man. I have found my true cause, my honor."

There was a charged instant between Christopher and Michael. The gray-vested knight-captain looked as if he might utter a bitter reply but said nothing.

Brynhild had been watching the confrontation with a growing smile. She said to Christopher, "You see? You rub people the wrong way, assassin. It's not just me."

Christopher led his horse away. "I'm not an assassin, god damn it!"

Brynhild grinned, shook her head, and whispered, "I don't know why he's always denying it." To William's surprise, she suddenly hugged him. "Prepare yourself, monk." Without another word, she turned and followed Christopher.

"A band of heroes," Amal said, smiling.

"I am no hero." William's face brightened, and he stood taller. "I'm a writer."

Amal watched as William walked away. Michael came to stand beside her, his face as brooding as ever. She said, "He is content with the part he must play. He knows who he is."

"We should be away from here," Michael said.

"Not yet, my Silent Knight. We shall descend the hill, and I'll help tend the wounded."

"It's too dangerous. Please, Amal. Let's ride away."

Slipping her hand into his, she said, "I'm no queen or warrior or writer of histories, but I, too, have a part to play, and play it I must, or it has all been for nothing. I must have a purpose, don't you see?"

The young knight didn't respond. He simply squeezed her hand tighter and swallowed the bitter tears threatening to break his resolve and tear down his heart. He watched the path of the crows through the rising smoke overhead and started to walk away, but Amal held him back. She looked at the same skies, studying the language of death as written by the circling carrion birds.

"Tell me about the sky metal," she said. "Tell me what it did to you. I wish to know everything."

45

The Battle of Castle Key

Laurence Tremain was the King of Canterbury, a husband, and a father. Of the three, fatherhood pleased him the most. His daughter had given him two granddaughters he loved beyond his ability to express. And his son was about to give him another grandchild; his advisors hoped it was a boy. They always hoped it was a boy.

Tremain stood outside his tent and gazed across the trampled fields at Castle Key two leagues away. He pulled at his pale-yellow beard, the color of pure, unadulterated flax.

No, that wasn't true.

His beard was no longer the color of flax. Now it was streaked with silver. Still, that was an insignificant thing. Age didn't bother him.

Another lie.

Age disturbed him greatly. He didn't like the heaviness settling on his bones, on his heart. Where had the years gone? It seemed like only a few short days ago that his son Patrick was running around, leaping on him from shadowed corners, pretending to be a tiger. The Tiger of Canterbury Castle. Fearsome. The king had laughed, thrown his hands up in mock fear and surrender.

There would be plenty of fear today, but no surrender.

Tremain had arrived too late to stop de Merlon from entering the Castle Key, but not all the madman's soldiers had attained the safety of the keep. Many had remained trapped outside the castle gates, and so Tremain's men and those of de Merlon were now fighting a bitter-pitched battle in the fields.

He thought again of his son, Patrick, his only son.

Another lie.

There was a second boy, a child born out of the holy sanctity of wedlock, a bastard, a son that he had never publicly acknowledged, one that he had secreted away, to his great personal shame. He sighed and looked up at the sweeping clouds. He heard a storm coming, though saw no sign of it in the skies above.

The king turned and entered the tent populated with a dozen of his military advisors, but the tall blonde woman, the yellow-robed monk, and the man in the gray knight-captain's leather armor, conversing quietly in the corner of the tent, attracted his attention.

King Tremain joined Brynhild Grimsdotter, William Barding, and Christopher Lewis. He rested one hand on Christopher's shoulder and said, "We are too late. I am sorry."

"You came as quickly as you could, sire," Christopher responded. "If blame rests anywhere, it lies with me. I failed to identify the threat in time."

"Nonsense, lad." Tremain turned to Brynhild Grimsdotter, a proud woman and as tall as the king himself, a little taller, if he were to be honest with himself, and today he had chosen to be brutally honest. "And how did you get caught up in all of this Princess Grimsdotter?"

"I like adventure and killing."

Tremain laughed. "I knew your father. Sagran Grimsdotter was a great man and a great king. A great warrior."

"And a wholly absent father," Brynhild said.

"Sometimes that cannot be helped." The king looked at Christopher. "We've lost some good men today, and the battle still rages. De Merlon's followers fight like men possessed."

"They *are* possessed," Christopher said.

"I cannot disagree. We have had reports of...unnatural occurrences, men with supernatural abilities. It seems Bruwaert was onto something all along. The fat bastard is inside the Castle Key, and while I have no love for the man, the Alliance still stands, and I will honor it."

The monk spoke up. "There are others inside with him, innocents. Rebecca, our friend."

"And who are you?"

"William Barding, Your Highness, of the Order of the Yellow Scholars. I travel with Brynhild in the hopes of recording her story."

"This is no place for a scholar, son."

William looked around at the gathered warriors. "Perhaps when this is over, I could ask you some questions about"—He glanced at Brynhild—"about Sagran Grimsdotter, as background for my book on his daughter."

Tremain smiled and pointed at the Norsewoman. "You stay close to her, boy, and you may just survive this. Then we'll have our interview, if she holds no objections."

Brynhild shook her blonde ponytailed head.

"We must end this here. De Merlon cannot be allowed to ride north," Christopher said.

Tremain nodded. "I understand."

Suddenly, there was a shout from outside.

"The gates are opening!"

King Tremain's advisers rose as one and looked to their king, who needed no second invitation. He rushed outside and mounted his massive black destrier.

Within a minute of the call, Tremain was leading the charge of one hundred mounted knights across the plains of flattened and crushed wheat and rye, Brynhild Grimsdotter and Christopher Lewis at his side. He turned to see the thin yellow scholar's robes fluttering in the growing winds, the monk's brown mare struggling to keep up. He might only be a writer, but the boy clearly had courage.

Tremain's mounted army thundered past the skirmishes still taking place between the king's foot soldiers and de Merlon's mad renegades, the horses splashing through pooling waters muddied with blood. Tremain raised his sword and brought it down as he sped past one such pocket of violence, separating the head of one of the sky-metal soldiers from his shoulders.

No supernatural ability was bringing him back from that, thought the king.

Tremain was brought up short by the sight of a thousand soldiers spilling out of the gates of Castle Key, clambering over themselves in apparent desperation to escape something within. The skin at the back of the king's neck prickled as he pulled his horse up hard. Screeching winds of a storm emanated from somewhere up ahead.

This was odd, he thought.

And then, a flash of light, like glass splintering in molasses, knocked the foot soldiers to the ground, and Tremain's horse reared up on its hind legs as a shockwave hit. The king nearly fell but held on.

Momentarily stunned, every man on the battlefield dragged himself to his feet and looked to Castle Key. Those men who possessed hair felt it whipped about their sweaty foreheads. For a dreadful few moments tension built, becoming unbearable. The power of the wind grew. And grew.

Men tried to run, but they only made a few steps before the screaming vacuum stopped them in their tracks. Every man, every horse, was inexorably pulled toward the center of Castle Key. Tremain's own horse, as powerful as it was, scrabbled for purchase and failed, hooves making long ruts in the mud as it fought against the invisible tether of rushing air.

But then, without preamble, the wind stopped. Men looked about, wondering whether to attack or run.

There was a lull on the battlefield, a moment within which men sat on a knife's edge of indecision.

Then somewhere, someone stabbed another man through the ear and twisted the dagger.

War resumed with a single scream, as it always does.

46

The Siege of Broadford Higgins

Men sprinted everywhere. The courtyard of Castle Key bustled with soldiers barring the gates and taking up defensive positions on the battlements. Others were caught outside, evidenced by the clash of sword on steel and the screams born from metal and flesh uniting.

King Tremain had arrived with his army to save the day.

But it was too late for the fat king Bruwaert and certainly too late for Rebecca Occitane.

Tristan Drogos de Merlon sat beside the laid-out body of Rebecca Occitane, his scarred head in his scarred hands.

There were two other corpses present in the courtyard. De Merlon couldn't see them. Jeremiah couldn't see them. But Broadford could.

Malcolm Dewar was back, bloody and eyeless, standing right next to de Merlon but staring at Broadford all the same. And beside the ghost of his best friend, the girl he had strangled, Hailey Smith. He hadn't forgotten. He had lured her out with promises of something special. Something about seeing sprites by moonlight. She was eager for an adventure with Uncle Broadie.

The man and girl approached the toff, hand in hand.

"Hello, Broadie," Malcolm said with a grin. The ghost licked at the blood around its mouth, blood dripping from the pecked-out holes where the eyes used to be.

Broadford said nothing. There were too many people around. If he were seen talking to ghosts, people would think he was mad.

Malcolm Dewar and Hailey Smith laughed. "Mad?" Malcolm said. "This whole situation is mad." He pointed at the weeping mother and child, Ainslie and Lachlan Bruwaert. "You have to save them. Save the boy and his mum."

"Fuck off," Broadford whispered.

"Not a good time?"

"Fuck off, Malcolm."

Malcolm Dewar grimaced in feigned disappointment. "You have to save somebody, Broadie. You have to right the balance, pay the debt you owe. Two lives for two lives." He cocked his bloody head and smiled. "You know it's the right thing to do."

Some things could never be righted, Broadford thought.

"You'd better do it soon," Malcolm said. "Save somebody. Otherwise, what good are you?"

Broadford furrowed his brows, keeping his eyes on de Merlon sitting with head in hands on the steps before the defeated king and his broken-down throne. He could probably do it. Leap at de Merlon with a concealed blade, take him while he sat there in a stupor, before he could react. He would take no pleasure killing the man. Then, he'd murder old Jeremiah, which would bring him a great deal of pleasure. Here was his chance, the chance to redeem himself, the chance to reveal himself a hero.

He did nothing but stare at the man who would be King of All.

Shaking its head and sighing in obvious disgust, the ghost of Malcolm Dewar turned its eyeless sockets toward the girl in the muddied white nightdress. "Tell him," he said.

The ghost of Hailey Smith snickered behind its hand and leaned forward, speaking low as if whispering a great secret. "She's going to end it all."

Then the incorporeal figures of Malcolm Dewar and Hailey Smith disappeared.

End it all? She? Who?

Tristan Drogos de Merlon slowly got to his feet, with his eyes on Ainsley and Lachlan Bruwaert. Broadford could feel their fear. He was afraid too.

Shoulders slumped, a shattered figure, de Merlon turned to Bruwaert and said, "They will all burn."

The fat king's wife screamed and struggled, and Broadford increased his grip on her shoulder. She whimpered. The boy was squirming and shouting for his father. Oddly, he was shrieking "king, king" and not "daddy, daddy."

Broadford thought there was something wrong with that. What child refers to their father as king and not father? If he were king, he'd have his children call him "daddy." None of this royal bullshit. There should be no distance between father and child, no cold gap between flesh and blood.

The little boy, Lachlan, kicked his shins. *Good on you, boy, you've got some fight in you. Won't be enough. But die like a man, boy, try and die like a man. It's all you can do in this horrific life.*

The Hungry King walked down the steps from the throne to the courtyard floor. With a flick of his fingers, he motioned for Broadford to let the woman and boy go free.

Broadford backed away as the wife and son sank to their knees. King Bruwaert struggled against the ropes binding him to his broken throne, his voice increasing in pitch, becoming a bizarre soprano of fear.

Flames licked around de Merlon's fingers.

Bruwaert screamed.

Tristan Drogos de Merlon pulled at his sky-metal armor, wrenching the gauntlets and cuirass from himself, exposing his naked torso and the two trinkets on his chest, the crown and the hand. His body began to simmer, to cook, heat waves washing off him. Ainslie and Lachlan tried to shield themselves from the oncoming heat, rabbits lost in a forest fire, turning this way and that, crying.

Why don't you just run? Broadford thought, backing away. *Get up and fucking run!*

De Merlon held his hands out, holding them above the woman and child. Bruwaert screamed again.

Broadford Higgins watched as the heat began to singe the hair of Ainslie and Lachlan, to burn it at the ends and work its way down, like a fuse lighting gunpowder. He felt sick. It was one thing to kill, but this was going to be slow and painful, a show for Bruwaert. Then something caught his attention, something so shocking it ripped off the emotional scab that had long since grown over his wearied heart.

Rebecca Occitane was struggling to her feet. She held her hand over the gash in her chest, stemming the blood. "You will not harm them," she said, staggering.

Tristan Drogos de Merlon whirled around. Bruwaert, Broadford, and Jeremiah stared. The girl was standing there, a disapproving expression on her face.

Tristan recovered his composure and waggled a flaming index finger in Rebecca's direction. "No. They will all burn," he said.

The girl stood straight, chin jutting. "You will not harm them."

"How are you alive?"

Rebecca took her hand away from the wound in her chest, blood no longer issuing from the dark spot on her tunic. She said, "My desire for vengeance is every bit as strong as yours."

Tristan clenched his fists. "No! My vengeance strikes down the gods!"

"Every bit as strong as yours," she repeated. Her body began to lift off the ground. Her aspect changed, her face darkening, as if the amber of her eyes were spilling out to color her features, stain her body the same dark hue.

Broadford Higgins walked backward, fear devouring his newly found heart.

Jeremiah walked forward, his face screwed in puzzlement. "What is she doing?" he said.

Tristan shook his hairless, scarred head. The Hungry King gazed upon the ungodly sight of the young girl floating off the ground, as mystified as anyone else.

Rebecca began to shimmer, and a cold wind started up, pulling at cloak and robe.

"What is she doing?" Jeremiah said again, horror eating at the edges of his ancient voice.

Tristan Drogos de Merlon, the Hungry King, just stared.

The wind whistled and grew in power. Dust flew toward Rebecca and disappeared when it touched her skin.

The Monk of Ulfur stopped moving forward, put his hands to his shriveled head, and began to back off.

The wind tore Broadford's top hat from his head. He grabbed for it, but too late, the black felt headpiece disappearing somewhere within the torso of Rebecca Occitane.

Which made no sense. None of this made any sense.

Jeremiah screamed. The old monk's robes fluttered and flapped in the growing breeze; his sandaled feet scrabbled upon the broken tiles of the courtyard floor. Broadford watched in horror as the old monk was dragged by invisible hands toward the floating girl above the dais upon which sat an equally stunned King Bruwaert, the fat old man's head jerking left and right, his mouth gaping open trying to breathe in the ever-growing vacuum.

Broadford's own feet began to slip and slide on the courtyard. He saw Rebecca Occitane, floating in the air, head thrown back, arms outstretched, white tunic fluttering like sails in a dry storm.

With all of his strength and weight, Broadford Higgins tore himself from the vortex of wild, keening winds. He ran toward the internal stables where horses shied and kicked at their stalls, sensing the oncoming storm. His own horse was gone, in fact half the horses were gone; he, apparently, was not the first rat to think of leaving the sinking ship.

Bastards had taken his horse, but there were others. Desperately, he tried to soothe a panicked tan gelding, whispering musical sounds and patting the neck of the terrified creature.

By now, several of Tristan's soldiers within the courtyard and on the battlements had noticed the bizarre wind at their backs. They turned to witness the scene. Amazement and fear spread through the soldiers. Men whispered of the witch in their midst and pointed at the hellish sight of the floating girl amid the unnatural winds.

Broadford Higgins had very little understanding of what was happening but knew it didn't bode well. The screams and shouts from outside the walls were echoed by the shrieks of panic from within. He mounted the gelding and pointed his way through the nervous throng of soldiers to the arched entrance of Castle Key. "Open the portcullis! Open the gates!" he shouted.

From within the milling crowd of nervous soldiers, Commander Roger Forbury pushed his way through on foot. "Are you mad, Higgins? Tremain and his men await outside. We'll be cut to pieces!"

"Then, we'll take our chances and fight our way out! Better that than to be stuck here like rats in rising floodwater. She's tearing the place down!"

"His Highness de Merlon can handle the situation. You will not abandon your king!"

Broadford could barely hear the slug-nosed Forbury over the shrieking winds. Looking back to the courtyard, he realized dozens of men were now caught up in the whirlpool of destruction emanating from Rebecca Occitane, their cries for help drowned out by the winds. The girl was pulling them in; she was going to drag everyone down to Hell.

The castle walls shook, warped. He had to get out.

He dismounted the horse, intending to winch the portcullis up himself if need be, and Forbury slapped him across the face. "I'm the commander! You will control your cowardice!"

Cold weight settled over Broadford's heart once again. He touched his face where Forbury had dared to lay a hand on him. "What's your power, Forbury?"

"Power?"

"The trinket," Broadford shouted above the winds, "gives everyone powers! What's yours?"

"I don't know. It hasn't had time to settle in!"

"Good!" Broadford said as he stabbed the commander in the belly, twisting the knife. Roger Forbury shrieked, and Broadford was

reminded of a pig being gutted, which was an apt description for
what was taking place, he thought. Even in the howling storm ripping through Castle Key, men backed away in horror at the sight of
Forbury jumping around on the end of Higgins's blade. The toff dug
deeper, twisted harder. The commander dropped to the castle floor,
guts spilling out in the dirt.

"Open the portcullis!" Broadford wrenched the phallus amulet
free from Forbury's body and put it in the pocket of his black gentleman's coat. He waited for an extra surge of warmth, of power. It
didn't come.

The two men operating the winch started winding for all they
were worth. The portcullis rose, its screeching protestations mixing
with the sounds of the vortex tugging at the toff's coat, even here by
the castle gates.

"Sir, what's happening?"

Broadford whirled around. Cracker Jackson was staring at the
corpse of Roger Forbury. "I thought we...why is Tremain attack-
ing us? I don't understand!" He stood warily eyeing Broadford and
the bloodied knife, not getting too close. He pointed at the body
still twitching in the dust. "I thought we were fighting for Tremain
alongside him!"

Broadford shouted, his voice being torn from his throat by the
growing winds, "I wish I could've done that a little more privately!
There's been some confusion in terms of loyalty!"

"You lied to us!"

Broadford slowly brought the knife up level with the man's frog-
eyes. "Don't get in my way, Cracker!"

Cracker Jackson held up his hands in a show of non-confrontation. "How did it come to this? Why does King Tremain wait outside
to cut us down? Who are we loyal to?"

The toff cleaned his knife and put it away. "It's...it's just war.
Look, it's every man for himself now, old son! But we have to get out!
The girl is going to destroy everything!"

The gates slowly opened, men crushing other men in their desperation to escape the shrieking maelstrom threatening to drag them all

down. The tan gelding bolted for freedom. As Broadford was carried outside in a wave of human panic and chaos, he saw Tremain and his men bearing down on them, swords held high and war cries on their lips.

Broadford glanced back to the central courtyard of Castle Key. Suddenly, originating from a point near or within Rebecca Occitane, a pulse of energy washed outwards, like a quickly expanding glass ring, knocking the toff and a thousand other men to the ground.

When Broadford got to his feet, he found himself standing in black sand, on a cold, windswept beach.

47

Among the Stars

Tristan Drogos de Merlon watched the dark waves rolling in slowly like thick oil. The sound of the surf was oddly muted; it gurgled and sucked at the black sands of the beach.

He looked down at his naked torso, felt the chill coastal air bite his scarred flesh, and wondered where he was. The two amulets on his chest, the crown and the hand, were glowing a dull black, pulsing pure darkness, a color he had never witnessed in them before. A moment ago, he had stood in the courtyard of Castle Key, watching the reanimated corpse of Rebecca Occitane rise from the floor, arms outstretched, head thrown back, mouth open, a hungry whirlwind surrounding her. Then there had been some kind of crystal blast.

And now he was here, on this dark beach with the oily waves slurping at the shore under a roiling, tumultuous sky. Behind him, the sand rose gently for half a league to meet a sheer cliff wall of obsidian rock that climbed forever into the ominous sky.

If it weren't for the flimsy, washed-out rays from the odd-looking sun above, a sun much larger than he'd ever seen but casting an obscurely dull light, all would be darkness, nothing visible whatsoever.

Tristan scanned a few leagues either direction along the beach and made out a figure dressed in white further down. He began walking, his feet scrunching on the sand as if it were old, hard sugar.

As he approached, he recognized Rebecca Occitane, her bloodstained tunic fluttering in the sea breeze, and she was not alone.

A man sat in the sand at her feet, holding a piece of driftwood and a knife, whittling one with the other. It was Robert Occitane, Rebecca's dead father, Tristan's former comrade-in-arms. The girl just stood there, acknowledging neither the man's presence nor that of Tristan.

"Robert?" He stood beside Rebecca. "Robert?"

The man looked up and smiled. "Hello, Tristan. I'm glad to see you, old friend." He went back to his whittling.

Tristan shook his head in disbelief. "How can this be? I thought he was dead."

"He is," Rebecca said. "He's dead."

"But he's right here. Aren't you, Robert?"

Rebecca's father looked up again, but there was an emptiness behind the man's usually bright amber eyes.

"He's not here. I made him up. This is . . . a dream given flesh," she said.

He stepped closer and touched Robert Occitane on the shoulder. He was solid. The man then laid his hand on Tristan's and clasped it tightly. Tristan turned back to Rebecca, a puzzled, inquiring expression on his ruined face. "But he *is* here. He has weight, substance. I can feel him."

Rebecca shook her head. "He's not real. This is a phantom."

"Does it matter?"

"*Does it matter?* My father is dead. That matters to me."

Tristan frowned. "But he lives here, in this place."

"This isn't real."

"Better an illusion than the pain of reality," Tristan said. "Give it to me."

Rebecca looked at him sharply.

Tristan went on: "I want to see my family again. If you can resurrect your father, then you can bring back my family."

Rebecca closed her eyes hard, and Robert Occitane disappeared.

"Are you mad? Bring him back! Bring my family back!"

"You tried to murder me. Perhaps you did murder me, and this is Heaven. Or Hell. Or somewhere in between. I'll never help you, you fleshless bastard. You don't deserve it. You don't deserve happiness or a family."

Tristan Drogos de Merlon curved his lips back in a snarl, his sunken eyes burning with fire, but when he raised his hands, no fire came seeping through his skin; the familiar rush of heat was gone. He clenched his fists and screamed, and that scream vanished into the heavy atmosphere, as completely as the phantom of Robert Occitane had vanished.

Rebecca smiled. "It seems your powers don't work here."

Tristan dropped to the sands. "You betrayed your father," he whispered. "You let him go."

"I'll never let him go!" Rebecca screamed. "I need no cold facsimile produced by the metal." She pointed at her own head. "I remember him. *I* remember."

"And I cannot. I've forgotten everything, their names, even their faces become indistinct. My family are shadows, obscured from me. But you can help me. You can bring them back. Please."

Rebecca turned her back on Tristan and took a few steps on the crackling sand. She hugged herself against the chilling breeze. "I can't. I don't have... I don't have your memories. I can't help you, even if I wanted to. And I don't."

Tristan stood gingerly. "So, that's it then, is it?" He gestured around the beach. "Just you and I here for eternity?" He took in the black sand, the oil-like waves and dark sky. "Where are we anyway? This place looks nothing like... anything I've ever seen."

"I don't know," Rebecca said.

"Look." Tristan pointed with a long-nailed finger at another figure making its way along the beach.

The hunched figure of the Monk of Ulfur scuttled towards them, looking left and right in alarm. He came up to them, breathing hard and scanning the surroundings, his gaze rising with the obsidian rocks. "You've opened a portal you foolish child!"

Tristan frowned and said, "A portal, to where?"

"Hell, for all I know! But we're not at Castle Key in case you haven't noticed."

"Calm yourself, Jeremiah. I have noticed."

Rebecca pointed and said, "Another arrival."

Trudging along the beach from the opposite direction that Jeremiah had come, was another shape, this one almost as tall as Tristan and wearing a coat darker than the sand.

"It's a demon!" Jeremiah shrieked. As the figure grew closer, the monk spat a thick glob of sputum into the sands and muttered, "It's just that bastard, Higgins. Would've preferred a demon."

Broadford Higgins, once again wearing his top hat, joined Rebecca, Tristan, and Jeremiah. "Where are we?"

"Jeremiah says I've opened a portal," Rebecca said.

"A portal? To where?"

Tristan looked around. "I'm beginning to suspect this is the home world of the metal."

"Home world?" Broadford said. "Are you saying we stand on another star?"

"That's what I believe, yes."

Jeremiah's mouth dropped open. "How do we get back?"

Everyone looked at Rebecca.

"You opened it," Broadford said. "Perhaps you can close it."

"If I have no idea how I opened it, how would I know how to close it?"

"We need to think this through," Tristan said.

"Why us?" Broadford asked. "Why are we here? I mean, us four specifically?"

Jeremiah snorted, as if the answer were obvious. "The metal. It's in our blood. We're bound to it. Enslaved, you fool."

"Careful who you call a fool, old one," Broadford said. "The last person that called me a fool had his guts turned inside out not too long ago."

"Enough," Tristan said. "We must work together."

Rebecca laughed spitefully. "Together? *You* tried to kill me. Jeremiah's a child murderer, which you turn a blind eye to, and in fact encourage by supplying him with innocents. Mr. Higgins seems the only decent one among you, but I'm not stupid enough to take appearances for granted. He's here for a reason. And I've killed people. I admit it. Cut their throats, stabbed them in the eyes. If this is Hell, then maybe we're all where we belong."

"She's right!" Jeremiah screamed. "Our sins have dragged us here!"

"Steel your sagging ball sac, old man," Broadford said. "This isn't Hell. There has to be a way back."

"There!" Jeremiah said, pointing a gnarled finger.

Two more figures progressed down the black nightmarish beach, hand in hand, one large in leather armor, the other smaller in a light cotton dress of green whipping about shapely legs, a purple shawl over her shoulders.

The four stared in hope and horror at the approaching two. Suddenly, Broadford spoke in hushed tones. "It's Michael. Michael Alaine."

"Who's with him?" Tristan asked, squinting.

The young soldier came to stand before them. With blue eyes, he looked over each person and came to rest on Rebecca. "I'm Michael Alaine."

Rebecca nodded. "The man from the hospital."

Michael turned to the girl in green holding his hand. "This is Amal. She has something to say."

"Hello." The slight desert girl hesitated. "You should know that Castle Key is falling. And not just—"

"How are you here, girl?" Jeremiah said, his voice cracking, screeching. "You don't bear the metal upon your person, and I smell nothing of it in your veins. You're no murderer. You don't belong among us."

Amal lifted her hand held tightly in the grip of Michael Alaine, his blood tethering her to this plane, allowing her access to the black beach of a distant world.

Jeremiah's yellow eyes grew wide.

"Why are you here, Amal?" Rebecca asked. "Please, speak."

"Castle Key is being torn from its foundations. Men are dying beneath the falling blocks of stone. But I fear that this is just the beginning. I can't be sure, but I think it's my destiny to save you, Rebecca Occitane. And quite possibly the world."

Rebecca looked down at the bloodstains on her tunic. None of this made any sense. She should be dead, but now she stood on another world. "The beginning? Of what?"

"A vortex is destroying Castle Key, but it's widening to include the fields and farms that surround it. I don't know just how far it will spread, but I suspect it won't stop." Amal waved her arm. "This world is destroying ours. We must close the portal, and quickly."

"Hah!" Tristan spat. "Let the castle fall. Let the world be dragged down to the abyss."

"You would see our world end to assuage your need for vengeance? You disgust me." Rebecca turned to Amal. "How can I stop it? I don't know what to do."

"From what I'm told by Michael, the sky metal, when awakened, provides each bearer with individual abilities. I believe yours is to bridge worlds. How did you start? What fuels the forge of your soul?"

"Vengeance!" Tristan said.

Amal nodded. "Then learn to control this need for vengeance, for if you fail in this, it will control you. You must forgive."

"No!" Tristan said. "Never forgive. Let them all die."

Rebecca put her hands to her head. "Silence! I need to think." She addressed Amal once more. "I didn't kill King Bruwaert. I refused. Surely, that's forgiveness?"

"I don't have all the answers. All I know is that you're the key to all of this."

Michael Alaine took a step forward, still grasping Amal's hand. "Rebecca, whatever you're going to do, do it quickly. The world falls. I feel my grip on Amal fading. She'll return soon, for she does not belong here."

"What should I do? I don't . . . please, Amal, tell me, what should I do?"

The desert girl looked down at her legs and gasped. Slowly, some invisible force began to pull her through the sand, her feet dragging inexorably towards the dark, oily waters. The young knight embraced her, held her close, but he couldn't arrest her progress.

"Don't let me go, Michael."

Rebecca stepped forward quickly and grasped Amal's hand, intending to add her strength to that of Michael Alaine.

The moment Rebecca took Amal's hand, pain seared through her head. She saw a fountain, blood and water swirling, dust and sand, black hair floating on stairs, Amal crouched in a closet. Rebecca witnessed the murder of Amal's family, the death of the father, the slow rape of her mother and sister.

Rebecca gasped in overwhelming agony and shock. Her back arched, the pain running through her like a thunderstroke, smiting her soul and contextualizing her own suffering.

How odd, she thought. *How so very odd to see one's pain set side by side with that of another. How odd to see the cold, stark comparison of one's life to that of a second soul.* She felt blinded by insight. She wasn't alone, not alone in the depth and breadth of her feelings or experience. She had a connection with another.

Rebecca bridged the gap between their souls and took a little forgiveness from somewhere deep inside Amal.

The dark sea no longer pulled.

She knelt at Amal's feet, her hand still held within that of the desert girl. She looked up and whispered, "You're . . . a priestess of pain."

And then, in the span of a heartbeat, they were all back in Castle Key.

48

 Monks

The black beach with its obsidian cliffs had been replaced by a long stone corridor lit by flickering wall torches. Jeremiah was somewhere below ground in one of the cold, damp subterranean tunnels over which Castle Key had been built. He inhaled the dankness, and a feeling of coming home washed over him. The dark places, the buried places of the world, yes, he preferred the comfort of the crypt to the open skies and fields above ground.

The sounds of battle raged within the castle walls above, and clashing steel echoed somewhere in the tunnels at an indeterminate distance and direction. Castle Key had been breached. Tremain's men were inside, and for all Jeremiah knew, the big king himself was perhaps searching for him at this very instant.

Deeper, thought Jeremiah. He had to go deeper. He couldn't let the king find him.

Just then, a fragile, fleeting thought, a panicked spike of emotion tainted with fragrant innocence, came to him in the moldy-smelling air. He stopped and listened.

It was the boy, Lachlan Bruwaert, scared and alone, close by, somehow separated from his mother in the confusion, seeking her. Jeremiah thought of ignoring the boy and simply fleeing to save his own life but immediately dismissed the idea. This was a gift from the gods, an opportunity too good to pass up, and perhaps his last.

Through the gloomy, moist tunnels, he followed the thought like a hound following the scent of its quarry. The lower levels of Castle Key comprised wine cellars, ancient dungeons now used as storerooms, and even servants' quarters.

Jeremiah no longer needed to use his mind to locate the child; the boy was whimpering audibly somewhere up ahead.

The Monk of Ulfur peered into a hastily abandoned room, most likely belonging to one of the stable boys. Different shapes and sizes of horseshoes had been nailed to the wall, as if the absent occupant were proudly displaying his collection of equine hoof wear to any who had an interest. Surprisingly, given the social status of servants, the room was equipped with the luxuries of a wardrobe and a bed on short legs.

The child's snuffling ceased as soon as the hunched black-robed figure padded into the room. Jeremiah looked from the wardrobe to the bed.

Which was it? He hoped it was the wardrobe. These days neither his back nor his knees made a habit of gently acquiescing to the physical demands of bending and kneeling. Still, the reward here would be well worth the effort.

Jeremiah sniffed the wardrobe. All that filled his nostrils was the odor of horse, so he reached for the handle and pulled—a dirty shirt, one pair of dirty shoes, but no child, dirty or otherwise.

He groaned in frustration and looked at the bed. "Child, come out. I will not hurt you. I'm a monk."

For a moment, there was no response from the bed, and then it spoke in a small frightened voice.

"You are with him. The burning man."

"No, no, no. He's not my friend. I served him, but that time is over. You must come out, it's dangerous, fighting all around. I'll take you somewhere safe."

"My mother, I can't find my mother." Despair filled the child's voice, a voice struggling to hold back tears.

"I can take you to her. She's waiting, come out, take my hand, child."

The boy snuffled. "Are you telling the truth?"

Jeremiah smiled and tried to put the smile into his cracking voice. "I'm a monk. If you can't trust a monk, who can you trust?"

"Do you promise to take me to mother?"

"I promise. Upon my eternal soul." The ancient monk stood back.

Lachlan Bruwaert slowly climbed out from under the bed. The child stood and gazed at Jeremiah with innocent eyes. The boy looked older than his eight years, his eyes tired, as if trauma had aged him.

Trauma does that, thought Jeremiah. The wizened Monk of Ulfur considered not killing the child, not feeding on the innocence within. He thought of telling the boy to run.

Then the madness left him, and he once again settled on his course. Here. He would do it here. While he still could.

"You promised," the boy said.

Jeremiah nodded and moved closer to the child. "If you can't trust a monk—"

"Who can you trust?" said another voice in the room.

Jeremiah whirled about. In his excitement, he hadn't sensed the newcomer, a man with a monk's tonsure, wearing yellow robes.

"Who are you?"

"A brother, one sworn to help those in need, as you were long ago. My name is William."

"What do you want?" Jeremiah's old heart pounded in anticipation.

"I'm looking for the boy."

"He's mine." The Monk of Ulfur produced a wicked serrated blade from his robes.

Lachlan's eyes grew wide, and the boy leaped back under the bed as quick as a rabbit.

"Curse you! Now see what you've done?"

William calmly folded his arms. "Leave the boy alone."

"Who are you?" Jeremiah asked.

"I told you. My name is William, William Barding. I belong to the Order of the Yellow Scholars."

"Hah!" Jeremiah spat. "Never heard of them. Just another cult. Just more mad monks."

"I'm not a monk. As the name of my order implies, I'm a scholar."

"Good for you. Does that mean you get to fuck?" His voice dripped with sarcasm.

William furrowed his thin brows. "Guard your language in front of the child."

"Right now, my language is the last thing either you or the child need worry about." He lifted the blade.

"Do you intend to harm the boy, Jeremiah?"

He looked at the weapon in his hand and sneered. "Is that a trick question?" The gnarled monk cocked his head. "How do you know my name?"

"That's not important. You will not harm the child."

Jeremiah stared hard at William. "I know you. Rebecca has thought of you, often. You saved her from Bruwaert's men, after they killed her father. Yes, I know you. You saved her, and though you make an admirable habit of saving the innocent, you won't save this one, monk. The boy is mine."

From under the bed, sounds of sniffling and weeping began once more.

"Not a monk. I'm a scholar," William said evenly as he reached within his butter-colored robes and revealed a dagger in each hand.

Jeremiah's forehead wrinkled up in surprise. "A scholar with knives? Mmm. Interesting order, the . . . which brotherhood did you say you hail from?"

"The Order of the Yellow—"

With lightning reactions that belied the old man's crooked frame, Jeremiah stripped a horseshoe from its nail on the wall and hurled it at William. The younger man barely jerked his head to the side in time to avoid the lethal projectile, which exited the room through the doorway and clanged into the darkness somewhere.

Jeremiah snarled. "I may look old and useless, Brother, but I can assure you the metal in my blood has provided a few surprises over the years, and not only in terms of mental abilities. If you thought to find a defenseless old man, you are very much mistaken."

"You're a child murderer. Nothing else matters."

Jeremiah grinned mockingly, the dry skin around his mouth stretching. "Oh, I'm much worse than that."

The old monk lunged with his knife, hacking and slashing with inhuman speed at the face and neck of William Barding. To Jeremiah's surprise, the thin young man deflected or dodged each thrust, his butter-yellow robes flowing about him like water. This man might be an academic, but he knew how to handle himself, and despite the twisted monk's earlier boast of his physical prowess as gifted by the sky metal, he found himself tiring rapidly. William was proving to be a skilled and dangerous foe. Clearly, today's modern monk received a different kind of training than Jeremiah's generation had been exposed to.

Both men sweated with effort, looking for an opening, not giving any quarter. Jeremiah's speed was nulled as William wielded two daggers and could double up his attacks. Slowly, the old monk gave ground, edging backward until his leg bumped against the bed.

Suddenly, Jeremiah dropped his knife to the floor with a clang and raised his hands. "I give up, young man," he said, panting like a dog. "William. William, yes...William is your name, isn't it? I'm not as young as...no, no, lower your daggers, please. I concede the fight, do not hurt this frail old fool."

The young monk looked away for a split second and eyed the knife on the floor. He moved a step closer to the discarded blade and made to kick it away.

This was the moment Jeremiah was waiting for.

He lowered one arm, released the second blade secreted within the sleeve of his dirty brown robes, and lunged.

William Barding took the knife in his eye. His eye globe popped, but the blade buried no further as he was already moving his head backward, not in a reflex moment, but in a sudden flash of warning. He had seen Rebecca Occitane releasing her blade from within her sleeve as she rode on horseback beside the assassin, Christopher Lewis. This forewarning enabled William to jerk backward—though unable to avoid a stab through his eye—and successfully avoid the fatal plunge into his brain. He stood, only one eye functioning, but he stood.

In attempting the death blow on William, Jeremiah lost his balance and tumbled forward. The younger man returned the strike by stabbing the old monk in the groin and grinding the blade upwards into his pelvis and abdomen.

The shriveled monk shrieked. "Bastard!" he screamed as blood spurted from beneath his robes. Any normal man would have been incapacitated in seconds, dead in minutes. He'd been hurt before, but nothing like this. Too much blood, his femoral artery sliced open. Still, the metal would come to his aid. He grinned through the pain, cackled, and stepped forward to finish the half-blinded yellow scholar.

Jeremiah's knee buckled and he staggered, only just righting himself before collapsing to the floor. His hands trembled, and he found he no longer had the strength to hold the knife. It fell clanging to the stone floor. Something was wrong.

The wound still flowed, blood rushing down his leg. The metal had forsaken him. Jeremiah stared dumbfounded at William and then crashed to the floor.

The scholar-monk sank to his knees beside the bed and put his hand over his eye to stem the vitreous that pulsed forth. "Boy. Come out. Lachlan!"

"No!" the child bellowed.

William felt his stomach churning. He vomited, his spew joining Jeremiah's blood and the fluid from his eye on the floor. "Please, boy."

Jeremiah curled into a fetal position, his life forces rapidly fleeing his body. His old, wizened frame shook, and he knew the metal was preparing to leave him, leave him after all this time. "Fucker." His voice was fading.

William retched again. "Lachlan, it's time to go."

The boy poked his head out and looked from Jeremiah to William. The ancient monk's voice was barely a whisper now. "Cunt."

"Please boy. I have a book to write." William held out his hand.

Lachlan Bruwaert reached out, and the monk pulled him from under the bed. The scholar and the boy got to their feet and stumbled from the room.

Jeremiah watched them run from the small subterranean bedroom. He felt the metal stretching at his veins, trying to break out, abandoning him. Darkness began to settle on the Monk of Ulfur, and his mind raced, trying to relive all the good moments of his life.

He was bitterly disappointed at how few those moments were in comparison to how long his life had been.

He listened to the receding footsteps of William and Lachlan. The old man cursed William Barding one more time with every shred of vitriol remaining in him.

"Fucking . . . monk."

Then Jeremiah, monk of the ancient Order of Ulfur, did something he never thought he'd have the courage to do.

He died.

49

Toffs

Broadford Higgins found himself back in Castle Key surrounded by the hacking and slashing of blades and the screams of the dying. He had decided to flee. Again. His first attempt had been thwarted by Rebecca Occitane opening a portal. Now, he was slipping and sliding on the blood-slicked tiles of the central courtyard.

His top hat fell, and a crazed combatant unwittingly kicked it away from Broadford's grasp. He cursed his luck, his life, his circumstances.

How had it come to this? Indentured to a madman, forced to recruit an army, haunted by phantoms, beaten, bruised. And he had lied to all and sundry—not a friend left in the world. Well, he *had* killed his only true friend for the trinket, so he couldn't really complain about that last part. But everything else stunk of life having it in for him. It really was all rather unfair.

Broadford scrambled, crawling over the blood-splattered ground, hoping a death blow wouldn't find him, and grabbed his hat. He gathered his feet under him and ran—ducking, weaving, dodging the flailing sword strikes of fighters from both sides as he made his way toward the open castle gates.

Some might call him a deserter, a coward, but he would put a knife in their liver to silence that kind of talk. This was just practicality. The practicality of survival.

He made the gates and exploded as fast as his long legs could carry him into the bloodied fields—top hat in one hand and sword in the other—straight into more fighting that had spilled outside. There was just no escaping the blood, death, and madness.

He sprinted past the melee, scanning left and right for any means of escape or any point of safety.

He thought of the last girl he'd fucked and wondered if he'd ever fuck again. This couldn't be the end. He wouldn't allow it. They could all go back to Hades: de Merlon, Michael, Rebecca, the freakish old monk, Cracker, Big Ted. He didn't care. He just wanted to be drunk somewhere in a tavern, alone. Just make the serving wench pretty and young, that was all. He didn't ask for much. Just good ale and a pretty serving girl.

And then salvation appeared before him.

His own horse was standing under a tree half a league away in a pool of non-violence, just beyond and unnoticed by the soldiers madly hacking at each other, like the visage of an oasis in a desert, beauty among the ugliness, order among the chaos. A way out. He had never named the horse but now loved it more than any other living creature. He almost cried tears of relief.

His heart pumped. His brain burst with sparks of color as he pushed his body beyond its oxygen capacity. He was almost there, almost clear of the killing and death.

And then a soldier scuttled onto the horse like a spider along the thread of a web. The man looked at him with a manic smile and dug his heels into the animal's ribs, spurring the horse away.

Broadford watched in shock and despair. He recognized the grinning rider, even from this distance.

Malcolm Dewar.

Broadford screamed in frustration, cursed his old friend, then, in his peripheral vision, caught the downward arc of an axe coming at him.

50

The Gallery

"This is macabre. What's the meaning of all this, this cruelty?" Rebecca said.

Among the arcane objects carefully exhibited on the plastered walls and around the room on plinths were fangs, tusks, skulls, the sprawled-out skins of great predators, small porcelain vases containing the ground bones of exotic animals, and in fluid-filled glass jars, preserved scrotums still containing the testicles of unnamed creatures.

Bruwaert withdrew his gaze from the wall. "It's a collection of objects I've gathered over the years, each purported to contain some kind of occult power, a kind of life-giving virility, but the entire gallery is worthless, I assure you. I've tried it all, worn it, eaten it, supped on teas infused with the powdered bones of near-mythical animals. I'm ashamed to admit that I even slept with the mummified corpses of some of them. Ainslie chose to retire to another bedroom, as you can imagine. But my youth fades, it was all hokum. All until . . ." Bruwaert stared lasciviously at the trinket hanging around the girl's neck.

Rebecca contorted her face in disgust. "This is all in the name of your fragile manhood?"

"I . . ." Bruwaert looked around. "How did we get here? The last thing I remember, I was bound to my throne in the courtyard. Have I taken a blow to the head? Where are my wife and son?"

"I can only hope Tristan hasn't found them. We need to hide. The game isn't over for him, not yet. He still seeks this." Rebecca grabbed the book resting on her chest. "He believes it will make him a god."

"And will it?"

"I don't know. I believe the trinket has awakened to its full potential. He must not have it. His powers mustn't ascend." Rebecca's face froze, and with a churning in his ample guts, Bruwaert picked up the sound of approaching footsteps outside.

"Conceal yourself," Rebecca whispered.

Bruwaert played a peculiarly terrifying game of hide and seek, but in this game, it was Death himself who peered in the small, dark places, looking for him. He realized with horror that he was too fat to position himself adequately behind any of the dozens of displays in the gallery.

And then, the Hungry King, as if walking on air, glided into the spacious hall of bizarre exhibits. Bruwaert had given up the attempt at hiding. His knees weakened as he found himself alone, staring into the sunken eyes of the tall, ghoulish Tristan Drogos de Merlon.

Tristan looked around the gallery and laughed. He raised his arms wide. "Tell me, Bruwaert, does the fountain of eternal youth reside within these walls? Is this your inner sanctum of potency? Do I stand among your own personal aphrodisiacs? It's all truly marvelous. I, myself, feel an erection coming on!"

Bruwaert scanned the room desperately, hoping to find a hiding place he had missed, but it was futile, much too late. He said, "None of it worked. I continue to grow old."

On Tristan's ruined, shipwrecked face, a mock expression of disappointment. "Ah, shame. A man does need his penis in working order." He brought his fist down on a glass case, which exploded in a thousand shards. He picked up a skull of some extinct animal, perhaps the last of its kind, and peered into the empty eye sockets. "I shall avenge you." The skull flared, flamed, and burnt to a cinder, ash falling to the floor. Tristan stepped through the gray dust and approached the terrified Bruwaert.

"Help me," the king whispered.

Rebecca Occitane stepped out from behind a plinth and walked calmly to stand in front of the trembling king. "Leave him be," she said flatly.

Tristan recoiled in disgust, almost unable to look at Rebecca. "You no longer seek vengeance. You've changed. I admire that, even understand it. But you would seek to stop me ," Tristan's voice broke with emotion, "from killing the man who murdered your father? You would seek to *protect* this man? Now, *that* is something I cannot understand. *That* makes no sense." Tristan breathed deeply, his naked torso heaving, sharp ribs stretching against papyrus skin. "Just step aside. Do not interfere. That's all I ask. Just do nothing."

Rebecca shook her head sorrowfully. "I never thought to be here. I hated him, that's true. But Amal's shown me another way."

Tristan looked down at his boots. He then raised his head and met Rebecca's powerful and peaceful amber eyes. Anger and confusion raged across his face. "What has she done to you?"

"She's shown me the path of forgiveness."

De Merlon grimaced, lips pulled back, teeth showing in a feral snarl. "Then, it's too late for you both! I'll destroy you!"

Rebecca lifted her head proudly. "You couldn't kill me before. What makes you think you can do it now?"

The Hungry King smiled through his wrath, his voice lowering. "Well, a knife doesn't work, that I know. Let me see if burning you to dust will prove to be more effective." He began to glow with flame, the fire licking from his exposed skin, building in ferocity. He raised both hands, fingers spread out before him.

Bruwaert ran. Before he got halfway to the door, a fireball erupted from Tristan's hands and flashed across the room, knocking the king from his feet, searing the flesh from his back. He screamed in agony, his charred flesh hissing, the smell of smoked meat permeating the room.

Rebecca put her fingers to her temple. The flesh stopped burning, and Bruwaert stopped screaming. He lay panting on the floor of his gallery of oddities.

Tristan glanced at Rebecca, fury contorting his face. He gathered his energies and sent out a mesh of flame that crashed down on Bruwaert like a fisherman's net on a shoal of tuna, setting the fat king's flesh to melting once more.

"Stop it!" Rebecca shouted.

Tristan responded by harpooning Bruwaert with a projectile of metal-hard fire. The fat king screamed a final time and died, his flesh sizzling obscenely.

Rebecca looked away. "No! You've doomed yourself, don't you see?"

Tristan sniffed the air and smiled. "I smell roast pig. Don't tell me you're not secretly pleased."

The girl shook her head in silence. "You're no different." She nodded to the melting corpse of King Bruwaert, fat pooling on the floor. "Seeking godhood, and power. Selfish, such selfish men."

"What I seek is righteous! I seek revenge! Plain and simple! You, of all people, understand that, or you once did. Power is simply a means to an end. When my task is over, I'll step aside. I'll gladly die, for I don't desire power for its own sake."

"You're a murderer," Rebecca said, her light brown hair falling over her downcast face. "You've lost your way. I had such hopes for you."

"Everything you can say about me would equally apply to you! Do not pretend otherwise!" The Hungry King sighed and gazed around the room of occult objects. "I'm fond of you, Rebecca, and I regret what I must do. I had five sons. If I had ever been lucky enough to have a daughter, I believe she would have possessed your spirit. I'm sorry for what must happen."

Tristan stretched out his hands, energies coalescing once more, flames leaping from his face. Rebecca simply raised her chin.

Brynhild Grimsdotter ran into the gallery, screaming something in the Norse language. Tristan turned in surprise and glared at the warrior princess. A second figure tumbled into the room, rolling, moving, taking Tristan's attention away from Brynhild and Rebecca.

Christopher Lewis came out of the roll, finding his feet, a dagger leaving his hand and slicing through the air.

De Merlon swatted aside the blade as if it were a bloated mosquito. He released a ball of fire at Christopher, and the assassin rolled again, narrowly avoiding Bruwaert's horrific fate, his gray leather armor spitting and hissing.

Brynhild had closed the distance to de Merlon, and her katana flashed out, only to be blocked by a shield of whirling flame in de Merlon's left hand, the katana bouncing wildly backward and almost taking Brynhild's nose off.

A blade of black flame flowered instantly in de Merlon's right hand, pommel and hilt forming first, cross guard and blade coming to life in a heartbeat thereafter.

The Hungry King slashed at Brynhild with the supernatural blade as Christopher moved in from behind, twin short swords in hand, in an attempt to hack at the exposed backs of de Merlon's legs. But as he got within striking distance, the assassin encountered an inhuman heat, as if the doors of a blast furnace stood wide open, forcing him back. Christopher had a split second in which to act while de Merlon was occupied with the Norsewoman.

He hurled one of his short swords at de Merlon's back; the blade hit an invisible wall of heat and clattered to the marble floor. The man had a fire-shield in hand and a wall of protective heat around him. If the knight-captain couldn't penetrate the heat-defense of the Hungry King in the next few seconds, Brynhild was dead, and he and Rebecca would soon follow.

Brynhild Grimsdotter swung once more at the burning skeletal warrior, only to have her offensive maneuver blocked. A riposte came slashing at her followed by another counterattack of inhuman speed. Her eyes were tearing from the intense heat. She had to put distance between herself and the burning devil or die, but he was pushing forward too fast, and she couldn't turn her back on him, couldn't create space.

Rebecca watched the battle and could see that Brynhild and Christopher were outmatched, only moments from inevitable defeat and death. She gripped the finely carved book given to her by her father, and closed her eyes, trying to find a weakness in de Merlon's mind, trying to find a way to shut down his power. But the man had set up mental defenses against any probes, no doubt placed there to keep out the ancient Jeremiah. Desperately, Rebecca swept up and down, along the outer perimeter, looking for cracks in the man's spiritual armor. She found none. Then she came upon something, not a weakness in de Merlon, no, she had located something else. She had found a strength in the assassin, in Christopher Lewis.

In the pocket of his gray leather breeches, the knight-captain had three trinkets, each of mild potency, only half-unlocked, half-realized. If she could just give them a little push, a little encouragement . . .

Rebecca screwed her eyes tighter shut. She whispered to the trinkets.

"Help him."

51

Of Kings

Christopher Lewis felt warmth surge through his body, easing the fear of death that had so recently swept over him. He relaxed his mind and saw everything happening as if he were an actor in a play performed a thousand times. He took in the scene around him in abstract consideration: Bruwaert was dead, lying in a pool of his own fat, Brynhild Grimsdotter on the defensive and about to join him, the Hungry King's blade of fire swiftly bludgeoning the Norsewoman into submission.

No other warrior could have survived the brutal onslaught de Merlon now brought to bear on the tall woman, but she was made of the finest steel. She fought bravely, always on the back foot but stood nonetheless. Brynhild Grimsdotter was the bough that would bend but never break.

And so, the madman's attention was focused on her, giving Christopher a chance, just one chance, one he must take, now or never.

The trinkets in his pocket spoke to him. At first, he didn't recognize the whispering. The murmurings became a single desire with the faint echo of a thousand other wishes behind it, both singular and plural, both here and now, both close and distant. He couldn't reconcile the voices, the thoughts in his head. They seemed like the inner workings of his own psyche and yet the babblings of multitudinous strangers.

But they provided the answers.

They provided the impetus.

They provided the insight.

Christopher Lewis put his hand on the soft splayed skin of some exotic beast hanging on the alabaster wall. From his fingertips down his arm, through his chest and stomach, he felt the power of the dead creature revive within him, set his heart to pumping, his lungs expanding.

He roared a primal beast scream and tore the creature's pelt from the wall, enveloped himself within it, using it as a shield against the heat emanating from the tall, ghoulish de Merlon. Christopher abandoned reason as he jumped into the furnace.

Tristan Drogos de Merlon turned at the animalistic snarl and witnessed the long-extinct southern sand leopard coming at him, its massive jaws wide and about to tear and rend. Instinctively, he flung his arm up to keep the creature from his throat, and the sand leopard clamped onto de Merlon's forearm and bit down.

The Hungry King's protective wall of heat faltered, and Brynhild drove her katana through Tristan's back. The burning man screamed in pain and anger, the agony clearing his head, bringing him back to his senses. He could now see that the sand leopard was merely a ruse, a disguise; it was the other man, the assassin hiding behind the skin, the assassin's short blade puncturing his forearm.

He'd been deceived by his own eyes.

The assassin had dropped the pelt and was removing his blade from de Merlon's forearm when Tristan kicked him in the stomach, sending him flying. De Merlon then turned and punched Brynhild on the jaw, the tall woman sent reeling backward through the air, the skin on her chin searing, her katana still inserted neatly through Tristan's torso. The assassin recovered his feet and leapt back into the fray, his blades plunging into the Hungry King's flesh several times before the Norse warrior hit the ground.

With inhuman speed, de Merlon grasped Christopher Lewis and dragged him into a flaming embrace and onto the blade still piercing the Hungry King's solar plexus. The heat shield built in intensity once more, healing Tristan's wounds, cauterizing cuts of internal organs and external flesh as soon as they were made.

Screaming in fury, a weaponless Brynhild tried to wrest the assassin from de Merlon's clutches but was again repulsed by the heat. Christopher shimmered in a ferocious haze as the heat shield continued to regenerate.

At that moment, King Laurence Tremain entered the room and shouted, "Let that man go!"

Tristan released his fatal grip on the assassin, letting him drop, smoking, to the floor. Brynhild dragged the unconscious assassin to safety by one foot as a smiling de Merlon rounded on the king.

"King Tremain, how very kind of you to grace us. I've been seeking an audience with you for some time." He reached behind himself and pulled the katana from his back. He held it up, his fist clasped about the steel blade, unconcerned by its biting edge, then let the bloodied weapon fall.

Tremain looked at the cooling gelatinous corpse of Bruwaert, then at the smoldering assassin. "You'll pay for this."

"Hardly. It is I who am owed two pounds of flesh. The first I have already extracted," Tristan said, walking toward the silver-bearded king, the blade of flame blossoming from his right fist once again. "And now I shall have the second."

Rebecca Occitane knelt with the Norsewoman over the smoking body of Christopher Lewis. She said to Tristan, "You can't let your suffering rule you. You can't carry your pain, care for it and water it like a living thing, only to send it out into the world to be amplified a thousandfold."

De Merlon turned and said flatly, "You and I, we once only lived to nurture our pain."

"You have to let it go." Rebecca lowered her head. "As I have done."

Tristin's smile had no malice in it, his voice quieted. "Without it, what am I?"

"You are what you've always been. Husband. Father."

"Bereft of wife or children, I am neither."

"Fight me," King Tremain said, "but leave the others be, leave my son alone."

Tristan looked sharply at the mortally wounded assassin. "Your son?"

The king nodded.

De Merlon looked from the father to his boy. The anger lines that constantly plagued his face, softened and disappeared; his eyes glazed over. A moment later, he seemed to snap out of a dream. He tilted his head as if listening to something, seeing something. Smiling, he allowed his flame-sword to diminish and disappear. He stretched his arms wide.

Brynhild reached for her katana, the hilt burning her hand as she gripped it. She did not let go.

De Merlon's heat shield went out, and he said, "I thought you couldn't do it. But I see them."

Rebecca swallowed hard. "I . . ."

"Thank you," Tristan said, tears falling from his sunken eyes.

Brynhild Grimsdotter approached de Merlon from behind and swept her katana in a swift horizontal arc.

"No!" Rebecca screamed.

But it was too late.

The Hungry King's scarred head separated from his shoulders and bounced to the floor, his body falling slowly, the alien minerals within his blood seeming to lay him down gently, the room cooling.

And then the sky metal departed the corpse of Tristan Drogos de Merlon in a brilliant fracturing of impossible colors, colors which swirled about his body for a few seconds before lifting, each minute teardrop beginning the long journey back to the stars.

Rebecca bowed her head and tried to focus on Christopher's dissipating heartbeat. She spoke to the trinkets once more, urging them to heal the burns, to rush to the aid of the dark-eyed assassin. Without them, he would surely die.

The king knelt and gently touched Christopher's red and raw hand. "Will he live?"

Rebecca didn't speak. She tilted her head, listening. "He'll live, but the burns will scar him forever."

Tremain sat back on his arse, breathing heavily. "I thank you both. If there's anything I can do for you, either of you, you have but to ask."

Brynhild cleaned and put away her katana. Shaking her head, she said, "I require nothing. Besides, someone once told me that honor is its own reward." She met the king's eyes. "I think I understand now exactly what he meant."

52

Endings

The battle for Castle Key had come to an end, de Merlon's men routed and fleeing, the castle once again secured but without a king to command it.

Ainslie Bruwaert held her crying child while Brynhild stood close by, biting her tongue, wishing for nothing more than to tell young Lachlan that his father was not worth crying over, that men in general had a habit of disappointing their children. But she let the boy grieve. In lieu of a real father, grief was all the boy would ever have.

She walked across the courtyard to the cracked and bloodied steps beneath the broken throne. Amal was kneeling in front of a seated William, bandaging the space his eye once occupied. Rebecca sat beside him, dried blood on her tunic, like flowers, and gave generous hugs to the embarrassed-looking yellow scholar. Michael, ever present at Amal's side, watched with a grim frown.

Brynhild patted the scholar-monk on the shoulder. "I believe a writer only needs one eye."

William winced, looked up with the one eye, and raised two gossamer eyebrows along with it. "Theoretically, yes. While I can't fault your logic, I shall miss it." He sighed and added, "At least now, I may finish my book."

The bandages in place, Brynhild pulled William to his feet.

Michael rubbed his hands through his blond hair, scanning the corpses strewn like leaves in the autumn wind about the castle courtyard. "This was all my fault," he said.

"You flatter yourself, boy," Brynhild said in amusement, and not a little disparagement. "Had your mother never shat you screaming into this world, another man would have found those accursed objects. Besides, it takes more than one fool to wage a war. You may be guilty of stupidity, but you are by no means alone."

The young knight scratched his head. "Well, that makes me feel better."

"You are welcome."

Christopher Lewis sat a few steps above the group on Bruwaert's broken throne, his hair and eyebrows gone, his skin red and angry across his face, throat, and hands. Since retaining consciousness, the assassin seemed lost in thought.

"Is it over, Christopher?" Michael asked.

The knight-captain snapped out of his reverie and shook his head. "No. The metal's infected many, among them will be men with unusual abilities, which will help them escape." He touched his burnt face. Suddenly, as if recalling something, he removed the three trinkets from his pockets and cast them to the courtyard floor.

Brynhild watched the trinkets come to rest in a pool of blood. "Is that wise? They're healing you."

"If I'd been given a choice, I'd have chosen to burn."

"Noble but foolish, as someone once said to me." The tall woman narrowed her eyes. "So, assassin, you're the son of a king. That's quite some secret you've been carrying around. I knew I couldn't trust you."

"The bastard son, if that makes any difference."

"Still a son." Brynhild tugged at her blonde braid and said casually, "The throne suits you, even a broken one."

Christopher glanced at her sharply.

She went on: "You must resent Tremain for never publicly acknowledging you."

"And you must hate your father for whoring around on your mother and dying on you when you needed him the most."

Brynhild shrugged. "We all have our families to survive." She paused and weighed up the assassin. "What are you going to do?"

"No idea. And you?"

"My biographer is back in business, so we ride north to my home-lands. Join us, provided you have no other pressing matters, nor are too proud."

Christopher met the tall woman's challenging gaze. "My arse is raw and I cannot ride, if that's not too proud an excuse."

Brynhild laughed. "We can wait until your riding muscles have recuperated. We suffer no need for haste."

The knight-captain nodded but said nothing more.

Michael put his hand gently on Amal's shoulder. "We should go."

"No," Rebecca said, interjecting herself. "The outlying lands are rife with sky-metal crazed soldiers. Wait until Tremain has hunted them down. Besides, I like Amal. I think we have much to learn from each other."

Amal took Rebecca's hand. "Please, will you come with us when it is over?"

Rebecca looked at Michael, who gave a nod. She smiled and turned to the daughter of Shae. "I'd be delighted to."

"Amal and I will head south," Michael said. "Back to the Great Southern Sands, perhaps Sil'Raka. We'll attempt to make a life there."

"I intend to set up a hospital," Amal said, her eyes bright, "and perhaps a place of worship where those in pain can find healing, both physical and spiritual."

"I'm your first disciple," Rebecca said.

Michael Alaine folded his arms. "The second."

53

One Man's Frippery

Broadford Higgins sat exhausted and breathing hard behind an all-too-naked tree. He had run ten leagues without slowing down, an astonishing feat and something he'd never come close to even in the prime of his youth. He now had an inkling as to what power the trinket had gifted him, apart from drinking all kinds of accursed liquor without a hangover. His lungs had expanded beyond the normal human capacity. He was a horse in human form. This was the only reason he was still alive. It was a wonder he'd never discovered it before, but then again, he'd never had to run for his life like this before.

Another thought plagued him. How do they know? How do they know who's on whose side? Tremain's men and de Merlon's were not, strictly speaking, uniformed combatants. How did Tremain's men know friend from foe?

The answer came to him in a flash of insight.

The sky metal. The trinkets. Somehow the men on either side recognized the enemy, the alien, on the other side.

All he had to do was throw it away. Throw away the key. He'd be unrecognizable then, could flatter his way back into Tremain's army and live like a sycophant the rest of his days.

But he couldn't do it. Couldn't give up the metal in his blood.

And so, it would be another run. How far to the nearest city? How far to the Freelands? Eighty leagues. He could do it. He could, but only without men on horseback in pursuit.

He thought about Cracker Jackson. Old frog eyes had gone down under a flurry of blows. Broadford had been close by, running for his own life. If he'd stopped and assisted, he might, *might* have been able to help Cracker.

It was a risk he wasn't prepared to take, and so he'd let Cracker die. And Big Ted and Spade.

He didn't feel guilty. Broadford Higgins was beyond guilt. That particular feeling had never inflicted itself upon him; he couldn't remember ever feeling it. He was immune, invulnerable to it.

Just as well, because the things a man has to do to survive . . . Well, those things are better left unsaid.

Riders nearby broke twigs under hoof fall.

Broadford tried to control his breathing and stay as silent as a corpse in a well-dug grave. The late autumn tree gave little foliage to hide behind, and so he dropped to his belly. Among the dead leaves and soil, he thought he could hear the sounds of worms burrowing mindlessly.

Futile, he thought. It's futile, my little friends.

Then the riders passed by, three on one side of him, four on the other, moving forward in a sweeping pattern. With horror, he realized one of the riders was carrying his top hat. He couldn't remember dropping it. When he looked closer, the man carrying it was King Tremain himself.

They hadn't seen him, somehow. Miraculously, they hadn't spotted him lying cradled in the roots of the bare tree. If he lay where he was, they'd pass by.

But it was *his* top hat. *His.*

Don't do it, whispered the metal around his neck and in his blood. *You'll die. There are too many. The king rides with them, he's still strong despite his years.*

It's mine.

Let the hat go. There will be other hats. Let it go. It doesn't matter.

A man has his pride. It's my hat.

It's futile, little worm, let it go.

What did you call me?

The metal didn't reply.

What did you call me? Is that you, Malcolm? You hiding up in my head somewhere?

Suddenly, he was tired of running. He stood and shouted at the receding riders.

"Hey!"

King Tremain and six heavily armed men on horseback turned as one.

"Why did Prometheus cross the road?" Broadford's challenge echoed through the glade.

The men stared, then drew long glinting swords and urged their horses forward.

Broadford thought of the girl from Dunedin, the red-headed waitress with the beautiful big tits. There had been a moment when they were together in the bed above the bar, before they dragged him from her embrace to give him a beating, when he kissed her lips and she returned the kiss with even more passion than which he had given it.

A moment when he saw a future beyond the drink and the whores.

A moment when all of his sins fell from him like the dirty travel-stained cloak and undershirt he shed that night.

A moment when he stood at a crossroads.

What was her name? Had he even asked? It didn't matter. Nothing mattered.

Broadford drew his sword. He had been frightened his entire life.

But he wasn't afraid anymore.

54

Homecoming

Tristan Drogos de Merlon approached the door and stood for a moment. He was going to knock. Though it was his own home, his own family within, he was going to knock. He had, after all, been away for over two years.

He raised his hand to rap against the simple wooden door before him, but a voice, familiar yet far away, made him turn.

Albert. . . he is the oldest. Then Terence, Geoffrey, Simon. The little one is called Matthew. Matthew.

Something about the voice reminded him of the color amber.

He turned back and knocked, his heart beating. He wondered who would open the door.

Standing there, taller, broader, stronger, Albert was the spitting image of his mother. The boy, no, young man of fourteen, cried and leapt into his father's arms. The other boys followed, grabbing at their father's legs, pulling Tristan down so they could kiss his face. The smallest of the children stood back, unsure.

Tristan smiled.

"You must be Matthew," he said. "It's nice to meet you." The boy teetered on his feet, puzzled at the stranger in the house. Tristan held out his hand, and the infant came. He kissed the boy on his forehead and gazed into his wide eyes.

"Papa. You've been gone so long," Albert said.

"I'm sorry. I came as soon as I could. Where's your mother?"

Albert pointed.

There at the gate she stood, fruit basket on her arm. Stella.

Gently, she laid the basket down and smiled. Tristan, accompanied by five excited children, rushed forward eagerly and embraced his wife. She smelled of lilacs on the mountainside, and Tristan felt his heart burst and the stars come down to collect him.

"Where have you been?" Stella whispered as she ran her fingers down Tristan's strong, full jawline.

"Here, with you and the children," he said. "I've always been here."

THE END

ABOUT THE AUTHOR

CAMERON SCOTT KIRK (*Christchurch, New Zealand*) is interested in travelling the world looking for lost treasure, meeting alien life, and wielding a sword against horrific monsters. In lieu of the real thing, he writes about it.

Kirk has been published in over a dozen magazines including Antipodean SF, Aphotic Realm, and Alcyone magazine to name but a few. A winner of Best of Fiction at Across the Margins magazine (another publication starting with "A"). He lives with his wife and daughter, who both think he should give up his silly writing and get a real job.

'

Made in the USA
Middletown, DE
08 November 2021